Heritage

A Collection of Science Fiction Short Stories

Nick Neim

New York
2015

HERITAGE

A Collection of Science Fiction Short Stories

Copyright © 2015 by Nick Neim

ISBN 978-0-9896417-1-5

Printed in USA
For information, please address nikneim09@gmail.com
Library of Congress Data is available
First Edition

Dedicated to Diana and David...

Author's Note

Dear friends,

These stories are written for you, those who like to dream of unusual things, to fantasize, to think, to learn something interesting – in short, soul mates. I believe that there must be a good number of us.

Opening the book, you have come to visit me, and as a welcoming host, I want to treat you to something nice – to arouse your interest instead of leaving you indifferent. Your feedback will show me whether I was able to succeed in this.

In this book you will find three main science fiction topics: a journey either from Earth or to Earth (to put it poetically – space travel), time travel and adventures in the Here and Now.

The human craving for the unknown, visits to distant lands awaken in each of us an interest in science fiction. And those who are lucky enough to encounter its best samples become its strongest fans. I used to be lucky, and I gratefully recall my "friends in paperback", opening to me the warmth of the human soul in the most unusual guises and places of the universe. I hope that this tradition continues in my book.

In the stories, you will find notes. Are they needed? Only for those who may wish a quick reminder of something once learned in school, who want to make sure that they correctly understand hints and who might need some help in distinguishing fantasy from reality.

I wish you exciting reading and a pleasant aftertaste.

Nicholas Neiman,
Or simply, yours,
Nick Neim

Table of Contents

Acknowledgment

With all my pleasure, I want to thank my friends and colleagues who helped me bring my stories into a publishable shape.

First, my editorial group – T. Schueler, V. Feyder, D. Israeli and L. Bliss – whose nerves I wracked despite my deep respect for their abilities and their work.

Second, my designer – R. Bonilla – who beautifully implemented my amateur drawings into the gorgeous, professional cover page, which not only adorns the book but exemplifies the mathematical mystery hidden within the main story.

Third, my computer specialist – L. Mizrahi – who prepared the Russian edition and whose advice I followed in preparing the English edition for print.

Finally, a special thanks to my indispensable Support Group.

HERITAGE

1. Victor

Heavily and slowly, **"Plop... plop... plop!"** And in unison with these tones – quickly and gracefully, *"Plop, plop, plop, plop."* Melodious chimes of dripping water woke Victor every morning. But, how disgusting it was indeed to wake up in the spring of 1945 in Buchenwald: cold, hungry, scared. As soon as one's tired body starts to sit up on the plank bed, a swarm of anxious thoughts comes flying from the nightmares and begins to buzz in one's consciousness. On the one hand – good news – the Allies approached, and the regime would soon fall. On the other hand, – bad – rumors that prisoner would be evacuated and executed to cover up atrocities and the campers' swinish conditions.

The possibility of imminent death forced Victor to continuously think about his secret. He strained his memory, and words and signs cherished there surfaced from the depth. He had always wanted, and now even craved, to recreate the thaumaturgic Kabbalistic formula – a prayer designed to save people.

In distant pre-war times, Victor had borne a long, pretty name. He was the rabbi of a small Polish town, then the chief rabbi of Eastern Poland, which suddenly became Western Ukraine. Then Poland had disappeared, and by the way, so had Ukraine.

Ghettos, camps and eventually Buchenwald – the Beech forest, a gigantic concentration camp on top of Etter Mountain near Weimar – the heart of German culture, appeared in his life. In this new world, the

1

prisoner began to be called Victor, either in consonance with his last name, or in derision renamed as a winner.

And the victor he was! At sixteen, an exceptionally young age, Victor was ordained as a rabbi, a tribute paid to his knowledge, and in fact, to a phenomenal memory. However, the boy's main quality was a passion for science. Not for mundane secular scholars' experiments, but for religious and humanistic research. Thus, the young rabbi continued his studies; he entered Krakow University with a philosophy major and completed a doctoral dissertation on "The Metaphysics of Kabbalah". By no means did all rabbis and Talmudists agree with Victor's views, but for him it did not matter; he studied the texts composed thousands of years ago, read and edited by generations of scientists to transfer knowledge from the very beginning of civilization.

In the university archives, fastidious Victor happened upon a manuscript written on material made of pressed plants. Victor had no doubt about the deep antiquity of his finding: the papyrus contained the ancient Aramaic text of the prayer, to summon the Messiah. Annotations to the manuscript stated that this prayer was the Sod – the sacred mystic core of the Kabbalah and that it required exegesis – the interpretation of the text.

Since he found the text, Victor continually pondered what constituted the exegesis. How to turn the ancient prayer into a key that unlocks the mysteries of metaphysics, the Kabbalah, and maybe even cosmogony? Many times had the rabbi and his disciples uttered this prayer: day and night, on holy days and weekdays, silently and aloud – but nothing happened. Only, Victor never gave up; he was convinced that the secret of the interpretation was implicit in the sound of the spell.

"**Plop... plop... plop!** *Plop, plop, plop, plop, plop.*"

Something incomprehensible in the chiming droplets bothered Victor. Of course, spring itself is a disturbing time of nature; and to meet it in the concentration camp is torture. But, it's not the first year. "May God make it the last one!" prayed rabbi. Or, "May God not make it the last one!" his late bunk neighbor, Lemel had sadly joked.

"So where do these worries come from? Do I fear death? Am I afraid not to survive until the liberation? Why such anxiety?"

Reflecting on this, Victor crawled out from under the thin blanket he shared with Bert, a newcomer who had replaced Lemel, and stepped down from the bunk bed on the cold, dirty floor. He shuffled with his wooden clogs, dragging himself to the toilet bowls in the corner of the hut. He had gotten used to easing himself publicly, but in the early morning hours most inhabitants of the barracks were still asleep, which created an illusion of relative privacy.

As the rabbi turned off the faucet, the rhythm of drops into the sink and melting icicles outdoors created a peculiar melody, and it dawned on him – the music! The prayer should be sung! And immediately another sharp and even seditious thought struck Victor. Words are just coded notes and knowing the melody one can pray in any language and even sing without words – God will hear!

However, there were no music pictograms on the papyrus. He remembered this for sure. Therefore, it would be necessary to identify a note for each word, i.e. to translate the numerical values of words into musical signs. The problem may look unsolvable for a layperson, but for the Talmudist and metaphysician it is not. For this task, he has to perform thousands of difficult calculations. Victor decided to talk to Bert. Indeed, it seemed that God had intentionally sent him in place of the deceased Lemel.

2. Bert

Bert was almost the last to wake up in the barracks. He could afford not to be in a hurry. To the envy of his neighbors, he wore wool socks, did not fight for a bigger slice of bread during the morning distribution; nor did he bribe the capo for a better work assignment. He was a "blue blood", chosen by fate. He hardly knew Yiddish, preferring to communicate in German. A native of Vienna, he had until 1943 owned a factory of precise mechanical instruments. Just before the war, he had

3

invented a new type of calculator, but the Anschluss derailed all his plans. The German authorities demanded he make modification to the factory at his own expense.

What could he do? He had to switch to the production of optic scopes. But who understands the Lord's intent? Were part of his blood not Jewish, he could just finish the war hating Nazis silently while apparently continuing to manufacture scopes for the Third Reich. How many such businessmen received a prison term after the war?

However, fate decided otherwise. The Gestapo accused Bert of having Jewish sympathies, Jewish roots, and of sexually desecrating an Aryan woman. And he thought naively that he had just simply loved Anna. His sentence was harsh and "fair": internment in the concentration camp, his factory forfeited. What tormented Bert the most was that his invention had gone for nothing.

Initially Bert sickened in Buchenwald, the camp of slow death. A heavy workload and scarce meals would gradually have finished off any athlete. Brawn had not related to Bert at all: he had never been a husky man.

In wooden shoes without socks, it was unbearably cold and slippery to trudge through the snow and ice to the quarries. SS-men beat and even shot to death the inmates who slipped and fell. Those who could not rely on their ability to balance took off their clogs and walked barefoot; they preferred a death from pneumonia to a death from battery. However, man proposes and God disposes: people rarely caught a cold but frostbitten feet happened aplenty. Bert escaped this doom too.

In the winter of 1943-44, tank scopes manufactured at the Vienna precision mechanics factory received high praise in the report of General Guderian, Chief Inspector of the armed forces of the Reich. Then somebody recalled Bert.

The camp commandant, Oberfuhrer Herman Pister, summoned Bert to his study to talk. To Pister's surprise, an inmate Jew turned out to be a German engineer and inventor, moreover, a Protestant like Oberfuhrer himself. The prisoner claimed that he had invented a miniature calculator that he could redesign from memory within a year, and then assemble an experimental model. The commandant quickly twigged that they did not have enough time to build the calculator by April 20, 1944, Adolf Hitler's birthday, but to present the Fuhrer with a never-before-seen toy by the same date of 1945 would be a great move! And he should not skimp on the cost.

The commandant switched Bert to a special favorable regime. In the first shift, he had duties as a technician at the factory, then he had a real lunch, and in the second shift, he worked at a Kuhlman drafting unit recreating the blueprints of his invention. The former engineer received woolen socks and a warm jacket. To his surprise, neither the criminals nor the communists took them away. His life started to show promise again. He recovered, became stronger, and, most importantly, the meaning of life smoldered in him. He again started to notice interesting talkers and pretty women.

He especially liked the 35-year-old green-eyed Italian, Emma, who lived in special barracks. He spotted her during the Sunday concert, which many called the mass. It was obvious that she was a singer, most probably an opera diva. Her voice, a crystal clear soprano, sounded like the angels' liturgy. Bert managed to make her acquaintance and even asked her to a movie. Emma initially refused, claiming she was too busy that evening, but promised to find time next Sunday.

Amazing how a human can immerse himself in hope when only hell surrounds him. Bert's thoughts switched again to his creation. "My baby", he called it lovingly. He dreamed about a time after the war when he would be manufacturing again... what to name the model? At one point, he wanted to name it "BERTHA" or "BERTA" in memory of his mother, just as his dad had named him Bert in her honor. Then for some time he wanted to christen it "ANNA", but his will melted away after the trial. Now a new thought sneaked into his mind. Maybe it could be "EMMA"...

3. Emma

U sually the sounds of rousing marches performed by brass bands banged out of the camp's loudspeakers early in the morning. The rumors went around that loud music muffled the sounds of the shots and cries coming from the pathology department's basements where SS-men carried out executions. Prisoners lined up in the campground for roll call, orders announcements, news, and work assignments. This type of activity did not apply to Emma and her cohabitants in the "special barracks", or in simple term, the camp's bordello. Radio speaker delivered them news; work and health issues were dealt with directly in the place during the weekdays. But on weekends and holidays, every single inhabitant of Buchenwald who could keep themselves up on their feet was taken out to the campground and stalled there even longer than usually.

"The Madame" of the bordello, the sturdily built Swabian of 40, called Nettie had a five-year term in camp for being involved in a bank robbery attempt. Under the rule of the previous camp commandant Otto Koch, who stole until he was imprisoned in Maidanek, criminals were in the saddle, and Nettie served as a capo in the women barracks. Here she became friends with the girlfriend of Walter, one of the camp's communist leaders. This connection helped Nettie keep her position when the new commandant changed capo-criminals to capo-communists. The new position provided an even better life than before, but burdened her with many more responsibilities. Nettie recruited new staff, taught good manners and rules of behavior, looked over their health, found light work during the daytime for them and continuously worked on the schedule; in short, she was never bored. Being musical and not vicious, she soon grew to love Emma for her humility and operatic talent.

Emma had been assigned to the special barrack not accidentally, but according to her indictment. She, a fellow of the Milan La Scala and the Berlin Unter den Linden, was sentenced and sent to Buchenwald as a prostitute. Perhaps it was not coincidence: the character of Cio-Cio San

6

was her favorite. When the famous Carmen Melis started to fade, Emma became her first student and was slated to replace her in "Madama Butterfly". But, love and pregnancy had entered her young life and, minutes before her stage entrance, she collapsed.

Her colleague, soprano Albanese, stood in for her and took off on a wave of success. Emma, however, became sick. Twice, one after another, she lost her unborn children, and then – her husband in the Spanish war. But she had to get back on her feet, so she started to sing again.

Albanese had already moved to the United States and Emma gradually gained recognition. Unfortunately, the war had gathered momentum, European tours practically disappeared and Emma entered the fellowship in the famous Berlin State Opera House under the direction of the renowned conductor Herbert von Karajan. She prepared herself for the character of Eve in Wagner's "Mastersingers of Nuremberg". News arrived during the height of the staging process: La Scala had been severely damaged in a bombing of Milan and would not be reopening soon. "How lucky I am that I live safely here," thought Emma, and studied even more diligently.

Then history repeated itself; it was not in the cards for Emma to conquer the opera world. The Reich Minister of Culture and Propaganda, Goebbels, came to a reception; he expressed compliments to the beauty and voice of the diva and directly proposed a night meeting for "an exquisite evaluation of her other charms." When Emma emphatically refused, Goebbels wry-smiled and sneered, "You believe that you are already Eve, but according to our data you are still a geisha…"

On the very same night, Emma was raped in her hotel room, and the police, who had only come to help the rapists, filed a report that a "madam" was illegally engaged in prostitution with "Herren Offizieren" asking 100 Reich marks from each. Banknotes with her fingerprints lay on the nightstand…

That is how Emma came to be in the camp. She first met Nettie during the "intake medical examination" and seeing the sadistic madness reigning there, understood that she had to obey Nettie and follow orders quickly. The women around her were embarrassed and reacted slowly. SS-men poured out dirty words, awarded women with smacks on their faces and tore off their clothes, leaving them in tatters. Then capos shaved them bald, dumped them down on the tables, and shaved their pubes. SS-men came by, examined their mouths, vaginas and anuses, and human beings were transformed into almost genderless creatures imbibed with fear.

The order "Take off your clothes!" she performed in a flash and completely.

"A prostitute?" asked a capo.

Emma shook her head and snapped out a "Yes!"

Something that looked like understanding flashed in Nettie's eyes.

"You will go with me to work in the bordello!"

Using scissors, she carefully cut off Emma's long dark curls leaving her with a short haircut, while whispering into her ear:

"Better they cum inside you, than come for you!"

Emma soon discovered the truth about life in Buchenwald and, shaking internally, agreed with Nettie's logic. There was no reason to torment herself with the question "Why?" It had no answer! Tens and hundreds of thousands of people were suffering because they were born in the wrong country or were of the wrong nationality. If one believed the stories told by prisoners transferred from other concentration camps, there are millions of victims! Personal "Why?" fades in comparison with collective grief.

Gradually Emma learned how to blunt her consciousness, lying under a heavy guard or a light prisoner, grasping her shoulders or breasts and pushing with frenzy his rage, despair and fear into her body. The only one thought bothered her: "Am I healthy?" Pregnancy has not occurred even when a client did not use protection. So hope whispered to her, "One day it'll be over; you will go home and have children…"

Children – it was her sacred word!

4. Children

The preparation for a concert usually starts right after an everlasting Sunday line up directly at the campground. Children crowded close to musicians, singers, magicians and jugglers. Only trained animals are absent. There are bears in the Zoo behind the fence, but after a gypsy was thrown into their cage to be torn to pieces, nobody even wants to watch them. Everything in this "plaza" looks interesting. Many will show their props; some even let you touch their things. Not everybody, for sure. Do not even approach a few; they are worse than the capos. There are also "classes" here; just on the ground, next to the stub of the giant oak, which succumbed to the bombing. One inmate teaches the children to pray, one to read, and another to steal.

Isaac loves to practice sleight of hand: nobody is able to detect how he takes a pfennig out of your pocket on a bet. After twenty wins, you collect enough for a ticket to a movie! Yves, the blind French boy, is sitting quietly aside waiting to find out whether or not they will play "La Marseillaise" today. The commandant approved it twice. After they first played it women were publicly whipped, and the second time Günter was hanged. It seems the commandant had better forbid playing it.

Yves does not work; he is a courier between blocks. They say he was in the Resistance and got blind after interrogations by the Gestapo. The "doctor", however, said that he lost his vision during his childhood; therefore, he is so well oriented; otherwise, he would have been clumsy like Tadeusz, who caught a butt stock blow to the back of his head from an SS-man. All the boys from the chorus are called now. The rehearsal is starting soon.

Yankel settled himself next to Istvan who was one year older. Together they manage to sing well. Yankel skipped low tones, but Istvan did the same with high pitches and they never sang out of tune. Both of them were transferred to Buchenwald from Auschwitz right after New Year, but Istvan lived in Auschwitz two years longer than Yankel, therefore the tattoo number on his forearm was smaller and consisted of smaller digits. You should remember this fact to set the right game rule: the bigger or the smaller number should win, depending on whom you are playing with.

Here comes Bolek! Actually, Vasya who sort of babysits him, like an older brother, brought him. But they could not be brothers; Vasya is Russian, and Bolek is a Pole. Every time they come, Haym from the Jewish "Small camp," comes running and watches from aside and once he even cried. Bolek is just a little kid and an underfed tiny chicken, but on very high notes, he has no equal. Even our prima donna from the special barracks cannot outcheep him, and she sings first class! Every senior boy is in love with her! She is a beauty: Marlene Dietrich is a long way behind! The wife of the former camp commandant Else Koch, who was called "The Bitch of Buchenwald", would never have tolerated such a beauty and with her beloved whip would either have mutilated her or beat her to death.

Well, we are starting the singing soon. Yes, Sol has come; there he is, as always. He works as an interpreter and "in spite of his small height" he speaks twelve languages. He knew six of them before the war and other six he learned in Auschwitz: he catches them on the move. He has a lucky number tattooed on his arm, all eights; but it does not help, everybody knows that, so nobody plays numbers with him. But Sol always knows all the news and so he gets an "extra income": an eighth of a bread allowance or half a cigarette.

Old Itzhak, the conductor of the orchestra and the chorus, got sick today. Nathan, a former cantor, substitutes him. Sol said that Itzhak had diarrhea in the morning. In case typhus has flared up again in the "Small camp", the quarantine camp, where all Jews are residing will be separated from the big Buchenwald and no fun will be left to the Jews. Just lie down and die from the blues! Many will follow that way... The quarantine camp was built on the soccer field so Jews were called soccers or suckers after that. The joke did not stay funny for long: soon it became incomprehensible, as the population of the camp changed so quickly.

Nathan announced that today we would sing Bach's chorales without words, only the melody. It's very convenient for everybody: no mistakes with words – one punishment less; and a chorale itself consists of two melodies – one for the low voice and another for the high, which means it's easier to sing it. Should we perform well the commandant will reward us with ersatz-bread with some ersatz-preserves. So, let's start, our nourisher, Herr Bach!

5. J. S. Bach

"**D**addy, Daddy, look what a huge beech!" exclaimed seven-year old Willie when the family of Johann Sebastian Bach, the concertmaster at the court of Wilhelm Ernst, Duke of Saks-Weimar, came out into a glade in the beech forest at the top of Ettersberg Hill.

"It's not a beech, but an oak," corrected Cattie, who was just one year older than her brother, but rightly considered herself the head of the Bach family kids' team. Yet, to confirm the authority of her statement, she tugged at the sleeve of her father's waistcoat and smiling alluringly, asked, "Right, Daddy?"

"True, my clever little one, but Willie made a mistake quite naturally. See, how many beeches are around here," said Johann in an accommodating spirit.

In this warm spring day of 1717, the air was filled with the fine aroma of fresh leaves, grass and wild flowers. As the days grew warmer the townspeople, recovering from odious limited winter mobility, flocked to the countryside for picnics.

From here, the top of the hill, trilling and at the same time calming view of Weimar, situated in the scenic valley, opened up as if to tempt painters. In the center of the landscape were the bell tower and the palace. It was only this morning that Bach had performed his newly composed fugue in the palace church. The Duke gave it somewhat reserved approval, but, frowned, refused the composer's request for a transfer to the vacant position of the Kapellmeister, the court musical director.

The composer's wife, Maria, tried to placate him, "Johann, calm down! You are such an explosive man."

"I am not explosive, I am temperamental!" answered Bach, "But where is the protestant honesty of the Duke, his devotion to God, where are the ideals of Luther? The Duke wants to appoint the late director Drese's goofy son to the position of his father! What sort of masses or liturgies will parishioners hear then? I will tell the Duke all this to his face!"

"Johann, please, stop. The Duke could punish you as easily as he would a common peasant."

"Then I will just leave Weimar! There will always be a position as organist available to me in Thuringia!"

The need to constantly think about financial security was an everlasting splinter lodged in the soul of thirty-two year old Bach. His eldest brother Christoph, the organist in Ohrdruf, had brought up his two younger brothers, when their parents had died. This was habitual in the big family of Bachs. The eldest brother of Johann Sebastian's grandfather has also reared his youngest sibling. Thank God, everybody became good musicians. Unfortunately, wealth did not stick to any of them. Johann attended a prestigious school only because of the scholarship, and often got his honorariums fighting tooth and nail. Even his last salary raise four years ago Bach acquired only by threatening to resign. And the marriage? Had he not received an inheritance from his maternal uncle Tobias, "may his soul repose in Christ", he and Maria, his third cousin, would have been collecting their orphan dowry for a long time while kissing in the organ loft under the pretense of music lessons.

But really, could these woes of life outweigh the happiness of his being in the love of God, Maria and music? These three hypostases of the one big feeling overwhelmed him like clear, powerful sounds of organs rising to the high ribbed vaults of the Gothic churches.

Music theory had captured Bach more and more over the last few years. He wrote forty-six preludes and chorales, for his future organist's manual, "The little organ book". Here he revealed an excellent contrapuntal technique, when different melodies and themes, playing together are represented by different, but compatible voices.

Gradually new thoughts started to overcome him. For music to sound heavenly, a stringed instrument should be tuned, tempered, not as by convention, but in the right way! Johann had obtained these ideas from the wonderful book of Andreas Werckmeister, and he himself drew it from a Chinese prince from the Ming dynasty. It was asserted in Werckmeister's book that true tune follows mathematical laws described by Johannes Kepler in his manuscript "The Harmony of the Worlds." Kepler wrote that harmonic proportions in music repeat harmonic proportions in astrology and that in the rarest moments of history "planets sing in full harmony." And then what? Is the Universe creating? Is the Messiah coming? Nobody knew the answer. Not Kepler, nor Werckmeister; not Bach, nor the prince from the Ming dynasty.

The sun had started to go down, and the children tired from running and eating were taking a nap on the warm rugs. It was time to return home. Maria's elder sister Frieda, a spinster, who lived with the Bach family, was their housekeeper. Now, she was caring for the two toddlers, three-year-old Carl Fillip and two-year-old Johann Gottfried. Maria missed them already, and Johann had work to do. After collecting their picnic things and waving goodbye to the beautiful fairy-tale oak, the Bach family hurried home.

Johann liked that they lived in a house just a five-minute walk from his work place, the Duke's palace. Close to the palace was the city's St. Peter and St. Paul's church. Bach's children had been baptized in this church. The godfather of Carl Philipp was the famous composer and theorist Georg Philipp Telemann; oh, how desperately Johann wanted to talk to him! Alas, he was far away. Bach would now talk to his friend and cousin Johann Walther, who worked as an organist in that same church. Tonight the maestro planned to reveal his new ideas to Walter.

The folio, which Johann had bought at Christmas time and since then slowly and thoroughly read, now occupied his thoughts more than ever. It was a collection of works, "The Jewish War" and "Antiquities of the Jews" by the famous historian of antiquity Titus Flavius Josephus. The Flemish explorer-Hellenist Arnoldus Arlenius found the Greek manuscript of Josephus during Martin Luther's time while cataloging the codices of the archives of Spain ambassador to Venice, Diego Hurtado de Mendoza. Arlenius had published Greek texts, which served as the base for translations into other languages. Such a book in German had charmed Bach. Initially he wanted to search the text for proof of Luther's accusations against Jews, but he found nothing like that in this book. Instead – "Oh, those predestined chains of fortuities!" – Johann happened upon the problem of death and survival whose mathematical formulation was similar to his harmonics. This puzzle was called "Josephus' problem". Well, who would doubt that problems concerned even Josephus?

6. Titus Flavius Josephus

D aylight no longer entered the cistern. Myriads of tiny droplets of sweat started to cover the face and body of Yosef. One could not endure this torment for a long time. The underground water reservoir allowed them to hide here for many days, but limited access to air would bring agonizing death to the whole squad. The scouts of the XV Apollonian Legion had already discovered the secret ventilation openings at the surface and were sealing them in with gravel and clay.

Thirty-year-old General Yosef Ben Matityahu, a rabbi and a nobleman, the commander of the Galilean Army and the fallen citadel of Tel-Jafat, had to persuade his fellow soldiers to surrender. He might as well have tried to persuade twenty-eight-year-old Titus, Legate, patrician, and son of the Chief-Commander of the Roman Army in Judea, General

Vespasian, to stop the assault. Nevertheless, Yosef had to undertake something to change his men's decision.

Firstly, he did not want to die. It seemed too stupid to him just to quit such an interesting life, filled with mysteries and exquisite feelings.

Secondly, from the very beginning he had been personally opposed to the Judean rebellion: fighting with Rome seemed to him a battle against civilization, culture and esthetics. He believed that all the iniquities against Jews came from ignorance and misunderstanding their religion, customs and traditions. Therefore, he saw it as his duty to explain Jewish values to the whole world. By debating such issues in the Roman Senate, he was even able to attain the release of several arrested rabbis. At that time, he had discovered Rome for himself and was charmed and captured forever by this magnificent, yet poetic city.

Thirdly, by surrendering he hoped to preserve the lives of his men, forty guards, who had survived in the secret cistern, hidden from legionnaires who had soaked the city in blood.

And last, the comet that shone in last year's sky like a "fire sword", which rebels read as a sign of luck, in Yosef's view was an omen of defeat. However, he did not run away from this danger. He obeyed the decision of the Jerusalem Sanhedrin and accepted the post of Commander. Indeed, the leader of the army should be educated and thoughtful, not bloodthirsty and impulsive like leaders of popular militia.

The General tried cautiously to discern if any supported surrender. None! The fanaticism of his soldiers burst forth with outcries, "Die together! Brother's sword, not Roman cross!"

Yosef pondered, "Are they really right? Is dying better than living, and dying together easier? Warriors, like lambs, are ready to accept slaughter from the hand of a brother-in-arms? It's mass madness, indeed!"

Only his personal bodyguard, and his loyal friend, Eleazar, whispered, "I am with you my master, whatever your choice. I will defend you till the last drop of my blood!"

"Well… at least one person supports you, following his own heart or mind.

…Through the mass of rocks blocking the exit came the muffled voices of the legionnaires, "Surrender and we'll dig you out by tomorrow morning; otherwise we won't even bother!"

"Men," said Yosef, "if each of us is ready to accept death from his brothers-in-arms, it should be performed in the way of old, and not as wild barbarians or gladiators would do it."

"Agreed! Tell us, General! Teach us, rabbi!"

The eyes of his soldiers turned to their leader, who in this difficult moment, provided support for their frenzied minds.

"Each of us will choose a number from one to forty one. Those who pick the same numbers draw straws until everyone has a different number. Then we form a circle, and start departing this world in sequence. First goes number one, then, moving from right to left, every third will be leaving this life: first, fourth, seventh and so on. The solders standing on either side help each brave heart to die quickly. The last two of us will help each other. And now it is time for silence: pray, remember the family, mentally bid farewell to loved ones and decide under which number you want to enter the Circle of Death."

A rumble of voices approved Yosef's plan. Now he faced the core problem: to identify the numbers of the two last survivors for himself and Eleazar. In almost complete darkness the general began calculating in his mind.

"The first dies; the forth dies; the seventh, the tenth and so on to the fortieth. Then let's skip number Forty-one and One. No! Number One has already died! Then let's skip Forty-one and Two. Number Three is going. Skipping number Forth… No, he was killed before; than the fifth and the sixth. The seventh dies; wrong, he is already down, and then the eighth is going… God! It's impossible to count this way because it's impossible to remember all the numbers. I should continue counting around the circle. After Forty-one is Forty-two, then Forty-three; and he is going to die. Then

Forty-six, Forty-nine, etc… It's possible to calculate the number of the last man to die. Every third person is killed; and there are thirty-nine such trios, until only two people are left. Therefore, the number of the last to die is 39 x 3 – 2 = 115. And the numbers of the two survivors are 113 and 114. I want to be One hundred fourteen! I want to! But what initial numbers in the circle of forty-one warriors correspond to 113 and 114?"

Yosef's head was splitting from the tension. In the darkness with no way to write, he could not solve the damned problem, which might cost him his life! Then the thirty-year-old rabbi, son and grandson of rabbis, decided that now was the time for prayer. The family treasured the sheet of papyrus carrying the words of the ancient prayer – a prayer nearly impossible to sing in its entirety, given the high note at the end. The legend had it that Moses moved the seawaters apart with the help of this prayer to save his people from the pharaoh's army.

Certainly, it was time for Yosef to pray, perhaps the last chance to pray. And he quietly sang that prayer as best he could and as long as he could. Then just to make sure he repeated the prayer silently. Nothing happened. It was still dark and damp, and breathing became labored. Then Yosef appealed to God as he would to his father, grandfather, rabbi, teacher, friend, guard, Sanhedrin, Roman Senate, mother, wife, courtesan, horse, dog – all the creatures whom he respected, loved or cherished. "Accept me into your essence, into your spiritual bosom, enfold me like incense, encircle me like a necklace… Like a necklace!"

Yosef began trembling, for indeed a golden necklace hung around his neck. It was a gift received in Rome from Poppaea Sabina, a passionate collector of exquisite sensations, a former concubine and then the wife of the emperor Nero. A jeweler's skillful hands had linked forty golden coins and hung a small turquoise bead to each. Later Yosef had added a Mogen David. The necklace was now composed of forty-one elements, conveniently beginning with a star.

Here was the key to life! The rest was just a matter of attention and order. Tearing off beads from every third coin – "killing it" – Yosef discovered numbers of the two elements left undamaged in the necklace: fourteen and twenty-nine – his and Eleazar's lucky numbers!

...In the morning, as Titus the Legate, himself had sworn to keep alive those who surrendered, the legionnaires dug out the entrance to the cave and met with an incredible scene: the thirty-nine corpses of Judean warriors and two unarmed living men, Yosef and Eleazar. No treasures were found in the cave save that, the rabbi wore a very simple necklace of Roman aurei, untrimmed, not even one turquoise bead. They all saw it – everybody...

7. Everybody

"Yes," Bert eventually said, "I agree!"

Long conversations and extended debates had preceded this short phrase. Initially Bert didn't even want to hear about calculations. "Is now really an appropriate time and place to scrutinize some sort of metaphysical theory?" asked the engineer.

"On the contrary, it's the most suitable," opposed the rabbi. "I am trying to strengthen spirit of people who believe that God is killed on the battlefields and incinerated in the crematorium furnaces of concentration camps."

"Well," replied Bert, "Let's say I would be able to calculate the melody of the prayer. Let's also assume it's the True Hymn – then what? Who in the world or even in the concentration camp will benefit from it? It will be senseless here in the same way as Champollion's work deciphering the Rosetta stone!"

"If it saves just one person, then the work is not in vain!" answered Victor.

His ardent reasoning slowly melted Bert's icy skepticism. After all, the calculator had been constructed and was now ready for a challenging run. "Is it really less important to compute music than to calculate an optic scope system?" Bert asked himself and calculated, calculated, calculated…

Gradually he discovered that all the numbers could be arranged into two groups, resembling harmonic rows. One sequence went in descending order, while the second ascended to an extremely high note. He showed Emma these hypothetical notes.

"Looks like Bach," she said, "but the first voice is too high, I would not be able to sing that last note. Where did you get this fugue from?"

"I wrote it myself," scowled the engineer, so Emma understood that she should not question him.

In the beginning of their acquaintance, the former singer was touched by his gentle invitation to a movie and – in the darkness – to his very sensual caresses to which she responded… But soon Bert discovered that he had fallen in love with a "julia", a camp prostitute. The bitterness of his disillusion extinguished his tenderness; he would've gone to the bordello to ravish her roughly, but Jews were not allowed there… Only the restoration work on "BERTA" – "Of course "BERTA" and no other names!" – supported him and gradually brought him, by Victor's definition, "to a state of pure friendship with Emma."

"You know, there is one kid who might be able to make this high note," suggested Emma, "but most of the first voice is too low for him."

During the council with Victor, they decided that Yankel and Istvan, teenagers from the choir, would sing the two voices, while the highest notes would be given to little Bolek.

"You wanted only Jewish children, didn't you?" Bert teased his neighbor.

"It's not a problem; in the camp everybody's a little bit Jewish, even you," Victor countered, unwilling to reveal the secret of Bolek's origin.

One way or another, despite the absence of joint rehearsals, the project progressed, and a trial run was set for April 8, 1945. Itzhak or Nathan would listen to the "new chorale without words" during concert practice just after Sunday line up. The only problem Victor anticipated was the high note at the end of the prayer. So far, no one had heard Bolek sing it, even though he claimed that he did.

However, disaster came unexpectedly. During the lineup, Commandant Pister announced that in the interests of Germany, the concert was cancelled and prisoners in columns of six must march out immediately from the campground to neighboring camps. SS-men started running, dogs barking; inmates were crushed and beaten into formation. The project had been crushed totally. Nevertheless, after the departure of the first several thousand prisoners, the process slowed. Remaining inmates were forced into their barracks and forbidden to exit.

Nobody brought them any food during the day. From time to time, the short bursts of machinegun fire, single shots and people's screams, were heard from the main camp. With night approaching, Sol brought news: the Allies are close, the camp in Orhdruf has already been freed, forty thousand of our prisoners have been deported. Later, in the darkness – no obstacle for him – came Yves passing information from the underground Camp Liberation committee. "Prisoners deported to die! Delay exit from camp, hide children. Commandant has already bolted."

That night everybody slept badly. Hunger, disturbing sounds and worrisome thoughts kept them awake: "Will we be destroyed or liberated?"

There with no reveille siren in the morning; bread was not dispensed and there was no usual line-up and roll-call! The air seemed strained, filled with human emotions. In the afternoon, people, in spite of the order, slowly started to creep out of their barracks. Two SS-men escorted a group of prisoners to the "Small camp" – among them Emma, Vasya and little Bolek.

"Can it be true that somebody ratted them out at the end?" thought Victor.

The two soldiers added to the group several teenagers from Barrack 56, including Sol, Yankel and Istvan and everybody proceeded behind the barracks to the grounds strewn with corpses.

"Sing! Sing!" cried Victor, trembling in fear that it might be too late.

8. The Contact

"Listen to what those idiots are singing," Hans grinned, "It's Bach's chorale."

"Extra proof that we are right. An inferior race should adopt the culture of a superior one, not the opposite; and even before their execution sing the superior's requiem, not its own degenerate hymn," agreed Fritz, loading a Walther picked up in the office of the run-away Pister.

"Do you think I would've let them sing their hymns? Yeah, right! Bach is fine. Let them entertain us for the last time."

"So be it!" said Hans, "Amen!"

At this exact time, by means of the portable radio transmitter assembled from stolen parts the underground Committee sent a radiogram to the Allies, "Message from Buchenwald! SOS! Help! SS want to exterminate us!"

Several times already Gwidon has tapped out this plea in three languages. Surprisingly, subtle Morse sounds could be heard amid the static.

"Not Russian," said Gwidon. "Not French," added Walter. "English; the third Army of the United States is sending help a.s.a.p." translated Harry.

"Hurray! And what does a.s.a.p. mean?"

"Who knows? Probably some sort of unit. The main thing is that they will come here soon!"

"We can start uprising now! Distribute the hidden weapons!" decided the Committee.

"A – a – a – A – A – a – a – a – a!" ringing in the air. These sounds became higher and thinner, ascending in the sky, space, the cosmos … Suddenly, silence – just an open mouth, goggle eyes and the inflated veins on Bolek's neck revealed the work of his voice box. The air behind the prisoners' backs vibrated as is over hot asphalt or during an earthquake; a blue gloving ring arose in front of the barbed wire separating the camp from the free land.

As the ring grew and expanded, in the space behind it, like on a movie screen, there appeared a wooden fence with a horse hitched to it. Next to the horse stood a tall, strong man with a golden mustache, dressed in a suede jacket and hat, yellow sharp-nosed boots and a couple of colt revolvers on his wide leather belt. He was looking at the group of emaciated people with an expression of anxiety and wonder on his kind, tanned face. He would have taken them for convicts because of their striped uniforms, except most of them were children.

"Hey! Who are you? Stick'em up!" yelled Hans readying his machinegun.

"Move aside!" Fritz commanded the prisoners, creating an open space to fire.

In fear for this handsome Messiah, so like a Hollywood actor, Emma threw herself into the gap between him and SS-men. A short burst and two single, but very loud shots, rang out simultaneously. Children were watching in terror and delight as both soldiers fell to the ground shot through the head. Little Bolek lying on the ground covered by Vasya, the breathless body of Emma and their rescuer, bleeding to death.

"Don't die!" Sol screamed in all the languages known to him, running headlong to the hero lying by the fence.

It was too late: a Schmeisser bullet hit his chest just beneath the spot where on the white cotton shirt was attached a silver Mogen David.

"Shhhit," faintly exhaled the man and went silent forever.

"Come back, Sol! Come back! The window is closing!" the children shouted.

Shuddering and sobbing, Sol tore off the Mogen David from his white shirt and ran back, smudging tears all over his freckled face.

"The Messiah was Marshall Montgomery!" he cried. "We have been liberated!"

Shots and shouts were coming from the Buchenwald side and a number of prisoners with rifles in their hands were already running toward "Small camp."

At the barracks, children told this unbelievable story to adults, but no traces of the Allies were found. It seemed strange as the underground Committee members confirmed that they had started a rebellion, expecting an American battalion named "a.s.a.p." to come to help. For two more days, hungry but already free Buchenwaldians waited for the American Army. On April 11, 1945, a Captain and three soldiers in a Jeep cautiously approached to the barbed wire fence of Buchenwald...

9. Sol

Mom called me from the University of Miami hospital. "Come," she said, "Sol has died."

The news was sad, but expected. My stepfather, Solomon Greenberg, a kind 75-year-old man, had been gravely ill for two years, struggling with cancer. On my way to JFK I remembered how he, a Holocaust survivor, outlived his first wife and raised two daughters, met my mom in one of the Florida Jewish Centers, which took care of immigrants from Russia. I thought that Mom's friendship with him and subsequent wedlock greatly affected our family. It brought fifteen years of happiness to my mom and provided me with Sol's guardianship and help. Not just help with learning English – every newcomer appreciates that – but French, Spanish, Polish, as well as the most valuable and subtle – lessons of life. Because of his efforts, I turned from a Moscow punk into an American linguist and UN interpreter. If it were not for Sol, who knows where I might have ended up after starting a career in a local Jacksonville pub gulping wineglasses full of vodka for spectators' fun.

I was expecting to see Sol's daughters, Emily and Jill, generally "not bad broads". But... they had always perceived their father's new immigrant wife as a caricature of their mother and a potential competitor for their inheritance. They always behaved arrogantly, aloof, well... in a sort of disgusting way. Four of Sol's granddaughters were pretty and looked at me with some interest. But all their "mishpokhe" believed that I was a "shmuck" and disapproved of any relationship with the girls. Anyway, they all lived far away, in New York, and local Florida chicks were close at hand.

No doubts Sol loved me. He always wanted to have a son, then a grandson, but he had no luck; and here was this flap-eared Russian boy, somewhat reticent and therefore aggressively impudent. Sol was always nice to me, like a friend. And he always said to my mom, "Michael can achieve anything he wants. Do not restrict him!" And Mom always echoed the Soviet era, "This isn't allowed and that's not allowed either..."

Sol told to me a great deal about the concentration camp and his fellow prisoners. Looks like Sol never had close connections with any of them, yet he knew almost everything about many of them. Victor had emigrated to Latin America and in the mid-sixties became the chief rabbi of... Argentina or something. The doctor, a former prisoner, who stayed to work in the infirmary after the liberation of Buchenwald, operated on Emma. She would have died of peritonitis, if the Americans hadn't come with their magic penicillin. Bert took her to Switzerland where he opened a calculator factory. They had two boys, but eventually they separated... Both Yankel and Istvan became Nobel Prize laureates, and that kid, Bolek, you would not believe it, became the chief rabbi of Israel.

Concerning Sol himself, he was very happy with his life. I often chatted with him about the Messiah, whose Mogen David he had taken. He generally avoided talking about this topic with other people, perhaps because Victor had disapproved of Sol's actions or maybe others took Sol for a fool. In same way, he hated to explain to nurses the meaning of the four eights tattooed on his forearm. Well, everything was now in the past...

After the funeral, Sol's old friend, a lawyer and executor of his will approached the family and asked everybody to his office the next day to hear the will of the deceased. To everybody's surprise, I was personally invited.

In the morning, the lawyer read us the will. Among the many expected chapters, relating to the house and bank accounts there was one chapter concerning me in particular. Sol had left to me "a dear souvenir of his youth." With these words, the executor took out a 2.5" x 2.5" jewelry box. Sol's daughters became tense, pursing their lips, while my mom raised her head proudly as if in victory. The lawyer opened the box, and to both sides' disappointment, everybody saw…

…"It's only a policeman's badge!" pronounced Emily, the elder sister.

"For $5.00 on eBay," added younger Jill.

On the black velvet lay a silvery Mogen David with the word MARSHALL in its center…

The plane was taking me home, to New York. So far, Mom had refused to move to join me there. I was still thinking of my inheritance. Now I understood why the Polish boy Sol thought of Marshal Montgomery, commander of Allies infantry. No boy in continental Europe would have used the word "marshal" for a policeman. I imagined how many times they later laughed at Sol…

"Well, suppose the SS-men were killed by rebels; suppose the blue shining was just a dream; but then from whom was the star removed?"

What explanation could I think of? Of the prayer's magical power, which twisted time and space and allowed an American marshal of the past to save innocent children of the future? My only rational explanation was that a kind American soldier, a former police marshal, later gave the badge to the boy. Everything suited me in this story except for one thing. I believed Sol.

To finally close the case, on my return to New York I went to 47th Street to consult to a familiar jeweler.

"How much do you think this is worth?" I asked. "It's from WWII or just before."

"That means it's already 50 bucks, but it's shiny not like a badge would have been, and it's heavier than a usual badge. Aha... this is silver, which means it is $100. But they never produced silver badges; therefore, it's a specially ordered commemorative service medal, which means it's even more expensive. You should investigate when it was produced and for what occasion. Do you mind if I clean the back side a little and look for a stamp?"

I did not mind. After a quick cleaning, he inspected it through an eyepiece and very suspiciously looked at me.

"Where did you get this?" he asked, his voice suddenly hoarsened. "Here is the stamp *F & H*. It's a rarity! 'Farrington and Hunnwell!' You should consult Sotheby's!"

I politely wished him good-bye and left. I had trusted Sol not in vain: "Farrington and Hunnwell Co" existed only between 1830 and 1860!

Perhaps it was now my turn to store this evidence of twisted time and space and to keep silent.

People on Sixth Avenue were hurrying about as usual. Next to the Hilton, statues of women's bodies chilled above the slick pool of autumn water...

JUST IN CASE

Slightly weary from her household chores, Hannah sat down for a moment on the dining room chair with the high, carved back and comfortable armrests, standing now at the head of the oaken kitchen table. Here she fed her family on weekdays, and in the dining room – on weekends and holidays. In the past, this honorable chair had been occupied by her first husband; then, after his death, by the second one, also deceased; and now it belonged entirely to her eldest son, Ike. He rarely stayed at his father's house, but on such occasions, the comfortable yet bulky chair followed Ike from the dining room into the kitchen, where it became an inconvenience to all cooking and serving.

However, this visit was unusual due to both its cause and duration. For more than a year, Ike had been hiding in his native village from the plague that had seized the capital and its surroundings. If he would only manage the farm and find a wife, his mother's joy would be boundless. Alas, the issue had long been decided upon and without any reconsideration, for philosophy and magic undividedly possessed the young man's mind. A scholarship for exceptional ability in math allowed Ike to have the best possible education, and his stepfather's inheritance let him live without worries for the future. Therefore, it couldn't be said that moving to the village greatly disrupted the steady flow of his life. Every day, starting from his school years, Ike had made a daily plan and, most importantly, followed it closely. He had brought books and tools with him to the village; however, his main luggage did not take up any space. It consisted of a heavy load of knowledge and countless thoughts about the nature of things, the matter of the universe, and the possibility of its cognition.

"There is a good reason why *Cartesius[1]* delineated the two substances, extended and cogitative, that make up the world. The first constitutes the universe and the second governs it. And the summit of the latter is God. But while the great philosopher separated them in opposition to one another, I, on the contrary, will bind them together. The consequences of this binding, however, are best kept to oneself and ought to not be revealed, even to well-wishers. After all, it directly means that God is in every point of space, in every one of its smallest particles or corpuscles. Therefore, by studying the structure of these corpuscles, we are actually studying God and by influencing them, we become godlike."

The young philosopher chuckled at his own thoughts. Everything looked so harmonious and wild at the same time that discussing it with anybody could be more dangerous than remaining in a plagued city.

"The difficulty lies in the fact that Man tries to understand the whole and manage it. But the smaller the part of the whole, the harder it is to understand and manage. God himself rules the particles invisible to the naked eye: their division into smaller parts is probably indefinite. At least, that's what my mathematical work proves. For example, let's take the method of *direct fluxions[2]*, or the *expansion of a function into an infinite series[3]*. Man is not given the ability to comprehend infinity, yet this is not necessary. For any job or calculation, it is enough to have only a few of the first terms. That is why it is impossible for us to reach or to cognize God in full. However, to come close to and understand Him well – but of course!"

"Ike, come eat! Breakfast is ready!" mother interrupted his thought.

---

[1] – a Latinized form of the name of Rene Descartes, a French philosopher and mathematician, father of Analytic geometry
[2] – differential calculus, derivatives
[3] – one of the main mathematical methods of the young scientist

"Mother, leave me something on the garden table, I'll eat later."

He had a long day ahead with tasks scheduled in advance. He wanted to organize his thoughts regarding a method of *reverse fluxions*[4]: calculate the length of a curved line, the area of a figure, and the volume of a body. If he had time, he would also draw up clear objections to the followers of Cartesius. But, the most exciting business for today would be to expand an ancient magic spell into a series! If the function of this spell is to turn a man into a disembodied spirit, then hypothetically, the main term of the series should transform him into a small living creature. And Ike desired to start with this task.

Hannah was not entirely pleased with her son's behavior. "Now that he has become a learned scientist, impressing his mother's will upon him would be the wrong thing to do and, in truth, impossible" she thought. So, reluctantly, Hannah brought a bowl of oatmeal, translucent golden apple jelly, and slices of bread fresh from the oven to the small table nestled beneath the shade of a sprawling tree. She had to rush: aside from chores around the house, she was burdened with the cares of the land and the farm.

Mother, along with the younger children, had already set out for the field when Ike stepped out into the garden. In the summertime, it was hotter out there than inside the house with its thick walls and closed shutters, but in return, it smelled pleasantly of fruits and flowers. The porridge in the faience bowl had long cooled. Bees flew round the jar of jelly. All of that mattered little to the young philosopher. He was much more troubled by the application of mathematics to the magic spell. Fresh from university Ike was not yet disturbed by the result, or the consequences; he planned to think these over later as needed. Only one thing bothered him now: in the case of a negative result, how would he distinguish a mathematical mistake from incorrect initial data within the spell itself?

Not noticing that the oatmeal had cooled and that the bees had impudently consumed his dessert, Ike, lost in deep thought, spread the jelly

---

[4] – integral calculus, integrals

over his bread and ate his breakfast. Formulas and series swam in his mind. The main term determined what the object would turn into. The second term described its base, probably food. Then, the third one… the components of the food and so forth down to the smallest *corpuscles*[5].

"Never mind these small terms," thought the magician. "We'll disregard them in this experiment; therefore we should just say…" And he mentally recited a portion of the ancient spell. The tricky part was that, according to the mathematical calculation, the spell should be cut short, halfway thro–

Ike did not understand what had happened. It seemed to him that he had fallen off the bench and he found himself sprawled beside the giant trunk of a baobab under a huge wooden shed resting on curved wooden poles. In fact, he was not lying, but rather sitting… in the pose of a sphinx. Bloody h…orror! The paws of the sphinx were coated in black fur and ended in sharp claws. He stretched: the claws shot out from his toe pads and retracted back inside. "Meow!" said the sphinx. And the philosopher realized with fright that the spell itself, and his expansion into series, had proven extremely successful and, damn it, now he was, in the eyes of all, not a graduate of the university, but just a black cat! This could not be true!

The discovery struck the unfortunate magician so deeply that for several minutes he wailed not just like a cat, but like a cat in heat. Luckily, there was nobody in the house to shoo away the mad animal. But, despite the fact that spring was long over, his pleading cries had reached the ears of the neighbor's tomcat. In one jump, he reached the orchard ready to help the stranger, and in another jump, he had landed on the cat's back. "Out of the frying pan into the fire!" Ike tried to squirm out from under the muscular body, which pressed him to the ground in an attempt to gain the cat's love. No one knows what would have ended their fight if Ike hadn't, with a purely human motion, thrown back his head into the tomcat's nose.

---

[5] – the scientist used name for microscopic particles

Snorting, the visitor bounced aside and hissed; "Now I'll get you!" But at this moment, the hand of Providence became the hand of a passing neighbor who splashed water out of her bucket onto them. Both cats disbanded with caterwauls. The cold well water doused the lust of the tomcat and the panic of the black cat, into which the philosopher had been transformed.

The doors and the windows of the house were shut. Alas, he had to return to the garden and climb the tree for safety. From a new degree of perception, coupled by the young man's fright, the tree looked like a baobab. In reality, it was just an ordinary apple tree bearing ripening apples.

Ike sat on a branch until evening. He had no luck. No spell helped. Even the mathematical formulas, which had always been his friends, refused to serve him. The magician recited the spell forwards, backwards in full and in short, yet to no avail.

In the evening, Ike's family returned. Lights and voices from the windows enticed him to come inside but Ike was afraid of his strict mother, who could not bear cats. She looked out into the orchard several times, cleared the small table, went to her neighbor's and eventually, in bewilderment, closed the front door. The poor magician did not know where to go. He wanted to eat and to cry but he already knew what this would bring from cats and humans, and kept silent. The first bout of panic had passed, and Ike mentally showered himself with every possible curse.

"Idiot! A philosopher with a tail! Who's to blame that you dared to experiment on yourself with the most sophisticated craft, alone and with no assistant?"

The night was cool. He could only rejoice that it was now summer, and not winter. "Lord, show me the right way," prayed Ike. "I swear I'll never challenge your prerogative again. Well, maybe I'll dabble a little in alchemy. That, at least, is not the lot of the divine, is it? I promise that instead of magic I will concentrate my thoughts *on natural philosophy*[6]!"

---

[6] – physics

31

To prove his sincere intention Ike stared at the Moon, shining in the sky. The nighttime patron of lovers and magicians was sending its silver light of hope down onto Earth. But this was possibly the first time that it had illuminated the path for a philosopher in a cat's body who was trying to immerse his curious mind in the secrets of the universe.

"The Moon, revolving around the Earth, is falling onto it at every moment; this means that the Earth influences its companion and causes such movement. Given that the laws of *influence*[7] and motion are the same for all bodies, one can compare the orbital acceleration of the Moon to the acceleration of a body falling from a height."

For quite a long time, the black cat thought of the topic, which was not only new for him, but far from most of his contemporaries in human form. But even cats get tired of thinking about philosophy and fall into salutary sleep. The young man dreamt that he knew how to return to his former state. He only needed to recite the magic spell in reverse. However, he had already no doubt that it was not enough to have only the main term of the spell's expansion into a series. Maybe two terms? What was the second, seemingly insignificant component? Food! What had he eaten? Bread and fruit jelly. So, he must to try to use that for his return to his original body! But what sort of jelly was it? He did not remember. Mother used to prepare many different kinds of jellies and preserves. Sneaking into the house, untying all the knots on the dozens of jars and pots, and tasting all the contents, had now become an unthinkably complex business. And, if in addition mother caught a cat licking her preserves... But, what if now he needed another food? Not human. "Hiss my ass!"

Early morning found the black cat in the apple tree. Not far away from him, a silly little bird was greeting the sunrise with a cheery chirping.

"If you were in my shoes," thought Ike gloomily, "you would have lost your joy at once. I'll show you!" And, in one leap, the philosopher covered the distance to the subject of his new interest. Alas, the human

---

[7] – attraction, gravitation

lacked the animal experience: the bird flitted away in the last second, while the cat just barely tried to hold on to an apple with his claws and teeth. "This is the end for me!" the thought flashed through his mind and the former magician, with the taste of apple in his mouth, in a final effort, meowed out his spell! An instinctive movement of his tail saved the scientist from a painful impact against the ground. He landed on all fours. But, following from above was the apple. Bang! It hit the cat on the head...

"Isaac! Wake up! What's the matter with you? You slept right here in the orchard! Where did you spend the night? Or have you found a girlfriend?"

His mother bent over him next to the small table beside the apple tree. It was all so strange. "Had I managed to be a cat? Or did I dream it all?" To answer this question he just needed to repeat the experiment. But, a real scientist always remains true to his word. After he made a vow never to return to magic and replace it with natural philosophy, this area of his new interests seemed to him quite attractive.

"Well, I'll have to schedule plans for today," Ike remarked as usual. "First, I'll finish my nighttime deliberations about the Moon's attraction to the Earth. If there is no mistake in the reasoning, then it is clear that the interaction is inversely proportional to the square of the distance. Then, I'll examine the beam of light. Based on how dawn changes its colors, one can infer that white light is composed of colored rays. I'll only need to drill a little hole in the shutter and play with the ray of sunlight. But first and foremost of all, it would be good to eat properly!"

"Mother, may I finish the leftovers of yesterday's dinner? I am as starved as a stray cat!"

And young Newton skipped towards to his house. A fresh thought suddenly struck him: a heavy front door should have a small light gate through which a cat may easily come and go without bothering the patron. At least if the cat also badly needs it... Well, just in case.

TOY MODEL

Bert walked over to the window and frowned. Rain was drizzling beyond it – it was gloomy there like in his soul. Indeed he never felt joyful, although he sometimes felt calm when nobody interrupted his play – laying out mosaic tiles in an order known only to him or imagining himself sailing far, far away to his home, his parents and sister, till aunt Sherry's voice drew him out of this state.

"Look at this!" she demanded not angrily, but firmly, "Do you like these little fishes I have brought you?"

Bert gradually yielded to her persuasion and began to glance out of the corner of his eye at the strange mobile little bodies, covered with golden scales. Aunty stroked his head repeating "Good boy, good boy! You should not pierce an empty space with your gaze when there are so many interesting things around. Let me read you a story."

She read him a fairy tale, and Bert gradually moved to his mysterious world, inaccessible to all others. It was cozy there. Nobody laughed at him. Nobody called him a loser and a stutterer.

There was kind, though always-busy Dad. And his wonderful gift – a round glass box with a rotating arrow. What did they call it? Such an amazing thing! The arrow always turned and showed the same direction.

There was Mommy. Soft and fragrant. Bert took her hand and put it on his head, and Mom... having guessed his desire, started to caress his hair.

He feels bad at school. Children hate and despise him. They all look alike. Nobody wants to be his friend. Bert could never play their games.

And he read badly. And talked scantily. Sometimes he got angry with the children – broke their pens and pencils. Once in rage he even growled and suddenly bit himself on the arm until he bled. The children were scared to death of him then and for several days did not approach.

Aunt Sherry is good. Pity that she does not play the piano and does not teach him, like Mom, to play the violin, but like Mom, she bakes Bert's favorite fritters with apple slices. They are so tasty that he could eat them three times a day, but uncle Robert returns from work, and they all sit down to dinner: you have to eat soup and main course, otherwise no fritters.

"How are you doing in school?" uncle Robert asks.

"You doing in school good. Doing good. Good," Bert answers.

The uncle looks at the nephew smiling, but Bert is staring in his plate in silence and indifference. The aunt appeals to her husband,

"Why do you confuse the child? Do we ourselves always know how we are? And today Bert composed very pretty patterns on the floor of his room."

"What are they? Like before?"

"Yes, but only more intricate. You should have seen them with your mathematical eye. It seems to me that simple game has some meaning."

Sherry shows photos of the mosaics to Robert, while Bert goes to his room and tries to express patterns with movements of his hands, like a conductor in front of an orchestra. His uncle's voice comes from the dining room, "You think it's only a simple game. Actually, he is constructing or creating something, maybe even not realizing it himself. Like nature. Anyway, those patterns consist of a sequence of decagonal numbers. And these... OK, we have to check. It looks like this set of numbers may convey the Möbius function. Has Bert ever depicted geometrical surfaces?"

"I think you ascribe more to his world than he intends. Do not forget that despite his computational ability the child is not quite fully developed."

"That's why I treat his games as a product of a yet unfamiliar brain activity. While Bert cannot express himself well in words, I am seeking to understand what he is trying to tell us in the images and forms he produces."

"Well, I have not seen any surfaces, but he portrays god knows what with his hands."

"I think I will consult Marcel. Two heads are better then one."

It was quiet in the smoking room of the Academy where Robert met his long-time friend, a professor of physics. The carpet and upholstered furniture muffled the hum of a few voices. The room smelled of expensive tobacco and coffee. From time to time, a waiter with a full coffee pot shuttled around the hall, topping off the white porcelain cups with the aromatic beverage.

"I agree with you," said Marcel. "These numbers are not random and can be described by the Möbius function. Now I would like to determine, whether they contain any connection between the theory of numbers presented here, and quantum field theory."

"Marcel, even for me such a hypothesis sounds too weird. These sequences in the mosaic patterns..."

"Let's also note that they are not just numbers, but numbers with an additional hallmark, a color!"

"And why is that important?"

"Just because it gives the system another degree of freedom. Therefore the validity of the mathematical theory of numbers can lead to the likelihood of new quantum states – put simply – of other dimensions or realities."

"And you think that the sick child invents an apparatus for changing the world?"

"I think that you think so. Therefore, you came to consult me!"

"But I do not think so. I... suspect that Bert is playing with numbers, unconsciously generating complex sequences with his unusual mind. And we two fools are trying to interpret his game."

"You know, as a physicist I would suggest an experiment. Let us drop off a flat flexible surface, say piece of rubber, into your nephew's room and see whether he will turn it into a simple and intuitive toy model of what he is thinking about. And we'll be keeping an eye on him!"

"What for?"

"Because the first numbers in your nephew's initial sequence described systems of simple dimensions: one, two and three. Now he has moved on to four, five and six. What's interesting is, is this the end or will he continue further with his mosaics? In fact, seven-, eight- and especially nine-dimensional space leads to string theory and to the possibility of non-spatial transitions. Moreover, ten-dimensional space affects time! So, I expect that Bert will soon ask for more mosaics because he needs hundreds of tiles... – Marcel scribbled something on the paper – 232, 297, 370, and for ten-dimensional space – 451 items!

"Well, I always believed that mathematicians have the wildest imaginations, but I see that physicists are no less so. I agree only on one point: to understand Bert better, we indeed have to provide him with a toy model. I will go and find for him a large elastic sheet of rubber... and more mosaic tiles. Let him lay out his combinations."

Sherry was tidying up in Bert's room. She photographed the mosaic patterns left on the floor, and then sorted the colored tiles and neatly put them back into their boxes. Bert did not get angry at her: this process had already become part of their routine. Recently Robert had brought for his nephew's favorite activity a lot of new tiles and a large flexible rubber sheet. Bert was terribly happy with the new mosaics. Sherry could see this in his spellbound gaze: he could not take his eyes off such a treasure. And from the strange movements of his hands it seemed that Bert conjures or imitating the magical passes of fakirs. But, Sherry was well aware that this was simply a manifestation of his illness.

The rubber sheet alerted the child. This was something unusual, alien in his room. Bert cautiously touched the new material, sniffed it and put it on the floor. The sheet lay down awkwardly, creating a ridge. The boy grabbed the edge trying to flatten the sheet and then rolled it into a tube. He looked through the tube, growled angrily and bent it into a donut. Then suddenly he threw it aside. The sheet flew over the bed and flopped onto the headboard, taking the shape of a complex mountainous surface.

"Do not worry," Sherry said to her nephew. "We love you, Uncle Robert and I. And we will always buy you toys. And do you love us?"

"You love. Love us. Love," answered the child in his monotonous voice, in which at this moment she heard an unusual mix of emotions."

"Poor boy," thought Sherry, "Losing one's family in a crash is a heavy trauma even for a strong healthy man, not to mention a sick child."

Bert had not talked after the accident for almost a year. Then he slowly began to thaw, warmed up by the tender attention of his aunt. She did not have her own children, and her husband Robert quickly agreed to accept the silent nephew in their family. Gradually he and the boy got used to and even got interested in each other, even though up to then Robert had been completely dedicated to his beloved profession.

Now, yesterday Bert had unexpectedly found that the rubber sheet could take a variety of configurations, and he played with it for a long time. But he did not forget about the mosaics either and posted a new complex pattern before bedtime. Robert was not surprised to see this, he just whistled:

"Is Marcel really right?"

After dinner Sherry, as usual, coddled the boy with his favorite apple fritters, sent him to his room, and then turned to her husband with a question, "Have you discussed with Marcel the new pattern?"

"No, not yet. I'll call now," and Robert started to dial his friend's number.

He gave up – no one answered.

"I'll going for a walk; to check out the bookstore. Did Bert build anything out of the rubber sheet?"

"No he did not, but he experimented with it for a long time. He put in it different toys like in an apron and watched how the rubber stretched under their weight. And he gesticulated a lot..."

"OK. I'll call later and discuss it with Marcel."

When Robert returned, Sherry was dozing in front of the TV.

"Sherry don't sleep! Marcel said that the boy is trying to reconcile quantum physics with gravitation, and we should not leave him alone, just in case!"

"What does that mean – 'just in case'?"

"Marcel suggested that if he gets the pattern of 451 tiles and expresses it with his movements, then he will penetrate into another space and time."

"Were you really in a bookstore? May be in a bar?" Sherry asked angrily.

It seemed to her, that Robert was saying something absurd, like a drunk man. Anyway, she opened the door and peeked into Bert's room.

"Where are you?" her excited voice could be heard.

Robert anxiously followed his wife, who was standing in a daze in the middle of the empty room. On the floor of the child's room, a mosaic pattern corresponding to a ten-dimensional space was glittering. The rubber sheet was stretched over the bedposts. In its center, a deep crater was closing up, as if a massive body was being sucked into it...

"Now, where has this child gotten off to?" Polly thought, tousling her unruly brown curls. "No, of course Hermy is not right. The boy is not foolish; he's just very easily carried away. That kind of boy would be staring at the giant hourglass in Herr Breguet's shop window and completely lose track of time."

At this point, the front door bell clanged and Polly's unkempt treasure with parted lips and dreamy eyes appeared on the doorstep of the apartment, dragging his schoolbag and his violin in its case.

"Albert," said his Mom, "Where have you been for two hours? I was so worried!" She kissed her son. Did some toy models in the shop windows enchant you again? I need to go shopping, and I have no one to stay with little Maya. Look after her. You may read your sister fairy tales and play the violin."

The little girl clapped her hands.

"Just do not try to teach her geometry. She is still a baby," smiled Frau Einstein watching her children, beaming with happiness.

REQUIEM FOR THE AMAZON

François was sitting at the small table of a cozy bar of the Temporal Academy. Penny warned him that she might be slightly late – you never knew in what conditions you would get out after training in the ancient martial arts fighting techniques.

François always admired Penny's ability to fight to the victorious end – regardless of any obstacles. He, rather, referred himself to a class of analysts and not fighters, preferring to calculate the required route and follow it without apparent effort. However, athletics and melee were obligatory subjects for everybody, and the ancient martial arts were extra preparation for Penny's graduation project "Amazons". Although athleticism in a woman never really attracted François, Penny was irresistible to him: well-defined muscles and adolescent breasts could not impair beauty of her curly brown hair, dark-turquoise radiant eyes and delicate skin.

Penny burst into the bar, and while moving, ordered juice, threw her bag on a hanger, jacket on a chair, greeted friends, and most importantly, kissed François furtively, but firmly, making it clear that this was not accidental touch,

"Hey, baby!"

She was slightly taller, but in their relationship, it did not play any role.

"Hi! Tell me how they liked your project."

He already knew the result but wanted to enjoy the details. Penny chose a difficult goal – to save the queen of the Amazons, Penthesilea, and to deal with contradictory myths surrounding several other queens.

According to some sources, Heracles killed Hippolyta during his ninth feat, while others argue that Theseus took her in Athens, but then banished her and married Phaedra. Others believed Penthesilea accidentally slayed her during the hunt. Homer describes the death of Penthesilea as occurring at the hands of Achilles. However, other authors have reported that she had not died, and took care of the mausoleum of Achilles on a small island White, later called Serpentine Island. For centuries, different states fought for this island until the International Court in the 21 century decided to transfer it to Ukraine.

"You know, I posed the question before the Academy. It seems that we are dealing with a human artifact left in the past, and this artifact is possibly me!"

"And what was the reaction of the Council? I know you can convince anyone!"

"You will not believe it! They permitted me to make a double transition: to Troy and to the White Island!"

"What about me? You want to stay in the past and leave me here?"

"And these are the words of the future Temporal sea dog? Is it possible to hide from a captain of a time cruiser? You can reach me in any time! But if we both run around from one assignment to another, it's likely we will see each other only when our vacations coincide."

Penny was right. The Academy did not recommend cadets marry colleagues for precisely this reason. In general, a person needs a home he can go back to after work. Preferably, a house under a big tree. And the music and the laughter of children, rather than the metal and plastic of the cruiser and a stimulator for emotions.

But one thought bothered François. "If Penthesilea on the White Island is Penny, then, according to Novikov's principle, the past will not let her go back as soon as she sets foot behind the Cauchy horizon... I wonder if they have a large tree on the island."

"Penny, then it turns out we have only a few days in our time?"

"And I hope to spend them like a real Amazon!"

François smiled with the corners of his lips. He knew they would torment each other...

Penthesilea viewed herself as a traitor. Though reared in contempt for men, she felt in her chest a longing when she saw Achilles in all the glory of his battle armor and later naked, like the god of war Ares. "Only weak women love men," the voice of reason whispered to her, but the arrow of Eros, fired by the well-aimed hand of a young god, has done its job. "How strange," Pente thought, "Women in our family are brilliant warriors, queens of the Amazons! But none of them are able to resist the male beauty and valor. And for their love they are paid with misery and death!"

Her two older sisters became victims of the two greatest heroes. Hippolyta in love with Heracles came to his ship and presented him with her gold belt. But the Amazons, fearing that Heracles would snatch their Queen, attacked the Greeks. As a result, the battle began, and Hippolyta was killed at the hands of... Heracles. During this battle, another hero, Theseus, king of Athens, captured Hippolyta's sister, Antiope. In Athens, she bore him a son, named Hippolytus after his aunt. When Amazons besieged Athens, Antiope died fighting shoulder to shoulder with her husband. The culprit of the most terrible misfortune in the family was Penthesilea herself. Hunting in the woods, she mistakenly shot and killed her younger sister, also called Hippolyta. For it, she sentenced herself to death and went to the Trojan War – to fight the Greeks. But now Pente felt she could not resist Achilles. Not as a hero and a warrior – she was not afraid of death – but as a man.

A warm seaside breeze ruffled the short-cropped strands of the two riders. Penthesilea, accompanied by just one Amazon, headed to the place where Achilles and his late friend, Patroclus, enjoyed swimming after sunset. She was not mistaken: against the darkening skies covered with burgundy clouds, she was able to make out the silhouette of a man, with prominent muscles, sitting in the pose of a thinker. A huge spear was stuck in the sand next to him; his shield was lying nearby.

"Peace be with you, leader of Myrmidons, renowned Achilles. Do we not disturb your loneliness?"

"Obviously, my spear is well known in Troy, if they recognized me even in the twilight," thought the warrior. – "Peace to you, Amazons! You cannot disturb someone whose lonely soul is waiting for its travel to the lands of Hades. What brings you to this deserted place at this late hour? Are you not afraid of attacks by ferocious Greeks?"

Penthesilea smiled. Polite, ceremonious words did not go together with a view of a naked man.

"Are not we protected by the famous hero? Did Greeks, during the truce, kill individual Amazons? And after all, are we so defenseless?"

With these words, the women-warriors demonstrated several techniques of unarmed combat.

"Wow!" Achilles laughed, but immediately turned serious, "Better not get caught by me tomorrow in battle."

"Let's not think about war today. Tomorrow, I myself will find you on the battlefield!" Pente said.

"Have it your way!" Achilles marveled at the courage of the young woman and extended his hand in a sign of agreement… "Ouch!" He had not expected such a forceful slap.

"Penelope, guard us from prying eyes!" Penthesilea ordered, sending her friend into the darkness. "I know, Achilles, the loss of a close friend is an immense sorrow; even a victory over Hector will not cure it. I also entered the war in search of death, grieving for my sister, who was killed by these very hands. Tomorrow you will quench your thirst of revenge, I'll go with glory to the kingdom of shadows, and now…"

"Oh, that's who my mystery guest is – queen Penthesilea herself," Achilles rose from the stone, not embarrassed with his nudity. "Well, enter with me these gentle waters, so loved by Patroclus…"

Without hesitation, she threw off her chiton and followed Achilles while faithful Penelope, or rather Temporal Academy cadet Penny, patrolled the deserted shore, where in the darkness resounded the kissing and moaning of people ready to come together in mortal combat the very next morning.

François in the outfit of Franz gasped and wiped his sweaty forehead with the sleeve of his blue, silver embroidered 18th Century Austrian waistcoat. It could not be worse: the capsule had frozen in the middle of nowhere and nowhen, beyond space and time. He, the Temporal Academy cadet, was ready for many woes and failures, but such an inglorious end to an operation that have not yet begun, he had not seen even in his nightmares.

"No fuss and panic!" he said to himself again and again, "Repeat the sequence of operations to return from superspace!"

All of this was self-deception. Test after test led to the same result: the system did not respond to commands, although there were no apparent reasons or damages. It was still too far to despair, but a flock of cats already scraped with iron claws at his heart. He knew that the next step was to enable the system alarm, but did not want to do it before making sure he was completely helpless. His graduation project had been repeatedly recalculated, the area of predictable causality verified, and François could bet that he would not lose face if he ascertained that Wolfgang Amadeus wanted to avoid death.

Of all the operations, Academy welcomed the most a classical scheme "Paradise" where the object, before his death, was seized from the past and replaced with a "doll", a biologically degradable precise anatomical body replica. A saved hero continued to exist and work in the future, while the past was not subjected to any changes. However, there had not yet been a captain who, during his cadet years, hadn't attempted to try other approaches.

All have long forgotten the days when scientists were afraid to affect the past by their actions. Opponents of the theory of impossibility to change past events did not exist anymore. Debates took place only in regard to the acceptable change limits. François, the other cadets and all the young captains reasoned as empiricists: "If it is impossible to change the past, why do we need such a strict and careful calculation of the Cauchy horizon? If the experimenter accidentally or even intentionally steps over the forbidden region, his actions are simply not realized and he... Well, depends on luck." All students have tried, and all the captains knew from their own experience: the past cannot be deceived or bypassed! The only requirement of Academy was not to create apparent contradictions, but who among the youth did not consider himself a virtuoso who knows better than any of the academician, how to protect people of the past from paradoxes or artifacts?

François pulled the powdery wig from his head. It's time! He tore off the seal on the console, opened the lid and for a few seconds pressed his thumb on the sensor. "Identity confirmed!" The alarm indicator flashed. "Push all the way!" No matter how much he wanted to avoid this, his trained fingers performed all the necessary manipulations without a hitch.

"When will they pull me out of here?" the cadet thought, mentally fending off a short and terrifying answer. A pilot could get stuck in his capsule forever. But one could not wait for help indefinitely outside of time and space. The homeostasis system, like the one present in all spaceships, was absent. Hibernation was initiated automatically... After all, most of the students were orphans, and only their friends lit memorial lights for their missing comrades. And he so hoped to prove himself as a Temporal sea dog!

His plan was simple. Under the guise of a messenger, or even the customer himself – Count Franz von Walsegg – he was to come to the sick Mozart with his next payment of a hundred ducats for the Requiem and initiate his antibiotic treatment. It has long been known that Salieri did not poison his friend, who died during a wartime epidemic. But, the sepsis and the strep that affected Mozart's kidneys could be fought.

Unfortunately, the geniuses of the past, exported to the future and separated from their time, loved ones, sources of suffering and inspiration, became depressed. Despite treatment, they never reached the past peaks of their creativity. But a cadet did not become a captain by not trying to save his heroes in the past.

"At least, I'll ask directly if he yet wants to create, or finds his path complete," thought François, planning the project. Now he had to ask the same question to himself. "Hey, somebody, come already!" he answered mentally, sinking into artificial sleep under the marvelous sounds of Mozart's Requiem.

Skirmishes between advanced detachments of the Greeks and Trojans continued well past morning. Twice already, troops went out from the city, repelled attackers and quickly retreated behind the impregnable fortress. Squadrons of archers under the command of Paris and the Amazons led by Penthesilea showered arrows on daredevils who approached the high thick walls, but the queen was getting more and more annoyed by this routine.

"If the Achaean army appears, twelve of you join me to confront the enemy!" she told her friends, "We will move right after the spearmen, together with the cavalry.

According to the traditions of the Amazons, they attacked the enemy from afar and inflicted significant damage, thanks to their clever shooting. Penthesilea developed a new method of attack: Amazons hit a selected target with high-angled plunging fire and while enemies raised their shields, hiding from the arrows falling almost vertically, women-warriors made a rapid leap forward and again hit the now vulnerable soldiers with point-blank fire...

Cavalry and foot soldiers appeared. There, Achilles's gilded armor glinted in the sun. The Amazons twice tried to use their trick, attacking the hero, but the myrmidon's bodyguards, sacrificing themselves, covered him on all sides with their huge shields. Pente noticed a warrior in rich armor near Achilles. It was Machaon, a Greek army doctor, skilled surgeon and hereditary healer. His elegant shield was adorned with a mosaic of a butterfly Swallowtail, composed of bronze and blackened iron.

"If I am not given to battle Achilles, let the Greeks know sorrow for losing their doctor," decided Penthesilea, directing arrows at the physician.

"See, how the Amazons are steamed up! They do not have enough men during the peaceful life, so they are looking for them in the war!" viciously as usual, croaked humpbacked Thersites, beaten not once for his sarcasm by Odysseus.

"Let's show them a real melee!" Achilles wedged into the Ethiopians, allies of the Trojans, his sword paving his way to the Amazons. His bodyguards followed him with their huge shields and his comrades-in-arms, left alone, immediately felt the wrath of Penthesilea's archers. One of the suitors of Helen, Podarkes, wheezed – an arrow pierced his throat. With a groan, Doctor Machaon fell from his horse, bleeding profusely.

Meanwhile, Achilles heated with battle, approached the Amazons, "I'll pierce you, my love!" he shouted, mad with blood, brandishing his death-bringing spear.

The Ethiopians, who lost their king Memnon in battle, did not withstand the onslaught and ran to the Scaean gate of Troy, dragging the Amazons. Several of them were already fatally stabbed by Achilles.

"Hold it!" Penthesilea shouted into his face, "You're craving not for their death, but mine! And I can't wait to fight you for the last time!"

Pursuers stopped in surprise, listening to the speech of the doomed woman, but everyone wanted to witness an unusual battle.

While the besieged army returned freely under the protection of the strong walls of Troy, the Greeks formed a large semicircle, within which Achilles was preparing for battle with the Queen of the Amazons. Three

Amazon warriors, who survived the battle, refused to hide in the fort and stayed to cover Penthesilea.

After a short welcome, riders raced towards each other.

"Bang!" the spear of the warrioress broke from hitting the mighty Achilles's shield, and Penthesilea flew into the air, knocked from her horse by the enemy's pike. Achilles sprang from his chariot to the ground, threw his shield aside and rushed to the prostrate body with a dart in his hand. Greeks cheered, anticipating a fatal blow. A dart whistled in the air, shook and howled like a bass string, vibrating in the soft sandstone of Trojan land: in the last second, the Amazon ducked, jumping to her feet under spectators' loud cries.

"A-a-a!" Achilles and Pentesilea cried out, drawing their swords.

"Watch out, Achilles! You don't have your spear and shield. Hades is waiting for you!" she roared.

"Beg for protection from the gods, braggart!" he shouted.

Blades flashed in the air, sparked upon impact, and suddenly everybody saw that the sword flew out of Achilles's hand. The air started vibrating from screams of terror and triumph, but in the next moment the hero caught his sword, parried Penthesilea's blow and struck twice: with his left fist in the bronze helmet of the Amazon and with the sword in the delicate cleft between her collarbones.

Viewers' cries shook the ground. Achilles had not heard anything and did not feel the pain of broken knuckles. A face of wondrous beauty who loved him last night opened to his eyes. And, he had sent her to Tartarus with his own hands! Trembling with rage and excitement, evoked by his memories, Achilles sprang upon the queen's body in a paroxysm of grief and passion.

"Achilles! You happen to be a hero-necrophile!" Thersites bleated as he came near, poking a spear in the face of the dead woman.

Achilles, pale as a corpse, smeared with Penthesilea's blood, bounced off the ground and struck a lightning blow to the bridge of the nose of the warrior. Bones crackled accompanied with a sucking sound, and the dead body collapsed to the ground. Staggering, Achilles walked along the wall, not seeing how the Amazons carried the body of their Queen into the city, how fellow warriors hung on Diomedes, holding him from revenge for his killed relative Thersites, how everybody yelled and waved arms to point at someone on the fortress wall. Achilles was alone in his infinite loneliness among the dead enemies, friends and feelings.

The first arrow shot by Paris, nailed his foot to the ground, the second hit in the chest, the third in the neck... His big strong body just winced each time until silenced forever.

Constanze cautiously opened the door to her husband's study, where Wolfgang sat for days. He had a great deal of work. The deadline for the Requiem was nearing. Ducats from the wealthy patron, who wished to remain anonymous, could not had come at a better time: for current expenses and for debt payments. Mozart usually didn't rush to carry out an order, but didn't tolerate tardiness either. Towards the end of the term, the composer's performance increased drastically, and he isolated himself in his office, piled to the top with sketches and drafts, annoying Constanze. And even now, despite his illness, work was in full swing. The composer, eyes closed, conducted, imagining himself flying through the ether and the cold to the stars, angels and God.

"Our Father... ta-a-a, do not be angry... ta, ta, ta-a, ta! We all come to you in our loneliness. La-a-a, Fa, Re, Re-e, Do-dies..."

"Wolfie, a gentleman came to see you," Constanze said, "I think, it's about the Requiem; the same man in a black cloak with a hood."

"Ask, ask him to come in! And do not forget to bring us a hot drink. I feel chills!"

Since September, when he conducted the opera *The Magic Flute* in Prague for the coronation of the emperor, Wolfgang felt horrible. At first it seemed like bouts of rheumatic fever, but he was getting worse. Dr.

Klosset twice performed bloodletting on the composer, but the patient only weakened.

"Good evening to you, Herr Mozart," said the soft voice with a subtle hint of a French accent, recognizable only by the exceptional musical ear of the genius. The visitor's face was hardly seen under a deep hood. And only a blue waistcoat with a silver braid, peeking out from under a black cloak, gave away the high status of the stranger.

"And good evening to you too, my patron," Wolfgang said, coughing and wrapping himself in a blanket.

"Here's another hundred ducats to support your work and your health," Franz handed the pouch with coins, "How is the work coming alone?"

"Not as prompt as I might desire, but no reason to worry. I can already hear the entire melody of the Requiem; it remains only to put the notes on paper. If I get bedridden, my disciple Franz Süssmayr will record my dictation. Everything will be according to the contract, do not worry, Your Excellency. Even my death cannot break it!"

"I worry exclusively for you, maestro. After the triumph of *The Magic Flute*, You do not appear in the opera and look much worse."

"Dear Count, my face became, pardon my joke, like a donkey's ass – swollen and covered with a rash, but the brain is still alive! And it still creates! Even now, I hear the arrangement of *The Requiem, Wrath of God*."

"Look, Herr Mozart, I would like to offer you an elixir that is successfully applied in the military hospital in Vienna. They say there is an epidemic, and the medicine literally brought back from the dead many soldiers who had swollen faces and feet, like you have now."

"Do not blaspheme, Your Excellency. God works in mysterious ways and no one can escape the fate that awaits him," Mozart crossed.

"What is the cost of the Count's assurances," Wolfgang pondered, "If he himself lost his young wife, the most precious thing he had. What kind of nonsense – to help swollen soldiers and not to save the Emperor himself, who contracted the disease during his visit to the frontlines and left this world. No, the dear Count is unhappy because of his loss and therefore he has compassion for everyone. And it saves his soul from loneliness. I'm married, I have already two sons, a sister, friends, but I feel myself a lonely wanderer in the vast sea of music and the endless ocean of the universe."

"Don't you want to recover and to write new operas?"

"Only if the Lord wishes that. Everyone knows how King Louis feared the number twenty one, but he was arrested June 21st, and he lost his crown on September 21st."

"Thank God, he didn't lose his head!" François indeed knew that Louis XVI's head would be cut off exactly on January 21st, in just over a year...

"It makes no sense to contradict Him! You know, dear Count, how many people are trying to help me with this disease? Family, friends, doctors... But I will just finish your order, and then... I'll be ready to meet Him."

"Have you considered composing music in the Paradise?"

"Thank you for preparing a place in Paradise for me, but if I get there I will not write a note! I will just listen! And now... Give me a piece of paper! Quick: La-a-a, Fa, Re, Re-e, Do-dies..."

François quietly walked out the door. "What a stubborn man!" he thought, "A damn fatalist! Operation "Paradise" is surely not for you, but let's try the medicine anyway."

"Frau Mozart," he turned to Constanze, "My lord sent tincture for your spouse. He said that it really helps for legs and face edema."

"I shall certainly make him drink it with hot tea right now."

When the stranger had left, Constanze took a deep breath. "What a good man is this Count," she thought, "Herr Salieri could have also sent something to his sick friend. I'll have to say to everybody, that it is Herr Salieri, who sent medicine to Wolfgang. Let Wolfie have at least some pleasure, either way he won't touch any remedies!"

"**A**ttention! Attention! Emergency mode! Cryostasis is disabled! Recovery phase!"

Mozart's delicate melody and François eventually came to. Penny stood in front of him in a chiton and Amazon armor, which highlighted her athletic figure.

"You were very lucky," she said, "I started later than you, and once in outer-space, received the alarm from your capsule. I didn't even calculate anything. The onboard computer led me to you. Do you know what happened with your capsule?"

"I only know the fact that it refused to execute commands."

"Then, under the statute, I must immediately evacuate you."

"On your way 'there'? And didn't you think to catch me on your way back?"

"No, I was afraid for you. If you got into the area of catastrophic disaster, then, no action in your past could save you."

"I understand, of course, and appreciate your strict adherence to the statute."

"Would you have done it differently?"

"Same. But now it turns out that we have to go back. So I suspect that the capsule malfunctioned not by chance, but according to Academy's plan to bring us home..."

"In that case, I won't be following the statute so strictly. You know how hard it is to turn me from my way. I think that we can first carry out our projects! Both of us. Throw me in Troy, deal with Mozart, and then take me on your way home from the White Island."

"Two projects in one capsule? You will remain without safeguards, my Temporal sea dog. This is the hotshot captain's way!"

"Already the Amazon's way, my dear Count! Aren't we the best safeguards for each other?"

And they pointed Penny's capsule to the besieged Ilion...

. . . **D**ark blue waves were crashing loudly on the rocky shore of the White Island – a small speck of land in the northwest of the Black Sea. White quartz sand turned pink in the rays of the rising sun. On the rocks, its facade to the east, Achilles mausoleum

53

dominated the landscape. A man was heading to it, sand squeaking at every step. On a green meadow, under a tall tree, stood a small house. A few goats and sheep grazed in the offing, under the watchful eye of the guard dog. The dog saw the approaching human and started to bark, but then at once kindly wagged its tail.

A young woman in a simple tunic came out of the house. Her brown hair was arranged in a tight bun at her nape.

"Hush, Cerberus," she said to the dog, "You'll wake up small Caystrius. Who do you bark at? No foreigner could appear here, in the midst of the sea, without a ship."

Suddenly her surprised gaze stopped on the stranger, on his statuesque figure covered in a foreign, short, tunic-like blue toga embroidered with silver snakes.

"Penny!" he called, "Penelope?.."

It was another woman. As tall and beautiful, as Penny, but different.

"Yes, I have been called that for four years now, after that night on the shore with Achilles when I got pregnant. Penny spell bounded me – persuaded me to exchange our armors before the battle..."

"Dad!" a kid ran out of the house, "Father came to pick us up!"

"He will take us to Olympus, a place where everyone is happy and where there is no death."

François understood everything in a flash: Penny always knew that she would save her hero, no matter what. No wonder she was able to convince anyone, from wise academicians to temperamental queens.

"We will fly on the celestial chariot," he said with tears in his eyes, "Inside it, music is playing, unearthly music – requiem. Requiem for the Amazon."

"A WONDROUS MOMENT I REMEMBER..."

Sachs was the most outstanding teacher in the Temporal Academy. For his ability to listen carefully to his students and to protect their sincere impulses from the overly rational administration, he was respected no less, if not more than for his scientific work. Everyone knew that the Law of Invariance of the Past would sooner or later be named after him. But, the cadets also knew that for many years to come, with Sachs's blessing, each undergraduate would be allowed one attempt to refute this law in a thesis project.

Class caught every professor's word about physical principles of Time, which Sachs illustrated with most interesting cadets' thesis ideas.

"The interface between the acceptable predictable changes of events and the unacceptable or unpredictable changes is called the Cauchy Horizon. According to Novikov's Principle, a man crossing the horizon will forever remain in the past and cannot return to his time. What's more, even the replacement of one person by another very slightly changes the course of events and causal relationships. This is analogous to the conservation of energy in a closed system. One can say that during the transition in time, the temporal continuum ceases to be isolated, so some changes in events become acceptable, leaving the Past, in general, invariant."

"Then why, Professor, do we so strictly and carefully calculate the Cauchy Horizon? If the experimenter accidentally, or even intentionally, enters the forbidden region, then his actions will not lead to a desired result."

"Because, for us, you are as precious as the greatest talents of the past! Nobody now is afraid that the past could ever change. Even in my youth, I barely came across a single adherent of this ancient misconception. We are afraid for you! The Future needs you as captains of temporal cruisers, not as replacements for the heroes of the past."

"That's true," Victor thought. "Nobody knows who we – the cadets of today – will become in the future."

The romanticism of rescuing the great persons of the past so captured the youthful imagination that many cadets risked their lives by engaging in the most perilous ventures.

The inseparable trio of friends – Alexandra, Marcel and Victor – were preparing a joint project. Defending it before the Council of the Academy was more difficult than presenting three single projects, but Vic was relying on his professor. Sachs had always supported interesting ideas; to understand the mystery of the duel and try to rescue from the tragic bullet the Russian poet Pushkin, a favorite of many generations – was a damn sincere idea.

Cadet Alexandra, the namesake of the poet and his sister-in-law, wanted to conduct a study on complex female characters and attempt to prevent the duel using the "factor of love". Four women – wives and mistresses of the duelists – were embroiled in the tragedy. The two Goncharov sisters, Natalia and Catherine, were wives of the poet and the Cavalier-Guard respectively. Pushkin's mistress was the third Goncharov sister, Alexandrina. The guard George d'Anthes's mistress was Idalia Poletika, cousin to the three Goncharov sisters.

Marcel's part of the project was to figure out the true motives of the duel between poet Alexander Pushkin and officer George d'Anthes-Heeckeren.

Baron Heeckeren was a secretary in the Dutch Embassy in Berlin. Once, he "accidentally" found the young French republican George d'Anthes, fleeing Paris after monarchy restoration and now dying from pneumonia in a small German Inn. The diplomat arranged his treatment, brought him to Russia, where the young man was headed, and helped to settle his enlistment in the prestigious Tsar's Cavalier-Guards regiment. The baron's good samaritan actions brought him a new position as the Dutch Ambassador to Russia. Later baron adopted George and gave him his name Heeckeren. Being very handsome, George had many affairs in the Russian high society. So had the brilliant poet Pushkin. But, when George d'Anthes de Heeckeren started to court Pushkin's wife, a first gage to the duel followed. It was cancelled, as d'Anthes was marrying Pushkin's sister-in-law Catherine. Nevertheless, soon Pushkin and his friends received letters, naming the poet a cuckold. A second gage followed. Pushkin was wounded and died of infection.

Marcel planned to take the place of the d'Anthes's second d'Archiac, in order to replace bullets in Cavalier-Guard's pistols with blanks. However, Marcel's plan did not seem dishonorable. Pushkin was considered a dangerous duelist: he constantly practiced shooting, hit the center of an ace from ten paces and trained his muscles to hold a weight in his outstretched right hand without trembling. Nevertheless, even though he challenged offenders to a duel fifteen times, he carried out only four. In three of them, each time after his opponent shot, poet fire into the air. To fearlessly meet the first shot and humiliated the enemy with his own magnanimity, gave him more satisfaction than a bloody vulgar punishment of his offender.

Victor took upon himself the third, key part of the project. In the guise of Doctor Arendt, Surgeon Ordinary to the tsar, who directed the care of the critically injured poet, Victor was to secretly inject Pushkin with penicillin.

Sachs liked the presentation of the tripartite proposal and its "triple support", but the project had to be approved by the Academic Council.

"Do you understand that you're going all in?" the professor addressed not just the three friends, but the whole audience. "If you are absolutely sure of the impossibility of changing the past, then in the situation with a dying person, it is best to apply the standard 'Paradise' operation."

The Academy supported the classical scheme: when the object of the experiment was seized from the past before his death, he was replaced by a "doll" – a precise anatomical and biologically degradable replica. The hero continued to exist and work in the future, but the past was not subject to any change.

"The dozens of witnesses in the Pushkin household preclude this method. But, it is quite possible to assure yourself of the Invariance of the Past. So, I will vote "pro" in the Council. Even a negative result goes into the piggy bank of your knowledge. In addition, you will find out what actually happened there and write a valuable historical work. Most important, do not leave any artifacts and do not commit paradoxical actions."

The reproachful expressions on the faces of the "old men" served as a signal to the professor, "Okay, okay, I'm joking. I know you're no longer freshmen, but only five minutes from becoming Temporal sea dogs," he finished to cheers and applause from the audience.

White fluffy flakes seemed to fill the entire space. They fell on the snow- covered streets, hiding traces of the rare passers-by. A doorman in an overcoat with braids and cap helpfully opened the oak door, and a tall, handsome man in a cloud of vanilla aroma came out from Wolff's Confectionery. The man was wearing the Cavalier-Guards regiment lieutenant's uniform and a highly polished brass helmet crowned with a silver double-headed eagle. One bird head was looking to the left and the other to the right as if to make sure its host is not under surveillance. Carefully holding a box of cakes, tied with a red silk ribbon, the officer turned the corner, where stood a carriage. The charming passenger, Idalia Poletica, waved her hand to approach, and the lieutenant in an instant found himself inside the vehicle.

"Georges, dear!"

He stopped Idalia's lips, kissing her as if for the last time, "Please wait, my darling. I have important news! I did not have time to wait for our usual rendezvous. Baron Heeckeren received a letter from Pushkin and has already consulted with Papá. Count Stroganoff acknowledged that with such serious insults there is no way to avoid the duel."

"What does Pushkin write?"

"He calls the Ambassador a pimp, and you – a syphilitic bastard..."

"My God, he's mad, Idalia, I cannot appeal to his reason. Count Stroganoff is right; I have to go for a duel. Worst of all, would be if Natalie, the Holy Simplicity, reported to her husband that I threatened to shoot myself if she did not give herself to me!"

"But she really did not yield, did she?"

"I do not need anyone but you, Idalia! I only said to Natalie everything that you told me to say to her."

"Lord, who would have thought that a silly vaudeville could turn into such a horror! Pushkin more than others believed in rumors designed for the court gossipers."

"Baron Heeckeren also believed that I should pretend to be flirting with this silly Natalie, and he even played along with it. It is scary to imagine that my affair with you might be revealed! Count Stroganov never gave you his name officially; but even so, he would never let you tarnish it. In the best case, my career would end. Do you remember Colonel Poletika's revenge? Do you really think that it's just an accident in the Regiment: a jealous admirer of yours tried to choke another admirer? Colonel will always find an obedient officer in his Cavalier-Guard Regiment who would be eager to tighten a leather thong around my neck!"

"I hardly think so. My husband is an innocent "ladybug". We avoided his jealousy, but instead we got insane jealousy of Mr. Poet."

"Strange... Alexander Sergeevich has never been so furious before. He always had a pretty calm attitude toward men flirting with his wife while he himself indulged in passions and affairs."

"You know, I think he was teed off about the November letters. The admission to the Order of the Cuckold was the last straw."

"But that scoundrel thinks it is my father's handiwork; but only because the stationary is similar to the embassy's."

"And the paper was ambassadorial, indeed. However, not from the Dutch embassy, but from the Austrian. Of course, no ambassador would allow himself such meanness. But, to get the paper and samples of the jester's letters to Mrs. Nesselrode was not difficult... She has hated Pushkin from the time of the epigram on her father."

"Yet Alexander should not have run amok."

"George, it's a secret. He believed in the gossip only because he allowed himself to do the same things. He lives with Alexandrina. She confessed to me. She loves him, as I love you, but I have the duty of being a wife, and she's – a sister."

"So, my silly jokes about his polygamy proved partially true?"

"Yes! Maybe that's why he has reacted to everything so emotionally. On the one hand, he believes Natalie; on the other, he thinks she is no worse than others as a mistress. And who would be the man to be jealous of? Only two men have shown their admiration for her: you and the tsar!"

"But how about, 'Caesar's wife is above suspicion'? Now the 'second wife' is also above suspicion?"

"And what about the third one? Did not you get her from the master's bed?"

"Idalia! Do not talk nonsense."

"God, all men are equal in their pride. My father stole my mother pregnant by him from her legal spouse, a Portuguese nobleman. In Russia, he lived with her and not with his lawful wife! My grandmother brought me – a bastard – up. The Portuguese king and the Russian tsar defended the honor of men! And everybody spat on the poor women! My husband, Pushkin, and you, all think of themselves as Caesars. You are only give lip service to political freedom; in fact, you seek to make women submissive and silent slaves! You call my words nonsense only because Catherine is your wife!"

"Idalia, believe me, at her thirty, Catherine was a virgin."

"Oh, poor thing, you had to torment yourself and... that's the reason for your marriage, a mystery which puzzled everybody!"

"I can reveal my secret only to you. She immediately got pregnant. I could not let my child be born illegitimate. Enough that my mother, like yours, did not have me from her husband, but from the great love of her youth."

"You want to say that this love is Mr. Ambassador, who adopted you despite the bewilderment of three countries?"

"Of course not. He only fulfilled the will of my father, Crown Prince of the Netherlands. Mother met him in Berlin, where he was studying at the Military Academy, and the following year visited Oxford... Of course, I carried reference letters to Russia, but the main support came directly from Amsterdam, from my real father. He is friends with the emperor..."

"Everything is so intertwined in this world! But, what is done cannot be changed. I just want to ask you one question, George. Do you have enough courage not to kill Pushkin?"

"I will answer you as a military man. I have enough courage not to kill him, but I doubt that I may not shoot at all: then he just will kill me."

"You're silly, who's talking about that? It's Pushkin who should apologize and cancel the duel..."

"I would have forgiven him his intemperate language and undeserved insults. But I cannot refuse the duel myself. Neither the Baron nor I will stoop to explain the true causes of our behavior to that jealous man or to assure him that we did not participate in that anonymous hoax. If I allowed myself jokes that Pushkin called barracks humor, it was only in response to his arrogance and treating my family as if they were nobodies of low character.

"George, I want to ask you as both an excellent shot and a military man: what injury incapacitates, but causes the least harm?"

"In the thigh, my darling. I promise you to aim there."

"Thank you. I will pray for you," she briefly pressed her lips to his.

It was time to depart, and Lieutenant d'Anthes came out of the warm carriage into the cold January evening. He did not notice that a cab with a lady and a gentleman in it followed Idalia Poletika's coach. On the box sat a man dressed in an unusually expensive coat for a cabman.

"**M**onsieur and Madame, you'd heard everything, didn't you?" Marcel appealed to his friends, "Now, we are the owners of a unique record of the conversation. It sheds light on the mysterious circumstances of the famous duel."

"So, it appears that Idalia was the main instigator of the intrigue around Natalia Goncharova-Pushkina?" Victor said.

"Sure! Didn't you understand? By all means she averted public attention from her secret relationship with d'Anthes, substituting another beauty – a girlfriend and a cousin," explained Alexandra. "That is exactly she arranged Natalie's meeting with d'Anthes at her home, immediately after meeting him herself. At the same time, Lansky was in the street "protecting the honor of M-dame Pushkin". He was supposed to signal them should Colonel Poletika return home. In fact, not knowing anything, he was standing guard Idalia's dalliance with d'Anthes."

"Which Lansky? Could it be...?"

"Yes, that's indeed he, the future second husband of Natalia Pushkina, the father of her three children, and now an actual admirer of Idalia. I've always said that that disenfranchised women of the past very skillfully managed their men by activating invisible leverages of their desires and passions."

"Anyway, Idalia certainly belongs to such women, and the Countess Maria Nesselrode, wife of the Minister of Foreign Affairs, even more so."

"And why should she have hated Pushkin and his epigram so much?"

"That epigram was written about her father, Count Dmitriy Gur'ev, Minister of Finance under Alexander I. The verse said that he stole from the royal treasury. Opponents of his financial and agrarian reforms not only spread nasty rumors about him, but also – by the way – attributed that epigram to Pushkin."

"And Pushkin was innocent?!"

"Exactly! The same way the Heeckerens were innocent of the November libels on Pushkin. Alexander heard from a friend, the owner of the printing house, that the letter paper was an expensive, 'ambassadorial' type. He immediately concluded that embassy was the Dutch one, and those who had called him a cuckold were father and son Heeckerens."

"I see… these intrigues are no less complex than in the novel 'Dangerous Liaisons'."

"I think we should rush to Pushkin's house," summed up Alexandra, "My namesake, Alexandra Goncharova, will now meet with Idalia. This is the best time to take on her image to influence Pushkin. Well, if he is in love with Alexandra, then maybe he'll listen to her opinion."

"Hi, Azin'ka! Come in, my dear friend!" Pushkin welcomed his sister-in-law, unaware that he was dealing with a Temporal Academy cadet. "Alea iacta est! – The die is cast; I sent him a letter. The duel is inevitable."

"O, Lord! Sasha, why? I'm so worried!"

"I could not stand keeping this dirt and filth in my soul any longer. After sending off the letter, I feel as if I'm revived!"

"Darling, you've come to life just to… die? What if d'Anthes is luckier than you? Neither Natalie nor I will be able to bear it! And if you kill d'Anthes, then Catherine will not endure it!"

Pushkin, who was just giving Alexandrina a hug, pulled back and looked suspiciously at her, "Where is your usual fire? You seem to be thinking like rational Katya or cowardly Natasha. One of us has to go. If I die, then that's fate and there's nothing to regret!"

"What are you saying, Sasha! You do not think about us, and all those who love you, about your friends, children – and me, finally."

"I do. And with your quick eye you can just see it..." the face of the poet took on a mischievous expression, "but also... I haven't yet picked my second," a grimace of discontent appeared. "And no money to buy pistols," his brows furrowed, "And see how much work is waiting for me!" Pushkin pointed to his desk, covered with piles of papers, but his face again brightened at this moment.

"Please, do not buy guns! Listen to me, Sasha. I spoke with Idalia. She knows from the Stroganoffs for sure that the Heeckerens aren't involved in the letters."

"And you believe that scheming woman? Yes, she covers both villains – the father and the son! The Baron has been friendly with the Count ever since Stroganoff has been playing tricks all over Europe and showing them Russian 'class'. For all I care, they can kiss my...! Is it befit for a poet be timid in front of a pistol's barrel?"

"But you – the golden quill of Russia – quail before the tongues of those you despise! You know perfectly well that your wife is not cheating on you! Do not be angry, Sasha, but it is not she, but you – cheating on her! That is why you so painfully perceive everything. Believe me, one soft word to the Heeckerens, and that's it – there is no duel anymore!"

"Why are you so sure Alexandrina? You're confusing me... with your entirely manlike logic. And how can you believe that if the old pimp received my letter of retraction, he wouldn't ridicule Pushkin before the whole world, accuse him of cowardice?"

"I'll talk to Catherine; we'll know for sure! And why the letter? Arrange a meeting to resolve everything face to face. Promise until then not to seek a second or money for weapons, I implore you! Help me, O Lord!" she devoutly crossed herself and ran.

"I promise... for now," Pushkin said, struck with Alexandrina's passion and rhetorical skills. "For how long will I have a strength to keep my word?" the poet wondered, looking at his study door, which had closed behind 'a piece of his heart'."

Pushkin could not even imagine how the fictitious Alexandrina had received a secret signal from the coach standing nearby on the Moika Street. But the signal was received, and it said that real Alexandra Goncharova was returning home after a conversation with her cousin, Idalia Poletika.

...The poet looked in surprise at Alexandrina, dragging a heavy bundle into his study.

"Have you already seen Catherine?" he asked, puzzled.

"It's meaningless to talk to Catherine!" the determined woman cut him off, "She is entirely on the side of her offended husband. I spoke with Idalia. It seems to me that she wants to shield the Heeckerens – both father and son. You know, the Baron is a friend of Count Stroganoff. The Count has already read your letter and concluded that the duel is inevitable. I know you cannot talk to Natasha about it, but I will support you not only in sinful bliss, but also in sinful torment! Here," she made a gesture toward the bundle. "This silver is from my dowry. You can mortgage it to buy guns. Sasha, Sasha! Take this chain for luck; let it be your talisman!" And the poor woman threw herself, in a surge of emotion, onto the chest of her beloved, showering his face with kisses.

This dramatic shift in the behavior of Alexandrina impressed Pushkin so, that he didn't even want to ask about the reason for this change. He stroked the pale oval face with its slightly pouty lips, salty with tears, which he covered with tender kisses and mentally thanked God, in this crucial moment of his life, for the presence at least one person to fully share his feelings. Maybe incorrect feelings, but representative of his understanding of this intricate human world.

Marcel was slightly worried despite the anxiety self-management techniques. Alexandra had finished her part of the project. Sacks would be satisfied with his student. She had collected material of great historical value, and had confirmed for herself the Invariance of the Past. Marseille had no doubt in his own readiness: in the guise of d'Anthes's second, Viscount Olivier d'Archiac, the Secretary of the French Embassy, he accompanied his ward to the dueling ground on the Black River. The real d'Archiac hired a sledge – driven, as it happened, by Victor – and now peacefully snored away in it. Alexandra provided direct sensoportation of what his alternate had seen and felt in the d'Archiac memory. Only one thing bothered Marcel: his exit from the situation must not be witnessed; but both combatants, both cabbies and Danzas, Pushkin's second, could be a hindrance...

The day was beautiful; there was only a light frost so the whole town was out and about on sleighs. Acquaintances of d'Anthes and d'Archiac chuckled at their leaving so late for a ride. On the road, to the displeasure of d'Anthes, Marcel-d'Archiac twice dropped the pistols in public, hoping that someone would notice and inform the police. But the bright sun had replaced the gloomy sky, and an instinctive kindness displaced the conventional suspicion of the townspeople.

They arrived concurrently with their opponents at the dueling place – the grounds of the summer residence of the Commandant of Peter and Paul Fortress. Leaving both sleighs behind the fence, the seconds found a convenient flat area on the grounds, and grumbling at their inability to resolve the conflict, began stamping out a track in the snow. Pushkin had insisted on converging from twenty paces and shooting at ten! In the case of a mutual miss, they would repeated the process until at least one of the duelists was wounded. Both opponents grimly awaited the start of the fight, each on his own side. Even nature became angry: a cold wind began to blow.

Pushkin's fur coat and d'Anthes's greatcoat were thrown into the snow to mark off their ten paces. Marcel at once liked his opposite, Lieutenant

Colonel Danzas – taciturn officer unpretentiously wearing a single Military Order. They quickly exchanged the ritual phrases; bitterly noting that while they had urged reconciliation, it was strongly rejected by both sides. Then – a cursory questioning of the two parties: did they bear any metal things, capable of deflecting a bullet – crosses, medallions, weapons, cigarette cases…? Of course not! Then the seconds approached each other and, side by side, started to load the weapons. Both had similar sets of two Lepage pistols with capsules. The misfire was out of question. Loading d'Anthes's pistols, Marcel managed to avoid lead bullets in the barrel; by sleight of hands, he slipped them back into their box. It seemed that everything was going according to plan, but Sachs was right: the system of causality began to change, keeping the Invariance of the Past.

"Fully trusting your actions and wanting to completely equalize the chances of both parties, I offer to exchange one pistol," Danzas said nobly.

"Of course," said D'Archiac, weakening and not finding a reason to refuse.

Now, both of the contestants had one unloaded "slapstick"-pistol in their sets. Each duelist silently took a pistol from the enemy's set; they quickly began to converge. Marcel was beside himself! So much effort for zero result. Moreover, now Pushkin held a gun with a blank charge! Suddenly, before reaching the barrier, d'Anthes fired. He was aiming low. Pushkin screamed briefly and fell – his gun's barrel buried in the snow.

"It seems to me that my thigh has been shattered," groaned the wounded man.

Everybody rushed to him, but Pushkin stopped them, "Wait, I still have enough power to make my shot!"

"I'm not against changing the gun," said d'Archiac.

D'Anthes approved this with a nod. Danzas indignantly remarked that there is no need both for d'Anthes's consent and for replacing the weapon, but still, just to play it safe, brought to Pushkin the gun he had bought instead of the former one. The Poet began to aim. Pushkin was aiming low whether from weakness or from a desire to strike his abuser in the place, at which he believed d'Anthes was really aiming for. The Cavalier-Guard probably noticed it. He stood half-turned to the shooter, holding his gun down, shielding not his heart, but those organs that "had managed" this tragic story.

The return shot cracked in the air. Now d'Anthes fell.

"Where are you hit?" Pushkin asked.

"I think, in the chest," the Cavalier-Guard replied.

"Bravo!" exclaimed the poet and lost consciousness.

Both seconds rushed to their parties. D'Anthes's wound was not serious. He had a perforating wound of the forearm and bruised chest. The bullet ricocheted off the silver button of his braces.

"It's bleeding severely!" Danzas's voice sounded.

"I can manage my wounds myself," said d'Anthes, "D'Archiac, please check, maybe there is more need for your help."

Marcel sprinted to the wounded man, regretting that he could not provide him the first aid of the future. Nevertheless, he took out a pair of handkerchiefs from his pockets and tried to pack the wound, pushing them through the hole in poet's trousers as deeply as possible. Pushkin's blood stained his fingers. All sterility was out of the question, but it did not matter. From now on, the result of the project was entirely dependent on the successful intervention of Victor-Arendt.

"Just a moment, Mr. Danzas, I will bring the cabman with the sleigh! We need to break down part of the fence!"

What could Marcel do? He went to the fence, where, on his order, two cabbies dismantled one portion, sufficient for a sled to pass through. No one noticed as Marcel disappeared among snowy trees from where the real Viscount d'Archiac, returned slightly rattled to no less depressed participants in the duel.

The coach of Nikolai Fedorovich Arendt, Surgeon Ordinary to His Imperial Majesty, arrived at the house of Pushkin for the umpteenth time in this night. Servants knew the Doctor and in the midst of the night, brought him to the bedside of their severely wounded master without reporting to the family. This time his assistant with a surgeon's leather valise accompanied Doctor Arendt.

In the study, a candle was burning. Pushkin was lying on the couch. In a corner, in the chair Ivan Spassky, the family physician slept worn out from keeping watch around-the-clock.

"Good," Arendt said, speaking to the assistant, "Do not wake him up. And stand at the side, right here."

The assistant, Temporal Academy cadet, Marcel, nodded to his friend Victor, shielding him in case of Spassky wake up unexpectedly.

Pushkin was in a bad way. He was panting; his pulse was weak and galloping. The best thing would be to take the poet out of the house for full treatment and surgery. But, a half day still remained before the historical death, and it was absolutely impossible to do this. Too much had not yet been said and not yet done: it would be both very easy and completely unreasonable to cross the Cauchy horizon. Sachs was right, as always: to take the poet out now was impossible because of irreversible damage to causality with unpredictable catastrophic consequences. Later, before his death it would be impossible because of the presence of dozens of witnesses. So Victor did not even try. His goal was to quietly inject the patient with a couple million units of penicillin and, if possible, to take a sample from the wound for bacteriological analysis according to medical protocol. The results would reveal sensitivity to antibiotics. However, to Victor this analysis seemed useless. Even a tenth of this dose of penicillin would prevent peritonitis. Anyway, this information could be useful in other projects, which certainly would follow. Victor firmly believed this.

Pushkin sighed when the needle penetrated into his muscle.

"A wondrous moment I remember..." the poet whisper, barely audible.

The pain that he was suffering practically masked the prick of the needle. Now it was necessary to take a sample exudate. Victor threw back the covers, exposing the injured area, and collected some pus from the wound. Then he injected antibiotic locally, into the inflamed tissues. Then he could not resist, and shot a dose of morphine.

"Whatever happens, at least three hours of calm sleep," he said to the assistant.

They left the room and headed for the exit.

"No need to wake anybody up; I'll be back later," said Arendt to the maid.

The carriage with the young effeminate coachman was waiting for them at the door. They still had to get to the country "shelter" without incident, where the temporal cruiser disguised as a sleigh was waiting for them in a barn. Their mission had ended. All that was left was to learn the result. To do this at home was just as accurate as here. Moreover, even faster.

"Today we congratulate our seniors with the successful completion of their graduation project," Sachs announced and looked with sympathy at the three sad friends. "All captains of cruisers and your teachers know how hard it is to give up your own dream. But, the actions of graduates are not just actions of scouts and diplomats; it is personal experience with the Law of the Invariance of the Past. No wonder the Academy allows each participant to observe the validity of this law directly. Your follow-up work will focus on the collection of historical data rather than useless risky games with the people's destinies. And now, please except my congratulations!"

"I am in the dump more than the others," said Victor, "Alexandra and Marcel were already convinced of the Invariance by the time Pushkin was brought back to his apartment, while I was relying on the miraculous effect of penicillin. Professor, can you explain the paradox – why did not the antibiotic work?"

"Paradoxes in science are marks on the way beyond its horizons," replied Sachs. "Didn't you feel pointless to test for sensitivity to antibiotics? And were you not surprised by the result of that analysis?"

"But it turned out that the bacteria were not only insensitive to penicillin, but even to the most powerful antibiotics today? How did those bacteria emerged in the nineteenth century?"

"The simplest explanation to this is a breach of a closed system. Entering the past, you converted its isolated system into an open one. The cause was your crew. It was your bacteria. Perhaps from the lips of Sasha-Alexandrine, but most likely from the fingers of Marcel-d'Archiac. These changes offset your impact on the past, allowing a slight distortion of causality, as always, to keep the past invariant.

Some initial claps from the audience turned into loud applause.

"Undoubtedly, the law will bear Sachs's name," Victor thought. "But I will never forget 'a wondrous moment' of my very first project."

Nobody around him noticed that the cadet furtively wiped from his eyelashes a small tear, treacherously welling up from the eye of the Temporal sea dog.

THERE, BEYOND THE HORIZON...

It was still chilly in the mornings, but in the afternoons, we threw the windows wide open and enjoyed the scent of lilacs blooming in the park of the Temporal Academy. In the physics Great Lecture Hall, Professor Sachs had been completing a series of lectures about transitions in time as well as commenting on thesis projects in which students proposed ways to contravene the Invariance of the Past.

"Here it is – the *Cauchy Horizon...*" Sachs said, hatching a complex figure. "Let me remind you," he continued, "It is the interface between ..." and he emphasized, "*the acceptable predictable changes in events and the unacceptable or unpredictable.*"

"May I?" I went to the screenboard and, right on the Professor's sketch, marked in red a small part of the trajectory of an event emerging from the future into the past.

"This is an illustration of my proposal," I said. "To check the Invariance of the Past one does not need to make energy-intensive journeys through centuries and epochs. It's enough to move into the recent past and shoot oneself. If the Invariance of the Past is violated, and the future I kills the present me, then... he can take my place."

"Bravo, Victor!" Sachs rejoiced, "Very simple and elegant. I will support your idea at the Council despite its 'bloodthirsty' veneer."

"Professor," Penny – the honor and conscience of our class – anxiously inquired, "Wouldn't you allow for the possibility of the bullet hitting someone? Or, at least a light injury?"

"You see, Penny, the closer to the present time a moment of interaction is chosen, the greater the range of the *acceptable predictable changes* will be. But, neither I nor the Council would permit bloodshed; therefore we allow for transfer to a selected point in the Past, which is..."

"In-variant!" the audience shouted in unison.

"All of you will witness *Novikov's Principle* in action," Sachs waved in my direction to invite me to demonstrate my knowledge of the theory.

And I continued, *"The limit of the probability of changing an event that already happened equals zero!"*

At this moment, the antique bell rang, traditionally marking the beginning and end of lectures in the Temporal Academy. The door to the hall opened, and into the auditorium, slightly limping, ran my double with the shipmaster's beard, which I was planning to grow after the prom. Reaching the middle of the auditorium, he drew a Colt, and like a hero in an adventure movie, pointed it at me.

"I am finished!" flashed through my head, but Penny knocked the weapon from the hand of the intruder. No wonder – in preparing for the visit to the realm of Amazons, she had become an expert in martial arts. A shot rang out: a bullet pinged sharply and disappeared out the wide-open window.

"Halt!" screamed Sasha, trying with a commanding shout to stop the maniac; and he, as if just waking up, threw a small Winnie-the-Pooh to her and turned to the door.

Before I could express to my counterpart's face, or rather, to his bearded mug all that flashed through my mind in response to my own damn originality, he disappeared, like a devil, leaving the audience with a wisp of bluish smoke and the smell of gunpowder. Even Sachs was surprised by such a rapid development. He hurried over to me, worried about my distraught look. Let me be honest: to discuss bravely how to shoot a double and mark the trajectory of events on the screenboard, hoping that Sasha would appreciate your courage is one thing. But, to stand defenseless at the gunpoint of a military weapon is entirely another.

Was the result really dependent on Penny's principality? She had celebrated my salvation, kissing passionately with her fiancé Francois, right in the middle of the audience. I imagined how the forty-five caliber bullet would have smashed my brain and immediately felt sick; to fertilize the garden and not dirty the floor, I staggered on trembling legs to the windowsill and literally collapsed on top of it. At this moment, the second shot rang out...

Vomiting brought me relief. But, it was too early to rejoice that the second bullet had whizzed over my head, knowing the persistence of this bearded bastard. Of course, I realized that theoretically, it was impossible to hit me as a target, but you never know what I might manage to come up with in the future to circumvent the Invariance of the Past! Still, I did not want to get a bullet in the head, where, for some reason, my double was aiming. I tried to dig into my inner self: am I a secret sadist? But such thoughts never came to me not even close. I was quite sure that in place of my alter ego I would shoot only at the legs of the unfortunate fugitive, as dictated by the code of honor of officers throughout all times. And we were only five minutes from becoming cruiser captains – and prepared to be real Temporal sea dogs.

Having found no grounds for hidden cruelty to myself, I decided anyway not to expose my head as a target and to sneak away from my double. But, not to appear cowardly, I stepped over the windowsill and tried to climb down the drainpipe to the park spreading out around the Academy. The height was considerable: the third floor! The cadets in the room crowded together at the window and tried to dissuade me to climbing down the pipe. Oddly, only Sasha did not take part, but she was worried more than anybody else – it was written on her face. I continued to play the role of the brave romantic man and started to climb down. The supports of the pipes clearly were not meant for such a load. The brackets gave in to my weight just as my stubborn double shot at me again from the far window. Alas, despite good athletic training, I did not have time to grab the hooks in the wall and dropped onto the lawn.

The pain in my left leg was unbearable. Falling from the third floor – even on soft ground – is no joke. I was saved by the blossoming lilac bushes and could only rejoice that the bullets had again not reached their aim. Astonishing, is it not? And I always shoot so well. So what is it that protects the past from changes? To my counterpart from the future, a succession of events may perhaps seem like random failures: first Penny intervened; second, I fell on the windowsill; third – a pipe broke. And for me the same chain of events represented lucky coincidence, protecting me from death. I wondered how long the hunt would last. Or, maybe everything had already ended?

I was hoping that in the eyes of Sasha I would appear a hero – though without a medal for my wound – and not a fool. The medics picked me up and took me to a nearby building – the Academy clinic. Even a cursory examination of the shin suggested a fracture and I was sent to X-ray. When one image had already been made, and technician was ready to take the second one, someone entered the dark room. I heard my pursuer's troubled breathing, then again the creaking of an opening door, and four muzzle flashes illuminated the wall. Very painful! Have you ever been smacked directly on your fracture? Four strokes hit the neo-aramid cassette containing the film, which had been placed against the foot to obtain an image in the lateral projection. There is no better protection than neo-aramid against bullets, but every shot echoed with burning pain in my broken bones. I screamed and fainted.

I woke up in the recovery room. My leg was still aching, but I could not call it a sharp pain.

"Well, hero," Dr. Clark turned to me, "I had to fix your fracture with a plate, but you can dance at the prom, I promise."

I had no doubt, knowing his skills and my tenacity. But, before dancing, I still had to learn how to walk again and succeed in my thesis project.

Such a project in Temporal Academy usually consists of an historical study, during which each cadet has the opportunity to personally test the validity of the *Invariance of the Past*. No doubt, it will eventually be named "Sachs's Law". No longer can one find a queer old fish, who still believes that the slightest change in the past leads to significant changes in the future. On the contrary, for each small change in the past produced by the object from the future, new changes arise to compensate its influence. Nature establishes a sort of barrier – the *Cauchy Horizon*, which protects the past from being changed. A forced intersection of this Horizon threatens indeed not the past but objects of the future, which we all would soon be during our thesis projects.

"Hey, Victor, how are you feeling?" I heard a voice and saw Sachs's huge figure in the doorway of the ward.

Our professor, of course, is not just an outstanding scientist, but also a rare personality. He has enough time for everything; he supports and protects every cadet against an overly strict administration. Judging by my adventure, he had managed to defend my risky undertaking in the future before the Council.

"Take two days to recover your mental strength, and then calculate the *Cauchy Horizon* for your adventure. I will check everything then," Sachs supported me and bid farewell.

"Nowhere near enough rest! But I'll have plenty of visitors in the next two days," I smiled at this prospect but immediately began to think about how I would hit the victim to spite all physics and violate the *Invariance of the Past*!

From one perspective, such a statement may seem silly and arrogant. Actually, I did not think that everybody else built *perpetuum mobile* badly, while only I could make a working model. Typically, each cadet's thesis project was an attempt to rescue heroes, prominent people of the past, or victims of injustice. Alas, the course of history was never changed. Nature stood guard to its laws, or maybe, on the contrary, the laws were guarding nature. Well, to move a prominent personality into the future in the first minute after death and resuscitate him while replacing the corpse with a biodegradable copy of the body was a favorite Academy mission. It was called "Paradise". In the course of such an operation, the past did not change, but it could be carried out only with the consent of the individual, who later often fell into a depression and might lose his creativity. Of course, I knew the theory and agreed with the Invariance of the Past. However, like any researcher and future Temporal sea dog, I wanted to discover the boundary conditions under which there may be some measurable deviations from the past course of events. Do you follow me? I just wanted to clarify the scope of the law or, perhaps slightly expand it. That's why I thought of this most simple and intuitive attempt to change the past. And, in the end, don't the real experimenters start with experiments on themselves?

By evening, I was discharged, and Marcel brought me home, where Sasha had set a small table for my return. The three of us prepared the project to rescue the Russian poet Pushkin from his death in a duel. Therefore, during that evening, a lot of discussions were about emotions: how it is to stand staring into the black dilated pupil of a barrel pointed at you. I then thought seriously, is it possible to calm yourself in the past? And how? It's the same impracticable attempt to break the Invariance!

At night, I slept badly. My leg ached and I dreamed that the bullet nevertheless hit me, and I woke up screaming incoherently. Sasha brought me a painkiller and ice tee to drink and be calmed, and I went to sleep again, clinging to her shoulder.

Gradually, I got better. During the first days, I went about on a scooter, then switched to crutches, and by the end of the month was already hobbling around, leaning on a stick. I was exempted from sports, so I stopped shaving and soon sprouted a short fuzz on my face. My calculation of the *Cauchy Horizon* showed that I would have practically unlimited freedom of action except, of course such actions as I had just tried to implement. Victor from the future could not get to me because in the future there were no outcomes from my wound because it did not exist in the present. And did my counterpart somehow manage to hurt me, he would cross the *Cauchy Horizon* and, I am afraid, such an injury would end for him much worse than for me.

Sachs withstood the battle with the administration. The Council eventually approved the experiment, although the firing of military weapons in educational institutions was never welcome at any time. Moreover, I was granted an additional temporary transition, while graduates were usually given only one independent attempt for the thesis project. Nevertheless, Sachs's influence was so great that any bureaucratic attempts found themselves powerless before him.

I spent all my free time on the development of my mini-project. "Do not forget," I told myself, "Your goal is not to shoot the innocent double but to find a weak spot in the Invariance of the Past."

"If there is such a spot," added the inner voice, sounding remarkably similar to the professor's speech.

It seemed to me that I had the advantage of knowing the order of the actions of all participants. I remember that it all started with the lame double running into the audience and pointing his Colt at me when Penny struck his gun with her foot during his shot. "That means I'll soon be able to run," I noted. "That's good." But, knowing what Penny will do, you can try to outsmart her. Will this change the past?

In the second phase, my double missed just when I felt sick and leaned out the window. So now, when I changed roles, I needed to hurry, or, else, wait: let my counterpart catch his breath, draw himself straight and then open fire.

In the third attempt, the drainpipe did not withstand my weight, so one must reinforce the brackets. Even if I do not shoot myself, then a successful descent down to the land would be in itself a violation of Invariance. I wondered what would happen then with my fracture. And with a metal plate screwed to the bone? With x-rays documenting the fact of the fracture? Although, if Victor did not fall from the drainpipe but fell in the garden and broke his leg, this would be *acceptable predictable change*, without modifying causal relationships...

Finally, if previous actions are unavoidable, are the events in the X-ray room, depending only on me, so inevitable? And if I shoot a technician? Probably, the same cassette with the film, which would be in his hands, will protect him. Eureka! And what if I do not go to the X-ray room at all, not shoot and not leave marks on the cassette case?

Sasha did not like my idea at all. More precisely, theoretically everything was sound, but to shoot at the double, well, as if to shoot oneself, was in her opinion wrong and ill considered.

"Don't you sense some kind of immorality in such behavior?" she said. "First, you shoot a man we... well, just I... love. But he has a lot of friends, and the Professor respects him. And this act makes of Victor another person, not the sort who is loved and respected! Secondly, somebody could misunderstand that the shooter is not a crazy man, not a terrorist, but the researcher Victor from the future... and cause you injury. And it could be me! The past does not protect you at all. And finally, third, what most worries me is that you do not care what you do to even slightly shake the Invariance of the Past. I do not know if you can do it, but if you manage or even accidentally cross the *Cauchy Horizon* – all of us expect big trouble. Don't you care?

"To be honest, not much," I thought. "Girls are always more sensitive to dangers and therefore tend to exaggerate. That's where their foresight comes from."

And I was more worried about the creation of a paradox, a small but measurable change in the past. And calculations derived from every little idea, of which I had an incredible number. But, alas, you could consult Sachs only on serious issues, not cadets' tricks. Although, if you think carefully about it, do tricks not sometimes lead to a revision of the serious issues?

Professor checked my calculations of the *Cauchy Horizon* and grunted:

"Practically…all correct. Have you noticed that the probability of injury to the leg is significantly higher than the probability of any other hit? How do you explain that?"

"I thought that the system took into account a much higher frequency of warning shots to the legs."

"Then the probability for each leg should be the same," said Sachs, "And as for the left leg, it is much higher, so the system assumes that the injury in the area of the fracture does not significantly change the picture of the events and associations."

"So it means that I can shoot him in the leg and not violate the Invariance of the Past?"

"Exactly! Therefore, for the net result you'd better not shoot at his legs, but aim exclusively at his head."

"Good suggestion, especially if it is someone else's head."

"Go ahead, shoot at my head," Sachs said quietly, "As you can see, nothing happened with it in the past. Recall the sharp ping of the bullet aimed at you. Understood? That was the invisible space-time barrier. But I want to warn you about one thing: you're certainly going to look for all sorts of ways to break the Invariance and bypass obstacles. That's as it should be. This is your project. But, do not try to shoot through your own body in order to injure anyone else. It will not help. Nature will find a way to protect them in the past. You have your own time, which artificially made a loop, but for you it continues its straight flow. Therefore, all your injuries and wounds will be real. Got that? Do not try to cripple yourself. Well, I say this just in case, like a boring teacher to a clever student who understands everything by himself…

Finally, the appointed day of the experiment arrived. Sasha persuaded me to spare her feelings in the past, and I promised, once there, to throw her a miniature Winnie-the-Pooh, the one that usually hung as a talisman from her backpack. Seeing Victor and Winnie's doubles, she would immediately realizes who this "psycho with a gun" was and what was going on.

In the morning, I did not go to classes but to the laboratory where the temporal capsule was situated. Transition to the past seemed to me a short ride on the high-speed elevator. My ears became obstructed for a moment. I swallowed and was ready to leave the capsule. Of course, the ride did not include the time for setting and synchronization. However, there was no need to transport or camouflage the capsule: I just slipped into the Laboratory of Temporal Measurements in the present and emerged from it in the past. The month before, when I came out of the capsule, the weather was clearly cooler than an hour ago, when I entered it, but the windows in all the classrooms were already held wide open so people could enjoy the fragrance of lilacs blooming in the garden of the Academy. The black 8-round Colt issued to me for the experiment weighed down my left trouser pocket. I was slightly worried, though I knew that nothing special would happen today because nothing had happened before. And the probability of changing an event that has already happened, you know, approaches zero. But, before trying to change such an event, I went to the Academy firefighter, Karel, and persuaded him to strengthen the drainpipe on the facade of the school building.

"Today we will climb it. Sachs knows that, but security never hurts!"

Then, making sure that he carefully attached the pipe to the wall with concrete nails, I went to the lecture hall. The bell would just be ringing.

I cannot say that I really wanted to shoot anyone, and even less my other self. Even meeting my "copy" was somehow scary. To cheer myself, I quickened my pace, and limping slightly, ran into the room where Sachs was lecturing on the calculation of the *Cauchy Horizon*. That very same lecture during which I offered to shoot to myself. "Well, now you feel the chill wind of it!" I thought and with my right hand drew a very realistic cap pistol. Perhaps I did not run in fast enough – my foot still ached a bit – but the face of my double standing at the screenboard with a marker in his hand was the grimace of surprise. "What an expression," I barely had time to think, as the cap pistol in my right hand flew into the air from the sharp blow from Penny's boot. Even though I had expected this blow, I could not counter her maneuver, so masterfully did Penny executed it. This is a real Amazon! But we also were not born yesterday: bang! – thundered a shot from the Colt in my left hand.

I could not blame nature or the Invariance: one should learn to shoot from the hip without aiming, like a cowboy in a western! The bullet pinged and then flew through the open window. I was a clumsy James Bond indeed...

"Victor...? Stop it immediately!" Sasha screamed.

Amid the cadets' confusion, I threw Sasha her little Winnie-The-Poo talisman and leaped out of the lecture hall, leaving an odor of devilry. I knew that Victor would now have gotten sick from scenes he had imagined, and I prepared a second shot to hit my poor double. But, imagination hooked me, too: my heart was pounding, trying to jump out of its cage, when I reentered the auditorium. According to my calculations, Victor would be standing by the window, breathing more calmly as he overcame his weakness. But, near the unfortunate guy, still leaning over the sill, Sachs stood, blocking him from the bullets. Then I remembered the words of the professor that it did not matter who I shot, and I fired at my beloved teacher though my hands were shaking like a Parkinson patient's before regeneration of his neurons.

Of course, I missed. Without any assistance from Penny. But the shots scared Victor from the past, and, ignoring the cries of the cadets, he climbed out the window, trying to escape from me in the garden. That was all right with me because the further I got away from the target, the more it turned into the "experimental object".

So, I ran back to the far window where I had a good shot at the fugitive, and fired twice. I knew that the drainpipe was already securely attached to the wall, so it wouldn't fall, and the victim could not escape. Just as I shot, my double – apparently doubting the reliability of drainpipes – tried to jump onto the fire escape. I am sure that he would have succeeded if not for the general tension: without ever having been under fire, this is not easy to understand. In short, his foot slipped off the crossbar, and the poor man dropped. Probably there was no one in the auditorium who would not sympathize with Victor, but hardly anybody could have been more upset than me: memories of my unfortunate fall were too fresh. And also, do you know what it is to have a twin brother? I felt this in the last few minutes. There was another person, who felt no less deeply for Victor. A tripping, a push, a sharp tug on the Colt's barrel, and I found myself on the floor, and the gun – in Sasha's hands. In my eyes there just flashed a figure fleeing into the corridor. That's bad! Or, the opposite, perhaps luck? That would also be a solution – to find the weapon and to return with it to my time with four unspent cartridges. That would be a documented change in the past! And I did not even know what consequences I might engender trying to cross the Cauchy Horizon. What if Sasha was right and nature would destroy an extra copy. I knew who was extra in this time! But as much as I'd like not to be affected by my own imprudence, I would reproach myself even more for Victor's fate: he would have to repeat my mistake in the near future. No – we will still go for it! I sprinted for the gun directly to the clinic where they would deliver the victim.

There was nobody in the corridor of the ER; then I just glimpsed a stretcher with the patient turning the corner where a luminous arrow with the word "Radiology" pointed. Peering around the corner, I saw Sasha and Marcel waiting for Victor in the hallway. They were arguing.

"It's up to you," concluded Marcel and left.

Then Sasha glanced around furtively and darted into the X-ray room.

In a few strides, I covered the distance to the X-ray room and slipped into the darkness. There, on a rotational platform, lay the patient. The image of his broken bone shone on the blue screen.

"Now I'll take a side view," said a voice from the loudspeaker, "And you will go to the surgeons in the OR."

At that moment, four lightings flashed – one after another – and four shots rang out. The patient on the platform gave a muffled cry and fell silent. The gun's wet grip poked me in the palm, and Sasha's voice reported, "That's it, 'Invarianter', the *status quo* is restored. Return to where you belong. And take these artifacts with you." The Colt was followed by Winnie-The-Pooh.

And I did so. I had no other choices left.

Coming out of the Temporal capsule in my warmer month, I handed over the weapon and left with a cute artifact in my hand. Its black eyes slyly looked at me as if passing greetings from the black-eyed Sasha. I pressed the bear's tummy, waiting for the familiar squeak, but I heard only a rustling.

"What is this?" I took out from the toy a crumpled piece of paper covered with Sasha's handwriting:

1. Victor-2 appears and shoots Victor-1 at the screenboard.
2. Victor-2 shoots Victor-1 at the window.
3. Victor-2 shoots twice at Victor-1 on the drainpipe.
4. Victor-1 falls and breaks his left leg.
5. Victor-1 is driven to the clinic.
6. Four shots in the X-ray cassette of Victor-1. Victor 2 disappears.

On the other side of the memo was a note for me, "Well, now are you convinced of the *Invariance of the Past*? Better prepare to save Pushkin – a more honorable task!"

Sasha, as always, was right: what are we looking for beyond the Horizon when here we have such good friends!

COMA

"Jack!"

Standing just in front of the school gate, Mom laughed merrily, waving to him. It was a surprise. How long was it since she came to fetch him? When he started first grade? What fifth grader, ha-ha, and, starting today – a sixth-grader, would allow his mom to pick him up from school in front of all his friends, just like a baby? But today, on the last day of the school year, it was nice – as a memory of childhood, which – now in the sixth grade – seemed long ago and happy.

"Let's go to a cafe to celebrate the end of the school year," Mom said, ruffling her son's long, Beatle-style hair.

"One more year, and Jack won't let me do that anymore," she thought.

They walked to the avenue and headed along the Central Park to the plaza in the form of a hexagon, five sides occupied by the terraces of cafes and restaurants, and on the sixth side, the edge of the park, a magnificent fountain – splashing and sparkling in the sun.

"Where will we sit?"

"Let's sit here, closer to the water. When we walked in the park on Sundays with Dad..." Jack started, but hesitated indecisively.

"I know you've always admired the rainbow in the fountain's spray," she said to her son and mentally remarked, "The topic of his father shouldn't be taboo."

"By the way, soon you'll fly to your dad for a month. A lot of traveling! Then for two weeks, you'll go to your grandmother in the village, and we'll spend two more weeks together, by the sea."

"Wow!" Jack imagined a cool summer full of adventure. "Sometimes two families is double the entertainment," he rightly decided, "And it would be nice to visit grandmother too."

In his memory flashed a picture of the village on the banks of a wide river where he had spent his childhood. "My September essay 'How I Spent My Summer' will again be the most interesting in my English class."

They both ordered juicy, bleeding steaks and cranberry lemonade.

"I'll get some coffee for dessert," Mom said, finishing her lunch, "Do you want ice cream?"

"Yes. But not the kind they sell here. Can I run to the fountain? There is a cart selling the world's crunchiest waffle cones with a sundae. I'll bring you one, OK?"

"Well, since we're having such a celebration..." Mom smiled. "Only, watch carefully, crossing the street."

"Mom! You treat me like a first-grader!"

And Jack, happy with such a good start to his vacation, rushed for his favorite treat. From his jeans, shirt and long hair it was difficult to determine from behind who this slim figure belonged to – a boy or a girl.

With flushing colored lights and wailing siren, an ambulance rushed into the courtyard of the hospital. As if in an educational movie, paramedics jumped out of the van, flung open its rear doors, and rolled out a stretcher carrying a patient. Not an adult, rather a child. Not a girl, rather a boy. Hurry! Hurry! Automatic glass doors parted before the stretcher. Right, sharp right, left, and now, the patient is already in the emergency room.

"MVA, boy, twelve years, fractured skull and limbs, cardiac arrest. Sinus rhythm restored! Consciousness, reflexes, spontaneous breathing absent," shouted the senior paramedic as the trauma team assembled with the ER attending.

COMA

First – the anesthesiologist inserted a breathing tube, so that a mechanical ventilator would force the boy's lungs to work again. Next – the surgeons stabilized the boy's neck, inserted catheters, took blood, and hung plastic bags with solutions. Then – the monitor's sensors cling to the boy's chest. And here we have all the data saved in the computer system. Specialists are consulted, tests and radiological examinations ordered. Everything is stat, stat, stat! Quick, quick, quick! Soon results will appear in the system, and doctors will draw their first conclusions. But, so far – it's a life threatening condition.

"A very tough case," the ER attending thought. "The paramedics did not even attempt to intubate the patient: did not waste time on it. They started the boy's heart, cleared his throat of ice cream, and gave oxygen. Intubation was very easy: absent swallowing reflex. Pain reflexes absent too. That bad. Reaction to light is present, but the pupils are narrow. If the blood does not reveal drugs, it means that the injuries are in the brain stem. Probably no bleeding: the blood pressure is only slightly low, strange though, he is very cold. We'll do a CT scan now; learn exactly what damage there is in the head and abdomen. If the cervical vertebrae are intact, then we can rotate his head and see how his eyes react. This is a job for a neurologist or neurosurgeon. But, it seems to me that the boy will not wake up even in six hours – so it's a coma. And on the Coma Scale he has only three points. Well, kid had no luck..."

The pale woman nervously smoothed the sheet on the boy's bed. The even paler cold arms of the child stretched along his body, surrounded by heaters, and, although his arms were limp – the woman was convinced of this – they did not "want" to bend at the elbows.

"Hi," said a man, pulling open the curtain, immediately brightening the unit. The dark circles under the eyes of the woman became noticeable. "I'm Dr. Mod, a neurosurgeon. And who are you?"

87

"I am Jack's mom. M-may I hope for something?" she said in a trembling voice, stumbling over the word "may" like a student who, in anticipation of a devastating test, tries to get excused by a strict teacher.

"So far, there is nothing that would even indicate some improvement in his condition. Your son is in a coma. A massive hemorrhage was not found, but rather a lot of pinpoint bleeding at all levels. The heart works by itself, and the breathing machine supports the lungs," he pointed to a ventilator. "Different centers in the brain have been damaged, so there is no consciousness or movement, and the brain maintains a low body temperature. To supply nutrition we will need to pass a tube from the stomach through the abdominal wall. This is a very simple operation; it is done without surgical incision, gastroscopically."

"Yes, I know. My father had a feeding tube. I will sign my consent." Her heart sank alarmingly: she saw how this feeding would end. "Doctor, how many..."

"How long Jack will be in a coma?"

"Yes."

The doctor shook his head sadly, "I do not think anyone can answer your question. We watch and hope that Jack will be better. And the first step – that he begins to breathe by himself."

"And then...?"

"Please, do not make me guess." Compassion set into Doctor Mod's eyes: "Some patients do not improve. Others... improve, but do not come out of the coma. Some come out by themselves or with medical help. But very few of them recover completely."

"Doctor, what do you mean 'with medical help'? What can be done?" For the first time, she looked at the doctor with hope.

"First, there is care and prevention of complications, and secondly – deep brain stimulation, which is still too early to discuss."

"But you will say when..." her voice broke.

"Of course," Mod sympathetically squeezed her arm, "We'll keep you informed of any changes in your son's condition, and we'll be delighted to tell you about any improvements."

The ICU doctor was preparing a transfer of the comatose patient to the neurosurgery department. There, comatose patients were cared for in a special section for traumatic brain injury.

"Doctor, doctor, come here quickly," the nurse called.

The patient, coughing and choking, was trying to push out the breathing tube.

"I was just clearing it as usual, and suddenly he started..."

"This can be a very good sign. If spontaneous breathing resumes, then there is some hope that other functions will also resume. Call the anesthesiologist for supervision, I want to remove the tube and check if the patient is breathing by himself."

When the boy's mother came back, the news was waiting for her. First, Jack had already gotten rid of the tube in his throat. The respirator, now turned off, was still standing next to the bed, now silent and useless, devoid of its usual huffing job. Secondly, Dr. Mod had decided to proceed with Jack's deep brain structure stimulation.

She believed in this word – *stimulation*.

"Now, I need your consent for the operation and procedure," the surgeon said. "It's not an easy decision. The operation – the insertion of electrodes is simple. The main problem is the outcome of the procedure: a stimulation is not certain. For some comatose patients it has been very useful in bringing them out of their critical condition. But, alas, not for all. Therefore, there is no guarantee that it will succeed. This is no longer an experimental treatment, but it is not yet the standard procedure. Patients may experience psychiatric complications: depression, hallucinations, decreased IQ."

"Doctor, are you kidding? Let him only go to school even if he studies for all D's," Mom shed tears. "I'm ready to do anything!"

"Well, your participation is not needed yet," Mod encouraged her.

"And how can I help my son? Blood? Spinal cord transplant? Anything!"

"No, no. I did not mean that. Let's proceed gradually. I promise, I'll tell you after the stimulation. Call me superstitious," smiled the surgeon, "but I do not like to discuss things in advance that are still too early to say."

"Mod, indeed, is a great doctor," the woman thought. "He actually predicted everything, but carefully, with reservations. I can understand him."

She could safely assume so because she had seen many tough cases in the neurosurgery intensive care unit in the past several months. Most of those patients could not overcome their illness or injury. Only her son's young age, according to the doctors, made him a favorable candidate for coming out of the coma. Maybe a child's brain treats and restores itself better than an adult brain?

The stimulation was successful. Gradually Jack began returning to consciousness. He slept for a long time now, but sometimes he woke up and asked to drink. He still could not hold a cup by himself, but he tried. He was primarily fed nutrient mixtures through the tube to his stomach, but his mother regularly gave him broth to drink. Still, Jack's body temperature remained low. Neither warmers nor warm baths helped. After each warm up, the boy woke up, "came alive", became oriented to his surroundings, recognized his mom, talked. But, after a while, he returned to his previous state, like a bear hibernating. Perhaps Nature itself demanded it: Christmas lights were already shining behind the windows.

One day Dr. Mod approached the mother.

"It's time now to talk about another method of treatment. This time it is experimental and concerns not only the patient but also the donor."

"Of course!" the woman's face lit up. "What do you want me to do?"

"Almost nothing... or maybe everything. You can share your brain signals with your son. It's almost the same as the previous method of deep stimulation, but now the signals are taken from the deep structures of the related brain. You know whose brain I'm talking about."

"Of course! I agree to any procedure; I'll make any sacrifice for my boy. I'm not afraid of any involvement and..."

"I am absolutely sure of your determination and your love for your son," Mod nodded. "Not to cool your enthusiasm, but I must tell you the new method is a double-edged sword. We will connect the structures responsible for thermoregulation in one hypothalamus to corresponding structures in the other. Your brain must, I repeat, must overpower the diseased brain signals and change its setting."

"But how do I do that? I have no idea how to change brain settings."

"Nobody has," Mod smiled sheepishly, "And nobody knows how to win in the battle of two structures. Alas, to tell the truth: not all experiments end safely. Just as not every deep stimulation results in success. But in the case of Jack, it did."

"Hence, this experiment will be successful!"

"Very good! I honor your faith, but by signing your consent for the new treatment, you should know that the result might be useless for your son, and disastrous for you."

"The main thing is that I don't hurt Jack! That would stop me. And the fact that there is a risk in the treatment... of course. As with everything in life, even buying ice cream..." her eyes filled with tears, but she quickly pulled herself together. "It's very good that you are honest with me, Doctor. I appreciate it. But you'd better teach me some tricks to deal with a sick brain."

"Only in the most general terms. Imagine that you need to fix a faulty thermostat, in a refrigerator. You have neither schema, nor tools, nor spare parts. You only have a hope that the refrigerator can understand your speech. What do you do? Ask it to fix itself, not to turn on the cooling chamber so often, and not to freeze so much. Do you understand?"

"I think so. I agree. What should I sign? And when do we start the experiment?"

S he was walking barefoot on the cold ground, covered here and there with frost – where is he?

"Jack!" the woman called, but there was no answer.

She quickened her pace, trying to warm up a little. Perhaps she succeeded or maybe it was simply warmer near the forest; in any case, the frost melted beneath her warm feet. The trees were bare, extending their leafless branches to each other. The sky scowled, hanging heavily over her head. It seemed about to snow. Suddenly – she heard someone behind the trees breathing heavily, as if after a run, and she rushed to the trees.

"Son, son, do you hear me?"

It was he. Thinner and taller than before, with a shaved head, dressed as she was, in a hospital gown.

"Mom, do not go out there; it's very hot there."

She took his hand. His skin was dry and cool.

"We need to go out of here and find an exit from this place," she insisted.

"I feel bad over there. It's so hot and stifling. Like in the summer."

"You always loved the summer, Jack! Do you remember how we rested by the sea, sunbathed and swam?

"Yes, I liked it then, but now I hate summer. I even feel hot in spring.

"And I am freezing here. Take me out, into the spring, let me warm up!"

The boy frowned, but did not argue. Turning into the woods, he plunged into a thicket. It was getting warmer. On the ground, the first blades of grass were sprouting here and there. Buds, and even new leaves, were appearing on some trees. A bird sang somewhere.

Jack was breathing heavily, "I dare not go any further, I feel bad even here."

"The doctor said you have to learn to love summer again."

"How can I do that when I can no longer tolerate the heat?"

"You will learn again. You only need to try it once."

"I have tried many times, but each time I was choking and stopped. I know the exit out of the woods is over there, in the heat, but I cannot make myself to go through it."

"You know, Jack, now you're not alone. I will help you bear the heat: I'll hold you with my cold hands, fan and cool you. We have to go to the river, where the summer is in full swing, and swim across it to the other side."

"I won't make it. I'll suffocate or drown."

"I'll save you. I'll breathe the air into you, and hold you up in the water. Together we can do everything. You really want to get out of here, don't you?"

"Yes. I do want to," the boy was remembering something – drops of sweat appeared on his forehead, "Let's try it together."

And hand in hand, they exited the woods and moved toward the river through green summer pastures.

When the head of the neurosurgery department looked into the recovery room, before his eyes appeared a "surgical idyll." Two patients, mother and son, blanketed in ice packs, lying on the beds, head to head. Corresponding electrodes implanted deep into each brain were interconnected.

"Well, what have you achieved with your experiment?" asked the Head to Doctor Mod. "The second day of the case. From one patient in a coma we happily got two," he shook his head and walked out of the room into the hallway, from which the cheerful sound of "Jingle Bells" came.

Mod paused a moment, and, taking both patients' hands, assured them, "That's OK; we'll keep fighting this coma, I promise you!"

His eyes widened: their fingers were warm and pleasant to the touch...

THE LITTLE ANT

The morning was sunny and clear. A green grass carpet, wet with dew, crept up to the horizon. The air filled with the sounds of plants rustling in the wind and the scent of flowers, calling insects to treat themselves to sweet juice and, at the same time, to pollinate them.

The lonely stranger rested his burden against a mighty green trunk vanishing into the skies. He did not feel the temperature, although it had gradually begun to heat up. His plans for the next few days were rather grandiose. First, he must find a good place to settle. Second, look for a girlfriend, and if he is lucky to find one with a good character – then take her as his wife. And finally... establish a... what? A dynasty? It sounded somewhat high-flown, but he could not find another, better word. "No, a colony is something else," his memory prompted him.

Memory... He knew that *it* had not always been like this, but he could not put into words when the changes had begun and what had changed. More recently, he was not even able to clearly visualize the images of his childhood or school, nor to remember his parents and friends. "Where are they all?" the thought floated in his mind, but he could not find the answer. However, there was no sense of uncertainty or error, so no anxiety arose.

After lunching on mushrooms that grew in abundance here, the stranger settled down to rest. It seemed to him that he vaguely remembered his mother walking with him along the streets of a beautiful, big city, as his father taught him... What? He did not remember it yet, but the confidence that all his memories would come back did not leave him. His friends from the house, the street, the school or the tribe... Fighting – no, rather battles with others began to appear in his reviving memory. Sometimes it seemed to him that all these were the dreams of others, so unfamiliar did they seem to him at first. But, after a while, the images took root, and it seemed strange that he did not recognize them immediately.

By the evening, the stranger realized that he knew where to go. It was not a blind choice, but a move towards the weak signals from his, as yet, unknown bride. Then, to expedite the meeting, he himself started to send out signals of his presence into his environs.

"I have to finish building this ant vivarium before Mom comes back," thought Vit. "Otherwise she will not be happy that I took everything that came to hand." He had chosen this project, for biology and social relations were his two favorite subjects.

Plexiglas cutting boards from the kitchen were ideally suited for making a flat transparent tank for an ant colony. He had read about a ready-to-use "Ant Farm", but where to find it? He had to spend more time searching the encyclopedia and doing everything himself. Not so nice and safe: Mom may scold about the Plexiglas, but it's more fun to "do-it-yourself". It would be necessary to pour good soil inside, and, in some places, to put a transparent jelly. Let them dig their tunnels and rooms. Tunnels that ants build in jelly are clearly visible. In short, it would be possible to study the life of these insects for a long time. Probably, it would be easier to find just a few ants and reproduce them in the "greenhouse". Better than many other creatures on land, ants withstand adverse living conditions and even radiation. Of course, not at such levels as in the former cities – where nothing was left alive living, but it would be worthwhile to look for them in the mountains. "If I find them, I will certainly boast to Ann. Interesting – has she ever observed ant life?"

Annie's image had appeared in his mind recently. At first just acquiesces, they became friends immediately. It was simple: despite their different hobbies, both, by nature, were researchers – that is what attracted them to each other.

Annie saw herself as a future "magician" – she wanted to become an expert on the fulfillment of desires. To do this it was necessary to master mathematical statistics, analytical programming, economics and psychology. She called her project "The child-wish-controlled bubble-blower": after all, some loved giant bubbles that slowly changed their shape and coloration in the air while others loved small quick bubbles, which flew up into the air, popping, and spraying down. And she loved cheerful, laughing children. "Someday I will have many children. That will be great! It's necessary to ask whether Vit likes a big family," thought Annie, going back to her calculations, taking the viscosity of soap solution as inversely proportional to the force of bubble blowing, which in turn, is directly dependent on the child's joy.

"Maybe the ants will feel very good in my artificial anthill: warm, dry and satisfied," thought Vit. "But we must take care of the offspring. Because they breed in flight, at some point, the farm will become their prison. But, what prevents me from opening the door and releasing the large queen with her frail elect to a mating flight? Who would have thought that the fate of the ant people may depend on one inconspicuous ant?"

"Vit, can you hear me?"

"I don't know, Annie. But I understand that you're calling me and you want to chat."

"Yes, I do. And where are you?"

"I do not know. I think I still live with my parents. I see our old house, my father with a pipe in a rocking chair on the front porch, and my mother, hurrying home from the market. And you?"

"I know that I'm alone. I ask everybody but no one answers me: nobody has seen my family. But, I'm not discouraged. I want to make bubbles for kids – bubbles that will decorate their dull gray world and replace the missing flowers and colors. It was my last school project."

"I was going to build an ant farm. Maybe I'll be able to do so now. I already know that in our kitchen there is Plexiglas, which is suitable. If only my mother would not get angry if I take it."

"**Z**eus, you have a dispatch from Earth," reported Hermes, the signalman of the spaceship Olympus".

"Does at least one living creature capable of sending telegrams remain there?" the Capitan was surprised.

"Of course not. However, the words and feelings of the bereaved residents are not lost. This is the first time we have encountered a request to restore humanity after a terrible plague. It is the only one among billions of electromagnetic scraps of thoughts and emotions decrypted by our scientific director, Athena."

"So, there was someone who thought more about the future than about their immediate troubles! Well, we can assume that the request is an official inquiry from Earth to the intergalactic community. Summon the Council, Hermes; we will approve a rescue project. Athena, what are your thoughts and considerations?"

"There is sufficient information about the earthlings in the database. There are two ways of responding to their plight: to wait till evolution leads to a restoration of mammals, primates and humans, or to take as a model any pair of a single species and transform them into humans."

"Biological reconstruction is not difficult, but what about psychological?" questioned the Capitan.

"Fortunately, we have samples of memory, feelings, experiences, and even conversation from these earthlings. Recently, we started experiments on interactions of these samples. The results are encouraging. I think we have enough material for at least one pair of organisms of different sexes."

"All that remains is finding biological beings suitable for transformation on Earth."

"Even this issue has practically been resolved. The species most resistant to radiation have proven to be ants from the Arthropod phylum."

"How many of them do we have?"

"Only one ant queen capable of producing abundant offspring survived."

"And what about the male? The man? The father?"

"So far the only candidate is too weak. He has been fed, trained, his formic memory has been restored, and he has been prepared to search for his bride. Let him think that he is the first hero of the ant world. I am afraid, however, that he will not be able to fly and fertilize the beautiful queen."

"I'll have to help him," declared Zeus. "After all, we both are the first."

A green grass carpet, wet with evening dew, crept up to the horizon. The air filled with the sounds of plants rustling in the wind and the scent of flowers, calling insects to treat themselves to sweet juice and, at the same time, to pollinate them. But, no bees or bumblebees could be heard.

A lone little ant rested his burden, leaning it back against a blade of green grass, and set his antennas to pick up the seductive pheromones of his future bride. He had no doubt that the beautiful queen would come to meet him. In the dark, faceted eyes see poorly, but the prevailing odors awoke deep feelings within him. At dawn, they found each other.

"Do you want to have a big family, lots of kids?" Annie asked.

"Of course, I am here for that reason," Vit replied.

"Then let's fly!"

And spreading their ant wings, glistening with rainbow colors like soap bubbles, they climbed into the clear air so that the people of Earth could continue to exist in the world of real things, not just as images living in the Universe forever.

PENNY LANE

1

From the report of John Connell, M.D., Colonel of Her Majesty's Armed Forces to Intelligence Service Section 5 (MI5):

*"...Presented is the postmortem examination of twelve bodies of children deceased between the ages of 24 days and 1 year; all with apparent **phocomelia** i.e. absence of the extremities, except for flipper-like hands and feet, sprouting directly from the body.*

An autopsy performed by me in the pathology department of the Liverpool Military Hospital revealed that six out of twelve bodies (group A) do not belong to the Homo Sapiens species but are in fact either an unknown-to-science kind of creature or a hybrid of human and extraterrestrial organisms.

Along with the internal organs presented in a normal human, the brain and liver are significantly altered. Unknown-to-science organs have also been detected in the abdominal and the cranial cavities.

All mothers of newborns from group A are younger than 21 years old and reside (or resided before marriage) within half a mile from the Penny Lane and Smithdown Road intersection roundabout.

Detailed anatomical description of all specimens, photos of sections and microscopy slides are enclosed.

Remaining six bodies (group B) do not bear any anatomical deviation from normality, except for above-mentioned phocomelia.

The Mothers' ages in group B range from 19 to 37 years old. Addresses of these women are randomly distributed throughout the city.

In group A, the cause of death in all instances are cardiac dysfunction and respiratory distress due to severe polymicrobial pneumonia, complicated with hemorrhages into the lung tissue."

This report represents the document of state importance. The code "Top Secret" is to be retained until special government instruction.

2

Paul comfortably reclined on a bench under a canopy in the center of the small square at the last stop of the bus line. He was in no hurry waiting for his friend John. It was their meeting place, familiar since childhood and teenage years. Here they waited for the bus to the center of Liverpool or to the University located in the faraway suburbs of Sefton Park. Here, in the church of St. Barnabas, little Paul sang in the choir. Here John's mother, a waitress of the nearby café, fed them something tasty – until she met her fate under the wheels of a car... Here local youth would hang out in the evenings: they drank beer, smoked the coming-into-fashion weed, and felt girls up under their skirts. Teddy joked once, "Like finger into a pie". Everybody laughed, but the expression "finger pie" caught on. "Well, bloody true, our stoned Shakespeare!"

The sky, the high sky radiated blue over the city, while the white fleece of clouds in the north had already started to darken, turning into black monsters of thunderstorm.

The chief of the local fire station jumped out of the hair salon across the street, and fanning his freshly shaved face, burning from cheap cologne, with the Queen's photo, headed to his station, around the corner. Since childhood, Paul remembered the gelled Kaiser Mustaches of the captain, his nickname "Brandmaster", his gold helmet, shining in the sun, and mainly, his fire machine – the dream and jealousy of all local boys. Ruby and platinum lights glistened at the top of the wonder-machine, not different from the identification lights of a jet or a spaceship. Boys grew up, but admiration stayed – no other suburb of Liverpool had such a marvelous red and chromed thingy.

Not every lucky lad could sign himself into the fire squad. Good lookers – Teddy and both his freckled brothers did it. Malicious tongues explained this luck by their relationship with the fire captain, but the brothers repaid it a hundredfold with back-breaking work, putting their best efforts into leaking clean the engine, pull-out ladders, pumps and many other mystic and beautiful tools including brass nosepieces and bells. Sometimes the captain gave a test to his crew: he put out the hourglass – and trouble awaited those who did not finish his task in time, dispensed by the rustling sand grains.

After the hardships of the day, the brothers came to the spot – the bus shelter at the Penny Lane roundabout. Here, in the summer time, they usually had their dinner of fried fish with potato chips, which were abundantly added to the serving of codfish for extra four pennies. Filled up and licking fat from their fingers brothers proceeded with the best desert possible – "finger pies". Well, the "bakery" always favored them.

Paul watched the sky again. If it starts pouring, he will have time to take refuge in James Bioletti's hair salon. The old hairdresser not only did haircuts, but was also fascinated with photography. Portraits with magnificent hairstyles adorned his workshop and small photos for passports, wallets or just "a present for mom" cost twice cheaper than in Goshen's studio, while looking not a halfpenny worse. Visitors gladly came, greeted each other and… stayed in the salon, transforming it into a one of a kind club of local importance.

3

From the reply of the British Medical Association to the Great Britain's Defense Ministry request:

"Total number of survived newborns with phocomelia in Great Britain is close to five hundred. Absolute majority of this number is a result of using medicine named *Distaval (Thalidomide)* produced by British "Distillers Company" under a license of West German *Chemie Grünenthal*. Some sporadic cases are not in conjunction with this medicine, but dependent on other factors. Percent of latter is very small and is about the same every year. Concerning the *Thalidomide* the history is as follows.

The drug was discovered by Dr. Heinrich Mücter, the main scientist of a small German chemical company *Chamoe Grünenthal*, and patented in 1954. It is difficult to explain why a completely undistinguished pharmacologist was accepted for such a prominent position. However, the decision turned to be very fortunate! According to the company statements, Dr. Mücter's discovery was serendipitous, when in the process of antihistamine search he found a tranquilizing chemical."

MI5 memo:

1. During WWII, Dr. H. Mücter was a young pharmacologist who has been developing a medicine for typhoid fever and performed trials on Polish prisoners, that cost hundreds of their lives.

2. The company Chemie Grünenthal was established in 1946 by soap manufacturers, twins Alfred and Hermann Wirtz, former Nazis, who bought a small part of equipment of disembodied IG Farben. Main part of the factories of this company was located in the Soviet zone of occupation and was taken to the USSR as part of the reparation.

3. The company IG Farben was a gigantic chemical corporation opened in 1925 (during the war – the fourth biggest income in the world after General Motors, US Steel and Standard Oil), where tragically infamous nerve gases Tabun, Sarin, Soman etc. were discovered and synthesized in great amounts.

4. Tabun (GA) was discovered in 1936 by Dr. Schreder, Sarin (GB) was discovered in 1939 by Dr. Ambros. Both specialists are world famous chemists and pharmacologists.

5. Dr. Ambros, after being sentenced by the Nuremberg trial and serving eight years, started working in Chemie Grünenthal in 1954 (the year of patenting Thalidomide).

"An intensive testing on animals showed "an absolute safety of the drug, absence of toxicity and harmful actions" therefore it was recommended for distribution and since October 1957 appeared in German drug stores under the name of *Contergan.*"

MI5 memo:
1. The name Contergan was bought from the biggest French chemical-pharmaceutical company Rhône-Poulenc, which was under Nazi control since the occupation of France.
2. From 1942 Rhône-Poulenc registered fourteen chemicals with the characteristic suffix "-ergan", unique to the company.

"British companies followed the German one, and soon the medicine filled up drug stores in thirty-seven countries across the world. Sales steadily rose and at the beginning of 1961, *Thalidomide* became the second most profitable drug in the world after aspirin. The company fought "sporadic" accusations in toxicity, affirmed that the opposite is true and recommended the product to children and pregnant women, to remove anxiety and stress. Nevertheless, US FDA did not approve sales of the drug in the USA on the ground of a reported possible *Thalidomide* neurotoxicity.
In April 1961, Dr. McBride from Australia sent a letter to Distillers Company that he observed phocomelia in newborns whose mothers were taking *Thalidomide* against morning sickness during pregnancy as it was advertised."

MI5 memo:

1. According to the company statement, the above-mentioned letter was never received.

"In May 1961, Dr. McBride convinced his superiors to forbid the medicine at the Women's Hospital in Sidney, where he worked. In October and November, he presented new cases. Then, in November 1961 *Distaval (Thalidomide)* was removed from the British market.

In December 1961, Dr. McBride published a letter in one of the most prestigious medical journals, *The Lancet*, accusing the medicine in teratogenity and induction of fetal malformations. In January and February of 1962, *The Lancet* published analogous letters from Dr. Widukind Lenz of Germany."

MI5 memo:

1. Dr. Widukind Lenz, a German pediatrician and geneticist by education served in the Air Force (Luftwaffe) Hospital during WWII, then was in a prisoner-of-war camp in England.

After returning home, he specialized in biochemistry.

Starting 1952 – chief pediatrician in Eppendorf Child Clinic.

Starting 1961 – professor of Pediatric Medicine in Hamburg University.

He is the son of Fritz Lenz.

2. Fritz Lenz – geneticist, a leading theorist in the field of eugenics and "scientific racism", whose works formed the basis of racial hygiene polices of the Third Reich.

Multiple articles in newspapers followed the publications in *The Lancet*. Under the public pressure, *Chemie Grünenthal* was forced to remove *Contergan (Thalidomide)* from the German market in the spring of 1962.

"Teratogenic effect of the *Thalidomide* has been proven when the medicine was taken from 34 to 49 day of a fetus development. Main organs susceptible to malformations are extremities, and less often: brain, intestines, ears and eyes.

Lawsuits against pharmaceutical companies were settled with indemnities. There are 6 – 8 thousand survivors at the present time. It is about half of all babies with phocomelia, besides unknown number of newborns killed because of "devilish appearance". The direct fault of the pharmaceutical companies was never established, not in a single case. In Great Britain an official discussion of the problem in the press is forbidden by the court decision for ten years till 1972."

4

George snuggled at the window of a bus and put his bag in the vacant adjacent seat. If nobody asked for it, Paul, as usual, would take the seat at the next bus stop, and then it would be more fun to go to school together. They met in the bus, when they found themselves attending the same grammar school – Liverpool Institute for Boys. Students, who successfully passed exams after graduating elementary schools, were accepted into it; all others had to continue studying in secondary schools until starting work. In the Institute, students were taught more literature, languages, art and could find more interesting jobs than just as an apprentice at a factory or a salesman at Woolworth department store. And guys were more interesting here.

George spotted Paul at once. He also was carrying a guitar, also was interesting in rock and pop music, but being a year older played in a senior band. What George liked best about Paul was his cheerfulness. On their way, they would scan familiar streets, houses and people while Paul made up stories, sometimes funny, sometimes mysterious, about what they saw.

"Can you see this pretty nurse with a tray of poppies?"

"Sure, she sells them for Armistice Day."

"No, George, she is just pretending, like acting in a play, but in truth she is in intelligence, which means she is acting anyway."

"You are kidding, aren't you?"

"Not at all! Her name is Beth; she was incorporated into the group of Nazis left over in Great Britain after Germany's defeat. Why do you think James, the hairdresser, makes photos of everybody? He is also from intelligence! And she has to discover the whole organization and then Secret Intelligent Service will catch them all at once, and Hitler – caput! Poppy is just a secret sign."

"What a secret sign, when everybody has it on the lapel?"

"That's the catch! Don't you know the story of Ali Baba? If there is a mark on every door then it's difficult to distinguish them. But what if the marks are different?"

"So, the poppies are different?"

"Of course! Well done, you've got it! There are simple poppies and opium poppies. Whoever knows the password receives an opium poppy. John has overheard the password, we can check!"

"I do not believe him. He does not want me in his band."

"Sure, you're just a freshman! But don't you worry! I'll tell him how cool you are playing "Raunchy" and you are in!"

"And what is this secret password?"

"How much is a poppy?" – She answers, "Four pennies." – And you: "I have only two pennies, but I need a poppy to put on my father's gravestone..."

At these words, Paul's voice trembled and his eyes moistened. George remembered that Paul buried his mom just about two weeks ago.

"You know, Paul, let me tell you something." Usually George, a quiet boy, preferred to listen, but now he felt sorrowful for his friend and he decided to share a story picked up from his older brother. "There was an article in a newspaper about the flying saucer, have you heard it?"

"No, I haven't. But so what? They always write about it."

"This time an article was not about a saucer itself, but about the man from it – an alien!"

"Come on, don't believe them!"

"Believe or not, but he was working in the bank at Smithdown Road. There in the safe deposit box he was hiding a jar with some fishy alien shit, either for food or for sex. From this substance our girls can get pregnant with alien babies."

Paul's eyes immediately became dry. He was looking like a young setter who picked up the trail.

"They found the jar accidentally. There was a checkup of all deposit boxes and this clerk by bad luck was out. It was raining cat and dogs, but he was slowly walking without umbrella and mackintosh. There, in Aquarius constellation, aliens need water like fish…"

"Then maybe it was caviar in the jar – it concerns food and sex at the same time," Paul laughed, "And the banker was a Russian spy who just wanted some caviar." Paul obviously preferred spy topics.

"Maybe," said George, "But the reporter wrote that they wanted to give the jar with a substance to the police, but the fire started. Our gorgeous fire engine showed up. The captain with his handsome nephews quickly extinguish the fire – lo, the jar vanished into thin smoke and was never found again."

"And what happened to the alien banker?"

"I don't know. Probably still works as a junior clerk."

The boys start laughing and got out of the bus at the last second, having nearly missed their stop at the Institute. The new school day had started quite well.

5

"May, May, come here, at once!" called John from the terrace.

May was frightened initially, fearing something bad had happened with Lennon, but then she calmed quickly, because John continued,

"Hey, leave everything! Look, what a wonder!"

May put on a T-shirt and climbed through the window, because they did not have a door for the terrace. Normally a process of her climbing out the window, especially half-naked, piqued John's interest, but not now. This time something unusual consumed him entirely. He was standing at the penthouse at East 52nd street, at the height of the seventeenth floor, buck-naked, staring into the night sky where a flying saucer was hovering. A traditional disc shape and a size of a small eight seat private "Lear" jet, which they took to come from LA to Newark, the UFO silently floated, a hundred feet from them, obstructing part of Queens' view.

"I can't believe this," whispered John, "Just look at it!"

The saucer came closer, and besides the central ruby light beaming from the top of its shallow cone, the small blinking platinum lights at the rim of a ship became visible.

"What a beauty!" said John, "and might, as if it emanates from the numen. Do you feel the karma? I would have departed with them!"

He spread his arms apart as aviators do at the flying field, inviting the ship for landing, but it flew above him and disappeared behind Manhattan skyscrapers.

"They did not take me again," complained John.

"Have you ever met them?"

"Of course, not," sneered John, "The saucer reminded me another powerful and beautiful thing from my childhood, which I was never able to ride."

"What was that?"

"The fire machine from Penny Lane in Liverpool. In our childhood, we all were lost in admiration of it. Paul even described it in the song."

"In *Penny Lane*?"

"Yes. You know everything… But what is interesting, Betty said that a couple of girls lied that they got pregnant from fingers of firemen-brothers, who were very handsome, but absolutely unfit for real sex!"

"And you believe in their immaculate conception?"

"I told you, "lied". Boys fondled them: at that time, it was called "finger pie", and some of the girls decided to get hitched with them, but failed. And it's a pity that these girls delivered crazy looking babies, who died soon. But these are old tales, and now we have a new one. I would not believe if somebody had told me the story of a flying saucer."

"Neither would they believe in your story! You'll better call Bob, he always gives good advice."

May Pang who worked before as a coordinator for Yoko Ono and now lived with John for a year, always wanted to arrange everything. She pushed John to resume his communication with his son Julian (they all even went to Disneyland in LA), fought John's drinking bouts, tried to fix old Beatles bonds and even acquired pair of cats named Major and Minor reminding John of aunt Mimi's house where he lived since his childhood. But at the same time, he recalled Yoko increasingly…

Bob Gruen, the famous rock and pop star photographer, who recently made John's shots at the Statue of Liberty in support of his struggle to dismiss his deportation from the USA. Bob listened to the story with the silent disbelief, and proposed, "Why don't you guys yourselves call to the police or a newspaper and report about the phenomena?"

"You want me, Bob, to call and say, 'This is John Lennon who just saw a flying saucer!' Can you imagine what this will start? They'll bring up my drinking bouts in LA, marihuana smoking in London and god knows what else!"

"O.K., O.K. Don't get started! You are right. I will talk to them myself, find out what this is about and then call you back. By the way, have your camera ready in case the saucer appears again…"

When Bob called the next morning and confirmed, that several people saw "his" saucer, John responded with delight, "I was a good boy and took a bunch of shots of the saucer last night. Just develop and print them!"

In the evening Bob called again, "The film must have been exposed to light, there is nothing there," he reported grievously.

John angrily kicked Major who accidentally caught his foot and hit the strings of the guitar. The minor chord sounded in unison with the unexplainable fillings in his soul, "It's enough to make a cat laugh!"

6

No doubts that humans are very strange creatures! They live in the backwoods of the Galaxy and think as backwoods people. Not that they insusceptible to high ideas and feelings. No. They just distort and remodel everything, and all good deeds come to nothing. The more developed their civilization becomes, the more difficult to influence it. How many human generations have we directed by introducing our "messiahs", "prophets" and "gods"? And what's the use? Humans do not change. They accept morals, religion, law and then slowly deviate from them, transforming all valuable ideas into "remembrance of the good". Predatory human nature nevertheless overcomes and sprouts through everything, even the kindest things. And the more time passes, the clearer the picture.

During the last century of my observation of Earth, humans killed a previously unheard of number of their own kind! They made uncounted profits on human exploitation that nobody had seen before. The Galactic Council insisted on creating a leader of the new faith, who will be able to shepherd others. But it's easy to discuss it there in the center of the Galaxy, than try to implement it here… So many years our group spent to join the community of a small city Liverpool. Last time we tried to repeat the Immaculate Conception and breed at least one superhero with no luck. All fetuses died from the medicine, which they developed as an antidote to their own deadly gases. Finally, they used it as an instrument of gain. The irony of fate, whims of an earthy "humanity" and the kindest works go for nothing!

The time of the observation for the superior ambassador – "the Brandmaster" together with "Teddy" and "the Banker" is over, and they flew away to our dear Aquarius. And two of us, who were subordinates, now take over and are waiting for more observers to come. But I believe that it's dangerous now to stay in the image of human. It seems to me that people started to take notice. They just can't assemble all the pieces of the puzzle. Devices spot spaceships, intelligence flags, press reports, but nobody cares to put everything together. Even in the song, people described everything so clearly, but still nobody understood a thing. Music is charming, though, is it not? I like to purr it inside my head.

Here is a typical earthy example: John, the kindest human being, a vegetarian on and off, who started a fight with the President himself against the war in Vietnam… kicks the cat. Not the unknown, wild, or stray cat but, let me underscore, his own dear cat! He kicks it with his own foot. And why? Because aliens did not take him to the spaceship. Shit! It was me, whom they did not take with them! They came to say farewell to me, not to him! Ouch! The flank is very sore!

ARENA

Ed braked sharply. That's it! He had had enough! How long can one drive on this endless dusty road? Initially, he had had no doubt that this highway led to Baldwin, where to he was contracted to deliver so-called dairy farm cans in which sloshed bootleg alcohol. The old engine of his newly renovated Ford pickup had been chugging steadily nonstop, running now like new, but after two hours when the town had long been supposed to appear on the horizon, an unpleasant feeling of being lost in a spooky place seized him.

Ed shut off the engine. Where was that Arena, which Liz was talking about? The highway was like a highway, the prairie like a prairie, but where the hell had he driven to? No forks, nor intersections? Where had all the signs, poles and transmission lines gone? There were no gas stations suggesting the proximity of residences and a well-deserved diner break. Why had he seen no cars during the trip? No salesman's new coupe outpaced him; no farm truck bearing freshly harvested ears of corn rushed past him. Only a gray sedan appeared in the mirror from time to time. But, apart from that, all around him was "dead space". The police, whom the bootleggers had advised him to avoid, were nowhere in sight, but as there was not even a hint of the Arena; it would be nice to clarify directions with somebody. Exactly how much time had he been driving? Ed looked at his watch. Its hands indicated the very moment he had taken his truck out of the shop... no, ten minutes after that, just when he entered the Baldwin Highway.

"What time is it?" Liz smiled, showing the dimples in her cheeks. "You are twenty minutes early to pick up your truck; I've not changed the oil yet."

It's rare that you come across a girl fixing cars in an auto repair shop, especially, such a girl. A fluffy mass of brown hair, exuding a subtle floral aroma, escaped from under her baseball cap boldly jammed backwards. A high clean forehead, straight little nose with a few small freckles, fresh rosy cheeks, and juicy cherry lips that would be the envy of any, even the most popular high-school girl. But, all these qualities faded against her eyes – the color of Caribbean waves – and long thick eyelashes.

This beauty ran the shop with confidence: it was no coincidence that she was the niece of the mechanic.

"Mark the time. At exactly ten, you can take your 'horse' with the new filter and fresh oil. We'll clean the windshield too."

"Are you sure it'll be ready?" Ed asked – a note of doubt in his voice. She nodded, not looking at him.

"And you're not afraid to bet…" Ed egged her on not finding anything else to say.

"You'll lose, Mister," the girl stated flatly.

"And what's the bet?" pressed Ed, already sensing that she must be right. "A wish!"

No self-respecting Texan could resist such a bet, though Ed would never allow himself to express his true desire aloud. He went outside and lit a cigarette, remembering how an unexpected incident had changed the course of his life.

Yesterday, running around the city in the pickup truck, inherited from his father, and looking to earn some money, Ed first saw Liz. He was waiting for the green light, and she was crossing the street. Not right in front of his car, but just past the intersection, at a distance, allowing him to fully enjoy the beauty and grace of this girl. The girl of his dreams.

Ed had not had time to realize what got into him. Usually he yielded to speed demons who loved to run red lights. But, this time he was sure those bastards in the black Chrysler-De-Soto, which raced down the road, with a flashing right turn signal, would a second later knock his dream girl down. So, without hesitation, Ed drove into the intersection to precisely place the worn side of his old pickup truck in the way of the chrome and glass of the nifty sedan. Everybody around screamed: the unemployed loafers sitting outside the shops were hopeful that their testimony might be needed in court. But, the passengers of the expensive car wanted neither attention nor police questioning. The driver, dressed in an expensive suit and hat – all sand color, beckoned Ed with a hand sheathed in a fine kidskin glove.

"I see, you are a cowboy," he said. "We won't argue whose right of way it was. Someone who knows how to apologize sometimes wins more, eh? In short, you can earn some money. Here is a deposit for repairs," he handed a couple of bills to Ed. "Come to "Fiorella" on Main Street at seven o'clock. If you bring a bill from the mechanic, you'll get the rest. And we'll talk about work. Are you interested?"

"I'll come for sure, thank you," Ed thanked the man, who now seemed quite decent. Feeling a bit sheepish, Ed had started to doubt the accuracy of his own intuition about them.

The passenger in the Chrysler, fat as a caricature capitalist, too perfumed, nodded in confirmation of the driver's words and added hoarsely, "Go to Charter Street. There's the girl's low price auto shop."

They sped away, leaving Ed again in doubt.

"Hmm, so they knew this beauty and she was not a random pedestrian for them. And they pretend to be friendly," his intuition again pricked up its ears.

But, the most enjoyable part of the story began when Ed returned to his mangled pickup truck to find the beautiful stranger relaxing in the passenger seat.

"I'm Liz," she said simply. "Thanks, you saved my life."

"Don't mention it; they actually apologized."

"Really?" exclaimed the girl. "That's not like bootleggers."

"Do you know them?"

"They put the squeeze on my uncle, a mechanic. By the way, let's go to our shop. Free repair for the brave defender!"

"Wow! Thank you! It's my lucky day. And what do bootleggers have to do with a mechanic?" Ed asked.

"My uncle developed a new car model that runs on alcohol, and they thought that he was their competitor – producing alcohol for sale, and... "

"And how did it all work out?"

"It didn't. My uncle opened a new business in Argentina, and I'm moving there soon."

All this was unusual and mysterious. Ed, of course, believed Liz, but still had his reservations. He suspected that her uncle indeed was involved in alcohol production, and therefore drew the bandits' attention. No wonder the mechanic had hit the road. But, why the bootleggers wanted to run over the girl still remained a mystery to Ed.

"Come back for the car tomorrow at ten o'clock in the morning," Liz said, handing him a bill.

The repair was also part of the riddle: too fast – just one evening without her uncle's help! Ed wanted to ask what she was doing tonight, but the question sounded silly. "It's clear that she'll be busy with the repairs," he thought and, saying goodbye to the charming owner went to "Fiorella" for the promised job.

A delicious smell of fresh bread, cheese, grilled meat and spices engulfed him. A waiter in a black shirt, pants, and a long, crisp white apron almost touching the floor, led Ed to a far booth, where his new friends were having dinner.

"A young man is asking for you," the waiter informed them politely.

"Sure, Gino," the fat one croaked. "Pull up a chair for the guy and bring him a glass of lemonade."

"I hope," he added, addressing his guest, "You respect homemade drinks, not just factory bottled soda?"

In these words, Ed heard a veiled reference to bootlegging, but nodded, not wanting to seem impolite.

"So do you want to make some money?" Fatso continued.

"Of course, sir," Ed said, "What do I need to do?"

"Take a load to Baldwin, that's all. The store address is on the invoice. You have to deliver cans of milk there."

"Of milk?"

"And you thought whiskey?" the men laughed, "No, just a dozen cans from the dairy farm. Do you think your truck can hold the weight?"

"Of course! And when do I go to the farm? Liz promised the truck would be ready tomorrow morning."

"Liz? Is that your girl from the auto shop? Excellent choice," the Chrysler's driver muttered. "You don't need to pick up the milk. The cans will already be on the truck, and the invoice – in the glove compartment. What's important is to drive safely and not mess with the police. When you come back you'll get the money for the work and the rest for the repairs," he waved the bill from the auto shop and slid it into the inside pocket of his jacket.

Ed stopped understanding: how will the cans get in his truck and the invoice – in the glove compartment? Why should one be careful of the police if the documents are in order? Wouldn't his new acquaintances cheat him?

These and many other questions troubled Ed, but it was too late to retreat. Especially if you are a grownup, independent person who needs to help his mother and aunt, as well as to pay for tuition, exam and a mechanic's license. But, it is one thing not to retreat, while entirely another not to be taken for a fool. Ed did not like any of this, so he decided that the best way is to keep an eye on the auto shop – how the repairs progressed and how the milk cans would be delivered. You never knew, maybe Liz would need his help again.

When he got to the already familiar auto shop on Charter Street, he was surprised to find the place dark and locked instead of ablaze with action. There was not a soul around and the place was silent. "What kind of joke is this? Maybe the pickup was moved to another place?" He began to peer through the windows, trying to make out anything in the dark. Luckily, one of the windows was slightly open, so Ed, without hesitation, climbed inside.

It smelled of gasoline, oil, metal and rubber – the usual car smells. The first thing he noticed was his Ford, standing over the pit. The side of the truck was completely flat and smooth to the touch. Not believing his hand, he struck a match: the pickup gleamed like new with fresh paint. Ed decided it was someone else's pickup, but the plate number was his, and hiding under the driver's seat, as always, was his shabby old military field bag with screwdrivers and adjustable wrenches.

"Another mystery," Ed thought, but suddenly the motor of a car rumbled at the door. The familiar voices of the bootleggers sounded. The hoarse voice of the Fat one said,

"Well, even our waiter would be able to open this lock!"

"Don't be too sure; the mechanic is a tough guy!" said the driver.

Ed heard the screeching of metal from outside: once, twice, third time. Without waiting for the intruders to appear, Ed slipped into the inspection pit and huddled in the corner, covering himself with a tarpaulin. The lock snapped, the garage doors opened with a creak, and the car's headlights lit the shop. The Fat man came in with a bunch of keys in his hand, the sedan slowly entered behind him, making the shadow of the big man grow to a giant size on the wall.

"Don't exaggerate their abilities; you're just too superstitious," the Fat man answered.

"What am I supposed to think when both ambushes happened after the repair? Hell! It's true, many died, but it's always from both sides, and these two times not one cop was even injured! The second time I found the corpses myself. Joe was still alive, he whispered, "That arena... and the dolls... is the show..." and died.

"Well, you never know what a person remembers before death. God rest his soul. Joe's words led to no clue. Therefore, luring the mechanic to the hospital to visit his niece was a good idea. It's a shame the damn boy interfered!"

"All for the best! You see, he also came in handy. With these cans and the invoice, the cops will find the auto shop's owner for us."

"And how did you turn the auto shop bill into an invoice so slick?"

"If you'd worked as long as me in Chicago, you would also know how. Capone's school is a university in our profession. Okay, now let's do it!"

And they began to pour alcohol into cans stored in the shop, and load them onto the pickup. When the work was finished, the gangsters sealed the cans, glued the "dairy farm" labels on them and covered the bed with a tarpaulin. The glove compartment door slammed, and the men, satisfied with their work, left the auto shop.

The sounds of the closing padlock and the departing sedan were a signal to Ed that he could leave his shelter and catch his breath.

"Now I'm done for! May they be ambushed the third time! And what will I do with the alcohol? Should I throw these cans in the river and leave the state?"

He also had to find affordable accommodation and not trudge home through the city, only to return almost immediately. Luckily, he still had the remainder of his bootleg advance. "Well, tomorrow is another day."

In the morning, after washing up and grabbing a hot coffee, Ed went to the shop. Accustomed to driving his pickup truck, he overestimated the time to walk to the shop, and got there twenty minutes early.

"Why did I make that bet?" Ed asked himself while smoking in the yard. "It will take Liz, with her fantastic repair speed, not twenty minutes but two, to replace the oil, although this should be impossible. And should I even tell her about my meeting last night, or is this dangerous stuff not for women? Should I try to get myself out of it?"

Still not having made up his mind, Ed stubbed out the cigarette and went back to the shop.

No wonder the bootleggers suspected witchcraft. His truck was in the air without any support, and waste oil was pouring from the engine into a pan on the floor, like a jet of dark beer from a barrel.

"Is this black magic?" he asked Liz.

"Oil is black, but it's no magic at all. Don't worry! It's advanced science and technology. I'm just in a hurry and don't care for disguises. Take a ride, see how the engine is running now," and she looked at him with her radiant eyes.

From this glance and maybe from the unearthly beauty of the girl, Ed felt at once so peaceful that he realized it was just stupid to conceal his thoughts from Liz.

"A car repair in a couple of hours is also advanced technology?" he asked and revealed everything he had seen and heard at night in the garage.

"If you are not afraid, which you've already proved with your courage and determination, we can retaliate by arranging a fancy show for the gangsters. They will not release your pickup with the alcohol unattended, so speed up and race harder. The bootleggers will rush you, and both cars will go... how to explain it... into another dimension... well, in short, in an unusual place, which the bandits called the Arena. Let it be so. The show will take place there. However, the gangsters don't understand jokes; they begin to fire and sadly end their 'adventures'... You, most importantly, must not meddle with anything. Can you do that?"

"I'll try. Does something really depend on me?" Ed asked. "Where should I start accelerating?"

"The exit from the main road onto the Baldwin highway is bi-level and very steep. Usually cars there barely trudge along. However, during these hours, the road is empty. You must speed up as much as possible to enter the turn and hit the gas even harder. You may even think that the truck wants to tip over, but everything will be okay. Don't be afraid, you will not roll over. My uncle lured the bootleggers two times that way. Do you trust me?"

"Yes," said Ed, wondering what the lost bet would cost him.

He still believed Liz's every word, even though he knew that there was little cause for it. But, on the other hand, there was quite a lot: he had just fallen in love.

To reach the junction took about ten minutes. As Liz expected, his old friends, bootleggers, this time in a gray sedan, followed his truck, which after the repair ran so fast that it nearly managed to get away.

In the morning, most of the traffic was going into the city, so his route was empty and, remembering Liz's instructions, he entered the junction at high speed, risking a rollover at a sharp turn. Indeed, at one point, Ed was sure it would happen: the horizon banked sharply and declined as in an aerobatic maneuver. Ed felt sick, as if on the "Russian Mountains" roller coaster in Luna Park. One moment – and everything was gone: he sort of woke up on the road, on which he had been... chugging along... already for two hours.

A delusion? It seemed he had just entered Baldwin highway, but not really – Ed braked sharply. How long can one drive on this endless dusty road leading to... Baldwin, really? He killed the engine. Where is the Arena that Liz was talking about? The gangsters' car crawled far away on a distant hill. But every moment the little bug was becoming bigger and bigger. Ed looked at his watch. The hands stood at the very minute he had taken the car out of the garage. No, actually, ten minutes later – just when he entered the Baldwin highway. He turned on the radio: there was silence on all the stations, but suddenly the shrill sounds of a circus march inundated him.

These sounds seemed to have served as a signal: the seemingly lifeless space came alive in an instant. Thousands of huge colorful butterflies filled the air. To the sounds of the music, they performed incredibly complex aerobatics, creating colorful patterns of a living kaleidoscope. At each pattern, applause from invisible spectators resounded until suddenly the butterflies crumbled to the ground in a rain of petals. Immediately, out of the ground, like fairy magic bean sprouts, climbed a forest of winding snakes. Their scales burned with many shades of multi-colored gold. The snakes intertwined and broke apart in complex patterns, as if they were parts of the same space mosaic. This entire phantasmagoria so amazed Ed that he could hardy remain in his seat. However, he remembered Liz's mandate – to do nothing. He did not even turn off the radio, just in case. One march was replaced by another, snakes – by fountains, fountains – by fishes, beasts, dragons, and finally humans. Lovely girls in gymnastic costumes danced and flew in space. Their beauty so agitated the gangsters that they jumped out of the car, trying to catch the charming gymnasts.

"Stop it!" shouted the gloved driver, brandishing a revolver.

"Girls, girls!" his companion echoed hoarsely, taking out a wallet full of banknotes.

One of the flying figures playfully pulled the wallet out of the Fat man's hand and slowly began to rise up, as if by invisible threads.

"Where...?" screamed the gangster in a fit of excitement and anger and shot at the figure.

The boom of the shot sounded, and the girl's body disintegrated into a myriad of sparkles, spraying both gangsters with... It seemed to Ed that he smelled perfume, but sniffing carefully, he realized that it was alcohol. Enraged with failure and distraught by what was happening, the bootleggers began shooting all around.

"Shoot that bastard; he is with them!" they shouted, running to Ed's truck.

At this point, the participants of the show had metamorphosed one last time: the gentle girls turned into warriors – looking like fairy soldiers from the Nutcracker's army. They swooped down on the gangsters, covering the renovated Ford with their bodies, and like rubber balls, bounced on impact. The bootleggers frantically opened fire on the clownish defenders who, in response, threw cans of "milk" from the pickup at the gangsters. Suddenly, one of the cans ignited. Fire spread to the people below, and the soldiers began to explode one after another, culminating the presentation in giant fireworks display.

Gradually, the music stopped, the smoke cleared, and when the applause of the invisible audience fell silent, Ed stepped out onto the highway. The bandits' bodies lay on the grass. It was the only thing left from the amassing phantasmagoria.

"The Galactic show featuring wild earthlings is over!" announced the radio in Liz's voice. "Come on!"

Ed obeyed; he got back in his pickup. As soon as he started the engine, he found himself back off the Baldwin highway and back on the city road. His watch showed ten minutes past ten.

"The truck's running great since the bodywork!" Ed thought. "Like new – really remarkable!"

The radio aired the news, "This morning, at the entrance to Baldwin, police discovered the bodies of two well-known citizens associated with illegal production of whisky. The cause of death was an explosion of the alcohol, transported in cans labeled dairy farm products."

Something vaguely familiar flashed in Ed's memory. He reached into the glove compartment and pulled out a document. It was a bill for car repairs...

When Ed pulled up to the auto shop on Charter Street, a lively scene reigned there. Workers were hanging a new sign above the entrance. Three cars were already in the pits, mechanics and assistants fussing over them; a cashier was writing out receipts, and a sturdy middle-aged man with a wheat-colored mustache was presiding over it all.

"Mr. Collins?" said the man. "I recognized you by your license plate. Liz left a letter for you," and he held out an envelope to Ed.

Sensing that the letter was a farewell, Ed opened the envelope and pulled out a sheet of paper. It retained a subtle floral fragrance.

"I am very sorry that we have not met before. I cannot stay. The shop was sold in advance, but the new owner according to the contract will train you and give you the salary of a mechanic. When you pass the exam and get a license, then you can decide if you want to work for yourself. The envelope contains a check to pay for the licensing exam. Think of it as a debt from your former acquaintances. And one more thing: in England, in Liverpool, lives a girl, also Liz. My uncle said that I am her exact double. I am sure that she, like me, will love you, and your family.

The remaining can of milk you may take home. It is very tasty and never sours..."

A SET OF TOOLS

The weather was cold and nasty, perfect for siting in a bar, sipping a hot drink and waiting for the right poker partners. And I sat. And waited. I'm good at these three things: sitting, waiting and playing. Before the war, I boasted quite different abilities, but after suffering severe injuries in Normandy, I walk with difficulty, cannot stand for long, and, therefore, am no longer any good as a mechanic. Rather than waiting for retraining from the government, I honed a natural dexterity in card playing and quickly became a professional.

The bar, in which I settled, seemed like an unsuitable place for a big game. Well, what could one expect to win in one of Liverpool's low-income neighborhoods, even a few years after the war? But, it was rumored that astonishing hands of cards were seen recently in the Fireside Bar, such rare combinations that only a beginner could believe in their accidental appearances. I consider myself a rather seasoned veteran, and for two nights straight, I killed time amongst the local amateurs – small fish in a Poker Sea – waiting for the real sharks.

All of the alleged "sharks" were ill suited for this title: neither the Capitan of the local fire station, nor master barber, nor the clerk from a nearby bank. The latter player interested me the most: I hoped that he would have his fingers in the till. Anyway, I had prepared my tools. In the old leather military field bag scratched with screwdrivers and wrenches, which I carried since my youth, now lay a few decks of cards with popular patterns favored in this bar. They were all marked with skillfully deposited notches and hidden nicks.

So, I was sipping mulled wine in the main hall and was not in a rush to engage in a trifling game. It was Friday, seven o'clock, and I was hoping for a meeting.

The bell on the door rang, letting in a firefighter, smart in his uniform, in a raincoat and a goldish helmet, covered with large drops of rain. His awesome mustache so resembled the Kaiser's that I mentally dubbed him the German word "Brandmaster". He politely greeted everyone, got a mug of ale and went straight into the far room, where players assembled. When in five or ten minutes the "Banker" came in, I already knew where he would go, and not waiting until he ordered a drink, moved to the gambling room.

The Brandmaster dealt cards. I and sat down at the round table covered with a worn green felt. The Bank employee holding a glass of whiskey soon joined the company. People at the table played with little stacks, cautiously and slowly, so I could safely prepare my tools. The barbershop's owner came – a bald Italian and after him – another man of uncertain nationality and appearance. Judging by the valise, in which medical professionals carry their instruments, the inconspicuous man was a doctor.

"Let's abolish the limit on bets, gentlemen!" the doctor suggested.

I was starting to like it. Everyone who interested me supported him; the two or three small-timers grumbled in dissatisfaction and left the game. After about an hour, the game moved with mixed success. I decided that it was time, and the first victim should be equitably the one who proposed to raise the stakes. The idea of cheating consists of precise distribution of rare high-rank combinations, seducing players to start batting. The main thing is to make everyone think that his combination is winning, and other players are just bluffing. Well, the best combination, of course, should be mine. I generously wished luck to my unsuspecting partners and began.

All was going smoothly until while exchanging one card for the fire captain, I threw him two instead. I could not believe I had done that with my own hands. It doesn't happen with specialists! Never! It's like a racer inserting the key not into the ignition, but the cigarette lighter, and not just inserting but turning it on! And his car would thus start up and drive backwards! That's about what happened.

Out of the two cards, the Brandmaster naturally chose not the one that was designated for him, but the one that was supposed to go to the doctor. The doctor then got a card that was prepared for me, and with it, his set could take the whole pot. After that, I did not draw myself cards, the barber folded and we were left four. My mood was awful. I cursed myself with the worst words in different languages, which I had picked up during the war, but it did not help. The first betting round, I still held out, and then left the game to not harm my pocket even more. The pot has grown to a size larger than I have ever seen, and when the doctor opened his winning cards, they all saw it – Royal Flush, the highest poker hand! Yes, that's why I was brought upon this bar.

Then I began to think that maybe it's me who "they" framed. I do not know who – "they" were, but with those who can make a professional misdeal cards, you trifle carefully. Better not at all! And with this thought I somehow lost all desire to rush into this game. I left the game for a while and was going to order a beer, as I heard the doctor say, referring to all partners in the game, "As a partial compensation you can tomorrow, at noon, get a free medical consultation in my office on Penny Lane."

No one but the overage Brandmaster was interested in it, and he gladly promised to come to the reception. I do not know why, but I decided to go too. "To recon!" I said to myself and signed up for a visit. After that, I went to the main hall, drank beer, chatted about this and that, and returned to the game. It was played with a different deck, but I had this pattern also. During my dealing, all the players had to get quads – four cards of the same kind or rank, but I had to get quad aces – the most senior.

You guessed right... When I put the deck before the bank clerk, sitting to my right, he took half the deck and by clicking on it with his finger, drove it into the remaining half, shuffling them completely. How he did it without touching the other half of the deck, I cannot imagine! Half of the cards lifted, letting its fellow cards into new places in the deck. After that, I immediately folded, the barber folded after the draw, and the rest again furiously bet until one after the other they conceded to the Brandmaster. They did not open their cards, and I did not understand if it was a bluff or not. Apparently, out of politeness the proposed firefighter offered the doctor a free checkup of his car. The doctor agreed with pleasure.

"I have a wonderful mechanic. Its my assistant, Teddy. He can check and repair any engine," said the fire captain. "I'll bring him on Saturday, and during my appointment he will check your car."

Suppressing a low desire to get drunk and make a brawl, I eventually finished my game for the day. After drinking tea with rum, I thanked every one of the company, the doctor and the barber – for the proposed checkup and a haircut, and left.

The next day, at noon, I rang the doorbell of the medical office. A pretty nurse, introduced herself as Betty invited me in, where the first patient with his outstanding Kaiser mustache – the captain of the fire department – was already waiting for the doctor. Next to him sat a tall young man with a lovely but freckled face, in the uniform of a firefighter, apparently, the previously mentioned mechanic Teddy. Waiting for the start of the checkup, I tried to chat with the captain. He was not talkative, answered in monosyllables, and judging by the place on his stomach, where he poked himself, I "diagnosed" him with liver problems. When the doctor came, Teddy jumped up and greeted him very respectfully. The Brandmaster also stood up, and after them, I did, not wanting to seem impolite. The doctor, in turn, spoke very friendly with them. He invited the fire captain to the examination room, and Teddy to the garage. I was offered coffee, tea, biscuits and the company of Betty, who stayed with me in the waiting room.

Soon the other patients came, and I was called to the examination room, where the Brandmaster's polished shoes could be seen from behind the folding-screen. The doctor put me on the couch, felt my abdomen, listened to my lungs and heart, and connected me to a newfangled machine for heart examination. While the machine hummed and recorded the electric activity of my heart on a moving strip, I was laying quiet, but, as the doctor pulled the piece of the paper strip and went to measure and calculate something on it, I could not resist and looked behind the folding-screen. There, on a chair, his back to me, sat the fire captain. From his right flank, dark green slush was leaking through a transparent hose directly into the doctoral bag, and another liquid, golden as a firefighter's helmet, was pumped back into the patient's body through another hose.

"Come here!" the doctor called, so I moved to his desk.

Behind the doctor's chair, through high windows of his office, I saw the patio and a car in it. Two things struck me: the car's appearance, and what the mechanic was doing. The car resembled the German F-2 missile on wheels, and Teddy... He connected this hybrid of a vehicle and a rocket to a metal chest with compartments in which mechanics usually keep sets of their tools, and, using two transparent hoses, exchanged gold solution from the car for a dark green one out of the box.

The doctor looked up from his papers and seeing surprise on my face, explained, "Teddy is a first-class specialist! He easily fixes even foreign cars!"

He sure could pull anyone's leg, but not mine. After several years, spent in the motorized units of Her Majesty's Army, I was well versed in cars, both ours and foreign.

"But let's talk about your health," continued the doctor. "I do not want to scare you, but you have a heart problem, a hidden one."

"Strange, I've never complained about my heart!"

"Nevertheless one unlucky day it can stop. You need, uh... a pacemaker, well; its production has not started yet. In a couple of years check with your doctor, how to get the pacemaker. Yet, if I would be in your situation, I would have worn on my wrist a bracelet with the words "If I lose consciousness hit my chest with a fist as hard as you can!"

I immediately recalled my sergeant saying, "Even losing consciousness hit the enemy..." You know where! I liked very much to quote my sergeant, but the doctor was worthy of respect even if only for his ability to play poker so classy. I said goodbye to everyone, came out of the clinic and walked slowly to the bus stop. I had to think about what had happened – in less than a day, I encountered several times a manifestation of superhuman professionalism. My tools happened to be not suitable, but "theirs" so perfect and incomprehensible.

I walked a couple of blocks on Penny Lane and suddenly appeared in front of the barbershop owned by James, my partner in yesterday's game. James was just coming out with a small suitcase in his hand.

"Again, a set of special tools," I thought, and asked aloud,

"What do famous barbers carry in their cases, their revenue?"

"That too," James answered with no surprise, "But more often, a set of tools."

These sets of tools have already started haunting me, and I, worked up the courage, and asked the barber, "Can I see what they look like?"

"Of course!" James replied guardedly. His eyes were far more eloquent, and I bet I knew all the words that it expressed.

The barber unlocked and opened the briefcase, and there appeared sets of razors, a grinding belt, hair clipper with different attachments, combs, scissors, cologne, shaving cream, brushes, powder, and all sort cups and napkins. But, in addition to all these hairdressing treasures, he had a German camera, "Leica"!

"You need it also for shaving?" I asked the barber.

"Of course, not. Customers like 'before' and 'after' portraits."

"All of them?"

"Well, someone would not like the pictures of cards early in the game and in its end, when they appeared tagged."

"Are you thinking of the doctor? He won a lot yesterday, and on an extremely rare combination."

"He won and lost. Rather, I am thinking about the one who really wanted to win and was waiting for appropriate players for the three days..."

"Well, you're right! Look what observational barbers live here."

"During the war I happened to observe even more unusual things while serving in intelligence."

"In intelligence of whose army?" I snapped.

"Do not worry, in that same army in which you also served – her Royal Majesty. You are Ed Collins, aren't you? I remember you well, wounded after the Normandy landing, entertaining soldiers in the hospital with card tricks."

Then I remembered that James's last name was either Briolini or Briolette and I met him in the hospital. James then also cut hair and photographed. Yes, he has indeed gotten older and fatter, and all his hair was gone...

"And now, once again, I entertain my partners in the game..."

"And why you, as I understand, a professional, did not win?"

"I ran into inexplicable super professionalism, and only thanks to good training did not get in the 'fight'. They would have me broke!"

"Who – 'they'?"

"I thought you were one of them, and I hoped that you would explain everything to me..."

"You see," James started, "Out of habit, and by the nature of working with people, I'm helping old friends from counterintelligence to identify Nazi agents. The fair captain and the bank clerk are obviously clean, but the doctor recently arrived from Argentina, worked a little here, and is going to move to the States. There is nothing reprehensible in it, but you know, many of our enemies are entrenched in Argentina. Doctor's contacts, however, are limited to card games in which I have always been involved and his patients that Betty keeps her eye on for us."

"Now let me tell you something," I answered. "I flew from the States to Liverpool for the funeral of my aunt, and old friends led me to the 'Fireside'. Often, very rare card combinations began to appear there, and this is either cheating or some secret code! As you yourself noted, the money went one way and then the other, that is, the players didn't win or lose much. I even doubted whether I have not been hunted. Sort of no! But, the most interesting thing I saw was in the medical office, where your Betty works," and I briefly told James about my visit to the doctor.

I cannot say that my story made a strong impression on him. Well, treated... Well, repaired... Yes, strange, unusual, but the world is changing so fast, so many new devices and machines appears every day. From his point of view, most important was it's not related to the enemy. But, I did not calm down,

"I still have to stop by the bank to pick up my aunt's jewelry from the depository, and in the evening I would like to inspect the doctor's car. Maybe Betty can lend me a key for the medical office?"

James thought it was foolhardy, but reluctantly agreed.

It was cool and a little bit dark in the bank on Smithdown Road. It seemed that the owners tried to save on heat and light even before closing the branch for the weekend. Entering the room, I noticed the familiar to me "banker" accompanying the "doctor" into the storage room. The doctor was holding his bag that I saw in his office, holding it gently in his clasping arms, like a newborn or a puppy.

"I need to enter the depository," I said to an attendant, presenting the necessary papers.

"One moment," he answered, "Once one of the escorts returns he will take you to the vault. Usually we do not let more than two visitors in there at a time."

At the end of his explanation, a girl in a suit and tie came, with a bunch of keys and, alternately opening and closing the door-lattice barriers, took me to the basement, where on both sides of the corridor were located personal safes. Slightly farther from me, the doctor was taking a glass jar with cream or God knows what from his valise. I was already tired of wondering and just grabbed my aunt's pennyworth inheritance. I wanted to quickly finish my business and return to warm Nevada. I yearned for Las Vegas, where legalized gambling bloomed and where Liz, a former nurse from a field hospital, the adoration of my military life and my postwar trophy, was waiting for me.

Until evening I worked to finish all my business related to the memorial for my aunt, and before returning home, I only had to inspect the doctor's unusual car. After that, I was going to leave the key, as we agreed, under the entrance pad, and from Liverpool airport report to James if my inspection yielded interesting results.

The lock gently clicked, and with a creak, the door of the old Victorian house let me into the dark interior. Somehow, I was seized by fear. Not the same fear as in a battle, which you expel with the excitement of the attack, not the card cheater's fear that retreats for the hope of winning, but the fear of a child gazing into the dark bedroom. I remembered the doctor's words that one day my heart would stop, and commanded it, "Hey, do not try to do it now!"

Maybe it helped, because the pressure in the chest eased a little. I walked through the hallway and kitchen to the door leading to the courtyard. Unfamiliar smells of an alien house disturbed my fainting heart. And here was the car. At night, in the ghostly light of street lamps, it looked like a huge sharp-nosed military amphibious vehicle. I pulled the handle of the rear door; it was not locked and silently succumbed to my tugging. At this point, the house lights came on. I had to dive into the car and through the window, or rather a porthole, I saw the doctor coming into the yard.

"Damn!"

I barely had time to hide myself behind the seat, which, to my surprise, moved to the side and up, freeing for me a cozy space, like a sleeping bag, in the lower compartment of the car. The doctor got into the front seat. Something hummed quietly, my heart again started beating with alarming interruptions and I felt nauseated. The doctor's voice sounded in my ears.

No! Not in the ears, but in the temples! He spoke in an unknown language, but I understood every phrase.

"The operation of the authority exchange is over. The fire captain took leadership of the group. Teddy has transfused information from the central storage to his archive and collected data accrued by his group. Hereditary material to create new Earth leaders is safely nestled in a bank vault. I request free access to hyperspace. Starting ignition sequence and departure from the Solar system!"

A vibrating tone rung out inside the car, the walls glowed with red and white lights, and once again, I felt my heart freeze and stop in my chest.

"Autopilot-calculator, report the reason of overload?" I heard and felt a jerk for a sleeping bag.

I could neither inhale nor exhale, and just out of the corner of my eye, appreciated the beauty of the night sky in the blazing lights of a flying saucer. In this, I had no doubt! The last thing I saw before my death, was the reproachful gaze of the doctor,

"Didn't I warn you that without a pacemaker you should not be traveling anywhere, especially into space?"

I woke up after a good night sleep in our house in Las Vegas. It was dawn. Liz sat on the bed near me, looking seductive in her thin nightgown. I was smitten with my darling, and she, wide-eyed in amazement was looking at the blanket, that bulged Mount-Everest-like, and was proud of me as in those days, before that damn attack. And maybe even more!

"Ed," she said, "What happened, did you win big? Yesterday you came half drunk, jumped and hopped around the house like crazy, and then fell asleep and did not even read the letter..."

"I jumped and hopped? On my crippled legs?"

The blanket was off in an instant! I jumped up and started hopping. These were my old legs, my old spine and my old... everything else.

"I am now able to work as a mechanic again!"

"Mechanic? Look in that letter, the position the Joint Council of Las Vegas casinos offers you! The Chief Consultant for Control of Card Games! Ed, what have you done there, in England?"

"I do not know, my dear, just went to the cemetery, had a drink at the Fireside Bar... and flew home. Oh, I also went to the bank for my aunt's trinkets. Here they are!"

I threw off the cover of my favorite military field bag. Its leather shined brand-new, not have a single scratch on it. And inside, as usual, lay my set of tools. Mine? As usual? The hell! The backs of all the cards were clean and the pack themselves were virgin new. There was also a simple canvas bag with my aunt's inheritance.

Rubies in platinum settings sparkled as *The Arabian Nights* treasures.

"This is for you," I said, swallowing the lump suddenly approached my throat, "I've always wanted..."

Liz threw herself on my neck and with a passionate kiss stopped my confession. And I gladly responded to her with the same!

A CAMPFIRE IN THE NIGHT

"*W*hat *a wonderful place this universe is! Happy and cheerful! How nice to take a rest here, feeling the fields of family and friends and sending them back your waves. After all, is there anything in the world more reliable than your friend's field of force? More exciting than interference with your loved one? More important than the development of the right gradient in children?"*

Thinking so, an ethereal mother was looking at her ethereal baby spreading out to the attainable infinity of the space. The infant enthusiastically studied their campfire, its sparks miraculously glowing in the night.

"Sonny, do not blow on the fire! It consists of material stars. Each spark is a star, such a short-lived substance, unlike us – fields."

But, go and try to refrain a child from mischief. With his ethereal wind, he again and again blew up the fire. As a result, supernovae flared up, black holes were born, stars erupted protuberances. Flows of particles and eddies of radiation swept across the universe, prompting matter to movement, activity and even aggressiveness.

The child did not know anything of this, while his mother believed that intelligence of matter was a terribly uncommon, quite unimaginable fluctuation of space-time, a mere invisible speck in the infinity. She thought that without a hesitation, one could disregard the probability of the existence of such intelligent matter not even mention its possible aggressiveness.

Meanwhile...

N ight fell across the ground as the Macedonian army, which had been pursuing the Illyrian troops, came out onto the plain. Alexander did not want to incur any risk by acting in the dark. Victory was too important to him. All the way up to the Danube, the army of Alexander, with its battle array and menacing sight, instilled wisdom within the not-too-combative Thracians, and scattered their small detachments. But, while order was quickly restored in Thracia, the rebellious Illyrians proved a tough nut to crack. Alexander felt that he should not just split its shell but squeeze the oil out of its core. That would be a convincing argument – a good lubricant for the squeaky wheels of negotiation with hesitant Athens and treacherous Thebes. Having secured the rearward lands in the north, he would quell the rebellious south, leaving the path east, to Persia, open!

"Tremble, Darius, you coward! You'll lose your arrogance before you lose your head!"

As down broke, a blossoming valley, flanked by forest on three sides – like a giant arena encompassed by an amphitheater – appeared to Alexander.

"Have the enemy troops been running away from us for four days, climbing higher and higher into the mountains, to bring us to this natural stadium where our army would have the maximum advantage? What suspicious thoughtlessness not common to the guileful Illyrians! Something is wrong!"

"It's a trap, Basileus!" his scouts reported.

The crushing power of the Macedonian army, the phalanx, was now located on a mountain plateau on which the surrounding trees hid the sheer cliff into the abyss. They had been lured into a trap; and an attack of the main Illyrian forces should be expected from the rear.

A wave of rage swept over Alexander: to drop the ball like a little boy, and miss the tactical maneuver of the enemy! It was necessary to correct the situation immediately. He realized that turning back to attack would lead them into the python's mouth. To sidle along the flanks of the slopes would be to lose the advantage of the phalanx and embrace the Illyrians' forest battle tactics in which the barbarians were strongest. There was only one option left – to fight here on the field, where the enemy could attack and retreat, and where the Macedonian army remained trapped between the enemy and the cliff.

"No, our war god Ares beats Illyrian Armatus! Think! Think!"

Alexander understood that the only right choice was to crush the enemy with the might of a phalanx on the comfortable natural arena, but... "We should force them... to fall on us... and... not retreat, as if behind them and not behind us was a mortal danger. So, a blow to the enemy would be unleashed behind their lines... by our cavalry, which would drive them to death!"

"Dionysius!" the young king summoned the commander of the cavalry and ordered him to leave through the woods on the flanks. "Circle round the enemy army, hit it in the rear and move towards us! The signal for the attack is a loud noise and the battle cry of the Macedonians. We only need to gain time. Time!"

The rays of the sun lit up the two armies. The Illyrians noted with disappointment that the enemy's army had already reconnoitered the area, and young Alexander grasped the situation. The armor-plated Phalanx, a giant metal square, stood alone in the middle of the field. No support forces, neither infantry nor archers, no jewel of the Macedonian troops – their cavalry – were to be seen.

"They cannot take cover behind the trees," grinned the Illyrian Strategos, "The forest is our natural element. A cavalry there would turn into infantry, and infantry – into minced lamb!"

As if in response to the Strategos' words, the phalanx saluted, raising their short Doric spears, wheeled left on command and began to advance towards the woods. The Illirian Military Council gazed in surprise at this completely incomprehensible enemy maneuver.

"See, their spears aren't very long, well, maybe only a little longer than ours!" noted Hadjo, the commander of the Illyrian spearmen.

The Macedonians in battle order reached the forest, saluted again – god knows to whom – wheeled around and again in battle order moved back.

Open-mouthed and wide-eyed, the Illyrians watched this unprecedented parade.

"The Gods have robbed Alexander of his mind," someone suggested.

This idea was fully confirmed by the actions of the Macedonians: the phalanx marched right – left, forward – backward, saluted, and even demonstrated tactical maneuvers.

"Well," said the Strategos, "It doesn't matter if they are healthy or sick in the head – they are still alive. It's is time to finish these hoplites."

And he commanded the attack. The phalanx in response... sat on their haunches – the men began pounding their swords against their shields and screamed the place down. Unexpectedly, coming from nowhere, the Macedonian cavalry hit the Illyrian army from the rear on one side, while the Thessalian cavalry hit the other side, precipitating a headlong run of the barbarians towards the "crouching" phalanx. And when only a hundred feet separated the Macedonians from imminent death, the phalanx suddenly lifted from the ground their hidden sarissas – twenty foot long giant spears – bristling with the sparkling death-bearing pikes.

"It's the end!" flashed through the Strategos' mind. Thousands Illyrians were strung on Macedonian sarissas. Others were hacked apart by the cavalry.

With this bloody battle, began the ascension to military fame of Alexander the Great, who marched during his life over the corpses of hundreds of thousands of people...

...the streams of particles, blown by the cosmic wind, yet again rushed into space, into the depths of the cosmos, to the distant, cold planets and their intelligent inhabitants – if indeed they existed at all.

"Well, sonny, I just told you," the Mother said, "The more you blow on the fire, the faster it will flare up and go out, and it will be not so nice here, and we won't have as much fun as we have now."

Who could know that...

A Campfire In The Night

They had been fighting nonstop for two days with varying success for a pair of small, useless villages on the left bank of the Danube – Aspern and Essling. For Emperor Napoleon Bonaparte, these villages were a temporary *place d'armes* for attacking the enemy. For Archduke of Austria, Karl Ludwig Johann von Teschen, they were a gap in his defense. As long as the French army occupied Vienna and remained on the left side of the Danube, and the Austrian army on the right, any capitulation was a long way off. That is why, the Austrian bombardiers tirelessly poured fire and metal into this gap.

Marshal Jean Lannes wearily closed his eyes. It was the seventeenth year of continuous war! The rise of a Gascon, a groom's son, a dyer's apprentice, from a simple infantryman to a Duke and Marshal of the Empire seemed to his entourage an amazing flight to Olympus. But his own life appeared to him like a chain of sudden advances from battle to battle. With a banner or a golden sword in hand, the brave heart led off, defended, won... Of course, he was the carrying out the will of the genius, his close friend and idol, but... every year Lannes thought more and more about the question: where will all this lead us, and why?

Here, in Austria, Jean Lannes had rushed from Spain with a heavy soul, despite victories in Tudela and Zaragoza. The view of the fallen in the besieged Zaragoza still shocked him: more than fifty thousand dead defenders! He, a former grenadier, wept silently in stifled anger at the stubborn townspeople, at himself and at his beloved emperor. In Paris, on the way to Napoleon's army, he was trying to atone for these sins by donating money to churches. Even the Empress Josephine felt that he was not his usual cheerful and straightforward self.

Despite the French having already won several battles here, in Austria, and even occupied Vienna, a disturbing feeling did not leave Lannes. He was not superstitious, but considered it a bad omen when he fell into the Danube during a reconnaissance, when Napoleon himself, smeared in mud and mire, pulled him to the shore.

Last night's quarrel with Marshal Bessière did not let him relax. Jean would have called the sneak to a duel for his long tongue and his sluggish obedience to orders. If not for the intervention of Senior Marshal Massena, who had banned the duel, Lannes – just over forty – would have shown what he was capable of.

Ah, to hell with it! His soldiers do a great job of beating the Austrians! The thrill of an attack never fails to rouse those daredevils. However, these Austrians are certainly not the same ones that were at Austerlitz; now they're giving us a severe thrashing.

All day yesterday, Lannes' Division had held Essling in bloody battles. In the evening, his soldiers fell to the ground asleep from exhaustion, but work continued around them all night.

The wounded were transported to the island of Lobau, where surgeons under the command of Jean-Dominique Larrey amputated limbs and applied bandages with unimaginable speed. Fresh French forces under the cover of darkness proceeded in the opposite direction across a single pontoon bridge – crippled with artillery and engulfed by the swelling spring Danube. They stepped onto the left bank ready to continue the slaughter the next morning. "A Battle of the Giants," as some scribbler would say about Napoleon and Charles.

"To call ours a 'giant' is ironic," the Marshal chuckled. "But Charles is smaller than he by half a head."

From early morning the fighting continued. The Emperor himself directed the offensive in the center; the flanks supported him, and the Austrians wavered. It would be another victory had not Archduke Charles shown extreme courage. Go laugh at him, suffering epilepsy: with a banner in his hand, he personally led the guards to attack. The French could only withstand the onslaught, not letting the Austrians push them into the river.

"No! I'm not going to dive again! Napoleon ordered to return to Lobau…"

Then, while the Marshal was discussing the best means of retreat with his old friend and mentor, General Pierre-Charles Puze, that which Jean had had a premonition and secret fear of – to lose someone dear, perhaps even Him – happened! An artillery ball ripped Pierre-Charles in half!

…Lannes, weak at the knees, covered from head to toe with blood and small bits of the general's flesh, sank to the ground. Cross-legged, panting, covering his face with his hands, he imagined his beautiful house near Paris, the Louvre and some unknown palace with huge steps and powerful pillars. He did not see the cannon ball that hit both his legs…

Jean woke up in the hospital after an amputation done with lightning speed by Larrey. Napoleon sobbed, his head on Lannes' chest.

"What are the losses?" asked Lannes.

"Twenty-three thousand from each side," someone answered.

"Lord," thought Lannes, "It's frightening to imagine: forty-six thousand killed in two days! Damn you! You will destroy us all!"

But, as usual, in dealing with the Emperor, he managed to keep his temper, and whispered, "Live on! And save the army!"

These were the last words that Marshal Lannes, Duke de Montebello, said to the Emperor, and beginning the defeat of Napoleon. But, before the end of the war there were still a million lives to be mown down…

. . . When Ali came from Algeria to Paris hoping to enter the Ecole Polytechnique, the situation was already critical. Any day now, guns would start talking. Germany was not slow in declaring war not only on France, but also on neutral Belgium. In addition to the Eastern Fronts – the Austro-Serbian and Austro-Russian – the Western Front opened. In the midst of patriotic hysteria, foreigners were banned from to the universities, but Ali found a workaround: he enlisted in the Algerian colonial troops, the service, which offered French citizenship. Now, before attempting to enroll in the Polytechnique, he had hoped to remain alive, and obtain citizenship. But Ali had enough optimism. He began military training together with two thousand of his compatriots, and three months later, they were all in the vicinity of the

Belgian city Ypres, by which time trenches had already bitten into the body of Old-Lady Europe up to the North Sea.

"Instead of a student bench I've got into a trench..." Ali stopped humming and sniffed around.

Lunch was brought into the German trenches at four o'clock. A North wind was blowing in the direction of the French defensive line, so everyone in Algerian Division knew that today the Kaiser was treating his soldiers to pork and cabbage in tomato sauce. Ali was always interested in what the German Muslims ate when pork was served. Did they get a special ration, or did they just fast? Anyway, the colonial Moroccan and Algerian troops were fed according to Sharia law, so no problems arose.

Traffic at the German side drew Ali's attention. Soldiers dragged small metal cylinders, lowered them into the trench, while leaving some on the breastworks. Usually lunch was not interrupted by preparation for an offensive.

"Abdul," he called his corporal, "What do you think they have over there?"

Good-natured Abdul, who worked as a cab driver in Algeria, spread his hands in surprise, but could not refrain from commenting, "Looks like shells, landmines or grenades. They are too big and heavy for grenades – cannot throw them far enough. They are too round-nosed for shells, and there are no guns in sight. So there is only one option left – they are landmines. So..."

"So the Germans have captured Belgian girls in their trenches, and are going to 'mine' them," Ali replied and added mentally, "Abdul-blab should drive, not fight! He loves vain talk, distracting the passenger while the cab's counter is on."

Ali noticed that after dinner, as usual, at five o'clock, the German side started shelling. "If lunch is at 16:00, but shelling is at 17:00, how much time is given to them for lunch, and how much for a smoke and the toilet?" Ali tried to calculate. One thing he knew for sure: the enemy trenches and latrines were much better equipped. The French dug trenches any old how, for temporary use; and Germans what, were they going to settle in them?

About five o'clock the order came: sit at the bottom of the trenches and don't stick out, let the Germans carry on shooting. The orders referred to the six-kilometer line, controlled by the Algerian 45th Division, positioned at Langemark and the Moroccan-French 87th Division – slightly to the west.

The wounded lay on stretchers, ready to be sent to hospitals. Suddenly the smell of corned beef and cabbage weakened sharply, as if the food from the Germans was suddenly taken away. Many started to sneeze and cough. Greenish mist crept along the ground, flowing down into the trenches and accumulating at the bottom. The wounded on stretchers gave a wail; a bout of coughing already shook everyone.

A barrage of enemy fire swept over those who first rushed up out of the trench. The remaining cautiously peered over the parapet, trying to crawl. Ali, leaning against the wall of the trench, covered his face with a crimson fez, which he usually wore under his helmet, and tried to breathe through it. A cannonade whooshed, especially sinister, reminding one that imminent death awaited at the top of a trench. The others on stretchers wheezed, unable to rise. Ten minutes later, all became quiet… Ali got up, begging God to spare his young life.

"Save my life, Lord; France will give me the citizenship, and I myself will handle the Polytechnique!" he whispered.

Surviving soldiers, coughing and covering their eyes, burning from chemicals, dragged to the rear.

"Hey, pal, can I hold on to you? I'm blinded," said someone close by.

The remaining fighters, like camels gathered in a caravan, trudged slowly, slipping on the bloody dunes of corpses…

In ten minutes, the two divisions lost about six thousand men, a miserable fraction of World War I sixteen million losses…

Taiko shuddered, "What was that?"
. . . A magnesium-bright flash lit the neat kitchen of her small house.

"Lightning? What lightning on such a wonderful sunny morning?" Taiko did not have a chance to think about it as a wave of heat scalded her. She would probably have taken it for one of the regular "hot flashes" which in recent months had repeatedly tormented the woman, but today's attack filled her soul with inexplicable fear. The heat was much stronger than usual, as if she had foolishly put not only her face into the stove, but her entire body.

But, Taiko did not really have time to be scared, because there sounded a loud clap and hum, as if a swarm of wasps had flown through her kitchen. It simultaneously burst the windowpanes and split the window frames, as distraught air broke into her apartment, tearing everything in its path from all surfaces and turning them upside down.

Not understanding what was happening, Taiko got off the floor, dusted off the glass fragments and turned on the local radio, but only crackling static came from the speaker. Then she ran outside in fear to ask her neighbors. They knew nothing themselves and in glass tottered clothes ran in a hurry to find explanations.

"An explosion, an explosion! We've been bombed!" someone shouted, "Look at the sky!"

A quarter of the sky was sparkling with the sun and azure, but three-quarters were covered with white and gray clouds that bustled and moved in accordance with their mysterious sky laws and then suddenly developed a huge mushroom hanging far over the building of "Hiroshima Gas Co". Pearly rays of all the colors of the rainbow came out of the cloud mushroom. It was so beautiful, but so scary!

Along with the others, Taiko, caught up in the general panic, ran along the streets, then along the avenue to the tram stop to go to the center, although she did not have family members there. Her husband had died with Admiral Ito aboard the "Yamato" sunk by the American aircraft in

April. Her son quietly served in the army in Manchuria on the border with neutral Russia. Her daughter had gone to help her aunt: they had a newborn and did not have enough help with the kids. On her way, Taiko comforted herself that she did not have to worry about her children.

They waited long for a tram, packed into it and rushed to the Miyuki Bridge. A woman in green held the sliced fragments of her dress together over her breast. A red bubble began to swell on the face of a skinny girl.

Security no longer allowed people on the bridge. Everyone came out of the car and saw a terrible picture: there was no the city behind the bridge – only a pile of shards and sand among the skeletons of separate buildings. The Kiobashi River overflowed with debris and disfigured corpses. People wept – some silently, others aloud. And, as if participating in the universal grief, the sky suddenly erupted with black mourning rain…

In just a few minutes in Hiroshima, there were killed seventy thousand citizens – one thousandth of the total losses of World War II.

Taiko could no longer stay in this hell. Instead of going home, she headed off on foot to the bus station to leave as quickly as possible to join her daughter and sister in Nagasaki, because…

…indeed, mischief with a campfire gives a child such pleasure. Yet Mother had insisted – an ethereal child should obey his parents. He is not a hypothetical matter creature from a nobody known universe!

"Just one last time, Mom, and that's it," promised the son and blew with all his might into the campfire, almost an entire eternity, so beautifully illuminating the cosmic night to space travelers…

Appendix. A brief glossary of intelligent cosmic beings:

Field – *a material medium (not matter!) transmitting interaction.*
Interference – *the superposition (or summation) of fields / waves.*
Gradient – *a direction of the quickest change (e.g. increasing).*
Ether – *a hypothetical medium that fills space.*
Induction – *the influence or generation a force throughout a field.*
Fluctuation – *a random change (or deviation from the mean) of a parameter.*

THE ROAD WE ARE GIVEN

Adam stared silently at the racks holding his favorite texts, melodies and images. To take these treasures with him made no sense at all. There, beyond the power field of "Eden", with no energy sources, all his electronic gems would become useless junk. Eve also looked sadly at the collection. Tomorrow morning, they would have to leave the station by Adoney's order, for nobody could disobey the Commander, even once, as she and Adam had done.

"I do not understand it," said Adam, "we violated the ban and therefore lost immortality. But why do we also need to go into exile?"

"Maybe he doesn't want to see how we will bear children whom we are going to love more than him?" Eve suggested.

"I don't know, maybe you're right – but Adoney is our father and creator. I will still love and respect him, even though he's sending us away."

"Or maybe it's Sutton's doing? Freed from the younger generation, he will have more opportunities to take over the chair of the Commander."

Commander Adoney was the brains of the spaceship, and the chief engineer Sutton, its driving force. The former never had any doubt and did not express his emotions. The latter questioned everything, honing his skills of sarcasm, yet was never able to attain the pre-eminence of his Commander. Obviously, it was he who beguiled the head of security, Serpone, into convincing Eve that the forbidden fruit was safe to eat.

It was unlikely that Serpone pursued personal gain. A representative of an ancient race of Dragonoids who had lost the capacity for deep feelings through evolution, he was suited to be an analyst, advisor, judge, but not the chief guard of several colleagues and thousands of androids. His punishment was overwhelming. Adoney limited Serpone's freedom of movement in space, leaving only a single plane where he could not even lift his head.

To tell the truth, Eve had never believed that the tree of life bore deadly fruit, and she was not mistaken. That incomparable joy of uniting with Adam, she would never forget! And what's more, that unforgettable experience she would seek again and again, as long as Adoney allowed her.

Frutt, the head of food services and supplies, was not taken into account as a conspirator. On the ship, he was the only representative of the thinking plants, whose interests were confined exclusively to his race. However, Adam suggested that on "Eden" Frutt could not have progeny under the total control of the system, and he secretly sought to ensure the independence of his descendants.

Anyway, tomorrow both of them, Adam and Eve, for the first time and forever, would leave the "Eden" and move into a new reality – absolutely unknown to them – called Earth. In the meantime, they had to think over what knowledge they might need to stock before leaving, and also prepare a list of all beings, animals and plants, wanting to accompany them.

To Adam's great regret, Fenix, the ship's doctor, who had been living a cyclic life, was to remain at the station. But his knowledge, updated at each of his revivals, could be vital where a new evolution and a struggle for survival had to start. As consolation for Adam and Eve, Fenix promised to bathe them with his healing tears and to teach them how to cry themselves. "Your tears will heal you from any grief," he said sadly.

All the team specialists and all the anhels – the heliolazer androids – had to attend the general meeting on thy "Eden". Adoney, as always, presided.

"You should have already realized, Sutton," he said, "I really appreciate your critical mind, your ability to turn everything upside down and consider a problem from an unprecedented perspective. However, that does not give you the right to make your own decisions disregarding my power. Before allowing the samples to reproduce themselves, we had to check everything and calculate the effects of possible outcomes, and not let things drift willy-nilly."

"You'd also reproach me that my ill deeds led to the Big Bang," joked the engineer.

"Don't play the fool, Sutton. Everybody knows that it was my right actions that led to it. In what continuums would our "Eden" have wandered, had I not created this universe, which an eternity ago had become a second home to all of us?"

"Adoney! You really are the greatest commander with whom I have ever served. And that's not a compliment, but the pure truth! Can someone name the creator of another universe?"

Silence was the answer.

"And yet, I want your wholehearted repentance and confession," continued Adoney.

"You're right about everything, Commander," Sutton cast down his eyes, "But at the same time…" a devilish light flashed in his eyes, "It was a divine pleasure to see their happy faces and your puzzled expression!"

"That's why you'll always be just an engineer of human souls, while I remain their creator," remarked Adoney impartially, touching Sutton's sore point.

Then Commander reviewed Serpone's and Frutt's actions, until each of them, under the pressure of Adoney's indisputable arguments, pleaded guilty of incorrect conduct.

"It always turns out in an interesting way," thought Serpone. "Commander's punishment is only half the trouble. His main goal is to break you down internally. And he always successfully achieves full spiritual remorse and suffering. How could I be so stupid to act as a

Sutton's puppet?" Serpone's moral torments supplemented his physical ones. Only the echo of his erroneous views persisted, "Let's see if he will still be able to deal smoothly with these babies, Adam and Eve?"

Frutt was philosophically calm. He was not involved in sabotage directly, and the fact that Adoney's favorite children disposed a "small fig" (Sutton would have called it "fico") from his farm was just nonsense... If Frutt had shoulders, he would have certainly shrugged them. But, despite the confidence in his own innocence, he also got his share from the Commander. Indeed, he's not some kind of guard-serubim, but a being equal in ancient origin to all other specialists, including the Commander, and perhaps even more ancient. And this meant something, for sure. "Well, he served me right. True for you, Commander!"

The Council session had ended. The specialists left first, and the rest of the listeners with anhelic smiles on their beautiful android faces were slowly leaving the courtroom. And the light automatically darkened thereof.

L eft alone, the Commander tiredly rubbed his eyes and sighed. Time was streaming so fast... It seemed that only yesterday they, Adoney, Toth, Horr, Seus, Bodda, Yesh, Ella, Krish, not to enumerate all – young graduates of the Commander Academy – were standing embracing on the marble steps at the front entrance... No, not the entrance but the exit. The exit into life. All that was left there, beyond the imagination, in another universe, in another dimension, in another time...

He was obliged to preserve the memory of these wonderful Commanders! They would come to people and their descendants in dreams, reveries and legends. He promises this. To ensure it, he has decided to conduct a full-fledged human experiment, but not to confine it to the hothouse laboratory conditions of "Eden."

"Full-fledged" means that Adam and Eve will be presented a whole world where – instead of immortality – toil, suffering and pain are waiting for them. However, each specialist who had somehow participated in the experiment should quite sincerely consider himself guilty for the expulsion of Adam and Eve and must atone for the harm that they brought about to them and their kin. As always, with the power of his intellect, Adoney has calculated how even the most intelligent of his associates will behave, and he has made no mistake. Moreover, obedient to the will of the conductor, all the instruments, including the premier violin, Sutton, have today played liturgy of remorse that the Commander wrote even before the creation of Adam. But, Adoney's most brilliant idea was new for everybody – this thing called love!

"Think again, has anything been forgotten?" the Commander asked himself. "They must be provided with the whole list of items, without losing even a little thing before tomorrow's... no, already today's transition."

He looked at Earth and smiled with the corners of his lips, "It came out nicely!"

In the planned site of displacement, it was getting lighter.

"Sutton!"

"Yes, Commander?"

"Is the energy transmitter filled up?"

"Yes Sir!"

"Attention!"

Adoney decided to take a last look with his watchful father's eye at his unwise children.

"Ready!"

Adam and Eve slept embracing. Beautiful, nude, cognizant of heavenly life and of heavenly love, prepared for a long and difficult road.

"Go!"

THE CORRECTION

The hot midday sun burned even the tanned skin of those who were used to it. Four pilgrims settled under the shade of a fig tree, not far from a spring, spouting out from under a rock. A caring hand had overlaid the spring with hewn stones, creating a reservoir. From there, water flowed into a wooden trough for cattle, and into a groove lined with potsherds and leading to the foot of the hill where the fields of wheat ripened.

Michael, the head of the group, put aside his blaster, disguised as a staff, lay down on the thick grass, closed his eyes, and with pleasure, fanned himself with a date palm branch.

"Well, Gabriel, what do you see there?"

Michael did not even need to raise his eyelids to know that his old friend and partner on special missions, Gabriel, a technical genius, as always, looked at the picture on the screen of his Guide and did not simply admire the surrounding world. This time Gabriel's company was the Marshal of Law Enforcement, Sariel, who usually preferred to discuss ethics with Doctor Raphael.

"Frankly speaking, the number of events is still so small that their conditional probabilities are easily determined: the total probability of each event is calculated, and the future can be seen quite clearly," responded Gabriel.

"Crystal clear," Sariel joked, referring to his Guide, a transparent orb that fit in the technical director's palm.

"Anything interesting?"

"Eve will soon be pregnant again. Abel will fight Cain and win."

"To determine pregnancy, a specialist does not need a Guide. It's enough to examine the patient," said the doctor, "Sometimes one simply questions her. For such a healthy woman, as Eve, delayed menstruation will undoubtedly mean only one thing – pregnancy."

"And what about the clash between the brothers?"

"A fight over a woman, as in any society."

"They won't violate the laws of honor, will they?" Sariel inquired.

"And if they do, will you interfere?" Michael grinned. "What laws are we speaking about for groups with so few members? Any rule is dictated by the conditions of daily life, and is broken by the primitive "I do not want it.""

"This does not mean that I'll permit murder or adultery," Sariel stubbornly shook his head.

"You see, Adam and Eve do every night, and already by law, that for which they were once expelled."

"In fact, they were already punished, and now they are free to do as they please: the law is not retroactive."

"If a person is cured of a disease, it does not mean that a relapse will not occur," put in Rafael.

"That's right," Michael supported him. "Who if not you, Sariel, knows that under the law, repeat offenders are punished more severely than others? But, near the isolated singularity, a value of the function often becomes uncertain."

"This situation is similar to a technical default," Gabriel added, "That is, you cannot, but you will be able to..."

"The fact is, in this situation, some uncertainty crept in from the beginning," Michael had decided that it was time to clarify their task. "Who are Adam and Eve to each other? Brother and sister? Father and daughter? Clones of different sex? Besides their creator, no one knows the answer to this question. It's not surprising that people, who violated a ban on love before all tests were performed, certainly mixed cards of the

Creator. Our task now is to make a detailed inspection and to correct deficiencies."

"But people always act in their own way. They are constituted so," Sariel said.

"That's his will," Gabriel summed up.

One might ask whose will he had in mind: the human, Michael carrying on the expedition attributes of supreme power, or someone else of higher rank? But, no question followed.

Cain plowed in into a new site. "Good land," he thought. "In the autumn, we can immediately use part of the harvested grain as seeds, and in the spring collect a second crop."

Unlike his father, who had had to do everything by himself, Cain and Abel, divided the work amongst themselves: Cain, as the elder, managed the land and the plants on it, and Abel – the cattle. It was very convenient: the division of labor multiplies people's wealth. However, it created some inequality that bothered Cain. Of course, who owned the bread – owned everything, but as life improved, meat, milk, butter and cheese once luxuries, became necessities. If initially, all the clothes were made of plants, (Cain chuckled at the thought of fig leaves) and sisters always begged him for cotton and linen fiber, then now everyone was asking Abel for more wool and leather. But, the greatest offense was that Awan, the younger sister, about whom he constantly dreamed and thought, not only allowed Abel to put new sandals on her feet, but also, to coil their straps up to her knees. He saw her cuddling on the lap of this brat. Everything should be straightforward. If they both wanted to take Awan as wife, then let a fight decide their dispute.

A year earlier, he would easily have won wrestling with Abel, but the girl was too young to get married. Adam would not let him. And who needs a baby in bed? It's like nibbling green peaches. But, during the past year, Awan's breasts had filled like September fruit and Abel's muscles became like melons, ripened in their beds. Cain thought to himself, "Alright, let's take a break, refresh, and then we can fight."

The sun was setting. When Abel drove the herd in from the pasture, the firewood was already ablaze. The brothers prepared to share a meal with God; Cain threw sacrificial ears of wheat, wet from the rain, into the fire. It stung the eyes: a nasty gray smoke drifted over the ground.

"That's how you treat the Almighty?" Abel was surprised. "It stinks! It's a sign that such a gift is not pleasing to God!"

"And your offering of lamb's wool stinks less in the fire?"

"Let's compare then!" Abel burst out. "Straw and wool – that's a cheapskate's offering!"

He grabbed a white lamb and stabbed it in the heart with his knife. Releasing his blood, the youth cut open the belly of the animal, snatched out his innards and threw them into the fire. Soon, the delicious aroma of fried offal filled the surroundings.

Cain frowned at the fire and roasting carcass of the lamb. The younger brother had humiliated him. So was he, Cain, with his bread and plants, not dear to God? Also, Abel made himself master of the common herd. Like a wolf, he had killed a lamb without asking advice from his older brother! Never would he have dared to do so, if he had not wanted to show who would be the leader of the pack, who would take Awan as a wife, who would decide matters of life and death. He had killed the lamb, and imagined the enemy! Me? "Lord, you have opened my eyes: my brother is my enemy!" Cain jumped to his feet, trembling with rage:

"Le-et's w-w-restle, Not, f-fight! The winner has everything! And Awan to wife!"

"Fighting? Now? Not even resting a while after a day of work?" Abel raised wondering eyes to his brother.

"That sly look, do not believe him!" the thought crossed Cain's mind.

"Oh, I know! You want me to gorge and weaken after the meal!"

"Since when do you weaken after the dinner? Even our father only occasionally went to bed after a hearty holiday meal."

"You mean he even puts our mother to bed!"

Pop!" resounded a face slap in return. Two mighty fighters locked in combat. They rolled, turned over, snarling and wheezing from the effort. Their hair swept aside like ears of wheat in the wind, their muscles bulged like bulls' napes and veins distended in size of grape vines. Cain pushed his knee into Abel's belly. Abel's entrails crackled as those he had donated to God, but he arched his powerful torso and in a single throw overturned his brother, getting on top of him. And now, the cattleman's elbow smashed the Adam's apple of the husbandman. Groaning, the elder brother lost consciousness.

The group of four men took counsel. Gabriel reported:

"If we want to stop a possible fratricide, we must rush into the valley where the battle between Cain and Abel will happen."

"I insist on it!" Sariel demanded, "Otherwise the sin will be on our heads."

"Do not jump to conclusions," Michael tried to cool him down, "We are given the task to inspect the system and in case we find a defect, to fix it, but not to change the path of the system's progression."

"But to watch the crime and do nothing is to be an accessory to it! We must make a difference!"

"First, you should make sure that the battle will lead to a crime. Gabriel, what does your Guide say about it?"

"The closer to the event, the more precise is its prognosis. So far, only one thing is absolutely sure: this is an unusual match. The brothers will soon become engaged in heavy combat."

"You say heavy? Can you specify?" Rafael was suddenly worried. "I have some thoughts..."

"Share them with us, please," Michael invited him.

"I have to start from the beginning," warned the doctor, "Otherwise, my hypothesis is unclear. The problem is that we do not know the degree of the relationship between Adam and Eve. The fact that Adam's genetic material was used to create Eve still tells us nothing. How much was it changed, or, conversely, how much remained unchanged?"

"Continue," Gabriel supported his colleague, staring relentlessly at the screen of his device.

"Well, Adam's Y-chromosome was transformed into Eve's X-chromosome, whereby, I presume, a change appeared in the genes. Let's call it a mutation."

"And the most common of them today..." Gabriel joined in, "leads to..."

"Hemophilia," Raphael finished.

"But neither Adam nor Eve have this disease," Sariel remarked.

"It says only that the X-chromosome of Adam is normal and a mutation occurred in another chromosome, which out of Y became X in the body of Eve. So, Eve is just the bearer, and half of her sons might be sick."

"But if your hypothesis is correct, one out of two of Adam and Eve's sons is possibly ill, and is likely to die from a serious injury."

"How can you talk so calmly about life and death?" Sariel was outraged.

"You see," Michael said philosophically, "Nature itself is involved in the selection, and we just stand on guard for its laws."

"Perfect! He has the right to die, but not to be killed. Hence, we must prevent the murder of one of the brothers. Let's hurry!"

And the whole company, burning with desire to crack the mystery, moved to support the youngest champion of justice.

Cain opened his eyes, but could hardly sit up. He cleared his throat and moved his head from side to side. Yes, he had lost... What do you know – a brat!

Abel was lying by the fire, where the lamb was starting to burn. "He will feast and celebrate his victory," thought the elder brother.

"Cain..." came to him a faint moan from the younger one.

And, as if there had been no fight, all anger and jealousy disappeared! How many times had he carried this kid on his shoulders, taught him to swim, fed and protected him from wild animals? How could he be so cruel as to beat his brother! After all, he knew well that Abel could not withstand blows, always becoming covered with huge bruises.

In an instant, Cain approached the prostrate body. Abel struggled to lean on his elbow.

"I cannot breathe," he croaked.

His stomach had swollen up, as if Abel had swallowed an unfortunate lamb whole.

"Lord, like a pregnant woman," thought Cain, touching the prominence.

But, no! Abel's belly, though swollen, was solid as a rock. A groan of pain escaped his dry lips, rapidly and greedily gasping for air.

"I will... now... burst," he whispered, "Ease my pain, brother."

"How can I help you, Abel?" Cain sobbed, ready to concede to his brother the harvest, the herds, seductive Awan, and even his life.

"Take the knife and release the spirit of darkness from my bowels. This is God's punishment for my pride and mockery."

Cain, poorly comprehending how to help the dying, grabbed from the ground the knife with which only a half an hour ago Abel had so masterly butchered the lamb, and with a precise short movement, stabbed his brother in the left flank. The knife entered the body to a depth of two fingers, and a jet of bright red blood spurted out, hot as the waters of a thermal spring.

"Thanks," whispered Abel, "Now... it's less sore."

A last gasp flew out from between his instantly whitened lips. Shocked, Cain clutching the bloodied body of his brother, rocked back and forth, howling like a wild beast:

"Am I my brother's keeper? I am my brother's keeper!"

He did not see how the four men in white robes, their heads bowed, humbly walked past him.

"Whosoever seeks revenge upon Cain, vengeance shall be taken on him sevenfold!" rustled the wheat ears and grass.

"Do you have time to repair Eve's genetic defect before she gets pregnant again?" Michael quietly asked Doctor Raphael.

On the fire, the meat of the sacrificial lamb has been slowly burning down.

THE ABORIGINES OF SPACE

(NOTES OF A WITNESS)

Have you ever headed out on an interstellar expedition? Not that it's a very joyful occasion, I'll tell you. Sure, one may be proud of participating in it, but the thought that never again will I see the Earth with its beauties, nor my friends, nor even unfamiliar people, whom sometimes you do not even want to look at – is depressing. My whole life will be spent in a large ship against the backdrop of a fabulous velvet sky, but... Just imagine that you are living trapped near a wonder of nature – a waterfall or canyon. You are trying to turn away, to hide from this unending wonder, but you cannot! And, after some time, you – an ordinary, normal person – find that you have a desire to spit into this miracle. Not to say that action heals, but at least for a moment, living becomes easier. However, here, even this, most simple and natural human protest, is impracticable. Like pissing against the wind.

It remains to outlive the grains of bitterness and anguish in oneself, and limp along the boring, routine life of a pioneer or a settler in space. You can't even take a girl for a walk. As in a remote village, "everybody knows everything about everyone." Even worse, surveillance cameras record your every move. Could one even inconspicuously get any privacy with someone – allow yourself some intimacy? I already know a biologist who has begun searching for a way to make alcohol. We probably have many more such searchers. People keep quiet: who likes it when they poke their noses into your problem?

THE ABORIGINES OF SPACE

Apparently, soon, we – astronauts – will intermarry. Of course, not all, but most of us. For some time it will help. Love and sex. I must say that astronauts were prepared for this – I mean sex in zero gravity. But, there is nothing to envy! One of the partners must be strapped to a bed, and the other must hold onto the rails, combining intimacy with inertia, wearing your arms to the bone. Yes, this is no fantastic future spaceship with artificial gravity. Each book describes everything so romantically, but the reality is such a grind!

It will probably be better when children are born. We will have someone to educate, to instruct, and on whom to vent our dissatisfaction. From these children will come a new type of people, perceiving the emptiness of space and the damned weightlessness as essential features of their only beloved birthplace, in which no one ever has a choice. I will be the dad of an aborigine who is just as comfortable defecating in the electrophoretic toilet bowl as I had been in a wild forest, behind a tree. Should I really be so hard on the children – are they really to blame? Let them at least be born healthy. That's where biologists and physicians work. In fact – the first full-fledged project: the children of weightlessness. Consider we are creating a new breed of human and doing this blindly. Past observations do not count: they were too brief, and gravity's absence was too haphazard. Who, in his or her right mind, would start offspring in such inhumane conditions?

Like every member on the flight, I know that if our infants are unviable, or simply different from normal children, then the ship must return to Earth. Those of us who had survived until this happy moment would again see our native land and regain the privilege to spit out of vexation and relieve yourself without having to be strapped in.

Theoretically, there are few people who could influence such a, I would call it, relatively favorable outcome. These are the children who were included in the crew with their parents. On Earth, there had been long disputes over the wisdom of including these children in the team. Yet the idea of having a small intermediary link between earthlings and "natives",

161

i.e. a second generation, won. To me, it only seems like a victory. If I had had my way, there would be no such middlemen. Apostasy – always a sure way to lose: it's OK with the natives – we continue the flight; it's a failure – we go back. Even so, who knows in what generation there could be a failure? At least, let's not miss our chance while we are still alive and can think with our old savvy earthly brains. Well, what if they liquefy after twenty years of weightlessness? Can you imagine? And the team turns into a flock of... I don't even want to imagine. And there is no place to spit. Better, I go take a walk.

"Hey, Bruce!"

This is Alice, a neighbor girl, nine years old. A future leader. The intermediate between us and them: earthlings and natives. She is the one who cannot wait for a brother. A local baby. A little aborigine. Well, good luck!

"Hi, Alice! How are you? Are your classes over?"

"Yes. And when do you lecture?"

"Soon, Alice. Next week is my turn."

This is also one of the problems. I mean – free time. We have so much of it that we do not know what to do with it. There is no getting rid of "teachers" and the majority of adults engage in self-education. Permanent studying protects their minds from idleness and, ultimately, from mental health problems. I'm sure these will appear. First of all – depression. We will learn how to produce moonshine, grow grass, and make God knows what kind of chemicals. Then will come all sorts of perversion and violation of biblical commandments. It is unlikely that you can steal anything, but to covet... and even kill in a rage, no one can impede you. Only yourself. Ugh, it'll be necessary to sign in for psychic support. Not, of course, to report, on my own thoughts and imagination.

"Are you free today?" I ask Linda, a pretty brunette of about twenty-five, who happen to be sitting next to me in a fruit bar on the promenade deck. A stupid question, of course, otherwise, she would be on duty. This comes from embarrassment.

The girl understands me. Perhaps even grasps the secret meaning embodied in this question. She nods curtly, sending her neat locks into motion, as if in a shampoo commercial, waves of floral aroma tenderly caressing my nostrils. The golden hairs on her tanned forearms excite me. "Lin-da, Lin-da," I roll her name along my palate, anticipating the sensation of her kiss.

For several months already, our ship, "Dragon", has been plunging into the depths of the universe, and all this time I have not had a single date with a girl, or even made a single attempt... I cannot say that this disturbed me much, initially. During the first few weeks, we were still under stress from our recent commitment – it's no joke, to go into space forever! Gradually people overcame their stiffness, and, as it usually happens in places with limited freedom, settled in and established roots.

I had the opportunity to become acquainted with almost half of the inhabitants of our spaceship; by face, of course, we all knew each other. But, oddly enough, in the first months of the flight, thoughts of intimacy never occurred to me, and only began to imbibe me in this strictly non-alcoholic fruit bar. Although, a shot of something stronger would not have hurt.

"Today I'm free," I continue to talk nonsense, rather than to tell Linda how beautiful she is.

I swear, I want her madly, but my feelings are tangled. On Earth, I would have known it long before, not just by the beating of my heart, but also by more... external signs, yet here, in the absence of gravity, you begin to doubt yourself.

To whom could I admit that during the whole flight an involuntary erection did not occur even once? Only recently, I tried to induce it myself, and to my own pleasant surprise, I achieved result – through "perseverance and diligence", as my schoolteacher used to say with respect to completely different things. It seemed to me that I was still not quite myself, and, although I was perfectly aware that conditions of weightlessness would not be easy for men, I never suspected such a high degree of difficulty; I credited everything to my depression and irritability.

"We can go to my place or to yours, Bruce, as you like."

She is also smart. What is there to like or not? All cabins are as alike as two peas. Just, in your own, you are more accustomed to doing things that confuse and worry you, as if you were a "late bloomer" at the most crucial moment of your growing up. And, in a girl's room, her favorite teddy bear reproachfully observes how you put on a vacuum suction with a rubber ring-lock... ugh. But, alas, another method in weightlessness (how I hate it!) had not yet been invented.

"Come on, let's get out of here, quick!" It seems that everyone in the bar knows why and where we go. Nonsense, of course, but... I remember the smell of grass and a tender young girl's hands. Hell, I'm like a disabled person of some sort. To kiss, it is necessary to cling to nearby objects, or if you want to feel female roundness under your palms, to snap on safety belts. Why be surprised? Even to take a leak, you can't forget to stick your boots into the fixation device, otherwise the rebound of your 'jet stream' will either slam your back against the door, or knock your head into the crossbeams, while the ricochet dumps you into your own urine, spilled past the receptacle.

Linda is truly a smart one. Without embarrassment, she immediately fastens herself to the seat of the sofa as if in a comfortable limousine. She then fastens me; we are in a rapture of kissing without fear of accidentally floating and raising bumps and bruises. The erection is still absent; my "shipmaster" slightly raises his head, like a drunk at a tavern table, but who, shackled in a dead sleep, drops it back again onto his hands. However, these hands are now a woman's. Apparently, I will need to use the humiliating inflator. Linda encourages me.

"Let's prepare everything in advance, and then continue in bed."

We move to a narrow bed, equipped with belts and railings, as if created for indecent paralytics. We even have to undress as if for a physical examination: neatly arranging our things. There's no theatrics there! Who, in the most interesting moment, would want a hit on the nose from the buckle of a belt or a jumpsuit, flying around the cabin?

My girlfriend is surprisingly pretty. The shape of her body is so beautiful, that I even wonder how it happened that she is with me, naked and ready for intimacy, and, perhaps for motherhood. I should not have wasted my time running left and right, saying that 'last goodbye' to all my former girlfriends, and even to girls I did not know, but instead, should have gotten to know my spaceship team. So what, then? What if I had fallen in love with her on Earth? Would I have discouraged Linda from flying? Would we now be living a long and happy ever after? Nonsense. Everything was perfect. The pre-flying party was gorgeous. I focus on this memory for inspiration, but "shipmaster" is still motionless.

"Lie down," Linda whispers to me.

She fastens me with a pair of belts as everyone does before going to bed, and she attaches wire cables, sliding along the railings, to a belt around her waist.

"Everything must be ready," she adds, putting a love device on me – one jerk of a cord and the air expands out of the case into the vacuum canister, and the blood from the veins of the pelvis fills the cavernous bodies.

In the next minute, the rubber ring elastically compresses me, and then, without losing a minute, Linda unzips its cover, and instead of its cool rubberized fabric, I excitingly feel the almost mystical tenderness of her hot womb. No – life is beautiful, even out there, where you can never spit overboard. But, I did it! Still waters, indeed, run deep. Am I really going to be among the first fathers?

I must admit that on New Year's Eve we celebrated perfectly. We started with a big banquet for the whole team, arranged in the center of the promenade deck, and ended up with a small neighborly, almost family-like party. Linda, having moved in with me, had become friends with Irene, Alice's mom. They were both preparing to be mothers of the first space children to captivate the attention of the entire population of the ship: the fate of the expedition depended on the successful development of offspring. Questions of erection and depression moved to the wayside. One era gave way to another.

Linda and I, like the rest of the parents, knew that things, were, if not bad, then a bit unusual. Babies in the absence of gravity developed differently. Whether their bodies lagged behind in development or whether the brain developed faster, the head of all the fetuses looked disproportionately large, and the medical team was preparing for elective C-sections. I felt ambivalent: on the one hand, as a father, I was worried about the child, and on the other – hoping that, our crew having understood the futility and even immorality of further flight with defective offspring on board would turn the ship back.

I will not describe the C-sections. We all have some idea about surgery, but not space-surgery, with dozens of manipulators bustling about inside the hermetically sealed transparent dome limiting the operative field and the surrounding space, and guarding every drop of blood from darting off the wall of the dome like a stray billiard ball. I was not concerned where our surgeons had trained, though these virtuosos impressed me. But the kids... The spectacle, of course, was not for the faint of heart – a head the size of the torso. Linda, like any mother, was happy, her arms around the baby, but she sensed my tension and, with her maternal instinct, interpreted it as hostility.

"I will not give him up, even if the child is sick! But, look, what a nice face, no signs of mental retardation!"

"Of course, that is out of the question. I only hope that we will have time to return to Earth and give birth to more children there."

"Back? That means our kids would be labelled as defective. That's impossible, I would not believe it! Look at our cutie! He looks so smart! His eyes do not even wander."

Even though I strongly doubted Linda's confidence in our "tadpole", she turned out to be not just a hundred percent right, but two hundred percent! Do you know what that means? Yes, all these newborns were champions in the development of their brains. Though, the physical abilities of the children left much to be desired, in terms of their mental capabilities, they far exceeded those of earth babies. And so it began! The whole ship threw themselves into raising this new generation. Some developed children physically, others designed them mechanisms for all occasions, and others taught them, and all together – studied them carefully. Gradually, even the more bull-headed, like me, realized that there was no turning back, and that our kids were not just smart, but brilliant, as if in one head they hid not one, but several brains.

"Our ship is called the 'Dragon' and not without reason: gradually there will remain only dragons. For now they are merely plush..." – bitterly remarked the biologist – who had finally synthesized alcohol from trash – and he quickly covered his head from my oncoming smack.

I wavered, but did not hit him, realizing that it was our common fear – never to see Earth again – that had come from his lips. No one even knew that it was my son – a preschooler – who told him how to modify one gene in a colony of lactic acid bacteria to cause alcoholic fermentation. I will not enumerate what else came from our little aborigines, but will go straight to what agitated the whole crew.

In the evening, after putting our son to bed, Linda and I usually discussed the day's events.

"I have to tell you something," said my wife, "It's about Alice. Irene shared her observations with me."

"Sure, tell me. What's the matter?

"I think she doesn't get enough attention".

"You mean her parents are preoccupied with their little aborigine?"

"Yes, that's also an issue, but it's not the main one. She's fourteen and..."

"She doesn't have a boyfriend? Is it that important?"

"You know, she's a smart girl. It looks like she is afraid that it isn't just "not" but "not and never will be.""

"Where did you get that? At her age every teenager goes through all those doubts and uncertainties."

"Yes, but not all are so smart as to find access to the ship computer's medical data to make sure that none of the young men on the ship, even at nineteen, are not interested in having a girlfriend. The absence of gravity kills the real men in them."

"I can imagine how upset the poor girl is."

"I'm afraid that things will get worse – she does not believe in the future; it seems to her that her parents do not love her, and she will never see Earth."

"You mean that Alice is in deep depression?"

"In any case, she was. But now she seems much better. It was her brother who noticed that she wasn't doing well..."

"I'll have to talk with our little aborigines, our son first and foremost."

Of course, the next morning, instead of talking to our son, we got caught up in, getting everybody off to school and work. And later everyone would find out how it happened.

Alice entered the vestibule of the docking module and blocked the inner door. The alarm tripped when she attempted to open the outer door. In the control room, they realized that she was trying to depressurize the airlock. The engineer wanted to shut off this operation, but the local command was stronger than the remote and suppressed it.

Alice heard the rustling sound. "That's it! The air has started to go out," she thought. "Forgive me, my dears..." Her head began to spin; the girl made an awkward movement and, losing consciousness, slowly began to rotate in the vestibule. As if through a haze, she saw how the inner panels fell away and two toddlers squeezed into the module. It's pretty cool when little kids know how to unlock that door, turn on the emergency oxygen supply, and... Well, anyway, you get who saved Alice.

As Linda and I learned later, Alice's brother had synthesized an antidepressant for her. Even he did not know that suicides occur most often when a person comes out of the doldrums.

A total population meeting was gathered at the request of the children. The eldest appealed to all the "aunts and uncles",

"It's time to turn the ship back home," he said, "It's obvious. Those who sent us wanted to hatch a new breed of people – Aborigines of Space who could reach the stars. But, too few children were born; the teenage boys have no interest in girls, the older sisters become depressed, and we are physically too weak to function in gravity. The success of any expedition consists of collecting new data and returning home. And without you, our parents, we are unlikely to be able to secede. We think that the command of the starship have instructions on returning home. We believe that the time has come!"

The commander nodded vigorously, confirming the speaker's words, and the audience burst into applause.

"The next interstellar expedition cannot take place before we learn to bring your kind of earthlings to the planets or adapt the spaceships and landing modules to Homo Sapiens Spacium," explained my son.

Well, have you ever heard such words from a first grader? I'm very proud of him.

Then the ship began to decelerate. Could you imagine our joy when the first tangible signs of gravity appeared? Everyone understood that this was the result of inertia, but what's the difference? Unfortunately, what was good and usual for us turned out to be painful for our children. A kind of "epidemic" swept them: they freaked out, wept, sought protection from their parents and, worst of all, began to deteriorate. What could we do? To be sorry, to love. Of course, we built a swimming pool, but how many hours a day can you spend underwater with oxygen tanks? The doctors advised exercises and muscle building, but how did it feel for those who had never experienced such loads?

As parents of space youngsters, we always shared what we learned about caring for our children in a force field. It sounds like nonsense, doesn't it? Our little aborigines were like dolphins stranded on a beach. We even thought that dolphin-nurses would be a good choice for our swimming pool... All the wonderful properties of the brain decreased as we watched them, the body, and the muscles grew, as if someone had launched the correct development program for them. The head seemed no longer disproportionately large, and the kids were gradually transforming into normal adolescents. I'm sure they will be able to bear adaptation to the moon, and eventually descend with their families to the parent's planet. And another thing: I saw Alice with her boyfriend. Well, you know, here "everybody knows everything about everyone!"

If it were not for the documents, analyses and videos, no one would have believed our story. They would think it a mass psychosis, the result of god knows what chemicals our little aborigines had synthesized, and only what plants had been cultivated! Gravity seemed so ordinary to us, but now see, how its absence affects the intelligence! And not only that... Wow! The tricks of evolution!

"Hurray!" the kids are shouting.

We have entered lunar orbit. They are back in their home weightlessness, and I remember with disgust that damn vacuum suction. Hopefully, for the last time!

LISTEN TO YOUR PARENTS

D anick, as we called Dan at home, was waiting for a friend. They were going to see a movie. But before that, they had to practice solving math problems for an hour, to strum a guitar for an hour, and to play video games for an hour. In case the balance among these three components got broken, then it would certainly not be in favor of math problems. We were not very worried for Danick, because his knowledge of math that he had studied in Moscow more than covered the algebra and geometry programs of any American school, up until calculus. Although his friend Juan was strong in history and the social sciences, he did not welcome much of Pythagoras and Wyeth. Strange, of course, but the boys become friends as if they had sat ten years at the same desk. Such luxury of studying together for such a long time is rare in America where classes are shuffled each year, and while every student knows all the others in his graduating class, there is less opportunity to build such a strong bond.

Danick didn't just have a friendship with Juan, but I would rather say a brotherhood bond. There are several reasons for this. Firstly, Juan, born in the United States, had plenty of relatives – Cuban immigrants – so he understood the problems of new Americans and didn't laugh at them. Secondly, the boys acted in tandem: both loved to play the guitar yet also managed to do their math and history homework together very fast, helping one another. And thirdly, Danick, like my husband, is partly Spanish, despite their fairly Jewish surname, Gusman. That, however, is a separate story, but one that is worth telling here.

I did not know my late father-in-law. He was a journalist in the besieged Madrid, where they called him "comrade Guzman". As it turned out, it was not a family name, but his first name – Guzmán. His last name remains unknown, as well as the date and place of his burial. His Spanish colleagues fled to various places in the world in search of asylum, while he was among those who considered themselves "lucky" to have escaped the Nazis to a communist Gulag. His choice was doubly bitter, according to my husband's stories, as Guzmán could have gone to the United States, for he was well acquainted with Hemingway, and had even named his own son Ernst in the writer's honor.

I also barely knew my mother-in-law. Rachel Gusman was the daughter of a Menshevik[1]. This fact earned her passage to the vast expanses of Siberia, where she eventually met "comrade Guzmán". They fell in love and even back then bequeathed unto their son the dream of a free life. Thus, my husband and I, with our son Daniel, emigrated from the Soviet Union shortly before the 1980 Olympic Games.

As I had already mentioned before, the third reason for the boys' friendship was our Spanish roots. Juan loved that Dan and Ernst could chat a little in Spanish. Well, you can't surprise anybody in New York with that, but I think a newcomer from Russia, who said to his classmate in Spanish class, "You (*Usted*[2]), are probably, a professor of Spanish!" would naturally win the sympathy of any Latino boy with that polite "*Usted.*"

But, the main reason, in my opinion was that Juan was attracted to Ernst. Juan's father and grandfather drowned before his birth during a storm, while they, along with pregnant Consuela, Juan's mother, fled on a boat from Cuba to the United States. A few years later, she got remarried. Juan's stepfather was a good man, a former Coastal Guard officer, much

---

[1] – Member of the socialist faction, opposing Bolsheviks – another, faction, under Lenin's leadership. After the Revolution, the Mensheviks were physically exterminated or sent with their families to concentration camps (GULAG) in freezing Siberia.

[2] – Spanish polite form of 'you'. To classmate, they apply '*Tu*' – usual form of 'you'

older than his wife. Juan had a deep respect for him. Despite this, with all his soul Juan reached out to Ernst and Dan, finding a great similarity between Ernst and his real father, a bearded man whom he knew only by a single yellowed amateur photograph. Ernst, having experienced first-hand the hard fate of being fatherless, also liked the boy and found him similar to Dan. You might laugh, but Juan and Dan do somehow look alike. I would call Juan a swarthy, dark-haired version of Dan. Juan also seems to get along with me; in any case, he kisses me hello and goodbye, as is customary with Latin Americans.

Ah, here he is – speak of the Angel: mwah-mwah! I put the stew on low hit and, commissioning the children to keep an eye on the pot, took the car and drove to the mall. Driving by myself was still a new and pleasant experience for a not entirely settled immigrant.

Ernst had recently started working in a good job – a company that repairs and adjusts computer-controlled equipment. Thanks to some knowledge of Spanish, he was often sent to the southern states and the Caribbean. This time he was off to the Yucatan Peninsula to inspect garment factories, and he hoped to enjoy going for swims in the sea in addition to checking production lines. Unfortunately, his plans for long swims in the Gulf of Mexico did not come true: hurricane "Kelly" was raging there. Parasailing and swimming far from the shore was dangerous. Every evening Ernst called from the hotel – we chatted for a long time about how one day we would go on vacation to those "banana-lemon" lands.

When I returned, the weather here had also deteriorated. The sky was overcast with leaden clouds, and a south-west wind was blowing in new ones. Boys had already eaten and gone to their movie, during my three and a half hours of absence. Of course, Dan was too embarrassed to take the large black umbrella. Well, at least he took his windcheater. I'm almost sure that Juan prompted him. He always says, "Listen to your parents!" If it poured, it would be necessary for me to go to pick them up. The TV continued to excite those who like thrills and counted how many roofs it blew away. Aha, this is already no joke – four people have died and two ships have not been found yet. It seems that again, Ernst will not fly home today. He mentioned that direct flights to Miami were still cancelled, but everybody was waiting for detour routes to open, bypassing the hurricane: west through Mexico City and San Antonio or east around Puerto Rico's San Juan and Bermuda's St. George Town.

Suddenly the view beyond the windows turned black, and a deafening noise broke out as millions of raindrops started drumming on all the surfaces. I hope that children are still in the movie theater: no umbrella will save them from such a waterfall. Half an hour later the flow of water from the sky slightly decreased and it became just a little brighter outside. No, it was the streetlights that had switched on. Just then the phone rang:

"Mom," said Dan, "There is such a crowd in the movie theater! Nobody's coming out; maybe we can see another movie? Without an umbrella we can't get to the bus stop, anyway."

"No second movie! Don't you have classes tomorrow? We also need to take Juan home. Wait, I'll come to pick you up!"

Before going out, I dialed the number of the hotel. Ernst was not in his room, so I left him a message, once again urging him not to rush, not even with a detour flight,

"Be careful, wait for the hurricane to subside. We also have heavy downpours. I'm going to pick up children in the movie theater. We'll chat this evening. Love you."

Do we really have torrents of water because of the hurricane? I have always been fascinated by forecasters' stories of struggling cyclones and anticyclones. Since childhood, I imagined them as fairy tales about the battle of good and evil forces, but never could understand whom we, the people, stand for – the cyclones or their opposites? Thinking about it while slopping along, I came to the car, sneakers and feet completely soaked, but I feared to drive barefoot. While I was folding my umbrella and climbing into our old Ford, the left half of my body also got soaked in the incessant rain. But, duty called, and without thinking about the danger, I started my journey. And immediately I was sorry I had gone shopping instead of staying home and advising my big boys. That I had not insisted on the umbrella. That Ernst is still in Mexico, that the car is old, and wind hasn't died down! Then I realized that I am very afraid, because never in my life have I driven the car in a tropical rainstorm.

It slightly skidded during the turns, but I remembered the rule and did not break, and corrected the direction by turning the wheel. Even worse – the wipers could not cope the water, and the visibility was terrible. I totally did not notice a figure darting in front of the car when I turned to the right, onto the avenue. I instinctively stepped on the brake and the car was dragged somewhere to the left under the blinding shine of the headlights and the wail of a siren, which smashed through first the door, then the seat, and eventually me. The last thing that struck me: despite all my efforts to withdraw the Ford from the hellish lights and the roar, my car stubbornly continued on its way until the light faded and the siren died. And then the pain disappeared...

Ernst knew that he would miss her call. Usually, he returned to the hotel quite late. Bosses liked it when you work from morning until night, so he tried his best. Even the proximity of the hurricane did not change his rules. Although Ernst had finished his main assignment two days ago, he paid daily visits to the last factory on his list just to do something useful. There, he was welcomed warmly as usual, both for his language skills and his Russian (Oh, Russo!) and Spanish (Ah, Español!) roots. After that, the revelry started, and the working day ended with a hearty Mexican dinner with tequila and bottles of beer with slices of lime. Several times since the beginning of the storm, Ernst had inquired about flights to New York, but the answer was always the same: there are no direct flights; we are waiting for detour flights to open.

At the hotel, a message from home was waiting for him, and, in anticipation of his return, he went to wash off the smell of smoke, cilantro and tequila. But, he was not allowed to relax for a long time – a persistent phone call pulled him out of the shower.

"Mr. Gusman, your wife is in critical condition..." he overthrew an open bottle of beer on the light carpet, "Taken to the University Hospital. The car accident. We are doing everything possible, but I'm afraid that her body cannot endure the severity of the injury..."

"Hello! Pan-American?" They already knew him. "When is the first flight to New York? Yes, any route! In forty minutes, with transfer in St. George? Great! I need one ticket... Yes... Ernst Gusman. Yes, yes, that's correct, I had a direct flight via Miami, please make the registration ready, I will be soon in the airport!"

His head was pounding, but he was thinking clearly: his stress destroyed the alcohol. Fear that he would not have time to see his wife alive paralyzed him. Ernst was sitting in a soft jetliner seat shrunk into himself; he imagined the hurricane picking up the plane and instantly transmitting it to the runways of Kennedy Airport in New York.

"Faster, faster!" he prayed to God, to the hurricane, to the pilot, to the plane and even to the digital cabin clock, whose neon numerals marked the inexorable passage of time.

"Please fasten your seat belts and stop smoking. We are entering an area of turbulence!" announced the pilot, as the airliner shook hard.

"Another hour and we land at St. George, Bermuda," thought Ernst *(shake, shake)*.

"Are not you afraid of the Bermuda Triangle?" asked the elderly over perfumed woman next to him. "Could we be sucked in there?" *(Shake-shake-shake!)*

"Don't worry *(shake-shake!)* Ma'am, that is extremely *(shake-shake!)* unlikely!"

"Too bad!" said the brave old lady. "I *(shake!)* always *(shake!)* wanted *(shake-shake!)* to learn, what was there *(shake!)* – another world *(shake-shake!)* or the same? *(Shake-shake-shake!)*

And as if in response to her display of interest, the alarm howled, and the cabin lit up with a blue light in which the bright, festive red letters "Exit" stood out. The aircraft trembled with a fine shiver like a kooky robot, and filled up with fog. Ernst could not tell if the outer air had penetrated into the cabin or if it was just his eyes dimming from the shaking. In this blue space, he could already not distinguish the passengers, the seats, the signs; and only the numbers on the digital clock – frozen at first, and then ran backward faster and faster, under the roar of the hurricane, turbines and ocean waves...

He woke up to the same sound of the surf, but it was calm and smooth like the deep breathing of a giant friend. A caressing breeze tousled his hair, bringing the slightly bitter odor and salty spray of the ocean.

"Amigo!" a woman's voice called out, and he saw a dusky beauty in her twenties with a bright flower in her blue-black hair. "Have they beat you?" she asked. "Does it hurt?"

He wanted to respond, but was only able to squeeze out an obscure groan.

"Carlos, Jose, help me," she said. "He must be hidden; I'm sure it's the work of Raoul's guards."

"What are you talking about, Consuelo? After several years, it's already a party! Fidel's party."

"Say even "the Communist Party!" After Raul shot the Independents with his own hands."

"Che also happened to leave... And where to put the stranger?"

"Let's take him to Grandpa Juan, in the fishing hut. Nobody will look for him there, and it's not far from Havana."

Two months later nobody would have recognized the lad. All his wounds had healed, his bruises were gone, a bronze tan coated his white skin and a golden beard gave his young face the features of a brave conquistador. One problem – his speech was still poor, though he understood everything and fixed the old fisherman's tackle so well that Juan's business prospered as never before. Consuelo thought of him as Enrique, though he called himself rather Eric or Ernst. Grandfather became very attached to him, and if not for the old man's bad temper, Consuelo would say that he loved Enrique. Or, maybe it was her feeling... Anyway, one day the grandfather started talking to her about their future. He said,

"You have to run with Enrique to the States."

"How about you, Grandpa?"

"I'm too old. I'll die if not today then tomorrow. I have nothing to do there."

"No, grandfather, I won't go anywhere without you! And it's more difficult for one man alone to operate the boat."

Then began their preparations for the crossing. Grandfather told her to take a picture of Enrique and one day, taking the photo, he disappeared into the capital. He came back with a gift – a passport for Enrique.

"And now you are married," he said and read a prayer of blessing.

Since then, the old fisherman often left for Havana, leaving Consuelo together with Enrique. The old fox was not mistaken. Love blossomed in the fishing lodge, and after three or four months, the grandfather said,

"We are waiting for a stormy night, when under cover of darkness, we'll head for Key West, and there – God help us!"

They did exactly as old Juan planed – on a stormy and gloomy night, the fishing boat with three passengers left the coast of Cuba and headed out... The old man was cunning. He made a loop, heading not north, towards the United States, but west, along the coast, entering neutral waters away from the patrol boats. This doubled the distance lengthened, but the risk of being caught by border guards near Havana greatly decreased. For sure, Juan considered them a danger and did not fear of menacing waves. He and Enrique, managed to control their small vessel, tossed like a chip on the ocean. Consuelo was quiet, scared and often prayed. Grandfather had supplied her with a lifesaver, and taught her how to untie it with one jerk from the mast if the boat capsized. Finally, after a couple of hours Juan began to turn north; it seemed to him that they had slipped past the guards, and there remained "one small final thing" – not to drown in the vast stormy seas.

"Get some sleep," the old man said to Enrique, "I can handle the boat myself; anyway we won't reach land until morning, and I have insomnia. Also the girl will be calmer if you sit next to her."

Consuelo looked gratefully at her grandfather and clung to Enrique,

"We have to reach the shore, or we ruin not only our souls, but one more – an innocent one."

In response to these words, he just put his arm around her.

The captain of the "Blue Bay" – Seventh District United States Coast Guard's boat-interceptor, Lieutenant Colonel James Sanchez, shook his head,

"Kevin, you think that we are soaking in this weather to no avail. Remember the "Titanic": the accident wouldn't have happened, had the lookout not been lulled by the "unsinkability" of the vessel. Do you believe there is nothing to watch for in these warm waters? Think of yourself as a lifeguard. We cannot judge the fugitives, or even smugglers, but we have to save them!"

The Lieutenant Colonel was on the verge of a well-deserved retirement, and at forty-seven, he could afford to teach young greenhorns, so he picked on the sailor on watch who shirked from his constant monitoring of the sea. Who, if not the old sea dog, taught by death at sea to value a human life, would grumble at young sailors? Over the past four years, the flow of Cuban refugees on boats had fallen sharply, but he remembered how four or five years ago, they were headed to Florida in any weather, like moths to a light bulb. Then, thanks to the efforts of the Coastal Guard, many refugees were saved. Sanchez was confident that at any day the flow would resume, so if you took an oath – you must serve! And, as if in answer to his thoughts, the watch cried out,

"Ahoy, Sir! 'The Flying Dutchman'!"

Sanchez looked at the "ghost" through his high-powered binoculars. Far away, in the predawn haze, could be seen the contours of a small fishing schooner tossed by waves from side to side. The bluish fog around it, apparently colored by lights from the top of the mast, seemed unusual.

"You know, Kevin," the Commander turned to him, "You're lucky to see that unusual phenomenon. The lights on the mast are an electrical discharge in the atmosphere. Since ancient times, it is called "St. Elmo's lights". But we still have to approach the schooner: it seems this boat is going to cross into our territorial waters."

And, turning on all her spotlights, the "Blue Bay" rushed for an interception. The scene facing the coastguards was bleak: on the deck of the boat, tied to the mast and clutching a lifeline, sat a beauty, pale as a ghost. No other passengers could be found.

Once on board the "Blue Bay", the girl, calling herself Consuelo, told them through tears and sobs, how she had fled Cuba with her husband and grandfather, roaming the sea and getting into a terrible storm. A giant wave had washed her husband off the boat, while her grandfather, rushing to save him, also drowned, and she did not have the strength to follow the men she loved. The crew was impressed by the girl's story, and the Commander even promised to help her at the immigration office in Miami. Kevin was sure that the "old man" just fallen in love.

"See how the weather's getting worse! Right before our eyes," said Juan. "We'd better get to the movies; or it'll start pouring and we might not get there."

"Yeah, let's go!" Dan grinned happily, supporting his friend, "Mom's not here; we can play parents."

Today was Juan's turn. He began:

"Have you washed the plates?"

"We have!"

"Have you put the food back in the fridge?"

"Yes!"

"Have you wiped the table?"

"Yes, we did."

"You didn't forget your money and bus cards?"

"We did not."

"Did you take the jacket and the big umbrella?"

"Oh, that's something! The real parent! It's OK to wear a jacket, but to carry a huge umbrella?"

"So we don't get wet when the rain starts. Anyway, you should listen to your parents!"

When I returned, the weather had already turned bad. The sky overcast with leaden clouds, and a south-west wind was blowing more in new ones. Boys had already eaten and gone to their movie, during my three and a half hours of absence. Wow, Dan actually took the large black umbrella. He was not embarrassed, and he did not forget his windcheater either. I'm almost sure that Juan prompted him He always says, "Listen to your parents!" The TV continued to excite those who like thrills and counted how many trees "Kelly" ripped off and how many roofs it blew off. Aha, this is already no joke – four people died and two ships have not been found yet. It seems that today Ernst will again not fly home. He mentioned that direct flights to Miami still cancelled, but everybody waiting for detour routes to open, bypassing the hurricane: west through Houston (Mexico city and San Antonio) or east through St. George's Town (Puerto Rican San Juan and Bermudian St. George's Town).

Suddenly the view behind the windows turned black, and a deafening noise broke out as millions of raindrops started drumming on all the surfaces. I hope the boys are still in the movie theater: no umbrella will save from such a waterfall. Half an hour later the flow of water from the sky slightly decreased and it got slightly brighter. Ah, those were the streetlights that came on. Just then, the phone rang:

"Mom," said Dan, "There's such a crowd in the movie theater! Nobody's coming out, but with our umbrella, the rain does not look scary!"

"Wait, I'll come to pick you up!"

"What do you mean, Mom?! We have a powerful umbrella! And we are not little kids anymore! Did we play parents for nothing? No, we'll come by ourselves!"

The boys were right, and for a new driver, like me, it was better to be cautious. I dialed the phone number of the hotel. Ernst had just returned; I got him out of the shower,

"Be careful, wait for the hurricane to blow over – don't even fly a detour. We also have heavy downpours."

"Well, darling, I will not fly!"

And we began once again to dream that one day we would take a vacation in those "banana-lemon" lands...

THE GOLDEN APPLE OF SADNESS

It was getting dark.

The first stars were beginning to appear in the vast expanses above his head.

"Look," the Man from Heaven stretched out his hand in the direction of a radiant golden point, "that is not a star. It's an unusual, cruel and menacing thing."

The elders of the tribes fell silent when he spoke – the most wise and knowledgeable, the most gracious and fair, their protector and teacher. Sometime ago, W'Il had descended to Earth in a cloud of smoke and fire, in the "rod" – a polished tower reaching to heaven – and started living among the earthlings. Since he came, people changed, as if they had matured. They divided the work, began to construct better dwellings, to cook tastier food, and even to think differently. The man from the sky taught them to ask questions, "What is that?" "Why?" "How?" and seek the answers around themselves, in real events and objects. He urged them to repeat "the magic spell" – "Your Heart Wants Heights" – to obtain knowledge, not to be afraid of the unknown and not to hide from it.

"The stars are distant suns. But, this 'star' is flying toward us – like an evil ancient dragon whose bones you sometimes find in the ground. Soon it will become a grape in the sky, and then grow to the size of an apple."

"And what if the apple falls on Earth?" asked one of the elders. – "Your Heart Wants Heights – I want to see it."

"You had better not. From a distance, the 'dragon' appears as a beautiful golden apple, but close up it turned into a horrifying fiery whirlwind... and vanquishes the sun. Then the world will descend into a very long night and winter." W'll did not specify that there would be no one living who could see or experience it.

"And can you manage to save us from the dragon? Will you protect the sun and the summer? Save us and our children from the harmful apple?"

"I think so," W'll sighed. "I will send my tower – my rod, as you call it – to kill the dragon, and then I'll stay to live among you."

"And when your tower returns..."

"It will never return. It is like an arrow that strikes the heart of the dragon, and the golden apple shoots off forever, and the Sun, as before, will give us its heat."

"May I draw you with the flying rod and a golden apple?" asked the artist.

The Man from the Sky nodded and smiled sadly in return.

"What?! Do they think I don't know this legend?" Cambyses was annoyed and therefore especially dangerous. "I, the King of Persia, Pharaoh of Egypt, the son of the mighty Cyrus, am advised how to behave, and behind my back am called a madman! I know that I'm the best marksman in the Persian army. Do I really need to repeat the exploits of ancient heroes to stay in people's minds? To split the 'apple of evil' on the head of an innocent child with 'the arrow of righteousness'? Zarathustra never taught this! Father was never required to make such a demonstration of his greatness! Croesus, you have always given wise counsel. Tell me, who has been the more prominent ruler: Cyrus or I?"

Croesus – the former Lydian ruler and the chief adviser already to the second Conqueror-King of the Achaemenid dynasty – froze. Since the ruin of the Persian army in Kush sands, Cambyses had not been himself. He acted impulsively and illogically. And, if one could never have called him "a kind man", then at least he had not raved in rage. Witness the recent unsounded execution of twelve nobles! It is clear that Cambyses was wroth: the luxurious feasts of the Egyptians infuriated him, defiling the memory of those soldiers eaten in hunger and of their fellows who had eaten them to survive. But, it was nonsense to bury alive youth from the best Persian families just because they were not on the march and the desert spared them!

"No offense, Cambyses. As always, I will tell you the truth," began Croesus diplomatically, "In deeds, you and your father are equally great, but you do not have such a son as he left us."

Pleased, Cambyses smiled, "The old fox knows how to talk to his lord, but he still cannot read my thoughts!"

"Bring Preksasp's son here!" he ordered, and the king's poor chef shook and shivered, knowing neither how to save his child's life nor his own.

"I will shoot at the child, who is not weary of me, nor do I have any evil feelings toward him, but I will send him to a better world to free him from future earthly burdens. If I get right to the heart of the boy, the transition will happen instantly, and then I'm not mad, but merciful. And, if people are right, and my mind did wander in the dark, I will not be able to get precisely to the heart and thereby demonstrate my exceptional accuracy and compassion. And then we will ask the father of the child, what kind of marksman I am."

Preksasp's spirit was already broken. His face, wet with sweat and tears, turned white, and the force left his body.

The boy was brought to stand in the doorway. The two mighty Nubians guarding the entrance dared not budge as Cambyses pulled the string of his bow. They merely stared into the space in front of them like genies, which do not touch the essence of mortal life.

"Teen-n-n!" the string sang its death song. "Mwah-ah!" the arrow squelched, penetrating the boy's chest next to his left nipple. The Nubians continued to stare blankly into space. Croesus, in disgust, turned away from the corpse.

"Sarduk, cut the body and make sure that the arrow has passed through the heart," Cambyses ordered his bodyguard, "Do not forget to show it to Preksasp; let him see that his son did not suffer. And you, Croesus, then tell me: who is mad? I or Persians, who mouth off in the bazaars?"

Apparently, the death of this child was the last straw for the wise counselor.

"You sacrifice even children! Watch out lest their 'crazy' parents rebel against you!" he blurted out and, without waiting for his master's reaction, run out of the chambers of Cambyses.

Wilhelm, barely restraining himself in his rage, loaded his bow with a recently sharpened arrow and began to slowly draw back on the string. Nobody noticed how he hid a second arrow in the folds of clothing over his chest. The guards of the Governor – the Vogt – Gessler had already relaxed, putting away their sharp pikes and swords pointed at Tell. This fleeting moment would have been enough to deal with the Vogt. However, the bowman had decided that if God did not give him the best of luck, and that the arrow would hit his son instead of the apple on the boy's head, then clinging to his own life would be meaningless, and would leave him only with revenge. A minute earlier, holding his uncharged bow, legs wide apart, Wilhelm was rotating his torso from side to side as if warming up, but actually trying to figure out how he would whip out his second arrow, and in one motion, swivel to the right, sending a messenger of death right through the throat of the arrogant ruler. Target height and angle imprinted into his memory, Tell whispered "Bolt, turn, corpse!" Oh, how he wanted to deal with Gessler right now, to show the villagers that human dignity is above birth status, and an even more alien title. But, the bowman was well aware that such actions would condemn his innocent son to death. "While the child is alive, the guards, no doubt, may well relax their watch – I won't do anything silly."

"Hey, son, close your eyes; don't be afraid!" he encouraged the boy and then thought, "Everybody believes that my bolt carries death, when in reality death is promised by orb of the power, as an apple put on the boy's head...

The child was pale and motionless. Not a sound escaped his compressed lips. Only the unnaturally pale cheeks and convulsively clenched fists of the boy revealed his internal stress and panic.

"Well, hunter, prove that you are a noble bowman, if you have never been of any other nobility," grinned Gessler. "However, for disobeying my order you will still have to add to the coffers. Granted, I could give you a delay."

Tell swore under his breath "Lord, keep me calm! A delay – that's the right thing. We'll meet on a deserted road. Then I'll repay you in full."

With no apparent effort, as if resigned to the strict order of the governor, Wilhelm pulled the string and with a light imperceptible movement of his fingers released the arrow into the apple. Stunned, the crowd could only gasp in response.

W'll was anxiously looking at the computer screen. The little yellow asterisk had turned into a bigger golden spot that was increasing in size with each passing hour.

"It's time to make the final decision," thought W'Il, "Option One: flight. Asteroid collides with the Earth. Immediate loss of all life in an area the size of half a continent. Earthquakes. Volcanic eruptions. Giant waves several kilometers in height repeatedly swept the surface of the Earth. Then – eternal winter: hopeless clouds shielding the lifeless land from sunshine and heat. But, sooner or later, creatures from the ocean will adapt themselves to live in this alien environment, and thus evolution will roll on. Who knows, maybe the human being in the new cycle of life will be more clever or skillful? But, what if it does not evolve at all? No, to slip away in good time from the giant asteroid and bring home a horror movie, be it the most spectacular ever shot – not my cup of tea.

187

Are these half-civilized people worth staying with forever, even as a ruler and a demigod? Never to see my homeland, friends, family? To have as many concubines unable to give me sons? Never to raise my own children? But, wouldn't the locals be like children to me? The whole planet – like a son for a smart and powerful father. Okay, you can make a long list of "pros" and "cons", but the solution to the problem has long been calculated. How many times have people sacrificed their lives and freedom for the sake of others? So what, if it's for the sake of primitive people? And even if not quite people but just sentient beings? Is it then I would be able to fly, run, throw them at the death? Well, I have no such force to push the asteroid off its path into open space or into the furnace of the sun, and keep my ship as well. That for this. Preserving the spaceship means preserving the asteroid while destroying the asteroid means destroying the ship. But, preserving the asteroid means destroying life while destroying the spaceship means preserving it! " It's simple. W'll laughed. He had already taken out the ship's equipment – at least anything useful for his future life with some residual features of his lost civilization.

"So, option number two: aim the spaceship at the asteroid and watch the phenomenon in the sky. Shoot a colorful movie through a satellite's telescope. Thus to obtain on Earth a 'permit' for residence without leave, but to save sentient life. As long as energy sources do not run out, the computer will receive signals from the satellite station.

Hmmm. 'Star Father (That's me) saves the 'earthly son' (that's them). Shoots a 'golden apple' right off his head. Looks like a tough father. Sad. Who will realize that the imminent danger is not in the shot, but in the apple? The shot – is just a safe harbor. Rescue for the son. And a 'sentence' for the father. Life without parole. Well, that is why people say no good deed must go unpunished, no matter how good it may seem to others."

Take off!

THE GOLDEN APPLE OF SADNESS

Golden Apple, sweet and sad,
Ship is leaving – crew gets mad,
Separation splashes its waves.
Tears in eyes: "Farewell sailors!"
Bitter smiles predicting failures,
Hope, bad things bypass our braves!

Golden Apple, hopeful sore,
Love me, honey, as before,
Let's meet on earth; not in the graves.
Yes, we travel o'er the abyss,
Yes, we're catching plague and rabies
And we view tsunamis just as waves.

Golden Apple, lone and still,
Keep in hand your steering wheel.
Let it clear! Cheer up, young wind!
Just imagine her dear face –
You are guarded by her faith
In blue skies, the golden sun is pinned.

THE EXIT

"Sign here that you understand everything," said the robot-guard and handed Jack a thin screen displaying a text. From its lusterless surface, like an enemy's army regiments in a battle order, aimed at him were three paragraphs.

Article 1

An individual who commits a crime against life, liberty, or human health is to transfer to hyperspace behind the Wall for a period determined for rehabilitation of the offender (the method of Mining) or for transition to another world (the method of Door).

Article 2

To return from hyperspace upon rehabilitation, the prisoner must successfully excavate a passage under the Wall. The difficulty and duration of this task are established in each case.

Article 3

To transition through a Door in the Wall, a prisoner takes upon himself the risk of moving into another world with all the consequent uncertainty.

"Ready! Aim! Fire!" Jack sized the electronic pen, signed the document and scanned his thumb. The uncertainty was the most disturbing. He looked out the window. Between the rows of poplars, one could see the road along which the old armored bus had rattled hoarsely to bring him with two other prisoners from the courtroom to the prison-forwarding station. Behind the poplars, like a new wonder the world, stood a giant white wall.

"When do you move us, officer?" Jack asked the robot.

"Rushing to do your time, are you?" quipped Pete, a pimply guy convicted of raping a young woman. He nervously cracked his knuckles, twisting his fingers while waiting for his turn to sign.

"I wouldn't be in a hurry; nobody's yet returned from out there! – as one twin said to the other during delivery," this – rather sarcastically – from an unkempt, lean tough boor, who had stabbed his wife with a file.

"The transfer is after lunch," the robot answered dispassionately. "First, we must conclude formalities and apply your restriction bracelets."

The dining room was small and clean, the food – simple but quite edible. Were it not for the complete unknown ahead, Jack would have taken his punishment for the death of the boy under the wheels of his trailer as deserved without hesitation. He ate and quietly leaned back in his chair anticipating a command; his hard-working hands, already equipped with the two "watchmen", dropped to his knees.

"Will you start digging or looking for the Door?" Pete grumbled, scaling at Jack sideways.

Jack almost blurted out, "Digging," but held his tongue. A quick reply would raise new questions, and he did not want to explain his choice as a desire to dig the grave for his dream of a son, but in fact, for himself.

"I'll look around for a bit, listen to old men," Jack replied cautiously.

He really did not know anything about life beyond the Wall. Erected soon after the discovery of hyperspace, it served as the frontier zone between the obscure but still earthly penitentiary camp and alien worlds.

"To look for what?" asked the boor, "You can dig or not to dig! I choose the second, to search for the Door in the Wall."

"Aren't you afraid to fly up an ass?" Pete glanced at him.

"To fear or not to fear – it's the same shit. We die here, man! It's all tales about Saps and Doors because officially there is no death penalty and nobody has fun feeding us forever. Who goes for digging will be buried alive, and who finds the Door in the Wall will wall himself in forever. Rehabilitation is for suckers, not pickled by drink. Yes, I drank! I drank a lot. And began to hear voices. But, I was treated, and almost recovered, if not for a trifle. The nurse missed her work – did not come to do the last injection...

"And besides her, they had no one who could stick your special flesh?" Pete cracked.

"I was sick of waiting, so I left. And as luck would have it, I met old friends. Then – as usual. And when I'm drunk, I'm evil. And she nags and nags. Here the voice told me, "There is the only remedy against a saw – a file!" Do you think I was not sorry for my wife? I was! But I felt even sorrier for myself that I could not otherwise get rid of the bitch, and once I started I could not stop. What will change now if I dig a hundred years? No, I'm going to look my Door, wherever it lids. Come on!"

At these words, there was a faint crackling and smell of ozone; Jack found himself with the passengers from the armored bus standing behind the tall white Wall that ran to the horizon. Scorched steppe lay underfoot. No tree or nor shrub to be seen. At a distance, a darkened craters and piles of earth extracted from the mines. The boor went to the Wall and with a shrug tapped it.

"Who's there?" said a mechanical voice, and a sensor's green light suddenly flashed in the Wall.

The prisoner silently held out his hand allowing the system to identify him from the bracelet. After a few seconds of analysis, a low narrow door with a bell appeared in the Wall.

"Do not rush, man," Pete said and raised his a hand in warning, "Your exit appeared too quick. Huh?"

"All my life I was nimble," said the killer and with one jerk opened the Door into dark space.

A bell tinkled faintly, and a vortex from the darkness sucked up the boor. The door paled and disappeared, replaced by a flat white surface.

"What happened to him?" Jack asked anxiously, but neither he nor the "pimply" found any answer.

Pete, spellbound, came close to the wall and knocked. The stone did not respond. Then he walked along the Wall and knocked again to no avail. Stepped – knocked, stepped – knocked. Again and again. Anew. Once more.

"Open up, you motherfucker!" he shouted.

There was no answer.

"One, two, three," Jack commanded himself, moving with the monotony of a digger. One – to immerse a shovel in the ground, two – to bring the soil to the container, three – to turn the shovel over. And from the beginning. And again. Muscles have tightened; body aching from fatigue and endless repetitive movements. Compulsive counting helped to fight off the obsessive thoughts.

First – about the boy. For probably the thousandth time, Jack is mentally replayed the episode with the short blow, scream and squeal of brakes, which tormented him at night. He could not explain nether to others nor to himself, how it all had happened. The rearview screen was clean, in the mirrors – not a soul, in the head – no sleep, nor hangover. Yet he had overlooked that rascal when backing up his loaded trailer. Blow – scream – screeching brakes! So into the ground – to the container – turn over! One – two – three!

Another thought was about the prison. "Where is he? Why does he dig, day after day, month after month? Maybe better to follow zonked Pete looking for the Door? Door to where?"

In the rare hours of leisure and feeding, prisoners exchanged scanty information. A few prisoners went along the Wall searching for theirs Doors. Most of them eventually began to dig a tunnel. This at least made sense of the prisoners' existence. The bracelets did not allow shirking –

electrical discharges quickly explained to the most "slow-witted", what was what. Sometimes everyone got excited at news about the some inmate's disappearance. Some stumble on the Door in the Wall; others, apparently finished rehab, found it where they were digging. What angered many was this purposeful uncertainty.

Pete started and stopped digging many times. He growled, "If I knew that the Door leads to Hell, I would dig tirelessly like a laborer. But now, who knows, maybe I'll meet some lame girl behind the Door."

Jack tried to convince him of the depravity of his approach, "Are we rehabilitating out of fear of the unknown behind the Door? I thought we just wanted to make amends."

"Except you, Jack, and another couple of blissful idiots, everybody here is innocent. Tell me, would that little man have killed his wife, had she not nagged him so much? Of course, you think that I raped a woman. And she is a poor victim. Lies! She hinted a consent! Do you know how it was?

I met her in the park. On the bench. It was immediately obvious she had no man. Of course, she was emotional with tearful eyes. I asked, "What have you lost here at this time? Have not you been waiting for me?"

And she says, "I've lost my son…"

"So let's make a new one," I say.

And she says, "I do not care…"

And this, in your opinion, is not a hint? Then, the bitch started screaming and scratching. In short, I've got into trouble…"

"In my case the boy neither annoyed me nor hinted to me. The fault is mine, that's for sure."

"Well then, dig, moron," Pete, angered, once again went looking for his Door.

And Jack persevered digging the tunnel, not expecting any surprises. And today there had been no special signs, when suddenly his shovel clinked against the metal surface. Jack frantically scraped away the earth and found a manhole cover. Another couple of minutes of fuss and it came off with a clang, opening the entrance to a broad dark pipe. "It looks like a sewer," Jack decided, but the smell was normal, slightly ozone, like his surroundings. "Should I call somebody?" he thought, but increasing electrical discharges in his bracelet did not allow him to move away from the hatch. "So it's my Door. And maybe that's the end?" thought the prisoner, and he climbed into the darkness. The hatch slammed shut behind him. A whirlwind caught and carried Jack away.

"Well, now it's really is a sewer," Jack grinned. The wind abated; now strong unmistakable odors wrapped him up. Under the thick soles of his miners' boots squelched stinking slime. All of a sudden, a faint light penetrated into this dungeon, and Jack perceived the contours of a shaft, rising vertically. Gathering his strength, he jumped up, caught the first bracket and climbed towards the light seeping through a gap at the top. The exit was blocked by a manhole cover, slightly shifted from its groove. Jack gathered his strength and moved the cover further to the side just at the very moment when a boy about ten years old ran across the street, crouching like a seasoned scout to the surface of the earth caught up with him. Jack barely managed to pull the boy into the hatch as a heavily laden trailer rumbled overhead, turned and sped away.

"Son, where is my son?" hysterically screamed a young woman looking around in a panic.

"Mom, I'm here!" the little boy yelled back, jumping out of the hatch to meet his mother.

"You frightened me, you rascal! Not yet enough to get under the dump truck! Where did you climb?"

"Mom, don't worry, a worker in the hatch was rescued me from the roaring dinosaur."

"Don't be mad at him," Jack said, "Children regret no less than we do".

"I do not have time to be angry," the woman said. "I have to rush now and give a very important injection to the patient; I cannot be late, or his treatment may be ruined. But would you like to come for the dinner and tea this evening? We will celebrate our lucky day!"

"Come, Mister, come! Oh, please!" exclaimed the boy. "That's our house, across the road. My mom and I will be waiting for you!"

"Thank you, I will come," Jack said, grasping a cold little palm in his great paw. "Now I need to hurry. I should already be sitting behind the wheel of that trailer. If my manager thinks that I had overslept then I'm in real trouble," Jack added and smiled widely.

MODULUS OF ELASTICITY

The first Sunday of October of 1795 dawned warm and sunny on Lower Saxony, especially on its southernmost city, Göttingen. Sixty years ago, in this very same place, the local Elector George-August, who became the King of Great Britain, founded a university, a hearth for free spirit and intellectual enlightenment! It was little wonder that students from all across Europe longed to be here: the best professors, the best library – all were here.

The Englishman Thomas Young dreamily shut his eyes. He was to continue his studies at Göttingen's renowned medical school. Life in a foreign city did not frighten him: he read German fluently and with time would soon speak as well as any other native. A sharp mind and an excellent memory allowed Thomas to grasp the essence of things and remember everything on the fly. The better his lectures were, the less time he needed to spend wearing out his pants in the library, and the more time that left him for other activities. Tom enjoyed playing music and dancing; he also didn't mind to earn himself a few extra thalers, using his gymnastic talents.

"Have you heard the news, Tom? The circus has come to town!" his boardinghouse neighbor hailed him. That was Carl Gauss, who had come from Braunschweig to study mathematics, "They're setting up stands in the park and raising a tent. I thought you might be interested."

"One cannot deny Carl's logic," Tom thought, wiping the sweat from his brow. "He might have caught me racing along the shoreline of Leine on a horse, tumbling on her back, but what he doesn't suspect is that last spring, in Edinburgh, I won a bet with a professional tightrope walker, repeating all of his tricks. Perhaps I could earn myself a bit of money here, too. The circus is a wellspring of profit for riders and gymnasts."

"Have they hanged any posters yet?" he asked Carl.

"Yes, they have. 'The Circus and Theatre of Riding: Clowns, acrobats, trained animals, and vaulting, by the famous Antonio Franconi!' Italians."

"I've heard of him," Tom said, "He's from Paris. Escaped from Robespierre's Terror and is touring Europe. And you're right about my interest, neighbor. Will you come and see my performance if they accept me into the troupe?"

"I'll bet a pint of beer... or even two that they'll accept you, but I'm afraid I won't be able to sever two hours from my math studies. No offense, my friend."

"But can science really take precedence over life? I forget everything when I read Natural philosophy, but medicine – that's even better. And languages? They send me out to other countries and times! And music, painting, gymnastics, and dance!"

Carl shook his head pensively, "I love literature and languages. But, mathematics is the queen of sciences and the Number theory is the queen of mathematics, and I am their servant."

"Well, I am the servant of other monarchs, but I promise that if I join the troupe, a free admission is on me. I'll tell you the most spectacular part of the show, so you don't have to snatch two hours from you mistress."

And they parted, each happy with his choice: Carl went to the library, where a recently published volume of Fermat's letters was waiting for him; and Thomas, in the hope of financial reward, went to the circus.

The transfer was instant and painless. Only a moment before, two inspectors, A'n and P't, had just received instructions from the Main Protector of Sirius's living space, when all of a sudden conical transmitters on their heads deployed and moved them to Earth, in a beautiful park.

"A pretty exact hit," A'n, the more experienced operative, said, looking at the small device in his hand, "The fugitive is within half a mile from us. It's a good thing that his homemade transmitter didn't send the boy off into that place where he was so eager to support 'freedom, equality and fraternity.' Try to save him there!"

"From the guillotine?" P't, the impressionable junior inspector, suggested.

"No, he has nothing to fear from the guillotine; the guy has 'hop-hop' with him," A'n said reassuringly. "But, the guillotine is not the only way to lose your life," he added. "Let's start exploring the surroundings."

"I'm quite sure he is out there, in the area where people are building something, moving about, and there are many animals in small wagons," P't reported.

"Fairly clever disguise," A'n approved. "A boy can hide in any of these creatures."

"It will be difficult to isolate him," P't sighed.

"Don't worry! Casting around in a big city would be harder," A'n encouraged his assistant. "Let's split up for a while: you patrol the area so as not to let the fugitive escape and in the meantime master their communication channels. I'll go into the thick of the crowd to figure out what's going on there."

A'n went toward the people who were pulling the canvas onto a frame around the assembled stands. While the scout slowly made his way to them, he picked up several of the languages used in this city, and understood that he was in Lower Saxony, Göttingen, in the city park, and that the people moving around the tent were workers and artists. Commanding them all was an energetic fifty-eight year old man, the circus director Antonio Franconi. A'n learned that the troupe was returning to Paris, liberated from the terror of the Jacobins. He also became aware that the circus lacked riders and needed more clowns, whose caps resembled the transmitters on the heads of the inspectors from Sirius.

"Mr. Director," A'n appealed to Franconi in Italian. "Do you, by any chance, have a couple of vacancies in your theater for two skillful circus clowns?" As he was speaking, he unscrewed his colorful pied head, tucking it, like a watermelon, under his arm.

"Oh, you're also Italian? Original! I mean – your trick. How do you do it?" Franconi asked. – "Ventriloquism?"

"Yes. Perhaps, you may call it so. My brother and I can entertain your audience with sketches and anecdotes throughout the show, pretending to interfere with the artists and get into funny situations, but if you like – we will repeat any of the most difficult tricks or somersaults."

"Do not take on too much, signor... what's your name?"

"Rankoni. Arlequin Rankoni, at your service." A'n set his head back in place, threw open the upper part of his skull, as if hinged, and pulled out of his head two fragrant cigars. "Would you like a smoke? Exclusive goods, product of Shlottman's from Hamburg."

"You are on, Arlequin!" the circus owner pronounced with a stentorious voice of an equerry; "You may come after lunch, sign the contract, and along with it introduce your brother. Is his name Pierrot, by any chance? By the way, where are you from?"

"His name is Pierrot indeed! How did you know it? We are from Venice," A'n without hesitation named Antonio's home city.

"Oh, I knew it! I could feel we share not only our national temperament, but also our Venetian artistry. Now, however, I have to hurry!" and he dove inside the tent, dispatching orders left and right.

"We've been recruited P't, congratulations are in order!" A'n telepathically contacted the colleague. "I am glad that you had already mastered a bunch of languages, but don't stop patrolling. In the afternoon, we have a meeting with the circus director. Do you need anything?"

"Yes," the junior inspector did not want to stint himself on pleasures, "Teleport me the same cool thing, that is smoking between your teeth, okay?"

"**W**ho can I talk to about the work?" Tom turned to the dark-haired young gymnast in tights wet with a sweat.

"Here, everything is decided by my father – Monsieur Franconi. And what can you do?" he replied in German with a strong French accent.

"I'm a good rider and acrobat," Tom switched to French.

"Great! Me too! And are you up to snuff, or are you just bragging? Look, in this matter, our family can't be fooled!"

"Well, for starters I undertake to repeat any of your tricks."

The young man's eyes lit up, "Fantastic! My name is Laurent. And yours?"

"Thomas. Thomas Young, from London."

"From London? And where did you learn to speak French so naturally?"

"At home. I can do much more, but I came here to study medicine, to know more and be able to do more."

Laurent Franconi looked at his peer with undisguised astonishment.

"You mean that you are fluent in three languages and crammed so much that you can go to college to prepare for medical school, but you also want to learn some riding in our Theater?"

"I speak six languages, and read eight more. I have already graduated from college and entered medical school. I do not intend to take lessons in your theater, but to make money performing!"

"Come to the arena!" temperamental Laurent exploded. "If you repeat my tricks, I myself will persuade my father to give you work. But if you're a skillful liar and only make good with your tongue, I swear, I'll show you that I am familiar not only with English racehorses, but also with the English boxing!"

"I agree," Tom said quietly with the shake of his locks, "Just to add spice to your bet: if you manage not to repeat my trick, then you'll pay for lunch at the 'Wild Goose'!"

And they raced to the tent, where in the arena there were already acrobats tumbling, while jugglers and tight rope walkers practiced on a high wire.

"Now they'll bring us the two horses," said Laurent, "And we will immediately..."

"...Start working up the animals," Tom finished for him.

"That's what I had in mind," added the young jockey, nodding approvingly, "At least you're familiar with horses. Now, we can stretch our muscles." And he threw his jacket and shoes on the rim of the arena and began to exercise somersaults, flips back and forth, cartwheels, splits and walking on the hands.

Tom also took off his jacket and shoes and repeated all same moves. Then into the arena entered two horses, a bay and a black, which galloped as usual around the circle. Laurent and Tom continued to exercise in the center; then Laurent caught up with the bay and effortlessly jumped onto her back upright. He turned his head to see Tom's reaction of the student. To his surprise, the Englishman was already standing on the rump of the black horse.

"Good for you, Tom!" called Laurent, "Let's repeat everything on horse's back."

And one by one they performed a series of somersaults. The artists and workers in the tent applauded, seeing the young men tumble synchronously on the horses galloping side by side.

"Consider yourself accepted," Laurent said, slowing the horses to a quiet trot, "I will talk to my father. At first, though, I didn't believe you. Where did you find the time for everything? Well, now you can demonstrate your trick."

"Here it is," said Tom, riding under the tight rope over his head.

He jumped up lightly from the horse, grabbed the wire and in a moment was standing on it. Deftly balancing and not stopping for an instant, he ran to the opposite side of the arena and jumped back onto his black horse, which was at this moment just below Tom. More applause resounded.

"They do not know that you've just earned your first lunch in our circus," Laurent patted his new friend on the shoulder, "If you're just as capable a teacher as a pupil, then I'll soon run on a tightrope. Now let's go, I'll show you our trailers, props and animals, and most importantly, introduce you to my father – he has the last word."

"Monsieur Franconi, Monsieur Franconi!" the elephant trainer monsieur Leken ran to the director, "I don't like the behavior of the Colossus."

"What's wrong with him? Is he sick?" Antonio was alarmed.

"I cannot say for sure. He twice tried to break the door of his cage and even bent its bars a little. Then, apparently, he stopped this, and without any command, stick or reward showed the workers all his tricks, even doing a headstand. I thought Colossus actually beckoned people to him with his trunk. So, just in case, I set the fence so that no one could come close to his cage."

"Do you think he's dangerous? Can he perform today at the opening?"

"No, he is not dangerous, but he is behaving strangely. I will bring Colossus to the arena; it looks like he wants to play, but let me have some back up."

"Be sure, monsieur Leken: the firefighters will be on alert, and I'll grab my gun. Thank you for the warning; stay calm."

"Well, of course! So now our elephant got sick – worse luck – in a new place and right before the premiere! Gosh, all the bumps for poor Franconi. However, not to panic! We've got out from even worse troubles," Antonio thought, lighting up the Hamburg cigar, the gift from the new clown.

The circus manager was not alone in his worries. Approximately the same thoughts disturbed a completely different creature – Dee – the mischievous adventuring boy from the Sirius system, who had taken refuge in the body of the elephant. He now realized that, without understanding, he had chosen the most powerful being in the crowd only to get into a cage from which he could escape only by contact with a new body. This has not worked. "Wait a bit, friend," he reassured the elephant, "I will soon free your body from your unexpected guest. It's not my habit to harm anyone else. I know 'Liberte, Egalite, Fraternite' are highly valued here. But you do not quite understand me, right? But you follow me anyway?" And to check, Dee walked on its hind legs; then made a stand on the front legs.

"Wow!" Tom said to Laurent, "You have a genius elephant: he's exercising too!"

"I guess the air of Göttingen affected him also," taunted the young rider, "Wait a while, he too, will register as a student. But why am I surprised? I myself wanted to learn your trick. And after Henry, my younger brother, meets you, he won't leave you alone... And here is my father."

They went to the large trailer, near which the circus director stood, surrounded by a crowd of men. All were vying to question him, scribbling in their notebooks. Undoubtedly, sketches and articles about the first performance of the French circus in this town would appear in the evening papers.

"Gentlemen, it is better to see everything with your own eyes. Come this evening!"

From the tent circus came the sound of music: the orchestra was rehearsing.

"Father, I found a great rider and acrobat for our troupe. You'll be very happy, believe me! We've already successfully practiced. If you want, he can start working in the arena tonight."

"Where are you from, young man? Introduce yourself."

At once, the reporters turned toward the young men.

"From England, Signor Franconi. I do not really want public to know about me – then Tom switched to Italian, once again surprising Laurent with his abilities – that a medical student and a member of the British Royal Society acts in the theater. I'll tell about myself and my family, but only to you and in private, not to a crowd of witnesses."

"Of course, of course, come into my office. Laurent, take care of our new rider. I'll join you in a minute."

Antonio waited while the two youths entered the director's trailer; then he turned to the reporters, "You have just witnessed the success of our new 'Theatre of Riding.' In front of your very eyes, the best rider from the

London Astley Troupe has joined our circus. Confidentially, I can report that he is a member of the British *Royal* Society. But his name is kept secret due to certain circumstances – proximity to the... family."

"Proximity to the Royal family," recorded half of the reporters.

Having made a splash with his statement and in no doubt that this would cause an additional influx of spectators, Antonio withdrew to his large trailer, finally releasing a fragrant cloud of cigar smoke.

G auss was returning home scowling in annoyance. No, the day was still beautiful, filled with the fading warmth of autumn. The bells of St. John and St. James's Churches melodiously rang the midday service. Carl was upset that he had forgotten about the shorter library hours on Sundays when he wanted so much to finish reading all the Fermat letters. Anyway, thorough work on this collection of letters would require considerably more time. Alas, Fermat had offered almost no proofs. In fact, he took most of his deductions for granted, as trivial. Gauss wanted an absolutely precise and unambiguous expression of thoughts. Well, then, the second half of the day, he will not read, but meditate. Maybe his neighbor, the Englishman Yung, was right that more attention should be given to the pleasures of life. He had already realized that short brakes provoked waves of clear thinking and creativity. Maybe today was just a day to drain a mug of beer with a friend and remember dear Johanna.

Carl did not have time to realize this Epicurean thought when he saw Tom with a young man heading towards the famous tavern "Wild Goose."

"Gaudeamus igitur!" Thomas welcomed the mathematician. "Come with us, there is much to celebrate. Your idea proved prophetic: I was accepted into the circus troupe; now I'm going to do gymnastics not only for my own pleasure, but even for pay! I invite you to the circus this evening – and now let's go; we'll try some roast goose. Laurent Franconi, my new friend here, is treating. Laurent, meet Carl!"

"Yuvenes dum sumus! Beer on me – for good luck!" Tom did not expect Carl's cheerful support.

"Are you also fluent in French and Italian?" Laurent asked?

"Of course. And I read in Latin, Greek, Hebrew and Arabic. And you?"

"Not in Arabic. But in Arabian…" the gymnast laughed, meaning his horses.

"Believe me, Carl; he's no less artful in equestrian vaulting than you are in mental arithmetic."

"Guys, you'll really like the circus," said young Franconi, "It's a world in miniature – with miracles and heroes. And I want…

"To treat them and save them," Thomas interrupted him.

"And I want to understand how numbers rule the world," Carl put in.

Laurent added, "To be in an atmosphere of beautiful music…"

Thomas went on, "To play instruments and calculate how to tune them…"

Carl: "To solve equations of waves…"

Laurent: "Shining lights and fragrant flowers…"

Thomas: "To explain the vision and smell…"

Carl: "To build geometry of different spaces…"

Laurent: "Among acrobats, clowns, fakirs, magicians headed by Egyptian queen…"

Thomas: "To read Cleopatra's name in hieroglyphs!"

Carl: "To develop a theory of numbers!"

Laurent: "Jumping, tumbling, flying under a circus dome!"

Thomas: "To comprehend the properties of an elastic medium!"

Carl: "To describe the motion of the stars in the sky!"

Beer, roast goose and dreams of youth – what could be better?

At the entrance to the tent gathered a huge crowd of spectators. To the sounds of the orchestra, waves of citizens, eager to see the wonders of riding, gymnastics, illusion, animal training and funny clowning, poured into the vast circus tent. From stalls, brightly costumed extras sold drinks, sweets, pins, turntables, caps and tweeters. Not only children, but adults gladly bought up trinkets and all the treats. The burghers sedately headed processions of their offspring under the watchful supervision of their marital rearguard. Circus lights glistened on gold braid, silk lapels and the gentlemen's fashionable top hats. The ladies fantastically adorned dresses, plumed hats and turbans, flashed with the fake luxury of a fairy world.

Talking excitedly, well-dressed people gradually took their places in the amphitheater, while a simpler and poorer audience, together with the student crowd, climbed into the gallery, up to the top of the stands. Carl in red and gold livery was opening and closing the barrier into the arena. Thanks to his natural physical strength and his new acquaintance, he received a one-time job tonight, but no matter how Laurent tried to persuade him, he would not agree to a contract.

Two eights of horses snorted behind the heavy velvet curtains. The blacks with golden harness and the dapple-grays – with ruby. They would open the show "Theatre of Riding." Quivering with impatience, the horses beat their hooves on the sandy flooring of the central passage into the arena. Behind them stood the clowns, Arlequin and Pierrot, ready to jump headlong into the arena after the riders. A'n and P't had long since identified in whose body hid their fugitive, and were continuously monitoring the elephant and everyone who approached him. To the convenience of the inspectors, the elephant was still isolated.

Then the riders, juggler, tightrope walkers, trained dogs and strongmen with huge weights prepared for their entrance. Behind them in the arena appeared the Egyptian fakir and a snake charmer with his assistant – "Cleopatra", who turned into a snake after the "bite."

Thomas and Laurent performed twice: their individual routine as well as in the final parade. As Tom listened to the sounds of the orchestra, he dreamed of how he would devise a new, more advanced system of tuning instruments.

"Get ready, now we are on!" Laurent commanded him, and the thundering voice of the master of ceremonies summoned them into the arena.

A sea of lights and roar of the public greeted the riders. One by one, they displayed miracles of horsemanship and physical control of their bodies. And when they were joined by Laurent's younger brother of and girls dressed as Amazons – the delight of the audience knew no bounds. Especially striking, Arlequin and Pierrot not only amused the audience with jokes and ridiculous actions, but also jumped upon the galloping horses, as if they themselves were highly trained vaulting riders. Minutes flew by as seconds, cascades of routines alternated with each other.

"Awesome!" Carl thought, operating the exit gate, "In the circus standard deviations evaporate, not obeying the laws of statistics. Minimal probabilities turn into the maximal, and events unrealistic in everyday life occur naturally here."

But even the most beautiful show comes to an end. The artists assembled in the arena for the finale. Finally, the handsome Colossus appeared. The audience greeted him screaming in delight. Standing on his head and front legs, he stretched out his trunk, over which leapt performing dogs. The Horses, obeying Laurent's orders, danced around the elephant on their hind legs, while acrobats spun in mad flips. At the command of Cleopatra, the python started to pull the rope that raised the trapeze carrying Tom up to the dome. The chimpanzee was waving the French flag with the emblem of the circus; clowns blew golden trumpets from which flames and jets of water escaped. The orchestra played a flourish of trumpets and the chief steward of the performance, Director Franconi, was about to say goodbye to the audience and announce the end of the show, but suddenly...

The elephant, as if by accident, touched a poodle with his trunk. The clowns immediately jumped to catch him, but the dog, frightened, ran into the stands, and in one second reached the orchestra where he licked the nose of a trombonist. At once as if going mad, the whole orchestra started playing tag, not stopping to perform the "Marseillaise."

"P't, hold them all at gunpoint – the boy has turned on his "hop-hop"! A'n ordered immediately, ready to grab each "newly mad" musician.

Modulus Of Elasticity

A drummer slapped the poodle, which jumped into the arena, knocking over the chimpanzee waving the flag; this pulled the rope out of the python's mouth. Audience gasped in anticipation of a terrible disaster. Tremolo of the kettledrums froze under the big top. The trapeze with Tom rocketed down. Antonio, Laurent and Carl rushed to the center of the arena, but the chimpanzee, already near the exit, spun around, threw out his arms, like a real magician, and Tom's fall slowed abruptly.

Before the eyes of Dee, full of unfulfilled dreams, floated the faces of frightened earthlings and cheering operatives. But the trapeze with Tom, unscathed, slowly and smoothly, as if in a viscous medium, descended into the arena to a solemn hymn and the deafening screams of the audience.

Almost no one noticed how the clowns comically put the chimp in handcuffs and some kind of fool's cap and took him backstage.

"Mom, why is that monkey's crying?" little Liesel asked her mom, but her words were lost in the final chords of the music.

In the evening, Carl and Thomas were returning home. After the sunset, it became much cooler, but friends were excited with the day's events.

"Of course it was a trick," Carl said, "But, I didn't really notice anything."

"At first I did fall," said Tom, "And then I felt as if I'd gotten into an elastic medium, well, with a different... compressibility... well, with another modulus... of elasticity."

"What are you talking about? I do not know these terms, but the normal distribution of probabilities was totally absent, especially at the end."

"And I do not quite understand what you're saying, but I agree that after a good shake-up it is necessary to sit down again for science. Natural philosophy attracts me a lot," Tom said.

"And for me – the theory of numbers," Carl added.

"But for me it's truly time to think about medicine! Finally, why did I come here – to explore elasticity, to invent a modulus, to perform in Franconi's circus?"

Finally, it got dark, and only a curious resident, leaning out of his window, would see under a dim kerosene lantern a typical picture of Göttingen: figures of disputing students. But Sunday had ended with the townspeople snug in their beds: who wanted to listen to some students arguing about some number theories and some moduli of elasticity...

THE PHILOSOPHER'S STONE

"Have mercy, open the door, please!" someone persistently knocked on the door, evermore slowly and softly with a weakening hand.

Schwinger, former alchemist at Prince-Elector's Mint, heard the horrifying shouts of approaching guards, "Who will protect the state criminal..."

At other times, he would not meddle and open the door to the fugitive, but now deprived of his work, having lost his health and looking forward to imminent death, more than ever he cared about the salvation of his own soul.

The man literally fell at his feet. The bloodstain on his clothes and a fragment of an arrow shaft in his right flank spoke for themselves.

The alchemist had no strength to lift the man onto the bench. Coughing and choking, Schwinger dragged his guest into the room, where – on the floor – he removed the arrowhead and treated the wound. His patient stoically endured the procedure and fell asleep after drinking a decoction of herbs. To change the compresses on the stranger's forehead all night long was beyond the host's strength: he himself been tormented with weakness and fever.

In the morning, Schwinger opened his eyes and stared, amazed: his guest was sitting in the armchair by the bed, reading the old alchemist's favorite folio about transmutation.

"Thank you, you saved me," said the man with an unfamiliar accent, "But I see you yourself are seriously ill."

He then examined Schwinger's skin, covered with sores and bruises, listened to how his lungs wheezed beneath his bony ribs, felt his enlarged liver and spleen under his bloated abdomen and shook his head.

"Are you also a healer?" the alchemist asked hopefully.

"You could say that. And judging by this book, your passion is turning base metals into gold."

"All my life I have wanted find the Philosopher's Stone. But not for gold – only as a way to understand the world. After all, the stone can transform into the elixir of life, so its solution is a cure for any disease. But, I fear that my life has passed, and there is still no elixir... I have not seen anything, but have only worked with the ore and metals.

"With the ore? Have you often seen bleeding miners?"

"Yes, stranger, it was not uncommon. I am tortured by this bleeding too. And, I see you are a knowledgeable doctor.

"Will you be able to get me out of town, into the Mainn Forest? There, in my temporary home, I'll try to help you," the man offered.

Schwinger was scared. He had little doubt that his unexpected patient was an inhabitant of another world. He would have liked to call it hell – he had spotted the small soft horns on the stranger's head, but the words failed him – this devil was so very much like a good man.

A door slid open in the thickets of wild rose to let them into the mountain to the stranger's temporary home – really a castle, which was beyond any Prince-Elector's dreams. Not in wealth, but in spaciousness and unimaginable wonders.

The stranger took a drop of blood from the finger of the frightened alchemist, smeared it onto a glass tile and began to examine it under various metal tubes – a small one on a table – and a towering one, like a cathedral organ's pipe, in the corner of his stunning alchemical laboratory.

"You have a blood disease; I'll put medicine in you with this needle. It does not hurt. Medicine is the very same gold solution of the philosopher's stone. People know how to make it there – where I live. Pray it helps – the disease is quite advanced!"

"A gold... from metals... you can also...?

"We can! From mercury, for example. But we do not make it that way: it's not worth it. It's cheaper to get it out of the ground and clean out the impurities."

"Could you make a piece for me with your philosopher's stone, as a memento?"

"With the reactor? I could, but it would be short-lived and revert to mercury again soon after."

Schwinger was sweating, "Whether he cannot or he does not want. How is it possible – to turn back into mercury by itself? It could not happen."

"Would you believe that I do not ask because of my greed, but just as a symbol of the victory of reason and knowledge over the human night of ignorance?"

"I believe you. So be it, I will make gold for you," the man replied and mentally smiled. Imagine how the alchemist would be surprised, when the gold turned back into mercury! But it is useful for the treatment of his leukemia – radiotherapy in addition to chemotherapy. – "Just don't even think about selling it!"

A few days later, Schwinger went to church to thank God for his wonderful doctor. Ulcers had healed one after another, his wheezing disappeared, and his swollen belly had subsided in plain view. His appetite had returned and so had his long lost joy in life – and with this a gold bar, the gift from his new friend, soothed the alchemist's soul with it soft shine. Then Schwinger decided to leave this place, get married, to live the good life he had newer had. Alas, he just did not have money for that. So he decided to sell his gold bar to the moneychangers...

Less than a day after this more than satisfactory transaction, the shining bar made its way into the presence of the Prince-Elector. This nobleman immediately suspected that something was wrong: "Apparently, the great surprise of the Elector, the bar soon began losing its golden shine and gleamed silver, like mercury.

"Arrest the fraud!" the angry ruler ordered.

Two dozen guards rushed to search for the alchemist, who was just about to leave his hometown to find a bride.

"Who dares protect the state criminal..." the terrible cries of the heralds rung out, "Here he is! Hold it! Stop! Shoot!"

"Have a mercy, open the door please!" Schwinger persistently knocked on the door more and more slowly and softly with a weakening hand.

"Will they let me in or not?" the thought flashed in alchemist's confused mind.

The bloodstain on his clothes and a fragment of an arrow shaft in his right flank spoke for themselves.

HOMEWORK

*J*osh cautiously crept into his father's study where the *Gravichron's metal helmet, resembling a hair dryer from a stylish beauty salon, mysteriously gleamed on a side table. At school, teens were not allowed to wear a helmet and travel through history. They were only permitted to view pictures of the past generated by this device. However, the three-dimensional movies could not be compared with fusion with a real historical person – his or her joy, sorrow, fear, pain, victory and defeat perceived as your own.*

"Why be so nervous?" Josh reassured himself. He planned to complete his homework assignment entitled "My Heroes are Creators of the Gravity-Time Machine" via dives into the consciousness of three people from a long list of prominent scientists and philosophers whose ideas and principles, (namely the quantization of gravity, conservation of mass-energy, multiplicity of worlds and mental purity with love for others) had led to the development of the Gravichron. He decided to follow the selected characters in the final hours of their lives, hoping to see, hear, and feel what might be their insights in the last minutes of their existence...

"**B**y the session of the Military Collegium of the Supreme Court of the USSR on the February 18, 1938, the defendant, Matvei (Matthew) Petrovich Bronstein born 1906, is found guilty of involvement in the counter-revolutionary fascist terrorist organization to overthrow the Soviet regime and to establish a political system, in which the intelligentsia as in Western countries would participate in the government along with other segments of the population. He also is found guilty of harming the Prospecting and Water Resources of the USSR. Therefore, he is sentenced to maximum punishment: execution by firing squad and confiscation of all his personal property. Sentence is to be executed."

At 8:40 p. m., the guards brought the 30-year-old doctor of sciences, the researcher at the Leningrad Physical-Technical Institute, into the courtroom where he heard those terrible words. Matthew's inflamed consciousness refused to accept such a wild, irrational mummery. The announcement of a sentence was the only thing even remotely resembling a classic trial. There was no jury, no defender, no last word or any other "artsy attributes of the rotten-hearted capitalist Themis."

At 9:00 p. m. Matthew had already been pushed into a Black Maria and was being driven back to Shpalernaya Prison. Matthew hated returning to his jail cell, which held 16 beds and about 160 prisoners. Here the scientist slept on the floor. But the more beatings he had withstood during interrogations, the farther away from the slop-bucket he ended up.

"I must contact Lidia without delay through the criminal channels. Let her ask her father to find connections to a good lawyer and apply for a pardon. Will that help? I am still thinking in the old-fashioned way. But now it's clear why our buddy "Johnny" has not returned from France..."

Only the first time, in October, was Matthew able to put his usual signature below the transcript of the first, "civilized" interrogation where he denied any guilt or association with enemies. That same night, he was taken for a "marathon", seven days of standing interrogation in the blinding light of a lamp and severe beatings. In the cell during the short hours of respite, someone gave him water, wiped blood from his broken face and reduced the dislocated joints of his tortured fingers, which had produced unrecognizable scrawls below printed "confessions" to sabotage. The investigator named dozens of arrested people, many of whom were completely unknown to him. Among his close friends, "Dau" i.e. Lev Landau. Among the colleagues, Vova Fok. And "Dimus" and

Kolya Kozyrev, old friends from the University, had already been convicted... "What an absurdity – crowds of scientists forming a fascist underground in our country!"

Matthew remembered his arrest in August 1937 at his parents' apartment in Kiev. The NKVD officer sternly commanded, "Surrender your weapons and poisons!"

Young doctor laughed in return; they confiscated "weapons" – a soap dish and a toothbrush, and "poisons" – a bar of soap and toothpaste.

But soon, very soon, his life became no laughing matter... Had Matthew believed in God, he would certainly have prayed. "With my nickname it would be just right." Friends called him Abbot in honor of Abbot Coignard sparkling with sharpness of mind and erudition. However, he was not up to poetry, languages or literature in the cell. Only physical concepts and hypotheses still swarmed in his head.

"Then... beating (and not being) determines consciousness," grimly joked Matthew, thinking his thoughts despite the pain and fear. "The Inability to apply quantization to gravity requires the rejection of conventional space-time ideas and their replacement by deeper concepts."

That is how extremely clearly and directly he expressed in a scientific paper long before Einstein's disillusion with unified field theory. Who would have thought that enlightenment comes even in the dungeons?

"Bronstein, exit with your stuff!" shouted the guard, and Matthew was taken from the holding pen down the iron corridors deep into the prison's maw.

"In a new unit? In another cell?" the prisoner was surprised, "Understanding the logic of the system comes only with experience."

The guard brought him to a small, solitary cell underground without any windows. The single bunk bed did not even have a mattress. Not that this troubled Matthew.

"Shit! How do I reach the criminals from my chamber?" he complained to himself, "On the other hand, it is quiet here and does not stink. Anyway... if the time variable t is replaced by..."

The clang of the door lock interrupted his thoughts. A major, dressed strangely, in the leather jacket like a revolutionary commissar, stepped into the cell.

"Idiots! A search? In the middle of the night – in an empty room, without even a mattress?" Matthew cursed inwardly, not suspecting that he was in fact in the death chamber, disguised with the plank-bed as a solitary cell, while the leather jacket of the major was just the executioner's overalls.

"Stand up! Face to the wall!" the overbearing shout sounded.

Matthew obeyed the order.

Thunder of the shot and a terrible pain...

*J*osh screamed and tore off his helmet. Sweat streamed down his face, his heart pounding furiously.

"So that's how it happened! Just as he realized how to quantize gravity in the new time, which we now call gravitime." Josh was gradually recovering, yet unable to rise from his chair. From his textbook, he recalled that Lidia, Matthew's poor wife had not learned that the sentence was executed the very day of the trial; she received the death certificate only twenty years later. She waited for her husband, searched for him, and then wrote a short epitaph for the nonexistent gravestone:

"So many times I've called on Death,

'Come; bring your cold and knife!'

What did not let me stop my breath? –

My man's eternal life."

After dawning a bottle of ice water and making sure that his parents were still out, Josh tuned Gravichron to a different era.

HOMEWORK

Antoine-Laurent de Lavoisier, chemist, member of the National Academy and the Bureau of Weights and Measures, commissioner of the Royal Arsenal, nobleman, banker, farmer... But, worst of all during a time of revolution – a tax farmer! An owner of one of the thirty-two companies collecting taxes in France. In November of 1793, as soon as a National Convention deputy threw a stone at the "fat cats", all former tax collectors were arrested, despite the fact that the tax farming system had been abolished two years ago.

Yesterday, during recess in Port-Libre prison yard, the warden handed Lavoisier a pile of notices to distribute amongst all the accused revenue leasers. With shaking hands Jacques Paulze, his father-in-law and partner, snatched a notice, skimmed through it and bitterly exclaimed, "The public hates tax collectors, so the Convention wants to deprive us of everything, including our lives. They accuse us of plundering twenty-two million livres by reselling wet tobacco. Rubbish! Lord, they will execute us for nothing! Each accused is given 15 minutes to defend himself. Just enough time to appeal for a pardon. No time for discussion! What a nightmare!"

It was difficult to watch his hysterics. After dispensing the notices, Antoine stepped away. "No doubt they are determined to execute all of us. 'Sanguinocrat' Robespierre would destroy all the undesirables at the same time with one gigantic guillotine, but it may be that a Higher Justice will spare me."

He felt no guilt neither before the government, nor before the public, whom he served all his life. His first scientific essay "How to Improve Lighting of Paris Streets" brought him candidacy to Academy. Is not his work at the Bureau of Weights and Measures considered a public service? And significant improvement of gunpowder? Was that for himself or for France? He spent years in agricultural study writing recommendations for farmers. He spent fifty thousand livres of his own money only to study the composition of water. But, with these arguments, it would be very difficult to influence revolutionaries, tearing apart society, science, morality and people. Tomorrow's outcome may prove to be bad, so...

Lavoisier decided to write a couple of farewell letters just in case. Fortunately, the chamber where he was incarcerated with his father-in-law had a small table, writing paper, ink and quills.

"My dear loving Marie-Anne," wrote Antoine to his wife, "life with you has been happiness! Remember that. They could not deprive me of what I learned and discovered. I have submitted to my fate... You will be living many more years; don't grieve as badly as yesterday during your visit... Just remember me."

Then – as his parents were no longer alive – he wrote to his friend and colleague from the disbanded Academy, mathematician Lagrange.

"It is difficult for me to identify my most important achievement. Oxygen? Hydrogen? Chemical classification? Theories of combustion, breathing, caloric? The future will answer these questions. It may be that 'the mass of all components is constant in reactions independently of the state of matter' is the core principle not just of chemistry but also of our entire world!

Yes, I will fight for my life and the ability to continue my work, but there is very little chance of convincing the machine of justice. Tomorrow at this time, the blade of the guillotine will already have separated my disobedient head from the perishable body. I hope, that an execution is painless as it was intended... I invite you, to come up to the scaffold among the lovers of axe whisper – the music of revolution, and watch carefully. If the consciousness is not connected to the body but belongs only to the head, it will wink at you. Let this salute be my last experiment."

In the morning, prisoners were taken to the Tribunal in the open wagon. One of them was already gone; it was too much for his nerves, and he stubbed himself to death. The others slowly rocked over the Parisian cobble-stoned pavements so loved by Antoine since his childhood. Here was the Louvre with the Academy of Science, where he worked for many years. And there, on the left side of the Seine, was his school, Mazarin College, where he first immersed himself in intense study forty years ago.

People followed their procession with mockeries and scorn. Some spat and even threw rotten eggs and leftover food. Guards shouted idly at the gawkers.

The Tribunal started at ten. A guilty verdict was announced every 15 minutes. "Guilty! To the Guillotine!" regularly sounded from the court hall, and mob at the street echoed these words with favor.

Antoine briefly consulted with the defense lawyer hired by his wife. They now had no documents to prove probity of Lavoisier, and to spend their precious minutes in sincere but unsubstantiated explanations seemed futile.

Tribunal Chairman, Judge Coffinhal, gave the floor to Lavoisier's lawyer.

"Your Honor, we are presenting a plea of mercy from the Bureau of Weights and Measures where the defendant has conducted important work for our country."

The judge immersed himself in reading for several minutes. "Is he really studying the paper or is he just killing time?" Antoine despaired.

Coffinhal finally looked up from the paper and said, "It has no importance for the Revolution!"

"Your Honor," immediately responded the lawyer, "We ask for an extension of two weeks, to present exculpatory evidence for Monsieur de Lavoisier. All his papers have been seized, so we need a search warrant."

"Extension is denied. You have one last opportunity to present the court something relevant."

Then the defender said in full despair, "Gentlemen, the scientist's achievements will make his death a national tragedy!"

"The Republic has no need of scientists, and justice must take its course," grumbled the judge, pronouncing another death verdict.

"But…"

"That's it! You are denied the right to reply!" Coffinhal terminated lawyer's last attempt to object.

"Lord, strengthen my spirit," Antoine prayed, realizing that his secret faith in the human mind had finally collapsed under the sentence.

At five p.m., twenty-seven men were brought from the courthouse to the Revolution Square where everyday a guillotine toiled. Ironically, the unfortunate opponent to the death penalty, Dr. Guillotin, had to change his last name when it became the name of a death machine.

Lavoisier was the fourth in the list, Jacques Paulze – third. As soon as the head of Jacques fell with a thud into the basket, the gendarmes at the scaffold clenched Antoine's arms more tightly. In an instant he was laid on a stretcher, straps buckled, stop screws tightened. A few meters from the platform stood Lagrange, his face contorted in grief. The Mathematician exclaimed,

"One second – and the head is cut off! And for another one like this to appear, even a hundred years is not enough time!"

Antoine heard the whistling blade and squeezed his eyes tight...

*J*osh puked. *He couldn't tighten his muscles so it was difficult to vomit. His eyes blinked randomly. "To switch the Gravichron to a movie viewing mode and quickly clean up everything," pounded in his temples, "before my parents have noticed."*

Mom came into the office when Gravichron 3D images of the Crusaders and Saracens were furiously fighting each other in the space as far as the horizon, and the little robot-cleaner had already crept into the corner.

"What's that smell?" she asked, "Freshener? Did you clean up dad's office? Or..."

"She guessed," flashed in Josh's mind, "She did same things in her school years..."

"You understand, sonny, we're not just afraid for your feelings, even though they may be hurt. You perfectly know that already three teenagers trying to save their heroes did not return from the past in nearly a hundred years of Gravichron use. Dad and I wouldn't want to lose you."

"Well, Mom, you yourself think that their possible disappearance in history contradicts the principles of the device's operation, and no one knows..."

"Because no one knows I'm scared when my son is immersed in the past."

"Don't worry, Mom, I did it briefly, and besides that, soon I'll be an adult."

"Please, postpone your travels until then, OK? And do not make trouble even then," summed up his mother, torn between honesty and authority.

Josh really wanted to be an obedient son, but the excitement of the search made him reconfigure the machine again. Now he needed the Middle Ages.

"**G**iordano Bruno ordained in the Dominican Order in the year one thousand five hundred and seventy-two, born Filippo of Nola, son of Giovanni Bruno, a soldier of the Kingdom of Naples, do you admit that you are guilty of heresy and blasphemy?"

"No, Your Eminence, only of erroneous thoughts and opinions, not of defiling the bosom of our church!"

Cardinal Bellarmine frowned. For several months after his appointment as Cardinal Inquisitor, he had been attended the hearings of the former Dominican Bruno. An experienced teacher and philosopher, Giordano was a master at disputing the judges' charges, but Cardinal's demand was clear: the heretic must either repent of everything or perish.

"You, Bruno, are a tough nut to crack," said Bellarmine, "Seven years spent in the darkness of the papal Tower of Nona prison is an ordeal, but you still persist. Truly, pride has overshadowed your brain. And you, stubborn monk, even don't realize that the Inquisition wants to save your life."

It was seemingly a simple task: Giordano Bruno was just asked to protect the foundations of the faith from his faulty deductions, to recognize them without exception as heretical, to repent, and to ask for forgiveness. The blasphemer was accused of perverting the sanctity of Jesus Christ, his resurrection and the future Second Coming; the denial of the Trinity and the Virgin Mary, the transformation of bread and wine into the body and blood of Christ. Moreover, he asserted the multiplicity and infinity of worlds, the transmigration of souls and the beliefs in magic and divination. One could add that he upheld the views of Copernicus, but the church had not yet developed its official position on this issue, and scientific disagreements and even magic were viewed only as isolated spots compared to the rivers of dirt, which spilled Bruno on the Catholic faith and its ministers.

"My son," the cardinal humbly appealed to the sinner, "Your education, knowledge and experience of lectures and sermons must indicate to you the correct pass. All your statements are false and ungodly, and therefore, should be retracted. This will help stop the spread of heresy. Understand, that only sincere repentance will save your soul and the souls of others who have yet not taken the wrong path."

"Father," politely answered Giordano, "I am ready to admit my mistakes and misconceptions about the dogmas of the church; I regret them. But what harm to the true faith is there in the knowledge of multiple endless worlds and the transmigration of souls? Is not the ascension of Jesus such a transition to another world?"

"Stop, blasphemer! You are either mocking the Holy Inquisition, or are possessed and do not know what you're doing and saying!"

Harsh words were ready to break away from the lips of the fiery Giordano, but the prisoner restrained himself by force of will. "Your Eminence, I humbly appeal to our Holy Father, Pope Clement VIII, with a petition for partial renunciation of my views. I am ready to swear on the Cross that I will never talk about other worlds, but I cannot accept that idea of their existence is a sacrilege and heresy!"

"You are signing your own death warrant," the cardinal whispered with vexation, "Appealing to the Pope, you only aggravate his plight. By sending me to court, the Pope entrusted the purity of faith to his servant, and you trying to shift it back to the pontiff. You probably think that the Pope, as a former lawyer, will mitigate the punishment. On the contrary, as a person with legal training, he would not want to assume responsibility before the church; he prefers capital punishment for heretics to desecration of the faith. Is the example of burning the miller, Mennokkio, less than a year ago not enough for you? The Inquisition initially believed Mennokkio and only ordered him to keep his mouth shut. But would talkers like you keep silence voluntarily?"

Then he added in full voice, "All right, my son. Your request will be transmitted to the Pope, but for the last time in the name of our Holy Church I urge you to renounce your heresy in full and repent."

"That will not happen! I hate hypocrites! I, like Christ, will go to Golgotha protecting the infinite worlds from dissemblers!"

"Take him away!" Bellarmine curtly ordered the guards. "He considers himself like Jesus, God forgive me," the Chief Inquisitor crossed himself, "And instead of love he keeps hatred at his heart."

As prophetically implied by the cardinal, the Pope adopted the position that Giordano Bruno was entirely guilty of heresy. However, as a clever solicitor, to avoid recrimination, the Pope referred the case to the secular authorities for sentencing.

On February 8, 1600, the City Court decided to burn heretic Bruno at the stake if he would not repent and ask for pardon. He was given eight days to reconsider. The fact that the sentence represented the path to apostasy enraged Giordano. Menacingly brandishing his clenched fists, his face disfigured in anger, he shouted,

"You, who deliver the verdict, are more afraid than I, who am sentenced!"

Whispers swept through the hall: the look and words of the rebel were terrifying.

On February 17, a huge crowd gathered in Flower Square, the central market square of Rome. In the center, on a hill, amid the ruins of the Theatre of Pompey was a pillar, surrounded by stacks of logs and brushwood. Giordano was pulled off the wagon and tied to a stake.

"I know as Jesus knew that there are other worlds and that the transition to them is possible. He was not afraid of this transfer," Bruno thought. "Must you die in order to see another world? But it must be a way without pain and suffering. Where is it?" Giordano wanted to shout, "I will follow Jesus, even if he was not a god, but only a clever magician!"

He opened his mouth, but a herald was in advance of him, completing the reading of the verdict, "...the heretic will be burned at the stake after losing the power of speech!"

At these words, the executioner pierced the tongue of the miserable man with an iron pin and, backed by the crowd's screams, lit the kindling...

*J*osh was not sure that he was quite all right. He was breathing frantically, sucking air with sobs; his skin felt burnt and tingled, his tongue seemed swollen and disobedient. "Undoubtedly, Giordano understood with some sort of intuition the principle of parallel worlds, but was he able to make the transition? These feelings are evidence that he was not. Like any die-hard, he was in a special field, such as that created by the Gravichron, but the state of mind should be far from fury of emotions. It must be love, love for the people!"

Father entered his study.

"Illegally immersed?" he asked immediately, "Do not answer until the weakness has gone. I can see for myself. I was also in high school. Here's my coffee, drink it. But let me repeat again many think it is possible that another reality takes over, and the young man disappears. Like you, the missing boys had pure intentions. Now their parents live with Gravichron images instead of children. Think about it – you may leave us with no other way to be with you."

"I actually just finished my homework, Dad..."

"Really? Then finishes the coffee, recover and come to dinner," he left his son alone with his youthful doubts.

Now, after so many trials, Josh realized that it was necessary to climb the scaffold with the person who has a perfectly pure soul and literally embraces the world with love. Well, he, a school student knew such a hero. Bruno also knew him, climbing Golgotha in his footsteps.

"But what about my parents? I feel that they understand me. Father even left me coffee. Of course, I'll be back as a lot of other people already

have in three generations. And if not? What to do? Should I not start the experiment?" Josh was terrified, "Oh, how the parents will grieve! And what if our reality could overpower the ancient one? I will save a person! No common one! Nobody knows such cases, not one person... But all four principals work! Come on then, lets go!

And Josh set up Gravichron on April 3, thirty-three A.D., known to all as the day of the crucifixion...

TRANSACTION

A riot of colors and sounds together with a sense of inexplicable wonder embraces a visitor to the Throne Fair in Paris.

Among this phantasmagoria, Martha's attention was attracted to a modest pink sign over the entrance to a small neat pavilion:

Fun game
"Become a princess!"

How wonderful! In her childhood, it often seemed to her that she had gotten into boarding school by mistake and that noble parents were about to come for her. Then Martha grew up to discover that such fantasies warm up the souls of many orphans. She learned how to deal with these feelings in middle school, but the appeal of the game still fascinated her.

"Come on, let's go!" Martha's girlfriends pulled her towards bigger attractions, tempting them with colorful posters. But, this simple sign seemed like an invitation specifically created for her, and the girl, rejecting the other proposals, pushed open the white plastic door with its little bell, and stepped over the threshold.

The room smelled sweet of lilacs, whose bushes were depicted on the wallpaper. Fields and meadows lay behind them, and in the distance, on a hill stood a castle. A wedding procession stretched along the road from the castle gate to the foot of the hill.

An aged man, with a gray mane, wearing a thick brown sweater and beige trousers, ironed carefully as if for a diplomatic reception, stepped towards the girl, smiling affably.

"Welcome to our game! In no other place will you find such a sophisticated computer program that compares two personalities bit by bit – yours and a selected character. You travel through time, and there is an exchange – a transaction: for a short while, you become the hero of the plot, and she – becomes you. At the end of each session, you can wake up and chose a new personality. And so on – as long as you do not get bored or you do not run out of money.

"I have no money, only a ticket to the fair. How many turns do I get?"

"Three, if you want to use them all."

"Follow me!" a majordomo in red livery pronounced, "The test will start tomorrow morning, but for now, by order of the Queen, you need to rest from your trip. I'll show you to the guest bedroom."

Martha timidly trotted behind the tall man down a corridor dimly lit by flames of a few sparse torches. The sharp shadows from massively framed paintings and from statues along the walls frightened her. Where had she come; where was she going? Maybe it was a trap, where lusty libertines or sadists were waiting for her?

But eventually, a door opened, and Martha entered a large room. Against the wall stood a wide bed with a canopy and a pile of duvets.

"Located conveniently, my fair lady. The better your rest, the more easily will you prove your noble birth, and the sooner I'll call you Your Highness! Good night!"

For a short while, Martha tossed about on the lovely feather bed, but nothing could prevent her from curling up and sleeping in anticipation of further adventures.

"Did you enjoy the journey into a fairy tale?" the owner of the attraction asked her.

"Yes, very much!" Martha replied. "Everything was so real! Only it seemed to me that this journey was for little girls and not for Lyceum graduates. And one more question: was I supposed to feel a pea, or was that a different tale?

"Of course, that's the one! It's just not your character. Will you try again?

"Yes, of course, but… May I have more romance?"

"Ah!" Martha suddenly woke up from a light kiss. She opened her eyes to see a young man bending over her. For the long tresses falling over his shoulders, his beard and mustache, the girl suspected that he might be a musician in a rock band, if it were not for his gold-embroidered waistcoat and his sword, adorned with precious stones. Martha sat up in bed in surprise to find that she had been sleeping in a crystal coffin in the middle of a great hall.

"Will you be my wife?" the prince proposed, gazing at her with his beautiful blue eyes.

"Yes," Martha replied simply.

Immediately fanfares blew, violins and harps began to play. The doors of the hall opened and, to the sounds of music, courtiers, brandishing bouquets of flowers, rushed to congratulate the happy couple. Prince again clung to her lips, and at that moment, Martha woke up in the room with lilac on the wallpaper.

"Is it the end of the session? It all started so well! Am I not fit for the role of the princess?"

"I cannot know this. The computer decides who best fits the character in this situation."

"Well, I still have the last turn... But please, more thrills! For adults!"

One could feel the speed even within this luxury limousine. Through the tinted glass could be seen the flashing lights of Paris. There was the light smell of cigars and brandy. Manly hands caressed her. Yes, yes! This was not a children's fairy-tale prince! But, what was that flash? One more, like lightning! A loud blow sounded like a gong, the ringing of shattered glass, the grating of gnarled metal. The space fills with the cry: "Dee-ah-nah!" and all is plunged into darkness.

Martha opens her eyes and takes a few steps. The owner of the attraction bows his head in respect. In front of him – still the same charming stranger, but something has subtly changed in her appearance: a statuesque posture, a proud poise, an intelligent and powerful gaze.

"Thank you, counselor. Your work will be appreciated," Martha says with a confident tone.

"Thank you, Your Royal Highness. The limousine is at your service. It will drive you to Orly airport. A private flight Paris – Riyadh. Your companion-elect will soon join you...

Without turning around, the princess leaves the room. The bell rings farewell. The attraction sign, obeying electronics, changes slightly. Now blue letters attract the candidates:

Fun game
"Become a prince!"

PROVING GROUNDS

The path winding along the brink of the mountain plateau was interrupted at places where the chunks of rock were split off the edge of the cliff. A couple of hundred meters down lay uprooted charred trees and bushes. Here and there among them could be seen trucks and excavators thrown about like toys, plus... something else – huge, steel.

"Here it is – the Devil's pit!" Nils thought.

People in the village said that this restricted zone had apatite mines, but all the old-timers were perfectly well aware that no zone was closed because of apatite. "Without a doubt, the war-dogs are trying out new weapons," was the general verdict, but in these northern areas lived silent people who did not like to wag their tongues in vain.

For Nils, no restricted zones existed in his native lands. His experience as a forester brought him to animal trails invisible to prying eyes. Having decided to explore the site, Nils skirted it from the north and came down to it through the rocky spurs of the Khibiny Mountains, from the side where no one would expect a man to appear.

The closer the forester came to the pit, the stronger the smell of burning. The rock underfoot also bore traces of fresh fire. Nils sniffed at a palmful of earth: it smelled of cinders mixed with some unfamiliar chemical. Rex also sniffed, to keep him company, but sneezed and turned away: chemical analysis was not a business for the respectful hunting dog. But, he, like his master, did not like this rock. Its blackened areas forced the dog to turn his wet nose away from the slippery stones. Nils wondered: the rock's edge shone, as if melted with... definitely not forest fire.

Landslides and forest fires were common things. In these mountains, the forester had seen earthquakes, inextinguishable wildfire, avalanches covering villages, and even volcanic eruptions. Yet, it was not the extent of the phenomenon that usually interested him, but the reason behind it. Nils had heard about recent tremors from seismologists; the split off rocks also supported the idea of an earthquake. But, what about the charred forest and burnt rocks? "The fire came from the lightning, and it could have started much earlier than the quake, while the melted rock suggests a fireball or meteorite. Or… a secret weapon. What else? Perhaps it would be good to walk along the whole rock fall area of the cliff, to see if there is any easy descent."

Forester took out an empty red tin candy box with shabby, golden letters "Red October", put in it samples of sludge and melted rock, slipped it back into the backpack, and started to search for a gentle descent. As his heavy boots slipped on a rock, he was glad he had brought along his alpenstock. Even Rex was breathing heavily, thrusting out his wet pink tongue, although he had no problems with climbing. He had grown up in the mountains and never questioned the routes of his leader. Only a family of red squirrels squeaked and chattered loudly in the charred pine branches, stealing doggy's attention.

"Leave them! Come on!" Nils said.

Rex, as always, agreed with his owner, and they began their descent, clinging carefully to every little irregularity of the surface.

"A-1, respond!" B-2, the navigator of the patrol boat, persistently repeated into the microphone, calling the captain, but there still was no response.

The planetary module with four scouts on board lost its connection soon after it discovered signs of nuclear testing on the third planet of the Solar system and started landing to take a sample of the planet's intellect. Usually this process took place by tacit approval: in the induced psycho-field, the consciousness of a thinking aborigine was exchanged with the consciousness of the first available local animal. The animal was then freely exported from the planet, without openly breaking any intergalactic laws, while another mad being was left on the planet.

B-2 was trying to guess the reason for the long silence. The beacon signal indicated that the module systems were functioning normally. Therefore, the problem was within the team itself.

"Very, very sorry!" calmly and prudently, as befitted a Space Marine, thought the navigator.

J ust when Nils had found a suitable slope, the clouds over the forest thickened and a thin prickly rain began to drizzle. "If it increases, it will be necessary, perhaps, to get out of this pit," decided the forester, but on the way down, they encountered a surprise – an entrance to a cave. "We can take shelter here!" Nils cheered up, boldly stepping into the darkness.

His torch lit a narrow tunnel leading deep into the rock. Nils carefully squeezed himself between the rocks and found himself in a small underground grotto, with a pool of dark water at its base. Rex, sniffing the shore, gladly began to lap from the tiny lake, while Nils began exploring the walls and vaulted ceiling. Suddenly a rumble came out of the entrails of the earth, and sand and pebbles showered on the forester from the ceiling.

"Rex come back now!" the man ordered.

The beam from his flashlight suddenly darted up and down the wall, drawing a wave, as if from a giant seismograph. The rocky walls jolted, crunched, grated, and within moments, the narrow entrance to the cave, covered with stones, ceased to exist. Now a convenient shelter from the rain had become a trap. Rex howled, and his master began stroking him, trying to reassure not only his dog, but also himself. He had, without panicking, to think over the situation, in which neither man nor dog could stay calm.

A-1, the captain, tried to pull the team out of their despondency. "Yes, the situation is non-standard, and we have to rely solely on ourselves. But, this is no reason for despair. We'll find a way to return to the ship and our former bodies! The air is fine, there are nutrients in excess, the gravity is suitable – so everything is in favor of survival," he said cheerfully. "And reproduction," he wanted very much to add, but he understood firstly what caused such thoughts, and secondly, did not want to offend this teammate, at whom he was already looking not as a comrade, but with an almost animal lust.

C-3, flight engineer, looked at A-1 in surprise, "And how are you going to restore the status quo?" he asked sarcastically, adding, "And with what?"

C-3 could barely restrain himself from pointing to new parts of his body: he was not sure what they were and also did not want to be rude.

D-4, the xenobiologist, made her proposal,

"First, we need to examine our new opportunities and understand how and with what we might open the module and get in."

"I totally agree!" captain supported her. He really wanted to start examining these possibilities with her as soon as possible.

"Yes, supposing that something in the module is still unbroken. Based on how these beast-rodents in our bodies are flying and breaking everything in the control room, we'll have no such luck," the intern, E-5 added.

"We should try to complete our task," the captain said, "Though landing the ship is irrational, our navigator might go for it."

A-1 strongly doubted this, knowing the psychology of his race. But, the new hormones were shaking his mental foundations, so he added philosophically,

"The main thing is to believe in yourself!"

Nils woke up as if he had been kicked. He raised his head and looked all around: it was the same dark cave. However, now it was filled with odors and sounds. Many shades – from the subtle scents of clay, sand, and water to strong, penetrating aromas of plants and rodents seeping through the rock fall from outside. A symphony of sounds struck him with a scale of fine rustles, which the forester well understood. Somewhere water was flowing over rocks into a lake, here a mouse was scratching in the ground, and there – his friend was breathing. He could see things much better too. He distinguished a palette of tones and semitones; the varied contours of walls and the water's edge, and... the body of a man lying next to him. "Who's this?" Nils, in horror, jumped to his feet. "Did I become shorter? Rex, to me," he cried and did not recognize his own voice – his throat struggled not to growl or bark. He looked down at his feet and nearly fainted: instead of his heavy forester's boots, his feet were now dog's paws with strong black claws. His body was covered with silvery hair and at the back ended with a quivering tail.

At the sounds of his voice, the sleeping man awoke and, shouting wild syllables, began scraping with his fingernails at fuzzy surface inside the sleeping bag, unable to open its zipper. His mouth opened, the tongue fell out and the eyes rolled, as if in an epileptic fit. Nils, trembling at a frightening thought, ran to the bag and reached out with what supposed to be his right hand; a claw hooked the tag of the zipper opening the bag and releasing the trembling man. What seemed to be a man jumped on all fours, reached Nils' hairy dog muzzle and began with all his might to lick it. Although the loyal nature of Rex had not changed with his new appearance, Nils with horror realized that even to unbutton the backpack and take out cookies and the thermos of hot tea would now be a daunting task for both of them.

"Fuff uh!" Nils howled.

"Auh! Auh! Auh!" Rex echoed.

A-1's body twitched in sweet convulsions. He could not think now of any job, duty, rescue, or heroism. The powerful animal instinct of procreation curbed all attempts of the brain to suppress such reflexes, seemingly so primitive. Now, not sparing anything, he stroked the soft red fur on the back of his lovely girlfriend. The voice of his colleague, xenobiologist D-4, brought him out of nirvana,

"How strange – to be in someone else's skin..."

A-1 just nipped her keen ear. But, the feeling of enjoyment gradually evaporated, replaced by a chill of alarm in the captain's heart:

"Who would have thought that we would take the place of experimental aborigines... If we can stay alive and return home, I certainly will create a League for Defense of Alien Intelligence!"

"First, we must return. And I've got an idea."

"Interesting!" the captain brightened up. He had completely recovered from the animal joy his new body brought him, and again felt himself to be the cold-blooded and calculating researcher.

"I watched the animals... well, you know, in whose bodies we found ourselves. They make enormous leaps from branch to branch, from tree to tree. It seems that they control their flight by manipulating their bushy tails."

"You want to glide to top of the module?

"Logic and reasoning are coming back to you. Yes, absolutely. I do not see any other way to get close to the entrance panel. I can probably engage the emergency airlock chamber opening in flight. But if I crash and cannot enter, you have to jump after me into the chamber. Find your way into the module and disable the psycho-field! That is the only way to recover our bodies, as beings dignified not only with cold reason, but also with warm heart. In fact we are now such things, right?" and she patted the captain on his dark red-brown fur.

"D-4, this is very dangerous, I will not let you!" he said, realizing that it was not a scout's logic, but an earthly creature's emotions talking in him.

"Maybe you're afraid for yourself? Or do you want to wait until the animal instincts overcome us again? Frankly, I would be so desirable to you for only fourteen more local days. Will you order me not to get out of the nest the whole time and take our pleasure?"

"Of course not! But...

"No 'buts', Captain. See you... my love!" and she bravely climbed onto a branch of straight carvel pine from the hollow where she had had this unforgettable night with A-1.

At the ground, right under the tree, glittered their module where several squirrels in the bodies of brave space explorers screamed and thrashed about.

At the same time, another couple of cosmic intelligences had located the two earthlings by their howling and barking behind the rock fall.

"While the captain and xenobiologist are seeking a path to the ship and a way to bring back our bodies, we should try to deliver a terrestrial intellect to the module," said the engineer, C-3.

"You make it sound like something you can influence, being in your new body," said the intern E-5.

"I can try to make contact with a fellow human being."

"In the best case, with a companion in misfortune. Somehow, we did not consider it a fellow when, with no consent, we stuffed the body of an animal with a human consciousness."

"No matter how changed my attitude towards the capture of a terrestrial mind, I'm still doing my job, intern, and I cannot question my orders."

"Does not our own existence in the bodies of local animals speak of the falsity of the chosen approach and the evident injustice?"

"Maybe it does, but we will solve that problem at home, if we get there. Meanwhile, we must pursue our goal and leave development of new strategies to the Council. We can take turns digging a tunnel to the creatures in there; our sharp claws will allow that much."

"And how are you going to communicate with the native? You not afraid of his beast?"

"No, E-5, I have no fear. The animal is now in the human body and it cannot catch us or damage us without human weapons. A man, even in the body of the beast, is reasonable. He would not attack us. Especially when I use my claws to draw geometric shapes and chemical formulas..."

Nils realized that some small creature was digging through the earth in the direction of their cave.

"Perhaps this is a way out," he thought, "At least it's worth a try."

There was no way to teach Rex to remove the debris, for the new forester's "hands" could not carry stones or wield the alpenstock. There was only one way out – to dig a tunnel with his paws. "If someone can get in here, so can we get out of here," thought Nils.

After two hours of work, Nils had dug a small hole. Initially Rex helped him as much he could: he was unable to dig into the hard ground with his fingers, but he could shovel out the material with his hands and reach with his hands into the hole until the passage became too narrow for him.

"To dig a passage large enough for a human, would take a prohibitively long amount of work," thought the forester, "It faster to get myself out and bring some rescuers."

The rustling from outside increased. Nils could not decide what to do about these unwitting assistants. "Let's say it's a mouse," he reasoned, "I could strangle it and even eat it."

But, Nils immediately rejected this image which made him sick.

"On the other hand, I could give Rex a mouse, let him eat it. A decent dinner for a hungry dog, but how will his new organism will take raw meat, especially with fur and guts? Won't he get sick?"

When after another two hours of work the tunnel significantly lengthened, fresh air blew in from it, and the muzzle of a squirrel appeared.

"A draught – it's the way out, and a squirrel – it's food for Rex," finally decided Nils and clamped his canine jaws around the neck of the defenseless animal – just at the moment when C-3 was going to display his knowledge of Pythagorean Theorem.

A-1 gazed sadly at the airlock chamber. His girlfriend was right – a special touch on the external sensors had deployed the emergency mechanism; the entrance to the module now gaped like a black maw embedded in the silver plating. Alas, alongside it spread a band of xenobiologist's red blood. D-4 had been right about that too.

The captain regrouped, sitting on the tip of a branch, ready to soar into the open hatch. He silently repeated the words of farewell from his darling. These has now become a reference point for him, something elevated, and at the same time, as natural as a new understanding of life, love, and self-sacrifice.

The airflow punched him in the face, forcing him to squint for a moment. A-1 pitched his four legs to the sides and swish-glided into the wide-open gateway to the module. His squirrel tail, performing rotational movements independent of the Captain's rational mind, maintained flight stability.

Suddenly, everything around the fearless scout buzzed and rang, and an elastic field surrounding his body seized him. The gravitational shock absorbers of the gateway had engaged, capturing the object which had flown in. Grasping franticly at the surfaces of this invisible environment, the claws and teeth of the squirrel ground down and twisted. A-1 squeaked, whined, moaned, but realized that the landing was successful, and the loss of a couple of teeth and claws counted for nothing. The squirrel's whiskers tipped with drops of blood bristled menacingly. Captain rushed to the psycho-field control panel.

"Hurry, hurry, I must bring back the consciousness of the xenobiologist before it is irretrievably lost in the dying animal!"

PROVING GROUNDS

Nils ran with all the power of the muscular, canine body. Twice he nearly fell off a cliff, and only by clinging heroically with all four paws to the ground and with his teeth to the bushes, saved himself from falling into the pit.

When he got to the edge of the charred crevice where he and Rex had begun their descent, he looked pitiful. "Like a beaten dog," thought Nils and smiled, "And who am I now?"

He could return by a direct, short route. Barbed wire and checkpoints were no hindrance to a dog. Nils had no idea about the reason for his strange metamorphosis, but intuitively understood that if Rex disappeared, then Nils would lose his last chance to return to his former body. He did not like to think about life in his new body.

"To eat leftovers from a bowl? To cover the neighbor's bitch?" It was awful. "To show people that you understand speech? Can read and write? They would immediately give you up for scientific experiments, or even put you in a rocket, like Belka and Strelka – and you vanish into thin air. Better to keep quiet, so as not to land in the knacker's yard."

All of a sudden, a small detachment came out from the trees: two soldiers with their sergeant, and together with them, Stepan – the friend and student of Nils.

"Rex, come to me, buddy!" Stepan patted the dog on his fury head, "See guys, and you did not believe that Nils was in the zone!"

"It would be better not to believe it! All the other people have long since evacuated, and now we climb into hell, looking for a fool to croak together with him!" the sergeant snapped, "The alarm is for 7:00; in five minutes an 'atomic' will explode! Even the concrete for the sarcophagus is ready to deploy! They," he pointed to the sky, "do not give a shit about any of us anyway, and even less if we catch high rads!"

"R-r, bow-wow-wow!" was the reply.

"Look, Rex is offended by you calling his master a fool," sighed Stepan, "Let's follow him. He is a smart dog, he'll brings us to the forester fast enough".

And they raced after Nils, hurrying back to save Rex.

A -1 was slowly making his way along the dimly lit corridor. The weight and size of the squirrel was not enough to automatically switch on the full illumination. But, the sharp eyes of the Captain clearly distinguished the surrounding space from the new and unusual perspective of a small creature. There were gateways to pass, he had to climb up the inner cladding until the sensors detected the presence of a living being and opened the door. However, A-1 was most determined – on his efficiency depended the life of the xenobiologist, whom the fates had decreed to become the Capitan's most cherished being.

"So, right, around the engine, bypass the control cockpit of the ship, to the next compartment of the psycho-field. The main thing is that the terrestrial animals in our bodies do not catch me," he thought, getting closer and closer to the target area. From the cockpit could be heard strange sounds produced by the squirrels dealing with the unfamiliar speech apparatuses of the aliens. Some of them ran around the cabin; others gnawed objects at hand. The floor and chairs were covered with filth.

In the psycho-field control compartment, all was quiet. Fortunately, the animals had not yet gotten there. A-1 scrambled onto the control panel and, jumping from key to key, began to turn on a system of reverse transition of animals into humans. He knew that misfortune had befallen the team, which was associated with an underground nuclear explosion and a complex interplay of fields. Now, he had to quickly get out of captivity and think about this new phenomenon. "Even without the seizure of the earthly intellect, we have discovered so many new things," thought the captain, "In physics, ethics, and emotions! Faster – into orbit and – home!"

The buzz of the aggregates was becoming more intense, when suddenly, the door of the compartment rapidly opened. The large body of the "brutalized" Space Marine, which A-1 recognized as his own, darted inside with a long howl. Evading pursuit, A-1 jumped to the side, the carcass after him – he lapped straight up, but the pursuer reached out the clutching hands of a madman and firmly grasped the twitching body of the

Captain. The forces were unequal, and A-1 froze with horror, now the teeth of a monster sank into his defenseless flesh... The animal sniffling, smelled him, and... the commander now realized that he held a small dark red-brown furry animal in his hands.

"Got it!" A-1 issued an exultant cry, not typical for unfeeling aliens, and, despite the growing rumble and shudder emerging from the earth, rushed into the cabin.

There, amid the devastation and unbearable stench, engineer C-3 was already engaging the engines of the module, the intern E-5 radioed into orbit, and xenobiologist D-4 silently gazed at the captain. Her eyes shone with new feelings – joy and love...

WORD OF HONOR

Quietly walking through the dark corridors of the Kremlin, the spy of Ivan the Terrible passed chambers, stopping and listening at every door. The Tsar should know everything: who is quietly breathing, and who is tossed by dream; who is whoring, and who is praying. Strength... it always comes from knowing things.

Behind Prince Ivan's door, a woman's voice was heard. It was Glashka, the chambermaid girl reading aloud. And reading what – a fairy tale! That's a laugh – next morning the heir is going to choose his bride, and the night before he amuses himself by fairy tales.

The girl was reading, "And the king ordered his sons to loose arrows – to learn their fate – at whichever house your arrow falls, there you will have to ask a maiden in marriage. The Tsar's son, Ivan, released his golden arrow, and that arrow fell into a swamp. Ivan rode up and saw that a marsh frog was holding his arrow. Prince Ivan was about to flee and abandon it, but the frog said to him in a human voice, "Croac-Croac, Prince Ivan! Come to me, kiss me and take me as your wife."

Saddened, Ivan answered the frog, "How can I take you as my wife? People will laugh at me!"

"You speak to them in your wise speeches; you do your good deeds, and they will follow you. In the meantime, keep your word to the Tsar."

Glashka noticed that the Prince had begun to snore and stopped her reading. Ivan was in a deep sleep. "God be with you!" she made the sign of the cross over her master and blew out the candle.

A breeze from the fields wafted fresh spring smells of awakening nature. The dirty snow was beginning to fade away and the first snowdrops decorated the thawed dark earth with their humble bells. Ivan, wearing only a quilted caftan and a sable rimmed hat, was sitting on a horse in the middle of the yard, testing the string of a heavy, gold bow. It looked as if his father was having a good laugh at his expense, by ordering him, as in the fairy tale, to loose the golden arrow, which would then point to his bride. No, Ivan could hardly believe these words, as they did not seem like the iron mandate of his father, Ivan the Terrible.

Today at noon there would be a parade of brides in Byzantine style. Again, from the Greeks. Sure – the Third Rome, aren't we! Today countless beauties will be brought to the capital city from all over Russia: each father wants to jump from nobleman to boyar. The Tsar would choose wives – for himself and for his son Ivan. With the younger, Feodor, quiet and pious, everything was simple: to whomever Tsar Ivan had nodded, she became his wife. But, with the older son, Ivan, there were only troubles – for the son tried to do everything his own way.

"Oh, no good will come of this arrow-guessing!" thought Ivan, but he did not dare to contradict the Tsar. He too well knew his father's temper. Sometimes, the Prince got not just the curses, but also a battering with the king's long staff. Didn't his father force his wives to take orders for their infertility – first Evdokia, then Praskovya – sending them to a distant nunnery in Suzdal? No matter how much Ivan grieved, how much he begged his father, nothing helped. Glashka, the youth that bathed and massaged him, had let slip that the king-father got rid of his young daughters-in-law not by chance... but was it possible to pronounce such words?

"Shut up, you fool, somebody will hear, report to the Tsar, and you won't ever see the light of day. Or even worse, on one evil day, the Tsar's trappers and horsemen will use you and then strangle you, God forbid..."

Ivan crossed himself in response to these sorrowful thoughts; he had not heard, as one archer whispered to another, "And indeed, there is no comparison to his father, Tsar Ivan the Terrible. The Prince is fit to hold not a bow, but a pen – to write 'The Lives of the Saints'[1]." – "Ah, our fate is bitter: Ivan Ivanovich is a hack writer, an ink-stainer; and Feodor Ivanovich, it's even worse – quite weak in his mind, he can only make bows to the Saints in the cathedrals!"

"Z-z-z!" whistled a golden arrow as it flew away towards the Devil's Ravine[2] and the Goat's Swamp[2].

"Moskva!" Ivan shouted the battle cry of the Moscovites, and spurring his horse, rushed in search of his arrow.

Clods of earth flew from under the hooves of his raven black stallion, as cries of alarm rose behind him. His bodyguards, hard put to keep up, cursed the impetuosity of the Prince.

The Bells of the great Cathedral of the Dormition, sanctified one hundred and one years before, tolled the matins.

The landing was forced. To repair their starship, they required the heavy, yellow metal that was considered precious and called gold on this planet. In the dark, it would be easy to collect it by hovering over the gilded domes of the cathedrals. The Commander would have done so, if the ship had not lost its maneuverability. By dawn, the xenobiologist was prepared to take control of the first aborigine to appear and use him to obtain the necessary gold. In order not to scare the humans, the astronaut had disguised their ship as a huge tree stump, and themselves as small amphibians, inhabiting this swamp. Croaking from time to time, they enjoyed themselves in this natural environment, soaking up the flavors of spring through their greenish pseudoskin. Even here, the Commander,

---

[1] – He wrote in 1579 the "Life of Saint Anthony of Siya" as well as the music to accompany it.
[2] – Chertolsky (Devil's) Ravine and Koz'e (Goat) Swamp existed in the 16th century near the Kremlin

distinguished from others by his large size, had comfortably installed himself on a hammock to bask in the gentle sun. Nobody expected new trouble: a flying object, made precisely of the metal so desired by the scouts, dropped from the heavens and pinned their commander to the ground.

"Oh, you poor creature," Ivan uttered, riding up to the great marsh frog who was plaintively jerking her legs in a vain attempt to get rid of his golden arrow, "Look, what trouble has happened to you! Thank God, the arrow did not accidentally hit a bride! Beauties come to the Kremlin, and the royal scion is fooling around with arrows! Was that not what my father was planning by ordering me to shot? Not easy then to implore forgiveness of God and Orthodox people for such a sin!

Reflecting on God's will and the royal guile, Ivan dismounted, squatted, and carefully, to avoid hurting a living creature, pulled the arrow out of the ground. The Frog stirred weakly. Then, he noticed that its small children were leaping as fast as they could toward a big stump in the swamp. Only one brave little frog climbed onto one of the Prince's morocco boots and looked at its parent with his clever, small eyes.

"Every creature of God has its own understanding!" Ivan thought, and looked into the eyes of the little frog. At that very moment, a whirlwind swept through the head of the Prince, and he heard a gentle, girlish voice,

"Help me, Ivan! That is not a swamp frog you shot, but the bewitched king from far over the seas. It is not an unreasonable, little frog who asks you, but the disconsolate daughter of the king..."

"Are you Vasilisa, or what?"

"Yes, Vasilisa!"

"Keep off me," Ivan thrice crossed himself, lightening-stricken by the talking frog and its story, so familiar from his childhood.

"Do not worry, dear Prince, we are not devils or demons; we are indeed like you, God's creatures. Help my father, and I swear I will repay your kindness. I know thy sorrow: be it unto thee today – the wife, not writ but welcomed, and she will bring you the long-awaited heir."

247

"What should I do, Vasilisa?" the Prince asked, losing all remnants of his will.

"First of all, cut off the arrowhead and free the king."

Ivan drew his sword from its sheath, deftly cut the soft metal and carefully released the large frog.

"Wait," Vasilisa said, "Do not throw away the pieces of the arrow. Take them with my father to the big stump."

Ivan, as in a dream, obeyed the orders of the little frog.

"And now – let's go get you married!" Vasilisa ordered. "Put me in your bosom, and listen to my advice. You aren't afraid to have a frog on your breast, then?"

"Don't I need to first kiss you?" the Prince asked timidly.

"You're a good man, Ivan, but I am still an amphibian," Vasilisa sighed. "You never know, we might kiss the bride together..."

Ivan jumped on his horse and headed back towards the Kremlin, just as the archers of his guard were galloping towards him.

"How lucky I am, that they did not see the frogs," the Prince thought, trying to comprehend the miracle which had happened to him. He could hear voices in his head. He heard the faithful Vasilisa protesting, while the other frogs stubbornly insisted, "Leave Ivan to himself and come back now! Don't wait, or the process becomes irreversible. Your mind will merge inseparably with the consciousness of this savage."

"But I gave my word of honor to the Prince. And I'm certainly going to keep it!"

A light, fragrant mist of incense drifted throughout the Cathedral of Dormition. The review of brides had already begun here, during the service of the sixth hour, ahead of the official ceremony. Rarely had so many beauties gassed a prayerfully into the all-seeing eyes of the holy icons. The Tsar together with his sons, court nobles, governors, and other courtiers began to appraise the best samples of the Russian women's beauty, charm, and grace.

"If the happiness of love is not written in the stars for me, then let me at least enjoy the pleasure of possession," Ivan, the Tsar of All Russia thought gloomily fixing his eyes on one girl after another.

Among the beauties, he had already noticed the daughter of his advisor, Feodor Nagoy[3].

"Oh, Maria, you'll be good, naked," he laughed at his own joke, "And the family is certainly coming from a long line of court nobility. With my son Feodor – everything was simple: he did not even need to look at row of brides. I took for him Irina Godunova, sister of my personal meat carver, Boris Godunov. Boris, Skuratov's[4] son-in-law, is still a faithful dog since Oprichnina. And if I also make him a boyar, then he will be completely ours, giblets and all. But, with Ivan, we always cross swords. He just cannot forgive me forcing his wives to take the veil. His wife's womb is dearer to him than the royal father's will! I shall hammer this son of a bitch!" The knuckles of the Tsar turned white as his staff shuddered convulsively in his clenched fist.

Prince Ivan stood a little way from the Tsar. His right hand fumbled sometimes in his bosom, as if he were scratching his armpit or trying to calm a chest pain.

"Unbecoming behavior," the king thought, looking at his son, "the ambassadors will be gossiping about that later."

Meanwhile, Vasilisa, like an experienced matchmaker, knowing all the brides without exception, broadcasted to Ivan,

"This one has only wealth in her head. That one, just dreams of being the queen. The one next to her came at the behest of her father to make him a boyar. But, wait, wait, this one is just for you. She likes you, and she wants to give you a son. She does not think about wealth and does not

---

[3] – The word 'nagoy' (masc.) and "nagaya" (fem.) in Russian means 'nude'.
[4] – Malyuta (Gregory) Skuratov-Belsky – head of the secret service Oprichnina.

serve her father. She has been an orphan for three years already: Governor Sheremet lost his head fighting at the walls Revel; her uncles are disgraced, so she is looking for your support as husband and master.

"How do I...?" Ivan started asking.

"Think, think! Do not speak aloud," Vasilisa snapped at him.

Ivan had already realized that he could talk to the little frog without speech, but he was not yet accustomed to this strange way of communication. Moreover, he had never, as yet, had such a wise counselor.

In the chambers of the Kremlin, Ivan approached his father. He looked at his son with a smirk, and raising his left eyebrow, sneered,

"Well, where's your arrow, Ivan? Did it find a 'red maiden' for a 'good fellow'?"

"It vanished in the swamp, sire."

Catching his father's mood, Feodor chuckled, "He was not looking for it: drank vodka, became a 'red-faced fellow' and went to the 'good maidens'."

"Ah, poor fellow, tsk-tsk-tsk!" the Tsar feigned pity for Prince Ivan, shaking his head and tut-tutting with his tongue in the Tatar fashion.

Then, to his father's surprise, the son deftly countered, saying:

"Poor in Bulgar is 'sheremet'. So permit me, Father, as you just suggested, to bestow my kerchief and ring upon Elena Sheremeteva, my chosen bride."

"What Sheremeteva? Elena? Daughter of Ivan? Do you know that all her breed are disgusting to me? All her uncles are traitors and devil's spawn."

"Her father was faithful to you, and she will be faithful to me! And she will bring me a son in less than a year," Ivan blurted following Vasilisa's tip.

The king scowled, thinking, "Ivan always wants everything his own way. My seed! We even like similar women. He has yet to understand, the little brat, that while the kingdom is mine, all the people, and their flesh, and their entrails are mine. Both men and women, serfs to nobles. And whosoever will choose to resist me, as Kolychev[5] did, shall follow his soul into the sky. I am their father and judge on Earth!"

"Well, Ivan," responded the Tsar, "I will not give you reason for complaint. Be it as you wish! But keep your word. If you do not make that young woman's belly grow, she goes to a nunnery. Mark my words!"

At a sign from the Tsar, the musicians began to play, the choir to sing, and a series of beautiful women sailed by Ivan Vasilyevich and his retinue, although the fate of the procession was already foregone.

The day was dawning. In the peace and quiet of the early morning, Ivan rose to learn marvelous things from Vasilisa. The Little Frog had long left the Prince, initially settled under the bed, and then completely disappeared, while Vasilisa remained to live in the Prince's head. She was now a kind of thought which guarded Ivan day and night, advised him, and trained him in all ways. Several times, he heard the voices of other little frogs persistently calling Ivan's friend to get back to the ship. "What ship are they talking about?" the Prince thought in surprise, but he realized that they were calling not him, but her, to sail to faraway lands. Once, there was even the voice of her father, the bullfrog,

"Xenobiologist, I understand your honesty and dedication to the idea. And I am immensely grateful for my rescue, but I have to continue our expedition. The only thing that I can do to help – is to leave a robot-conservator of the genetics and to call rescuers to this orbit."

Ivan understood almost nothing of this speech.

"Who is it – 'Xenia Biolog'?" he asked Vasilisa. "Sophia Paleolog[6]

---

[5] – Fyodor Kolychev – Metropolitan Philip II. Deprived of his rank, exiled in Tver and there, in a monastery, strangled by Skuratov on the order of Ivan the Terrible.
[6] – Daughter of the last emperor of Byzantium, the wife of Tsar Ivan III the Great, the mother of Vasily III, grandmother of Ivan IV the Terrible.

was my great-grandmother. Father keeps her library and sometimes allows us to flip through the ancient scrolls and papyruses... And you, planning to go? Will you abandon me?"

"Do not worry, Ivan, I'll never leave you. I can't, even if I wanted to. I share with you the single body now. I'll explain the different words and I'll help you to read the manuscripts."

"Vasilisa is my guardian angel!" thought Ivan. "The wondrous miracle and a fount of wisdom."

Ivan's speeches in the Duma earned him recognition. The people listened without smirks, not like before – "just blub, Ivan-the-fool" – but nodding their approval. Increasingly, the court noblemen sought his advice, to the displeasure of the Tsar. But, the knowledge was the least of the Prince's transformation. He became softer, kinder; he stopped attending interrogations and tortures. Vasilisa had taught him how to love his wife with unearthly love, and Elena, as if she had drunk a love potion, showered her husband with love and conceived on the first night of their nuptials.

"I am the happiest person in the world," Ivan thought, "I have both Elena-the-Beautiful and Vasilisa-the-Wise!"

Tsar Ivan felt that his son irritated him more and more with his wisdom, coming from nowhere, and growing influence. Everyone praised the heir as if the Tsar's hours were already numbered. The new Tsarina became no joy to him, and he put her out of sight, threatening to send her to Uglich if she made so much as a squeak. His eyes strayed increasingly often to the pregnant Elena. His son had kept his word, and the Tsar could not find any pretense to impose his desires onto his daughter-in-law. The spies reported that the Prince often left his wife and went to sit in the living room, even before dawn, but what he was doing there was unknown.

"It's clear what – he is plotting treason!" Ivan the Terrible thought, "Just listen to his speeches! Even the words he uses!"

Just the night before, in the Alexandrov Kremlin – the Tsar's country estate, the former capital of the Oprichnina – the Military Council was debating whether to go for a truce with Sweden and a respite in the damned Livonian war[7].

Then, the Prince dared to accuse his father, "Had the Tsar of Russia more tolerance for the Catholic faith, I, and not Stephan Batoriy[8] – our foe – would have been sitting on the Polish throne for five years already. And with Allied Poland, the Baltic Sea would have been ours long ago. And we would have beaten the Khans together!"

"O, you think yourself clever, to argue retroactively! Where was your mind when Stephen studied at the University? Or maybe you can boast of your military victories?"

The Prince wanted to protest, but Vasilisa did not let him, and told him to keep his eyes down. But it was too late. The Tsar hid his anger, looking like a vulture.

Early in the morning, when Ivan left the bedchamber for the hall, the king, dragging his feet, leaning on a stick and grunting with every step from the pain in his spine and all his joints, climbed up to the chamber adjacent to the bedroom of the young couple. Suddenly, Elena came out towards him wearing only her camisole, revealing her heavy breasts, already prepared for feeding. Ivan the Terrible, extremely excited, as he always was when preparing to attack his victim, roared at his daughter-in-law,

"How dare you, shameless! I'll give you a stick! But which? This one?" King grabbed his hill-standing robe, "Or this?" he shook his oak staff, which often battered his family and servants.

"My father, Ivan Vasilyevich, have mercy! I did not expect or know... Not in soul, nor in mind!"

"On your knees, whore!" Ivan lashed her belly with the thin end of his staff."

---

[7] – The war of 1558-1583 with the Nordic countries and the Commonwealth exhausted Russia

[8] – The Prince of Transylvania was elected King of Poland in 1575, graduated from the University of Padua, and achieved significant victories in the Livonian War.

Elena howled in pain and threw herself at the feet of her rabid father-in-law. "Not like that, you fool! With your back! And lift up your shirt!" the Tsar wheezed, continuing to strike the flanks of the unfortunate woman.

Not realizing what she was doing, Elena pulled the hem of her shirt over her head, trying to protect herself from the blows hailed down on her. At the view of her bare flesh, the Tsar went completely mad. Due to the stiffness and severe pain throughout his body, he was unable to get down on the floor and master this wanton, godless yet so desirable of a woman. With his left hand, he furiously jerked his genitals, ready to burst from the strain, and with his right, smashed the sleek body that hid in the depths of her womb; another future contender for the royal throne. His throne!

The cries of the suffering woman became a prolonged howl. Suddenly, the door burst open and Prince Ivan broke into the chamber.

"Stop, Father, for Christ's sake, please! Do not be a beast!" he cried in horror at the scene before his eyes.

With one leap, he wedged himself into the space between his wife and a mad creature that he could not consider, at this moment, a human, much less his father. But, his veneration of royal power did not allow him to strike the lecherous old man. He only tried to protect the body of his wife and their unborn child. Elena's belly, covered with purple welts, started to move, like dough in the hands of an invisible baker, and streams of blood, diluted with water, poured onto the floor from under the legs curled against her abdomen. The bestial roar of the autocrat reached its climax. Swinging with all his power, he hit the left temple of Prince Ivan with the knob of his staff. A crackle of broken bones, familiar to both, sounded, and the Prince, with a short groan, fell prostrate on the floor on top of the body of his wife. An expression of annoyance appeared on his face, like in a child who, given a new coveted toy, unexpectedly had the gift withdrawn. Perhaps this plaintive appearance of the son roused in the soul of his father the last remnants of human sense. Ivan the Terrible threw aside his weapon of punishment, and overcome with the pain wracking his body, lowered himself to the floor beside the motionless Prince. A tear flowed from his twitching, senile eye and slipped down alongside his long, hooked nose to the gray beard, with remnants of red hair.

"My son, my flesh," he whispered in a broken voice, "God knows I did not want to..."

With a still powerful, but trembling hand, he touched the face of Ivan, pale as chalk.

Thick, dark blood mixed with a strange, greenish liquid that was leaking from the wound on his temple.

"Is this your new mind that comes out?" the king was astonished.

He had watched thousands of tortures and executions, but had never encountered such a thing.

"And you still did not consider me a human," the Tsar said resentfully.

The Prince opened his eyes,

"Farewell, father. I forgive you..." he managed to say with his last effort.

At this moment, the window of the chamber swung open, and a white dove flew into the room on a stream of cold air. Expertly, without any bird-like bustling, he landed near the bodies of the Prince and Princess.

"The Holy Spirit has descended," the Tsar thought in awe.

The pigeon, mincing forward, approached the puddles. With straw jutted from his beak, he picked up a fraction of the blood from each puddle, and then a little bit of green liquid.

"It's not an angel but a demon," Ivan Vasilyevich thought, "But who will distinguish that for sure? Save us and have mercy on us! No more will I set foot in this damned estate!"

He went about quickly calling for doctors and servants, again giving countless orders, and making sure they were followed to their execution. A new day had started.

Meanwhile, the white dove had completed his job, spread his wings, fluttered to the window, and rose into the gloomy, November sky until he completely disappeared from sight.

LUCK'S DESCENT

"Hurry, hurry! Stop your goddamn incessant manicuring!" Commander Com implored his wife Maxi, his only help, the astronaut-researcher, and – most importantly – the Maximizer of their mission.

The landing on a giant planet where they intended to restock halogens for the spaceship's engine had turned into a mishap: the combined thoughts and desires of intelligent beings inhabiting the planet had created a completely unforeseen factor of influence on the spaceship's movements. The halogen reserves necessary for sintronium oxidation were melting away, the vehicle's engine was losing power, and a few more minutes would prove to be or not to be a catastrophe.

"Now my old air pilot skills should come in handy," Com thought feverishly, managing, by some automaticity retained from youth, to control the descent of the ship. Notwithstanding his maneuvers, Maxi remained the commander's main hope at this critical juncture: the Maximizer, capable of optimizing the interaction between psychofields and matter, could significantly increase the chances for their success.

"Will we make it?" he asked his steadfast companion.

"As always!" Maxi assured him, trying to find loopholes in the planet's psychofield and tacking to bring the ship to a soft landing unscathed.

The alarm roared for the last time and died on a high note, shut off by Com's firm hand – he had to save every quantum of energy. Meanwhile, Maxi had already been "seeing" the optimal trajectory, so she stepped into the management of the landing with no hesitation.

The picture of continents and oceans on the screen gave way to a view of a huge landmass. The lights in the cabin flickered and went out. Only the plasma flashes on the protective shell illuminated the tense faces of the explorers.

"Away from that big city!"

The surface of the planet approached inexorably. Their speed was still dangerously high. In the best case, impact threatened the ship's hull. And this would lead to inevitable and unwanted contact with the local civilization.

Com mashed down all the controls to the max. The ship, obeying orders, dropped its speed in a last effort and, through a huge gap, smoothly entered a colossal hangar. The flight ended with creaking and screeching in a giant depot filled (oh, horror!) with haphazardly bulked metal objects but also... (thanks to Maximizer!) with cushioning stuff.

The Astronauts embraced: operating in tandem had once again allowed them to escape, with honor, all sorts of scrapes. However, the ship...! Its body – scorched, covered with carbon deposits and crumpled during landing – had come to rest on a flat, albeit pitted with irregularities, cellulose surface. Marked with multicolored geometric shapes, this area resembled an airfield around which in various rigid poses stood colossal robots, each as large as a spacecraft.

"Maxi, they may become our allies! If we make them move, these titans should be able to transport the ship to a safe place and straighten its stabilizers."

"And I believe – the mechanical part is the most simple. It seems that my optimization on this planet is just beginning, but I hope it will take us to the finish line!"

"Let's initiate our antigravs and fly. You take over this android type robot, and I shall occupy that furry monster. We can always communicate on the π-wave!"

J ames pulled up alongside a neat house, entering the parking lot with the lop-sided sign "Customers only" on the fence. As long as he could remember, Mrs. Tuff's pharmacy had been a meeting place for lovers of a tasty breakfast with the gourmet home-brewed coffee for which the shop was famous, even before countless machines captured the coffee business. Large jars filled with amazing candy and chocolates, several stands holding books and comics, and a discounted toy section had long attracted children here. Rarely did a customer leave the shop empty-handed after digging into its treasures.

Jane's car was already there in the lot. They'd agreed to meet and have coffee before going to court where, today, they would have their divorce case hearing. Despite the peaceful nature of the process, the two parties were far from relaxed. Anyway, James could not forgive himself for not leaving as soon as he learned about Jane and Mitchell's affair. Yet, was there really anything to regret? When she confessed that Dory was not his daughter, the situation became unbearable... Moreover, circumstances now allowed him to live independently of his wife's income, and even "nobly" to repay her the cost of his college education.

"Hi, James!" Mrs. Tuff called him, looking like a strict teacher over her spectacles. "Meeting with the family in our pharmacy always benefits your health," she recited the old motto of her establishment.

The meeting indeed looked like a family breakfast. Jane came not alone, but with her father, who, after retirement, devoted himself entirely to his daughter. Well, tribute must be paid to old Ted. His support was not superfluous at all. In a result of her "game", Jane had lost both her men; not to mention, the fate of small Dory would be decided tomorrow in the operating room.

James felt uncomfortable about this situation, prudently trying to avoid it after all those nasty and stupid things that he'd rattled off in fits of anger to his wife. Dealing with his son, Dick, had been easier, but after the father left the household, the boy started to cast angry looks at him. Was that really what James had once expected from his marriage?

The Participants in the parley exchanged greetings reservedly. The aroma of coffee already tickled their nostrils. However, it mingled oddly with the faint smell of something burnt, not typical for the cozy shop.

"Are the coffee beans scorched, Mrs. Tuff?" James asked.

"Do not offend me, son. Since when have I forgotten how to make coffee? I think someone is burning leaves outside. I should not have kept all the windows open when I unlocked the pharmacy this morning."

Reasoning thus, Mrs. Tuff deftly swooped up cups of coffee, a milk jug, and a sugar bowl from an antique tray and arranged them on the small table at which the guests had settled in the corner of the shop.

"I won't create any problem for you," James said quietly when the hostess had walked away to the register. "I promise. You'll get the divorce with visitation schedule as you want; have it your way. I also agree to reasonable child support – you know my income. But if you insist on wild amounts, we will get into an expensive and unnecessary litigation."

"I won't, don't worry," Jane sipped aromatic coffee. "Take the children..." she paused, "Whenever you can. But if they want to visit you together, do not refuse them."

She looked right into James's eyes and for a moment, he felt something very familiar and elusively warm in those once beloved green whirlpools.

It was a good idea to meet in a neutral territory where everything, even the bitterness of the gourmet coffee, helped mask the bitterness in one's soul.

"Erm..." grumbled Ted, "Let's go and look at toys for the kids," and he limped off in the corner, where in large cardboard boxes were piles of children's treasures.

"There are new acquisitions in the box closer to the window," suggested Mrs. Tuff, but Ted – driven instinctively by an engineer's intuition – had already removed from the box an old, almost prewar, metallic Meccano set.

"I'll take this set and this striking, model rocket," he said. "I have always maintained that the old toys aren't as colorful as the modern, but are made much more realistically. And here's the proof!"

In truth, Ted had long wanted to teach his grandson to construct toys rather than to spend hours playing computer games. Constructing together seemed to him to be twice as interesting as sitting alone in front of a comp screen.

James followed his father-in-law and chose two toys from the top of the piles filling the box. He unerringly picked out the Barbie, a doll with the same green eyes as Jane and Dory had, as well as a plush dog, an exact copy of a real spaniel, Tarzan, who have moved out with James.

"Do you mind giving this to Dick when you meet him after school?" he asked Ted, handing him the puppy.

Ted did not mind. Jane also, with no resistance, took the Barbie for Dory, whom she was heading immediately to see after the trial. In fact, the meeting went by unusually calmly. Mrs. Tuff turned out to be right: such coffee brought benefits to all.

"All rise," announced the bailiff, and as everyone stood up, a tall stately man in a black robe entered the Courtroom.

"Hearing a divorce case..." clerk announced.

"Do you realize," the judge addressed the spouses, "that by trying to reduce legal costs by not using lawyers, you put yourself at a disadvantage. Your mistakes, incompetence, or unprofessional actions and poor decisions will not be a reason to appeal or ask for a new trial."

"Understood, Your Honor."

"Now, do you still want a divorce? Mrs. Barton, you first."

"I would like to be second, if you don't mind, Your Honor."

The judge thought for a short while. Usually to oppose him was only to harm oneself, but he did not notice the spirit of contradiction in Jane's behavior. After all, hesitations by the parties in such a process were quite natural and understandable. He could exercise a certain procedural discretion.

"OK. Mr. Barton, please."

"Your Honor, I believe in justice, but –"

"Mr. and Mrs. Barton, I saw during our previous session both of you were clamoring to speak and accuse each other. Now neither of you has the audacity to be first to insist on the divorce. The Court sees this as a positive change, but would like to know whether any new circumstances have arisen."

Jane opened her large bag and fumbled there for a white envelope with the hospital letter prepared for the court. It stuck in between Barbie's hands, as if she were passing it to her new family.

"Let me show you the document, Your Honor," Jane said.

The bailiff took the piece of paper and handed it to the judge. It was a letter informing the Court that Dory Barton was receiving treatment in a cancer center and tomorrow would undergo a tumor removal, along with possible amputation.

"That's where the shoe pinches," thought the judge. He had frequently observed that once-staunch opponents humbled their fervor due to confounding factors. Nothing prevented him from extending the probationary period and postponing the hearing, but ceding to a habit developed over the years, the judge sought clarification:

"Mr. Barton; do you still think that your spouse's behavior is the cause of the divorce?"

"No, Your Honor, I do not."

"Do I understand correctly that you have changed your opinion about the reason for the divorce?"

"I cannot really say so. But, I am fully aware that my alcoholism and rude behavior altered my wife's attitude towards me. However, she did not stop supporting me financially, even then."

The judge laughed to himself. These yuppies – their university diplomas still in hand – believe that they can replace professionals in everything. You see, they do not need lawyers in court. This young man does not even know that his statement means that almost any request for alimony may now be denied. However, the judge refrained from comment and turned to the wife:

"Do you, Mrs. Barton, agree with the assessment of events made by your husband?"

"No, Your Honor. Despite the behavior of my husband, I shouldn't have made that short flirtation out to be a real affair, nor lied to him that our daughter wasn't his."

"Shit!" thought the judge, "are you kidding, or did you drink a truth serum?" Of course, he did not say any such thing aloud, yet only summarized:

"Considering the change of positions of both parties, the Court adjourns the case for three months and defers judgment to the respective date. Both parties have the right to withdraw their applications for divorce at any time before final judgment is rendered."

"Bang!" he struck his gavel on the bench, imagining how his colleagues at the club would guffaw...

Small Dory felt buoyant in her ward.

First, Mom had surprisingly come to the hospital with Dad. Not with Mom's Dad, but with Dory's and Dick's dad. Oh, it was so great! She was not even afraid to go for surgery tomorrow.

Second – Barbie. Mom got her out of her bag and said, "Daddy himself chose it for you in the pharmacy of Mrs. Tuff." The doll with Mommy's green eyes and Daddy's slightly snub nose seemed so dear, as if she had long lived with Dory and kept all her secrets. Dory would never have traded this Barbie for a brand new one in a crispy wrapper, a cold, detached stranger from the big toy store.

Third, Dick called from Grandfather's apartment and promised to bring something. Dad had given him a toy dog, an exact copy of their Tarzan. And Dick decided to let Tarzan guard Dory. Together with Grandfather, they had fixed the toy rocket, an exact copy of a real one, like out of a movie. They straightened its bent stabilizers and cleaned off the carbon deposits from its scorched body. Dick would bring the rocket to Dory, so she could look at it and get well faster. In addition, he said, "We have at home a fresh game: an old metal Meccano set with a lot of pieces. We can build anything we want. Real! And it's as cool as playing comp!"

Finally, Dr. Green appeared with his assistants. He showed Jane and James pictures, lab results and explained that Dory was a very brave girl and fully ready for the operation.

"This doctor will make you sleep and not be afraid," said Dr. Green, introducing the anesthesiologist. "Let him examine you once more; we'll wait outside."

"Come into my office," continued the surgeon in the hallway. "You have to sign an important document, the consent for various surgery options, depending on the size and position of the tumor. You know, this is a very rare case: this tumor usually appears in older boys, not little girls. And if it metastasizes to the lungs, the prognosis is very poor. Dory has only a primary tumor in her leg. This is a relatively good situation, but if the tumor has invaded through most of the bone's diameter, then, of course we have to sacrifice the extremity to save the child. For this, I will need your written consent."

"I never thought that things had gone so far," said James, turning cold, "Did you know this?"

Jane silently choked with tears and only trembled.

"What about the pictures?"

"The images indicate significant tumor growth over the past two months. However, the results of CT-scans of the abdomen and lungs are absolutely normal."

Jane suddenly stopped crying and asked, "Doctor, and when did you take the last pictures?"

"A week ago. They have the greatest tumor size."

"Can you repeat images before the surgery?"

The doctor flushed slightly, but otherwise showed no sign that he was annoyed by the parents' disbelief. "Do they doubt my competence? Or is this their last hope?"

"Technically, you can," he agreed, "But we do not have any reasons to do this. So your insurance will never pay for a new study."

"I'll pay for it then," James said with confidence. "You know, I had severe leg pain in eighth grade. Old Dr. Ferguson suspected a tumor, and he found something on the X-rays, but all the symptoms slowly disappeared. This is our last chance, doctor; you cannot deny a mother's request. We will sign the consent before the surgery, tomorrow."

"It is a pity that I did not know you and your story earlier. I would have suggested that you do a comparison of your and your daughter's genotypes. Well, there is such a gene TP53… This is interesting from the scientific point of view."

"Before, I probably would not have wanted to do this analysis, but now it's not a problem. If you still want it, I can do it. Even tomorrow. I am quite sure that both I and my daughter have the same lucky gene."

Dory had not been able to fall asleep that night after so many events. To begin with, there was Mom and Dad coming together to visit her. Then Dick and Grandpa brought her Tarzan as well as the beautiful brilliant rocket, which now sparkled in the silver moonlight on the sill of an open window. And when everybody had left, Dory was taken for the CT-scan. Barbie was lying with her under the sheet, whispering words of comfort to the girl, "Do not worry, you will get better soon, no need to operate on you." And Dory imagined how they would live again with Dad; and a real Tarzan would return from the city and lick her cheeks and nose. Then she probably fell asleep and had an amazing dream.

Barbie and Tarzan cautiously got off her bed and climbed onto the dressing table near the window. They slowly and carefully picked up a bottle of iodine and, like acrobats, ascended with it onto the window-ledge, where the rocket stood. A hatch had opened, and the toys carefully poured the contents of the "canister with fuel" into the tank. And then, in a single synchronous movement, they dove from the window-sill to the chair, leaving behind two tiny silver mites, which in all haste, like sprinters at the finish line, fled to the giant spaceship.

The warm morning in the small town brought to all the characters in the story pleasant surprises, joy and wonder. Only Maxi and Com continued their long journey through bottomless space to distant mysterious stars. They were in no way surprised.

The Commander checked the stable operation of the sintronium engine, preparing the ship for a jump into hyperspace. And Maxi, with a soft brush as usual, charged her reality optimization capacitors, located, as in any woman, in the nails of both hands.

"I always knew that I had the best wife in the Universe," Com recorded his thoughts for future memoirs. "My only help-meet, the astronaut-researcher, but – most importantly – the unrivaled Maximizer!"

MY CLOWN IS DEAD...

If someone looked from outside, through the porthole light into the Intergalactic Starship, he would be amazed with the unusual setting on board. A curious observer would notice a spacious, top-notch kindergarten room filled with toy treasures – soft animals, dolls, and other unspecified rolling, wheeling and squeaking things. A little, red remote-controlled zero-transporter for preschoolers waited, ready to move you at any moment to the compartment of your choice.

However, looking closer, one would notice neither joyful children, nor kind teachers or busy babysitters. The comfortable space shelter's walls have never heard kids' voices or noises of a game. The ship could be called uninhabitable, if it had not had one living organism, which in the starship's registry was designated a "heartlet", and in the ship's log – a passenger.

It was a girl of four and a half years. All this time, after coming out of a black tunnel, the ship was moving in space towards the sun. The baby was nicknamed the "heartlet" because her creators generously infused this human organism with the best female qualities: love, affection, kindness and tenderness.

KIT and Clown called the girl Baby, and she willingly responded to this household name. KIT (Kind Intelligent Tiger) was registered in the Catalogue as a "brain" and looked like a soft and fluffy tiger cub. Under the guise of a children's toy clown, was hidden the most advanced robot with "superhuman" strength, agility and endurance – the "hands" of the system. The "brain" served as the knowledge and intelligence of the mission, the "hands" were the mission's protector and the executor of

266

tasks, and "heartlet" was its soul. This trio represented all that was left of human civilization, which barely had time to send a ship into the subspace, moments before annihilation.

"Ding-dong, ding-dong," merrily rang bells inviting for breakfast.

"Baby, it's time to eat before classes," purred KIT, straightening his antennas. Each of his hairs hid a self-perpetuating system of information stored in nucleic acids.

The girl stroked the big cat's silky fur, "Let's go, Kitty, and call the Clown."

Clown, as always, tirelessly inspected the ship's intricate systems when he wasn't busy completing his mistress' orders.

"We will send him a message, and he will quickly arrive directly into the dining room," KIT said.

"Puff!" Clown materialized on the red cart.

"Good morning! We are starting the astronaut's breakfast! 'Nothing's tastier'!" and he put an apron on the baby, hoisted her to her high stool at the table and poured milk into her mug. The next moment he drew fresh muffins from the oven, filled a bowl of fragrant porridge from the pot for the girl and put a cap of sour cream in front of the tiger.

"Look, Baby," said KIT, "everything you eat now is very easy to prepare. Milk is yielded by animals with udders. Bread is baked from pounded seeds like these. Porridge is cooked from them also." And he showed on a huge screen how similar animals from different planets were being milked, cereals were collected and threshed, flour was grinded, and bread was baked.

"And where do we get tools for all of that?"

"To provide them is my job," Clown said, but KIT suddenly noticed,

"Good question, Baby. Well done! I will immediately begin a survival course," and he started enthusiastically explaining how to get fire, make pottery, grind grain, and knead the dough.

By the end of breakfast, little girl already knew a lot. And after the meal she had to learn the calendar, sculpt figures, draw, read, count, and so on, until the flute lesson.

Joachim Neander, pastor of the Lutheran Church of St. Martin, looked at the clock – it was not long before the lesson would start. But, he was ready. As always, Joachim mentally selected excerpts from psalms for his music lessons that he gave free of charge to city children, on Sundays, at his church. The custom of such training he brought with him from Düsseldorf, where a year ago he served as rector of the gymnasium. On weekends during the warmer months, Neander went out of town to the valley of the river Düssel and, inspired by the beauty of nature, composed hymns, played music, and preached to the mushrooming audience of local Calvinists fans. Despite the sincerity of his intentions, to preach before being ordained was risky. This angered the church school leadership, and the young teacher was forced to leave his beloved job and return to his hometown, Bremen.

The son of a Latin poet and a grandson of a musician, Joachim inherited the poetry of his father and musicality of his grandfather. Maybe, that's why parishioners loved hymns he wrote. Citizens adored the delicate motifs and heartfelt words of his songs. The author's popularity was growing. Soon, the whole of Germany learned the name Neander (a new man), a name remodeled into Greek manner from Neumann by his grandfather. Newfound fame flattered the young man. Only one thing bothered him: in the warm May days of 1680, he was not feeling well, waking up nights in a cold sweat and choking with a persistent cough.

"And when will the lesson start?" the voice of Karl, a boy from the choir, a great lover of singing and church music, interrupted his chain of thought.

"Soon. Be patient. Is everybody already gathered?"

"Not yet, but the donkey who "sang" together with us last Sunday is again tied to the nearby fence.

Joachim remembered the funny incident. During the last lesson, a few local animals "joined them in singing" – a donkey roared, a dog howled, a cat mewed, and even a rooster in a neighboring yard wailed. All the parishioners laughed, but Neander turned the joke into a parable, saying that the psalms not only reach the soul of man, but also captivate all of God's creatures. All that week, Bremen rumored that Neander makes animals sing and become better creatures. Did they possess Divine Sparkle?

The pastor did not support these ideas...

"Congratulations," said KIT, "Today you have turned thirteen. You've become quite grown and pretty, and from now on, we will call you Sweetheart." Indeed, who would recognize the former Baby in this teenage girl? Only her daily companions, teachers, and defenders: KIT and Clown.

"And why are we taking so long? Isn't it possible to get there faster?"

"We are moving in ordinary space for a reason. During the flight, you will grow up to be young adult, and by the time we arrive, your babies will be born."

"And will I be able to have children by myself?"

"Yes. You're going to be the first mom in the new homeland. And babies are born out of cells, which are, so far, dormant inside you. There, on the third planet from the sun, there should live people very similar to you. Your genomes differ by less than one percent, but who knows, one defective gene – and the progeny may not appear. That's why you yourself should reproduce your own kids first, and then nature will rectify everything."

"And what if my children will not be able to intermarry with the local people?"

"Then you will start a new breed! Scientists have tried to make your offspring strong and healthy. You and your tribespeople will be taller and slimmer than local people. You will walk longer and run faster. And you will communicate better. But, the locals are stronger and tolerate pain easier. Their hair is red, the color of fire, and black, the color of the night, and yours – the golden color of our star."

"Is all of this so important?"

"Probably, yes. It's more important to run away from a very strong opponent than to fight him. And your ability to act together, strategically, will help to defeat him. Pain will serve you as a warning until it's too late, and golden hair attracts loving hearts."

"And there are no more differences?"

"There are some more. The special genetic information is recorded in a form of a ring introduced into your cells. It transmits only through the maternal line and helps to cope with the microorganisms. You'll be less hurt by wounds, though it will be harder to endure pain. Who knows, suffering can become a source of inspiration. And, sometime in the future, using the ring label, scientists will be able to find out who belongs to your lineage, and by deciphering the coded entry, calculate where it came from. But it is too early to explain all this to you, okay?"

"Nobody but you, KIT, know what to do and when to do it."

"You are clever, Sweetheart. You will grow up and realize that people are not driven by their knowledge, but by their desires."

"Oh, is that so?" said the little mistress of the ship as she dragged the big cat to the soft, plastic floor and began to tousle and caress his silk, faux fur. KIT only screwed his eyes and growled in response. Clown, with a bunch of flowers from the greenhouse, found them rolling out of pleasure on the floor.

The following article is written for theology students in order to enhance their education that suffers from censoring of latest paleontology information, as well as from poor explanation of newly discovered artifacts. The article is published for the tenth anniversary of these unusual findings.

As we know from eyewitness accounts, in August of 1856, workers of limestone quarries located in the Neander valley of river Düssel struck the wall of the cave and entered an underground grotto. There, under a layer of clay, they found fossilized mud, panned out by the river. Delving into it, workers ran into a piece of skull and coarse bones, which they mistook as belonging to a bear. Animal bones have been found before in Devil's cave, nearby. Usually, they were picked up or bought for pennies by local fortunetellers and soothsayers, but unexpectedly, this time things took a different turn.

The venerable Herr Johann Fuhlrott, Professor of Natural Philosophy in University of Tubingen, a Catholic and a widower, acquired the bony remnants. They interested him at once. Fascinated by natural sciences from his youth, he realized that the bones were human, but not part of a usual skeleton. Fuhlrott decided to consult a specialist and showed them to a colleague, Professor of Anatomy in University of Bonn, Herman Schaaffhausen.

The anatomist immediately confirmed the antiquity of the bones. After discussing the discovery, they published an article in the Annals of university papers in February of 1857. The bones were named "remains of Neanderthal man". We cannot recognize the name as a suitable one, because its meaning is the "ancient man out of the valley of the new man". However, mindful of the Joachim Neander's contribution to the development of spirituality of the nation, we did not dare to oppose the newly coined term.

But, a different thing is surprising. According to Dr. Mayer, Natural History Society of Prussia and Westphalia, black specks, which, under a lens, seem to be formed of very delicate, fern dendrites that have been growing on Earth for more than twenty, or thirty thousand years. By the logic of some "experts", these bones are related to the same time as the ferns. How can this data be true when every good Christian knows that the age of discovery is not supported by the story of Genesis? And it gets even worse!

Three years after the discovery, in 1859, quite a seditious work of the English naturalist Charles Darwin emerged. It asserted that modern species were not created by the Divine plan, but originated because of evolution of ancient species. The contagion started to spread!

Based on this "work", William King, an Irish geologist from Royal College in Galway, in 1864 suggested that the bones of Neanderthal man do not belong to the human species Homo sapiens, but to an intermediate chain between an ape (just imagine!) and a man, a species which he called Homo neanderthalensis.

No need to emphasize the obvious blasphemy and anti-scientific nature of such works and statements. Be aware of the moral damage this information can cause to the younger generation!"

Clown, following KIT's orders, aligned the telescopes. They had less than a year left to fly and wanted to see, with their own eyes, a new star with its planetary system, and especially the third planet and its inhabitants. KIT showed his student the images of giant reptiles and amphibians that reigned in this world millions of years ago, who were then replaced with mammals and primates. Have they evolved to develop intelligence?

The seventeen-year-old beauty, Milla, threw her heavy, gold braids behind her back and leaned over the display. The pursuit of science, sports, and arts faded into the background. Under her mentor's supervision, she learned how to resolve complex conflicts that depended on the cultural development of the aboriginal people. Soon, Milla became proficient in space diplomacy, but day after day, KIT invented new, more intricate problems for her training.

"Attention, KIT!" the voice of Clown sounded, "First telescopic data is coming in. One of the former planets of the system is missing; instead I am seeing a huge number of asteroids."

"What do you think? How will the shards affect our maneuvering?" KIT asked his student.

"In real space, it all depends on the momentum of bodies, i.e. their masses and velocities. From small or slow bodies we will protect ourselves with a power field or high-speed maneuver, but from the big and fast – we will escape into hyperspace."

"Unfortunately, a hyperspace move is unsafe near large masses like planets. If we face a collision, you will have to be evacuated in an individual capsule."

"And you?"

"The capsule is designed only for you, Milla. Robots will not last long without powerful sources of energy. In case of an accident, we will stay in the spaceship, try to restore it, and land on the second planet. Love does not die! Someday your kids will find us there."

The girl was not superstitious, but a chill of fear touched her heart. KIT never asked questions without a reason… Immediately after the break, Milla started to acquaint herself with the construction and management of the capsule.

Paul basically did not need to prepare for tomorrow's seminar on biochemistry. His presentation was called "Mitochondrial DNA and Mitochondrial Eve". Materials – ten on a penny. "Where to start?" he thought. "With mitochondria – microscopic energy stations of each live cell? With their unusual ring-form DNA, different from human nuclear DNA molecules? Or, with their origin? Some scientists believed that bacteria contaminated our cells with their genomes, which assimilated in suitable conditions. How well would it be if we didn't catch diseases because of affinity with bacteria," smiled Paul, "But only medicine, and not family ties, helps against diseases."

Mutations, changes in bacterial genes, occur more frequently than in humans, therefore, by finding an unmodified DNA, one can determine not only immediate family, but also distant ancestors.

"Here, I probably should tell about the fantastic transmission of mitochondrial DNA in the female line."

We receive the hereditary material from both mother and father, but why not the same way with mitochondria? It turns out, that after the maternal and paternal cells merge, special proteins destroy paternal mitochondrial DNA. Somehow, nature needed to tag the maternal mitochondrial DNA and store it unchanged.

"To me, this looks like science fiction. Well, if it wasn't God, then who protected inheritance of the first woman from the dissolution in the male genes?" Paul thought, but there was no answer yet.

"Oh, tomorrow my students will make fun of the topic and ask tons of questions. And what shall I answer: do not ask me questions, ask nature?" For thirty years since the discovery of the mitochondrial DNA, scientists have learned a great deal about it. Today, no one doubts that these molecules can establish who is whose relative on Earth, and in what generation; when they all descended from a single mother. "They'll show you this 'mother-father'!" an inner voice started to bitch again.

"No, of course it's wrong to understand mitochondrial Eve as a biblical character, moreover, as a single woman. Initially, it could be not one woman, but a group of relatives, carrying the same mitochondrial DNA," said Paul's mental antagonist. Many years he was puzzled over this riddle, trying to "reconcile" science with mystery. But, the practical application of this knowledge changed everything. After the publication of his article in the prestigious European magazine, he could talk about it.

On the night between July 16 and July 17, 1918, the family of the former Tsar Nicholas II in Yekaterinburg was moved from Ipatiev's house, where they had been held since April, down to the basement. The fate of the Romanovs was sealed. Together with the deposed Nicholas, his wife, daughters, son, family doctor Botkin, and several servants were shot. The maid, Anna Demidova, held a toy clown. According to the memoirs of one of the soldiers in the fire squad, the young prince whispered, "My clown is dead."

Dead bodies were found in 1979, reburied, and found again in 1991. It was then that an international forensic examination was performed, enabling confidential identification of remains. Paul, as a specialist took part in the examination from the Russian side.

"I'll tell boys and girls how mitochondrial DNA has helped to establish the truth," thought Paul. The basis for the examination was identity of mitochondrial DNA of Tsarina Alexandra Romanova, born

Princess Alix of Hesse, her children and living relative. Let me tell you who he is. All of you saw him on TV. Alix was the sister of Victoria. Victoria's grandson, Prince Philip is the husband of Queen Elizabeth II. Tall, thin, very elegant old Prince, remember?"

And some straight-A student will ask: "I do not understand, how did they identify Tsar Nicholas by the female DNA?"

"Well, good question. His mitochondrial DNA from the queen mother, Maria Feodorovna, born Danish Princess Dagmar, is identical to the DNA of her sister Alexandra, transmitted through the female line to her great-grandson, our contemporary, Sir Carnegie, Duke Fife of Scotland..."

Paul has long sat over the sheets and edited his presentation as a courtesy copy of a respected European magazine, with his article, mysteriously gleamed on his desk, reflecting the light of the old table lamp with a green shade.

"It's warmer in the cave than outside. Fire is difficult to maintain, but it is necessary," thought Lon.

Even near the equator, where the tribe roamed, snow and ice lingered for a long time. But, the fire warmed and drew away predators and intruders from a hostile tribe. Lon was sitting, wrapped in furry Mammoth skin on a bed of dried herbs, near Mother. Everyone called her so. Lon remembered that she referred to herself differently, but now her name, Millo, was used for the ritual structure of stones, on which the Mother sat during Courts and Councils. The same word meant a route from the hardships of hunters and gatherers' life up to the god-ship, in a distant starry sky.

Lon had already started entering the age when one decides in which of his sons to pass his power. Then, he could spend more time with Mother, listen to her stories, and learn her wisdom. But so far, he still firmly held a powerful club in his hands and darted a light spear farther then anyone in the Tribe. This throwing technique, which his mother taught him as well as everything else, saved their entire race from wild animals and cannibal neighbors. How many times have they attacked the Tribe, attracted by the beauty of its women with their golden hair, and as many times left with nothing? Collective combat tactics frightened enemies incapable of organized staged actions. Thus, they could rarely strike down a mammoth fighting without plan, only with bare force. But, if not for the protection of the Mother, they would have killed the Tribe children, one by one, before Lon and the others grew up. Not once, sprinting has saved them from the hairy, powerful, but clumsy people who then furiously crushed and devoured each other, both men and women, the soldiers that they were. Wise Mother took in her Tribe their red haired children, at the time when wicked parents died from illnesses and injuries. Growing up under the laws of the Tribe, they have become their own, learned to talk nearly as well, but died early, and the red-haired women did not give offspring from golden-haired men.

"Lon, come to me," Mother said, "Tomorrow is your birthday, remember?"

"Yes, Mother Millo," he specifically referred to her so as to please her, "Have you not taught us to keep a calendar?"

"I want to show something to my first-born," she said. "Gods have a custom to present each other with pretty, but unnecessary things. Just for fun."

"We are not gods. Pieces of smoked meat, flaps of skin, a pike for a spear, scrapers, berries and roots – these are our gifts."

"But we must imitate them. Look what I've made for you," and she handed him the figure of a lion-man. "Let it be your sign," she said, "You're just as smart as K-It, and strong as K-Lawn."

She called "KITties" all the lions, tigers, bobcats, and other wild animals whose cubs did not bark but meowed, and K-Lawn sounded strange. Lon thought that was the name of his father, jack-of-all-trades, but the mother never went into details, not wanting to upset her son. Lon went out of the cave. "Tomorrow will be mammoth hunting. Tribe men will drive and kill one animal. And it will be a feast in his honor, the chief, and Mother would play the flute made of a bird-bone, and women will sing.

Then, there will be dancing and orgies, and Mother would lead children away to paint animals on the walls of caves. And the usual succession of days will stretch after the holiday."

Lon suddenly felt an urge to make a gift to his mother. Such silly and unnecessary, but as gods taught, comforting to her heart. He decided that he would obtain a little kitty, even if he had to fight his parents. Lon imagined how she would snuggle a cub against her large, pendulous breasts that nursed dozens of children, embrace the kitten with her calloused hands, and stroking his soft fur, whisper strange words of memory and love, "KIT-ty, KIT-ty, my Clown is dead."

And when people fall asleep, the blue morning star in the sky gently winks to all loving hearts in the world.

A GENIE FROM PLANET JIHAD

Hassan

"Aaaa-*aa*-aaaa. . ." The mournful melody poured from the loudspeaker. It was almost time for the morning namaz. The muezzin was already on the minaret balcony to call the faithful to prayer. Today, he would do it himself, although more often than not, he turned on the recording. The Quran didn't say he couldn't.

Hassan was laying out freshly laundered rugs for himself and for Ismael, his late mother's younger brother, but he knew that however hard he tried, Ismael would still find an excuse to lay into him. "True it is that boys have an ear on their backs—they listen better when they're beaten," Ismael would say over and over again, and he boxed that ear long and hard. "Even the donkey cares more for me than my own uncle," Hassan thought. "He's never done anything to hurt me, and he's never said a mean word to me. Not that donkeys ever say much. . ." The beast brayed loud enough, though, when after a day of hauling heavy sacks to and fro, he would come home with Hassan and instead of a nice handful of hay would get a kick in the rump from Ismael. Then it was Hassan's job to calm him. He would wipe the sweat-soaked back, bring water and fodder, and watch as his four-legged friend munched his supper, his big, sad eyes asquint, as if he was asking, "The master's gone, yes?"

The donkey officially belonged to New Soap, which was Ismael's company. From sunup to sundown, the two of them, Hassan and the donkey, would be carrying loads from here to there. Everyone in Jaffa knew them. The boy made the rounds of the workshops with his donkey, bringing them sweet-smelling things to put into the famous soaps of Jaffa, which even Napoleon had admired. Or so they say, but that could be a joke. What was for sure, though, was that he had treated the Turks to a good lathering in Jaffa and then ruthlessly executed thousands of prisoners, starting with the governor.

Sometimes Hassan was delivering something else, not only additives for Ismael's soaps. He knew that on certain days the sacks would be heavier than usual and not just because of the perfumes. But the bomb-sniffing dogs never caught the explosives. They would sneeze and turn up their damp noses, bothered by the sharp odors, and the soldier would smile at Hassan and send him on through.

Hassan had no faith in Ismael. A true Muslim did not kill people. He loved people and wanted them to be better than they were. Ismael loved no one but himself. And to Allah he gave only lip-service. When Hassan's parents had died in the Territories, Ismael hadn't wept for his sister. Instead he dug his fingers into Hassan's shoulder and whispered, "We shall avenge, you and I. Ten for one! Or a hundred. The more, the better, Our vengeance is holy."

He slapped the boy across the face and when the tears of fear, pain, and loneliness began to flow, said to him, "Remember that feeling. It will pass when you have your revenge."

Ever since then, Hassan had lived with Ismael, who fed him, yes, but often beat him too and tried to teach him bad things. Hassan didn't want to kill anybody. The donkey didn't either. Hassan knew the simplicity of the donkey's thoughts, and asinine they were indeed: they were all about nipping at fresh grass, running in a meadow and . . . chasing a ball. "He wants to play soccer," Hassan thought, and he would have liked that too, but when was there time? All day long he was making his deliveries and having to listen to those nasty soap boilers telling him what a fine mujahid he was growing into. "One day you'll be a worthy avenger," they said. "Soon, soon your time will come."

Hassan didn't know what to do. If he'd been all grown up, like Ismael, he would have gone straight to the police and told them about those bad people. But young as he was, who would believe him? Then the soap boilers and Ismael would simply kill him. And think nothing of it. They'd even murdered Zulfia for refusing to go and blow up a bus. But before they did, they made her hurt. A lot. Eight men, one after another. What kind of believers were these? But Hassan believed in God. He wanted to be a teacher like his father, and…

The namaz began, and Hassan started carefully reciting the prayer of the dawn.

Ismael

"One day that accursed boy will be the death of me," Ismael was thinking. "He sticks his nose in everywhere, more like a Jew than a righteous Muslim whom it behooves to follow blindly the behests of his elders and betters."

The day before, just as Saeed, one of the soap boilers, was removing a pack of plastic explosive from a sack of fragrant powdered lavender, Hassan had come back unexpectedly and caught him.

"Shaitan, spawn of hell, what did you forget?" roared Saeed.

"I forgot to tell you that Ismael can't wait forever for you to repay your debt. He wants either the debt in full or interest payments."

"Tell your uncle that the payment will be ready in two days. He can collect it near the new cultural center, and you can be the courier."

The message was clear as day. Ismael knew exactly what it meant. Saeed had been pushing for them to load a donkey with explosives and send it and Hassan to some crowded place. "You'll be short two asses after that, but the Center will pay you well, and in dollars too," he said. Ismael agreed, and it wasn't the money that tempted him but service to an idea to which he would willingly have sacrificed his own children. But he had no family, no children of his own yet, and his nephew had been getting on his nerves from day one. He was different. Either his father, the teacher, had instilled the wrong kind of knowledge in him, or Israeli propaganda had corrupted his feeble spirit, but an avenger he would never be.

"Well, then, if not by thy will, then by God's." Ismael grinned as he worked on his plan.

It was simple enough: Saeed would drive Hassan and a loaded donkey in his minibus to a big public celebration. That would be the grand opening of the new Shimon Peres Cultural Center that was scheduled for the very next day. The organizers were expecting some of the city's dignitaries to come and large crowds as well, which, of course, meant that a whole lot of police and soldiers with dogs would be there too. But, who would pester a poor youngster selling flowers and little flags, or search his donkey's pack? Even if there were walk-through metal detectors, the plastic explosive would just breeze on through and the donkey's shoes would make a good distraction. The key to the operation would be to hustle Hassan and his cargo off the bus and drive away in a hurry, so none of the gawkers would be able to connect the donkey with the vehicle later. But that would be Saeed's problem in any case, because Ismael had no intention of showing up there with them. He was going to arrive alone, observe from a distance, and, when the time was right, press the detonation button. The one thing he hadn't yet decided was what to do about Saeed. First, the man owed him a good deal of money and wanted this operation to take care of that debt. Second, someone might actually remember his minibus and the boy clambering out of it with his donkey. But to avoid any unpleasant consequences it would only take a hint to Yusuf that Saeed had given himself away over the explosives, and his body would be found at last somewhere in the Old Town. But then Ismael would have to take care of the debt all on his own. . .

The Donkey

The waves are lapping quietly on the shore. From here, from Jaffa's old port, there's a lovely view of Tel Aviv, of the sea and of the cliffs rising from it. Hassan loves to walk here in the fresh air before going home after a long day's work, and I always keep him company. Sometimes the tourists—the ones who are brought to the old port every day to be told the story of Perseus, Andromeda, Pegasus the winged horse, and the monstrous whale-like thing that turned into a sea cliff at the very sight of the Gorgon Medusa's head—want to put their children on my back and take photos. Those children have no idea that I know the tale just as well as any tour guide.

Hassan lets them have their way, and for his trouble is given loose change that he plunks down for a fresh flatbread—or, on a day with lots of children, for a falafel-stuffed pita. Hassan always shares with me, and he never beats me. No wonder Ismael and Saeed call him a donkey. I'm so calm around him. It's a pity I'm not a boy, or I'd be his friend and play soccer with him (I can kick with the best of them, you know). When I feel good, I sing a joyful song. When I feel bad, the song is sad. "Ee-yah, ee-yah!" I cry. And so Hassan calls me Yah-kub. But there's not much singing to be done at home, or else Ismael will come running and kick me in the you-know-what. Then Hassan strokes me and gives me a piece of bread. But here on the seashore, I can run and sing all I want.

The sea is tepid at best, but Hassan wades out knee-deep and looks dreamily at the cliffs. Yes those cliffs. Sometimes I imagine that instead of a boy called Yakub, I'm Pegasus the flying horse. I catch up Hassan, my Perseus, and we fly away, to a wondrous land where Zulfia, our Andromeda, is safe and sound and waiting for him, and the monster Ismael is becoming a sea cliff. I sing aloud in my joy, rearing up on my hind legs and waving my forelegs in the air. The tourists laugh and snap photos of my futile attempts to fly.

But Hassan is going after something in the sea. Could he have seen a sea-monster, a whale? No, he has picked something up out of the water. What is it? A treasure from the land of make-believe? Maybe the sword of Perseus? We could make good use of that.

"Look!" Hassan calls out. "Look what I've found!" And he shows me something oblong with green hair that stirs like snakes.

"A head!" I think. "He's found the Gorgon Medusa's severed head!"

Hassan is cleaning the seaweed from this thing that's foul with slime and barnacles.

"It's an old copper pitcher. Or maybe an amphora," he says.

"Ee-yah, ee-yah!" That's me, saying "yes."

I know that the junk dealer will give my friend money for his find, and then he and I will feast on sweets. But for now it must be hidden, so Hassan tosses it into the sack on my back and covers it with rags and leftover lavender. Tomorrow we'll take it to the big city with the rest of our load and sell it. And I laugh and make a lot of noise. And all the tourists guffaw and hold their noses. I don't know why.

The Genie

O, my heart's delight! O, nightingale in my rose garden! Sing, sing louder! Salvation is at hand. Now the owner of that shrill and repulsive voice will unscrew the lid, and my vengeance shall be terrible. Only a voyager who has spent thousands of years in a defective capsule could ever know what this is like. At first the energy reserves are vast, and you have nothing to fear. But the hatch will not open from the inside, which makes it impossible to engage the photon space-time transducer. You call the whole world to your aid, promising happiness to your savior and all his kin. But the years pass and no one comes. The energy reserves that support my existence are melting, melting away. And I realize that I can no longer keep the promise I have made. So I cast a spell to annul that vow and commit to another, which is to grant three wishes to whosoever shall deliver me. That in itself is no small matter, especially since in the random world of men, even one wish hardly ever comes true. But time flows inexorably on, there is less and less energy, and it is apparent that my essence will shrivel away to naught irrespective of anyone's ability to open that hatch. Whether I end my life's journey within or without is of scant importance now. But some pitiful remnants of energy still remain to me, and again I change the rules.

"Whoever releases me from here to die in freedom, I shall reward with a fearsome death for the sins of his forbears, who hardened their hearts against me in recompense for my bountiful gifts."

But that hatch is still jammed. Though I hear the rasping of a clamp on the hatch thread, nothing comes of it.

"Harder, try harder," I urge my savior telepathically, yet all he does is roar in an ugly voice and strain so hard there comes a booming noise from his nether regions.

Finally, my capsule goes flying through the air, and I slam into my vessel's walls. So we have touchdown.

"Lord give him the strength to unscrew the lid and learn about Jihad, about the true Jihad," I pray, but all to no avail.

Jihad

At exactly nine in the morning, a silvery Suzuki minibus stopped a few blocks away from Friendship Square, where the new cultural center was to have its grand opening in an hour's time. The paunchy Saeed, his eyes cutting this way and that, got out and opened the rear door. Hassan hopped down and propped two boards against the back bumper to make a ramp that Yakub descended with wary steps. Saeed made a point of putting on the pack saddle himself and loaded it with a tray full of flowers and flags. Then he jumped into the driver's seat and sped away.

To the donkey, this was an unusually heavy load.

"What are those flags made of?" he wondered. "Drudge, drudge away, like the silly ass you are—no Saturdays for you and no Sundays either. It's true what people say. Donkeys have no god. Because how could a donkey god permit such injustice?"

Hassan led his dun-colored friend to the square, crying his wares as he went. Because the townsfolk flocked around to buy both flowers and flags, it was a while before Ismael was able to make out the two familiar silhouettes. The boy and his donkey were slowly making their way toward a checkpoint between a side street and the square. Traffic had been re-routed, and pedestrians were everywhere. From a distance, they looked like bees scurrying about their hive.

"Soon, soon enough the honey will be gone from your lives," Ismael was thinking, astonished that so many half-witted true believers were enjoying the spring day and that idiotic celebration every bit as much as the shifty, huckstering Jews. He felt like an outsider, not like one of them.

He could not have cared less what was going to happen to those manikins who were frolicking out there for no reason he could see.

"You pitiful, corrupt creatures! Why am I even the same species as you?" Ismael wondered, all the while regretting, zealot that he was, that he couldn't switch the plastic explosives on Yakub's back for a nuclear bomb.

But Ismael hadn't planned for what followed. Hassan stopped close to the checkpoint, rummaged in his pouch, and took out a strange object that turned out to be a copper pitcher stained green by time. And Ismael, looking on, turned green too, but with rage. Why had he not checked Hassan's pouch? Where had Hassan got that thing that could derail the entire operation? Even if it didn't start the metal detector pinging, the very look of it would make the police suspicious. And if they thought it was a bomb, they'd give the boy and his donkey a good going-over, and the operation would a bust. The soldiers would disconnect the detonator, and then you could press the button all you wanted but nothing would happen.

All he could do now was set off the explosion ahead of time, but his vanity forbad him to botch such a brilliantly planned operation.

Scornful of the danger and the chance of being recognized, Ismael charged toward his nephew, the donkey, and the pitcher, Iblis and his minions take them all.

Hassan had never thought that Ismael would be in his face even on a holiday.

"Give that here!" Ismael seemed to have appeared out of thin air, and now he was snarling at him and grabbing the pitcher.

But Hassan was not going to give in this time. "Let go!" he yelled, "It's mine!"

They tugged the pitcher to and fro while the astonished townspeople looked on. And Yakub couldn't resist joining in because, after all, enough was enough. But no one expected what came next. The pitcher flew from their grasp and landed with a resounding clang onto the asphalt pavement. The warped lid popped off and black smoke began to seep out.

"Bomb!" a woman screamed.

As if on cue, the crowd scattered and the soldiers, Uzis racked and ready, rushed toward the mysterious object on the ground.

Knowing now that the plan was wrecked, Ismael spoke the name of Allah and jabbed frantically at the detonation button grasped tightly in his pocket.

Epilogue

Thanks be to thee, Creator, that my journey continues! I was prepared to keep my word and before I met my end grant the last pitiable remnants of my strength to my savior—or no, not to one only, because there were three of them, on eight legs. But inscrutable are thy ways. I was suddenly surrounded by the first glimmerings of a reaction. In a matter of moments, those glimmerings would become a surge and would fill the space around. With not a second to lose, I sucked that life-giving flood, all of it, into my capsule, knowing then that the poet spoke true: What you give away is indeed yours forever. I had wanted to give them my life and the remains of my strength, but what I gained back was a hundredfold greater. Not as in the days of my youth, of course, when I could have brought joy to them and their kinsmen too, but of my maturity, because I could, and would, grant the three wishes. But there were three saviors here, so, then, one wish for each. The boy had wanted to be grown, the donkey to be a boy, and the man to be no longer of the human species. Then have your wishes: I have simply changed the husk you wear. Live in joy. I am glad to have kept my word. I leave this world now with a sense of duty done and return home, to the planet whose name is Endeavor, or in the language of these parts, Jihad. And now you can wish me a safe journey and a happy landing.

...An astonished soldier stood over the place where the strange object had been.

"Well, look at that! A crumpled newspaper. . . A trick of the light. It's always this way—when there's a panic, people see what they fear. Even the donkey was so scared he shit himself."

"Hey, you with the braying donkey, shut it up. Give it a swift kick."

"No, that I'll never do. I beat neither people nor animals," Hassan said, putting an arm around the shoulders of his nephew Yakub. "Ismael, stop that racket. All you want to do is frighten everyone. And you're not even carrying a heavy load and it's such a lovely day. Once we're home, I'll have some fresh hay for you. Hey there, who wants flowers and flags? No charge! I'm giving them away."